A Page in Your

By Keith A Pear

CW00504635

For more information about the author and to receive updates on his new releases, visit …

www.keithapearson.co.uk

1.

As I crunch through my last mouthful of cereal, Devon FM's breakfast show presenter, Robbie, introduces the lucky contestant, Lisa. She's offered a choice of categories for the Big Breakfast Quiz: pop royalty, or country music legends.

Lisa goes with pop royalty.

Robbie confirms the rules. One by one, he will reveal the names of four music acts and Lisa's challenge is to name a UK top-forty single by each one.

He reveals the first: Queen.

"Too easy," I mumble to myself. "*Radio Gaga*."

Lisa goes with the obvious and *Bohemian Rhapsody*.

Next up, Prince.

"*Purple Rain*."

Her answer is the same as mine. We're both right.

Robbie then ramps up the pressure by reminding Lisa there's a thousand-pound prize at stake. He then confirms the third artist: King.

"*Love and Pride*."

Lisa throws a curveball with *The Taste of Your Tears*. It's a track I haven't heard in years, and I make a mental note to add it to my Spotify playlist later.

Three correct answers. Just one more to go.

Robbie then requests the name of any top-forty single by Princess. Only one comes to mind.

"*Say I'm You're Number One*."

There are plenty of umms and errs but no answer. A digitised voice begins a ten-second countdown and as the seconds ebb away, so too does Lisa's dream of a long weekend in Paris.

"Who are you talking to?" Carol asks, as she breezes into the kitchen.

"Just playing along with a quiz on the radio. Why are you still in your dressing gown? It's nearly eight o'clock."

My wife of twenty-five years is a stickler for punctuality. It's not like her to be late for anything.

"I'm working from home today."

"Oh, okay."

She turns her attention to our outrageously expensive coffee machine. Not my choice.

"You've got that meeting with the board this morning, haven't you?" she calls across the kitchen.

"Yep, at eleven."

"What time will you be finished?"

"Not sure. Why?"

"I might pop into town later. If you're around, we could have lunch?"

"Sorry, but it's unlikely we'll be done much before one, and then I've got a report to finish by four."

The coffee machine hisses and spits as the aroma of dark roasted Sumatran beans drifts across the room. Carol then joins me at the table.

"Never mind. It was just a thought."

"We could have dinner out tonight?" I suggest as a consolation.

"We'll see."

She plucks her mobile phone from a pocket and taps away at the screen.

"Who are you messaging at this hour?"

"No one. I'm just replying to a tweet."

"You're not responding to Piers Morgan again?" I chuckle. "Remember the last time?"

"I do, and I'm still blocked."

I glance at my watch and puff.

"Anyway, I'd better get going."

As I stand to leave, Carol places her phone on the table in readiness for the perfunctory kiss on the cheek we share every morning.

"Good luck with the board."

"Thanks. See you later, and let me know what you decide

about dinner."

"Will do."

I'm just about to leave when Carol catches a thought.

"Oh, and Sean, message me when you're out of your meeting. I'd like to know how it went."

"Sure."

Grabbing my briefcase and car keys from the hallway en route, I step through the front door to the cobbled driveway of our cottage. I say cottage, but that makes our home sound small and twee when, in reality, it's a substantial house with an acre of landscaped gardens. We've lived here for over a decade, and in that time, we've spent an eye-watering amount of money on improvements. Even so, there's no end in sight to the improvement campaign as Carol's idea of perfection seems to shift with every passing year.

I'm sure folk pass judgement when they see our home and the seemingly idyllic lifestyle we lead, but they've no idea of the sacrifices we've both made, and continue to make. Sixty-hour work weeks are not uncommon, with each of those hours burdened with stress and pressure. No company pays the salaries we earn unless they're taking more than a pound or two of flesh in return.

Beyond the physical and mental strains, our single greatest sacrifice came in a decision fourteen years ago. Carol's company offered her a promotion just as we reached the point of planning a family. Both in our early forties, time was fast running out if we were ever to hear the pitter-patter of tiny feet.

In the end, Carol decided to take the promotion. I'm not going to deny her decision didn't sting, but I married an ambitious woman who always gets what she wants. Experience has taught me there's no sense complaining when I happen to be on the wrong end of her wanting.

We never talked about it again as we slipped seamlessly from parents-in-waiting to plain old Sean and Carol Hardy; that childless couple with the lovely house.

I get in the car and gently lay my briefcase on the leather-clad passenger's seat. The vehicle itself, a Mercedes-Benz EQC, is only six weeks fresh from the production line and my first-ever electric car. Even now, I find the lack of engine noise when I press the ignition button disconcerting. Still, I'm doing my tiny bit for the planet.

Shifting the automatic gearbox in to drive, I dab the accelerator. The car glides silently towards the brick pillars which mark the entrance to a rural lane. A right turn leads towards the centre of Bridford Village, but I turn left and begin the ten-mile journey to my company's head office in Exeter.

I joined The Hestia Hotel Group twenty years ago as deputy head of accounts. I'm now head of the entire finance department and responsible for the ebb and flow of millions of pounds every month. I'm also tantalisingly close to securing a seat on the board, which is why this morning's meeting is so important. I'm six years away from retirement and promotion will ensure those six years are the right side of comfortable.

The traffic is kind, and I arrive at the office on the dot of half eight.

I park up, grab my briefcase, and make my way across the car park towards the entrance.

To look at our featureless head-office building, you'd never guess it houses an operation managing over four hundred hotels and almost ten thousand employees. Like the hotels we operate, everything about The Hestia Hotel Group is low budget.

I traipse up to the third floor, and the cramped office I hope to leave behind — the director's offices on the fourth floor are twice the size.

Right on cue, my assistant, Eve, pokes her head around the door.

"Good morning, Sean," she says crisply.

"Morning, Eve."

Not one for excess pleasantries or small talk, she sits in the chair opposite and flips open a notepad. Even though she's two years younger than me, Eve has a distinct school governess vibe going on — a model of efficiency but mildly terrifying.

We go through the day's schedule, and I give her a list of tasks to complete while I focus on the final preparations for my meeting with the board. Eve heads back to her desk and, just as I'm about to begin prepping, my mobile rings. The name on the screen is Andy Marshall.

"Hey, Andy."

"Morning, Sean. How's it going?"

"Not bad. What can I do for you at this early hour?"

"I know you're probably busy so I'll get straight to it: are you free on Saturday evening?"

"I think so. Why?"

"I just got a call from the landlord of a club in Truro. He had a band booked for Saturday, but they've just cancelled on him."

"He's offered us the gig?"

"Yeah. You up for it?"

"I need to double-check with Carol, but I don't see why not."

"So, I'll tell him we can do it?"

"It's been a while so sod it. I'm in."

"Great. I'll email you the details, and we can catch up later."

"Nice one."

I end the call and make a note in my diary.

I've been the lead guitarist of Busted Flush for close to a decade. I learnt to play the guitar at school, but it wasn't until university I first performed in public. Together with a couple of mates, we set up a band and briefly harboured aspirations of making it big. I then met Carol, and my teenage self lost interest in the band. Years later, I met Andy at my local pub, and one drunken evening, we decided to form Busted Flush. There's no chance of fame or fortune but the dozen or so gigs we play every year are always a laugh and a great way to counter the stresses of work.

Perhaps this Saturday I might be playing lead guitar as the newly appointed director of a national hotel chain. We shall see.

For the next hour, I try to focus on my preparations for the meeting, but I'm interrupted every five minutes by another crisis which can't be dealt with unless I intervene. At ten o'clock, I tell Eve I'm not to be disturbed under any circumstances. My attention then turns to a PowerPoint presentation which succinctly highlights the reasons I see myself worthy of a seat on the board.

Only then do I realise I've got a problem.

I spent two hours working on the PowerPoint file at home last night, but the one I'm looking at doesn't contain any of the data I edited. In short, the file I'm looking at is wholly inaccurate. I must have saved it to my laptop's hard drive but not the file-sharing system. That laptop is at home.

Grabbing my phone, I call Carol's number, hoping she can email it to me. It cuts straight to voicemail.

"Shit!"

I give it a minute and then call her again, and then again. Four failed attempts over five minutes. Glancing at my watch, I know there's only one guaranteed way to get my hands on that file before eleven o'clock.

Snatching my car keys, I dart from my office and inform Eve I'm heading out on a mercy mission. I don't hear her reply as I'm already through the double doors and dashing towards the stairwell before she can catch a breath.

Pulling out of the car park, I offer a silent prayer the traffic gods are kind to me. If I push it, I can be home in twenty minutes. One minute to grab my laptop and then another twenty minutes for the return journey. If all goes according to plan, I can be back at my desk with time to spare.

As I drive, I make several further attempts to call Carol, but they're all diverted straight to voicemail. Perhaps she's turned her phone off to focus on work.

A mile from home, I give up trying.

Two minutes ahead of schedule, I turn in to our driveway and pull up as close to the front door as I can. I scramble out of my seat and leave the car door open — every spare second counts. As I unlock the front door, I'm hoping Carol is in the study and doesn't notice my return home. I don't have time to stand and explain why I'm here. I just want to grab the laptop from the lounge and get back in the car.

Leaving the front door open, I dart towards the lounge, but a sudden sound echoes down the stairs. I stop dead in my tracks and replay it in my head. Was it a shriek, or a yell, or just the squeal of a door hinge? I'm about to call out Carol's name when a similar sound bounces off the walls. Definitely of human origin but not a shriek or a yell. To my ear, it sounded more like a squeal, and one born from pleasure rather than pain.

I remain rooted to the spot and listen with canine-like intensity to a series of low groans and enthusiastic expletives. Unless Carol is watching a porn movie on high volume, there can only be one explanation for the sounds emanating from upstairs. Suddenly, another squeal fills the silence, and I know, without doubt, it came from my wife's mouth.

My blood runs cold — Carol is upstairs, having sex with another man.

Despite the overwhelming evidence, it's too implausible to believe. We've been together for thirty-four years, and I know my wife better than I know myself. If she were having an affair, I'd surely have spotted the signs? Maybe this isn't an affair. Perhaps it's just an impulsive moment of weakness, and some random lothario has tempted her into breaking our marriage vows.

Heart hammering, my hands ball in to tight fists. Some bloke is fucking my wife and penny to a pound he knows she's married. For that sin, he's going to pay with a swift smack in the mouth. As for Carol, I can't even begin to process how I feel about her betrayal. As it stands, there's now too much anger clouding my thoughts.

I creep silently up the stairs, so a sudden creak doesn't steal the element of surprise. Judging by Carol's now enthusiastic groans, she wouldn't hear a helicopter land in the garden.

"Ohh, you're so, so good," she purrs.

Whatever this piece of shit is doing to my wife, she evidently loves it. That assumption stokes my rage.

I reach the top of the stairs and focus on the source of the soundtrack — our bedroom. It's sickening enough to know another man is having sex with my wife, but the fact it's happening in our marital bed beggars belief.

As I move silently across the landing, it becomes apparent my wife is getting close to her happy moment. Not that we indulge often enough these days, but I know her vocal accompaniment to the nearest pant.

I get within a few steps of the bedroom door; ajar by three or four inches.

"Oh, my God. Don't stop! Don't stop!"

It's the coldest of comforts, but if I move now, I'll rob the arsehole the satisfaction of fulfilling my wife's pleasure.

With adrenalin coursing through every vein, every limb, I barge forward.

I cover four feet of Wilton carpet and come to an abrupt halt. "What the fuck!"

The scene is the opposite of the one I'd imagined, and the reality arrives like a punch to the gut.

There are two naked bodies sprawled across the king size bed. Stunned faces stare up at me. One belongs to my wife while the other, only inches from Carol's nether-regions, is that of Andy's wife, Vicky.

Time appears to stand still. Both women then scramble for their clothes, strewn across the floor.

If the circumstances were different I'd apologise and make a swift beeline for the door to protect Vicky's modesty. However, I'm not in the mood for apologies and her modesty ship set sail the moment she decided to cheat on her husband, with my wife.

Mouth agape, all I can do is stand and watch the scene unfold before me. I know what I saw, know what I heard, and I know how I felt, but no part of this makes sense. The confusion has fried my wiring. What is the correct reaction to a scene you can scarcely believe?

I've never known Carol to dress so quickly. Within seconds, both women are standing side by side on the opposite side of the bed, facing me. They have the look of cheating partners who've been caught red-handed and thrown on clothes with extreme urgency: flustered, yet sheepish. No great surprise, considering they're both guilty of said crime.

Carol is the first to speak.

"I'm sorry you walked in when you did."

With no hairy-arsed man to punch, I aim my rage in her direction.

"Are you kidding me? Of all the reasons you have to apologise, poor timing is way down my list."

"I didn't mean it like that," she replies with an air of defiance. "Don't be childish."

Now the initial panic and shock have passed, Carol's true persona has reactivated — the same hard persona which has fuelled her highly successful career.

"If you go and wait in the kitchen, we'll have a conversation," she continues. "I'm sure you've got questions."

I do — many questions.

"Please, Sean. Go wait in the kitchen."

I can't bear to look at her a second longer and storm back down the stairs. Only when I reach the kitchen do I remember the reason I'm home. I need to make a phone call and furnish Eve with a plausible explanation why I won't be at the board meeting in fifteen minutes.

Seeing as Carol is the reason I'm missing the most important meeting of my career, I blame her by saying she tripped over and I'm tending to a bump on the head. It's impossible to tell if Eve believes me, but as long as the directors do, I might be able to salvage one part of my life.

I grab a bottle of water from the fridge and slump down on a chair at our Italian-designed table. From the hallway, I catch muted voices and the sound of the front door closing. Vicky has left the scene, it seems.

Carol walks in and sits down opposite with the air of an interviewer about to grill a lowly job applicant.

"Okay," she sighs. "I need to tell you the truth."

2.

I can still remember the exact moment I first met Carol Shanley.

We were both aged twenty and studying at Exeter University. A friend, Patrick, invited me to a party one Saturday evening in late October. I had a practice session with the band the following morning, but Patrick wouldn't take no for an answer. He was single, and keen to hook up with a girl he knew would be at the party. I was in a long-term relationship and promised my girlfriend I'd stay clear of parties. It wasn't so much a matter of trust, but she'd heard the tales of student debauchery from a friend's sister who studied at Manchester.

As it transpired, she was right to be concerned.

Reluctantly, I tagged along with Patrick as we headed across town to an address on the outskirts of the city; a three-storey townhouse rented out as student digs. When we arrived, Patrick repeatedly knocked on the door before a young woman opened it. That young woman knew Patrick from the debating society, and he made the introductions.

It didn't take long for my friend to find the girl he'd set his heart on, and he left me to my own devices. I wasn't much of a drinker, and three cans of piss-weak lager were enough to fog my thoughts. If I'd been sober, I doubt I'd have stayed more than an hour, but the music and the atmosphere were just as intoxicating as the lager. I ended up in an armchair; content to watch the party unfold around me.

That's when the girl who'd greeted us at the front door plonked herself on the arm and said hello — that someone was Carol. And so began a friendship which would mature into an intense physical relationship within months.

It still amazes me how little Carol has changed from the girl who perched on that armchair in 1986. The spiral perm and dark eye makeup are gone, but the elfin face and penetrating hazel eyes remain. Expensive spa treatments and an obsessive gym regime have helped stem the tide of time, to the point her physique has barely changed over the decades. Less can be said of mine.

Sitting here now as a fifty-something couple, I no longer recognise the woman across the table.

"Let's hear it then," I snipe. "What is it Vicky has that I don't, apart from tits and a fanny?"

"There's no need for that tone."

"Oh, you think? What exactly is the right tone for a man who walks in on his wife having sex with a woman?"

"As I said, I'm sorry you had to witness that. It's not exactly how I wanted you to find out."

"Wait … what do you mean, find out? What is there to find out beyond what I just witnessed?"

She closes her eyes and pulls a deep breath.

"We want to be together," she then declares.

"Together, as in a couple? How the hell is that going to work when you're both married? Not to mention you're both heterosexual."

"Don't label me, Sean."

"You've been married to a bloke for twenty-five years. It's not a label; it's a fact."

"Well, the facts have changed, and I can't help the way I feel. I'm sorry, but I love her."

"No, you don't," I reply dismissively. "It's just a phase, like a mid-life crisis."

"We've been seeing each other for over a year. It's no phase."

"I … what? A year?"

She nods.

It feels like I'm tumbling down a flight of concrete stairs. Just when I think I've suffered the hardest blow, another quickly follows, and then another. How many more will I have to endure before the tumbling ends?

I don't know what to say. In lieu of anything constructive, I let my mouth continue, unsupervised.

"This isn't right. You don't suddenly wake up one day and decide you're a lesbian."

"I'm not a lesbian, I'm bisexual," she shrugs. "Just because I happen to be married to a man, it doesn't change who I am?"

I leave my mouth to continue the argument; brain disengaged.

"How the fuck do you know you're bisexual and this isn't just some ridiculous whim?"

"Because I dated a girl in college, and I had a brief fling with a woman before we got together."

Another stair, another blow.

"And you never thought to tell me? Unbelievable."

"Did you tell me about your love life before we met?"

"There was nothing to tell. I had one girlfriend, one sexual partner. Anyway, I'm not the one on trial here."

"And neither am I. These things happen, and I'm sorry I've hurt you — I truly am — but I never planned to fall in love with someone else."

We reach an impasse as the emotional winds change direction.

"If you just need some time and space," I say meekly. "I'm willing to wait."

"Wait for what?"

"Until this … whatever it is, runs its course."

"You're not understanding me, are you?"

"Obviously not."

"This isn't a fling or a phase or a fad. I've met someone and fallen in love with her. And, we're no different to any two people in love — we want to be together, live together, grow old together."

"That's what *we're* supposed to do together … you and me. We had it all planned out."

"The only plan I have in mind includes Vicky."

"But …"

"Stop, please. There's no easy way to say this, but I want a divorce."

"Good for you. I don't."

"Well, that's unfortunate. I hope, in time, you'll come to terms with my decision. I'd rather we parted as friends than enemies, but if you can't cope with that, I'm willing to fight tooth and nail."

"So, it's threats now, is it?"

"It's not a threat because the last thing I want is acrimony. Your emotions are understandably raw at the moment, but once the dust has settled, I'm sure you'll see things differently."

She stands up.

"Where are you going?"

"We could sit here all day and talk, but it won't change anything. I've told you how I feel and what I want, and none of it is negotiable."

"I don't get a say?"

"In this instance, no. It's my life and my choice."

"You didn't answer my question. Where are you going?"

"I said I want to be reasonable and as you've done nothing wrong, it's only fair I leave. Vicky has gone home to tell Andy, and then we'll stay in a hotel until we can sort out temporary accommodation."

I put my head in my hands.

"This is a nightmare. Please, tell me I'm about to wake up."

She places her hand on my shoulder. It's a touch of consolation rather than affection.

"You'll get through it and, who knows, maybe one day you'll look back and thank your lucky stars this happened. Everything happens for a reason, Sean."

A thought occurs. Actually, it's more the desperate lunge of a man mortally wounded in battle. At best, I might leave a scar.

"You do realise what I've given up for you?"

"Sorry?"

"I gave away the chance of fatherhood to make you happy,

and now it seems that sacrifice was in vain."

"No one forced you to stay. If you were so desperate for kids, you could have left, but you decided to stay with me. That's on you — don't try and guilt-trip me."

The hand slips from my shoulder; likely the last time my wife will ever touch me.

"I'm going to pack a few things."

She strides away. I know what comes next.

I sit motionless for God-knows how long until I hear footsteps on the stairs. Carol appears in the doorway; a small suitcase at her feet.

"My solicitor will be in touch later this week," she says without a hint of emotion. "I'm going to suggest we split everything fifty-fifty, but leave our pensions out of it. I hope you agree that's fair."

It's a statement, not a question. I don't reply.

"As soon as I've sorted out a rental place, I'll arrange for a removal company to pick up my possessions. If you draw up a list of items in the house you'd like to keep, we can discuss who gets what."

I look up from the table.

"Whatever."

"Goodbye, Sean."

She turns on her Louboutin heels and strides across the tiled hallway to the front door. Seconds later, she's gone. Gone for good, I fear.

The silence in the kitchen is crushing. I look around at the space my wife created. She chose the gloss-white units, the Corian worktops, the German-built appliances, and the limestone tiles beneath my feet. Her dream kitchen, her vision, yet she's willing to walk away from it for the love of ... I still can't believe it.

Just over three hours ago, I ate breakfast in this very chair; utterly oblivious to my wife's infidelity. It's easy to be angry at her, but how could I have been so blind? I've known Andy a long time but our friendship never really extended beyond the occasional gigs with Busted Flush and a few pints now and then. That was until two years ago when Carol and I received an invite to Andy's fiftieth birthday party.

Thinking back, I was chatting with the other members of the band, while our wives, bored of the blokeish chat, drifted away to a nearby table. I noticed Carol laughing and joking with Vicky, and I was pleased to see her enjoying the evening. There's nothing worse than taking your partner to an event and sensing their boredom. With Carol being so committed to her career, she'd always struggled to find the time for friendships.

So, a few days later, when Carol told me she was meeting Vicky for coffee, I actively encouraged her.

Idiot.

They continued to meet regularly for coffee, and every other Saturday they went shopping together. Should I have suspected something?

As I ponder that question, a moment of savage realisation arrives.

In September last year, one of Carol's clients gave her two tickets to see the musical *Wicked* in London, but I couldn't go because of work commitments. Rather than waste them, Carol suggested she might go with Vicky and make a weekend of it. My overriding emotion at the time was one of relief as I knew Carol had always wanted to see *Wicked*. I told her she absolutely should go with Vicky.

A few days before that weekend, I happened to glance at an email on Carol's laptop. It confirmed her two-night reservation at a five-star hotel in the West End. I remember mentioning a problem with the booking — a double room rather than a twin. Carol laughed it off and said she'd kick up a fuss when she got there in the hope of bagging an upgrade. I never gave it another thought, like I never gave much thought to the spa weekend they arranged a month later, or the various other trips they've taken together over the last twelve months: yoga retreats, theatre breaks, concerts, and a four-day wine tasting experience in Burgundy.

If Vicky had been a man, my suspicions would have piqued at the frequent meetings for coffee, but why would I suspect my wife of having an affair with a woman? How was I to know she'd already passed bi-curious and sampled bi-actual?

Then, I'm not the only fool who didn't have a clue.

Right this second, in a village on the other side of Exeter, Andy is probably kicking himself just as hard for not spotting the signs. Is he going through the same futile motions and begging his wife to change her mind? Is he currently reeling from the same seismic shock? Is he being pummelled by a raft of emotions he can barely process?

One thing is for sure: I can't see Andy and I ever playing in the band together again. It's easy to say we might become closer as we share our mutual pain, but I know where we'd go after that. At some point I'd mention that email and the double room booking, and Andy would look at me, confounded. He'd then question why I never told him. Likewise, there must have been times when his wife slipped up, but he overlooked it. In time, we'd grow to resent each other's failings. We'd both know the other missed an opportunity to nip the affair in the bud and, rightly or wrongly, we'd begin apportioning blame.

Minute by tortuous minute, further conclusions arrive — this is not just about my wife finding love with someone who isn't me — it's the complete and comprehensive deconstruction of the life I've built with Carol. Our home, our friends, our plans, our hopes and dreams; all gone. One moment I had everything, the next, nothing.

It might be page one of a new life, but it feels more like the end.

As it stands, only two people get to live their happily ever after. I'm not one of them.

SIX MONTHS LATER...

3.

I'm sick and tired of signing paperwork. So, when the foreman hands me a clipboard, I scribble my name at the bottom of the delivery form without reading it.

Although their work is complete, the three men in sweat-stained polo shirts appear reluctant to leave. It dawns on me why, and I take out my wallet.

"Great job, lads," I smile, handing over thirty quid. "Have a beer on me. You've earned it."

"Cheers, boss. All the best."

They file out of the kitchen, leaving me with a stack of boxes to unpack. Still, they've got a long journey ahead of them, all the way back to Exeter.

Putting off the unpacking, I take a slow tour around the two-bedroom apartment. Up until this morning, it belonged to a theatre director by the name of Lucas. Now, the deeds bear my name.

I scan the unfamiliar view from the lounge window and, in the silence, take a moment to reflect how I got here.

The weeks after *that* morning remain a haze. I continued living in a state of denial for days until the promised letter from Carol's solicitor arrived. In typical fashion, my estranged wife managed our separation like a work project; a series of tasks and milestones with me the unwilling stakeholder. I made several attempts to delay the process in the hope Carol would change her mind, but my bloody-mindedness only fuelled her determination. By mid-December, I had to concede defeat — divorce was inevitable.

Before I knew it, Christmas Eve arrived. I don't think there's a worse time to be alone than Christmas, and I knew it would be tough spending it on my own for the first time in my life. As hard as it was, I mustered just enough enthusiasm to venture out to the pub in the village, hoping the combination of mulled wine and cheery Christmas tunes might raise my spirits.

When I arrived, I made straight for the bar and ordered a drink. I then scanned the room in search of a quiet table where I could observe rather than participate in the festive celebrations. That's when I saw them — Carol and Vicky chatting and giggling together at a table in the corner. To anyone looking on, it might have appeared they were simply two friends enjoying a night out together. I knew different, and when Carol discreetly stroked Vicky's thigh beneath the table, I lost it.

Foolishly, I thought it a good idea to storm over and confront them. During the rant, I'm sure I used the term 'selfish bitch' at least once.

After I'd blown myself out, Carol calmly stated I'd have to get used to seeing them in the pub as they were renting a house in the village. They'd set up home barely half-a-mile from our cottage. Any progress I'd made over the weeks since we split evaporated in that moment. I tipped nearly an entire pint of Bishop's Finger into my wife's lap and walked out. I didn't know it at the time, but it would be the last visit to my local.

The New Year dawned and my emotional state no doubt contributed to the mistakes I began making at work. Those mistakes cost the company money and, with that, any chance of a place on the board. In truth, I was lucky to keep the job I had. Despite my problems, I worked all hours in the hope it would prove a distraction, but I soon became the target of water-cooler gossip.

The more ambitious of my subordinates smelt blood, and the harmless gossip evolved into malicious muck spreading. If I couldn't even keep my marriage together, how could I possibly be trusted to manage my department? Every minor mistake I made ended up being magnified ten-fold and reported back to the board through a chorus of Chinese whispers; my reputation and authority undermined continuously.

Work became a distraction but for all the wrong reasons. It became a living hell.

By February, when the decree nisi arrived, I'd made a

decision. I had to get away. When you've lived most of your adult life in one place, it's impossible to escape the constant reminders of the past, and every part of that past included Carol. My wife became a ghost, haunting me wherever I went. On top of that, there was a sense of failure, of humiliation. I could almost hear the sniggers whenever I ventured out — there's that bloke whose wife set up home with another woman. It was probably no more than my paranoia, but I couldn't live with it.

I handed in my notice and decided to relocate.

Then came the decision on where I would spend the rest of my days. The only family I have is an older brother, Stuart, but he emigrated to Australia decades ago. I wanted to get far away from Carol, but I'm no fan of forty-degree heat or venomous spiders. Not an option.

I drew up a shortlist of possible towns but quickly whittled it down to one. I grew up in Guildford, in Surrey, and it's also home to a headstone engraved with my parents' names. They moved to Bournemouth while I was at uni, but they both wanted to be buried in their home town when the time came. Little did I know that time would arrive prematurely.

So, here I am. One hundred and fifty miles away from Exeter, in a town where no one knows my back story. I'd like to say I'm relishing the clean slate, but in truth, I'm not.

Although I don't want to grow old alone, the thought of entering another relationship terrifies me. The last time I went on a date, there were only four television channels, and I sported a glorious head of sandy-blond hair. The only hair on my head these days is a greyish goatee-style beard which helps to hide a few of my chins. My once speedy metabolism has slowed to a crawl — there's now fifty per cent more of me than there once was.

When I look in the mirror, I don't see an object of desire — I see a fifty-four-year-old wreck who's eaten in too many restaurants and supped too much ale over the years. A man who has never much cared about his skincare regime or whether his clothes were fashionable. Happily married, he had no reason to preen or polish.

Beyond the damning aesthetics I see a man who lost his wife to a woman.

I've been told a dozen times by a dozen different people I shouldn't let that get under my skin, but it does. Perhaps it's because I know what I'd think if it had happened to someone else: what an abject failure as a husband.

Maybe my view is a bit simplistic, a bit old-fashioned, but I can't help it. I feel a lesser-man, and my confidence is in shreds.

"Pull yourself together," I snap, my voice echoing off the bare walls.

Over the last six months, I've developed a coping mechanism for times like this. With that, I rip the tape from a box which journeyed here in the boot of my car. Although the removal company provided insurance for all my worldly belongings, the box contains a priceless collection of cassettes and compact discs — every single *Now That's What I Call Music* compilation album ever released. Each edition includes an eclectic selection of chart hits from the year of release; a musical snapshot of my life at the time.

I bought the first one when I was seventeen, on cassette, and then the second and third albums on the day they were released. I took my fledgling collection with me to university, and by the time I graduated, that collection had grown to nine albums. Carol never understood why I continued to buy each new release on compact disc even after we entered the age of digital downloads. Although I stored my collection in an unused bedroom, she'd continually complain the rows of plastic cases were a dust magnet, and I should sell them on eBay.

Now, every album feels like a familiar old friend. Sad as it is, they're my only friends, so I'm glad they're here with me.

I open a second box which also travelled up in my car. It contains a portable stereo I've owned since the early nineties. As far as sound technology is concerned, it's rooted in the dark ages but unlike its modern counterparts, it can play both cassettes and compact discs.

After plugging the stereo in, I peruse the options in the box. With new beginnings in mind, I select the very first album from 1983 and carefully extract the case. Choosing cassette one, side one, I slip it into the stereo and press the play button.

It begins with Phil Collins' version of *You Can't Hurry Love*.

If I were to ever appear on Mastermind, my specialist subject would be the *Now* albums. I'm sure I could name every track on every album, in order. I must confess I favour the first forty-seven albums over those released post-millennium. Those later releases don't resonate in the same way as they lack the musical diversity of the earlier albums. A point in question is the album I'm currently listening to as it contains tracks from Malcolm McLaren of Sex Pistols fame, Madness, Howard Jones, Mike Oldfield, KC and the Sunshine Band, The Human League, Rock Steady Crew, and The Cure. It's like a journey through musical genres.

The earliest *Now* albums will always be my favourites, and here now, the first of the series will provide the soundtrack to my unpacking duties. As Phil Collins hands over to Duran Duran, I tear open another box.

I made a conscious decision to bring as little with me as possible. When starting a new life, the last thing I wanted was to fill it with reminders of the old one. Alongside all my clothes and personal possessions, I chose a few items of carefully selected furniture. As a consequence, my new apartment errs towards a minimalist style. I've got a double bed, though not the one Carol and I shared for obvious reasons, a chest of drawers and bedside table taken from our former guest bedroom, two armchairs which previously resided in the conservatory, and that's it. Carol took full responsibility for the interior design of our cottage, and although I liked the odd painting or two, there was nothing I liked enough to fight over. I guess all those carefully collated pieces now reside in my ex-wife's new love nest.

Part of me hopes Vicky detests Carol's quirky tastes in interior design. It would serve her right.

It's late afternoon by the time I unpack the final box. I then slowly pad around each of the rooms in an orientation exercise. I wouldn't exactly call it homely, but everything in the apartment is here because I alone chose it, and I want it here. Over time I guess I'll make an effort to inject some character into the place, but the bachelor pad styling will suffice for now.

Hunger strikes, but I don't have so much as a loaf of bread in the kitchen, nor do I have the energy for a trip to the supermarket. I open the takeaway delivery app on my phone, and a reminder of my previous life immediately greets me.

Because of our busy work lives, we used to order in a takeaway three or four times a week. Over the years, we must have tried every takeaway in the Exeter area and honed our preferences down to one favourite for each type of cuisine: Chinese from The Lotus Flower, Indian from The Bengal Grill, Thai from Blue Mango, and so on.

All of those takeaways remain in the app as my favourites. In the unlikely event any of them deliver to Guildford, I wouldn't want to eat a meal I'd only ever consumed in my wife's company.

I delete the list. Now, I literally do have a blank page.

Scanning the options on the screen, I stop when I reach Domino's Pizza. Carol hated pizza, so I can't recall the last time I tucked into a thin crust Hawaiian. I update the delivery address and order a large one, along with some garlic bread, being there's no one around to complain about my breath.

My phone pings a confirmation message just as the final track on cassette two begins: *Victims* by Culture Club. I know both the takeaway order and my album of choice are metaphoric bookends: the music I used to listen to pre-Carol, and the food I can now eat post-Carol. Admittedly, it's a narrow slip of land to inhabit but preferable to the bleak landscape I endured in the weeks after our break up.

While I attempt to build a new life, I can find solace by embracing the musical memories of life before Carol and celebrate the positive aspects of my new-found freedom, however insignificant they might be.

Keen to test the theory, I set up the television in the lounge, knowing I, and I alone will have full control of the remote control.

"Small wins, Sean," I whisper, as I untangle the nest of leads. "Small wins."

4.

I'm now used to waking up alone, but it's disconcerting waking up in a strange bedroom. I hadn't realised it faces east and the curtains are an inadequate filter for the early morning sunrays. I squint and look away from the window, but the previous owner clearly had an aversion to colour as every wall is brilliant white. There's no escaping the assault on my retinas.

I can add curtain shopping to my to-do list, which also includes a trip to the supermarket and the not insignificant challenge of setting up a new business.

After I handed in my notice, I spent a week browsing job websites in the search for a suitable position in Surrey. There were plenty of opportunities for a candidate with my skill set, but not necessarily for candidates with my mindset.

While my contemporaries were burning cash supporting their offspring, I invested a large chunk of my disposable income in a pension. I'm six years away from that pension paying out, and I now fancy coasting those last six years.

The prospect of starting a new job and proving myself, while also justifying a generous salary, held no appeal. I concluded I'd had enough of office politics and career advancement. Besides, I've already endured far too much work-related stress over the years, and I'd rather avoid a heart attack or stroke this side of my sixtieth birthday.

So, I made another life-changing decision — to set myself up as a freelance finance consultant for independent hotels. After years of creative penny pinching for my previous employer, I estimated I could save the average hotel owner tens of thousands of pounds in operational costs, thus justifying the fee I intend to charge them. I've spent weeks formulating a business plan, and if that plan is accurate, I only need a dozen or so clients to earn a reasonable living. I've no mortgage, fortunately, so besides my household bills and the car, I've no real financial liabilities.

A positive consequence of my career change is a renewed

sense of focus, and there's plenty to keep me busy as I set up my new venture. The spare bedroom will become my office, so I need to kit that out. Then, I'll need a website and all the other marketing paraphernalia required to attract clients.

Plenty to do, but this morning there's one task on my list which takes precedent over all the others.

I get up, grab a quick shower, dress in seasonably appropriate attire, and leave the apartment.

My destination is a couple of miles north of the town, so I hop in the car. There are two waypoints I need to visit. I use the car's in-built sat-nav to identify a street to the north of the town centre where a coffee shop and a florist are only a hundred yards apart, and I can easily park.

I pull away from the bay outside my apartment and revel in the novelty of driving through the streets of Guildford. I didn't pass my driving test until the last year of university, so for the eighteen years I lived here, I had to rely on public transport or my dad if I wanted to get anywhere. The streets themselves are still vaguely familiar, but many of the buildings aren't. Much has changed.

After bolting down a toasted bagel and a coffee, I head to the florists and leave with a bunch of brightly coloured flowers, plucked from a bucket just inside the door. I don't know if they're appropriate, but I'd like to think their cheerful hue best reflects the kind of people Ian and Ruth Hardy were.

Back in the car, I set the sat-nav for my ultimate destination: Stoke New Cemetery.

I've always thought my parents' final resting place had a peculiar name. It hasn't been a new cemetery since the Second World War when it first opened its gates, and geographically it's nowhere near Stoke.

The journey is brief, and I can still taste the bitterness of the coffee as I park up and make my way to the main entrance.

Like most cemeteries, Stoke New is a flat expanse of mottled grass, interspersed with monotone headstones and evergreen trees. There are benches and bins and a well-maintained path which cuts through the centre towards a small chapel. In this corner of Guildford, nothing has changed.

I wander up the path and cut left towards the boundary. Ten yards short of the hedge, and currently shaded by a tall conifer, is my parents' grave.

I squat down and brush away the organic detritus the wind has failed to clear from the foot of the headstone.

The limestone is probably millions of years old but only been employed in its current role for twenty-seven years. It's showing the signs of age now, darkened by the elements and a far cry from the pale pristine tablet unveiled all those years ago.

To my shame, this is only the third time I've seen it up close. The first viewing coincided with my parents' funeral, with Carol by my side as a girlfriend rather than a wife. I also had Stuart's company after he flew back from Australia. There were a few dozen other attendees: some distant family members I didn't know or didn't care to know, plus my parents' friends, former colleagues, and assorted acquaintances.

We were all here to share our mutual grief and our shock.

Five weeks prior, the future looked rosy for every member of the Hardy family.

I was twenty-six at the time, and I'd carved out a decent life with Carol down in Exeter. My parents were enjoying their retirement, and they'd constantly tease me how they intended to blow my inheritance on a decadent lifestyle. They sold the family home in Guildford and bought a luxury seafront apartment in Bournemouth. Being much closer to Exeter, I got to see them more often, and we'd go out for dinner or drinks, and I'd hear all about their plans to travel the world.

On the 17th February 1993, those plans were well underway as my parents climbed aboard a ferry in Jérémie, Haiti. They were embarking on a grand tour of the Caribbean and were heading towards Port-au-Prince, Haiti's capital city, where they intended to stay for a few days. As they neared their destination, a storm broke out, and the ferry capsized. We found out later it was only licenced to carry six-hundred and fifty passengers, but that night, almost two thousand souls lost their lives. That toll included both my parents. They were only in their mid-fifties; maybe a year or so older than I am now.

I carefully lay the flowers against the headstone and stand up.

Some people can sit at a grave and chat to their dearly departed for hours on end. I'm afraid I don't possess either the belief or the conviction to talk to a cold slab of limestone. I wish I did, but it's just not me. Religion has never been part of my life, and it would be hypocritical to assume I can cherry-pick the parts I want to believe in just because the circumstance suits. There's no getting past the truth here — this visit is about easing my conscience rather than an opportunity to say hello.

There's only so long you can stare at a headstone, but it feels wrong to depart after just a few minutes. Instead, I turn and cast my eyes across the cemetery grounds. Over a hundred and fifty thousand people live in the Guildford area, but I'm the only one currently appreciating the tranquillity and mild May weather. It's a Tuesday morning, so I suppose most are at work.

To all intents and purposes, I'm alone. Not just here in this cemetery but in every sense. My parents are long gone, and so is Carol, albeit her departure was for a different life rather than a mythical afterlife. And, with my brother now a fully-fledged Aussie enjoying his retirement on the opposite side of the globe, I have no family.

I turn back to the headstone and forsaking my principles, mumble a few words.

"I miss you both terribly. I'll try and visit more often."

Swallowing hard, I walk away. This was never a visit I wanted to make but one I felt I had to make. I'm glad it's over.

As I get back in the car, I'm taken by a sudden need to be amongst people. It wasn't on my list until later, but I decide to go grocery shopping. I leave Stoke New Cemetery behind me. I don't intend to return until the first autumn frost arrives.

After an hour spent wandering the aisles of Waitrose, I head back to the apartment and unpack the shopping. Nothing yet has a designated home, so it takes a bit longer than it would otherwise.

I make myself a cup of instant coffee and retire to the lounge. Using my mobile phone, I waste an hour browsing a dozen different websites before ordering a desk, office chair, and a filing cabinet. Next, I call the broadband company and book an engineer to visit on Thursday. Another tick on the list. The third most pressing task involves hiring someone to build a website. I'm a bit of a dinosaur when it comes to the internet — I don't even have a Facebook account — but I do know a decent website is essential in this day and age.

I search for local website designers and call the first one listed in the results. A woman answers.

"Good afternoon, Gresham Web Marketing."

"Hi, I'm looking to get a website designed, and I don't have the first clue how to go about it."

"No problem, Sir. Can I get some details and we'll see what we can do?"

I quote the requested details, including a basic overview of what I want the website for.

"Seeing as you're local, Mr Hardy, would you like to come in and have a chat? It's often easier talking face-to-face."

"I'm quite keen to get this sorted as I know it'll take a few weeks to do whatever you people do. With that, how soon can I pop in?"

"Can you hold for a second and I'll have a word with Kian."

She nips off to consult with Kian, whoever he is, and returns after a minute rather than a second.

"Would half-four today work?"

"Perfect."

I end the call and check the time; three and a bit hours to kill.

Returning to my to-do list, I realise there are several tasks I can't complete until I've sorted out the website. I can't get stationery or business cards printed until I know what my website domain name and email address will be. Thinking about it, I don't even know what I'm going to call this new venture. Do I give it a corporate-like name or use my own name? I've no idea.

I guess most of my questions will be answered later. With nothing else better to do, I open the Amazon app and work my way through a list of items I need for the apartment, including new bedroom curtains, a coffee machine of the inexpensive variety, and various kitchen utensils. I relinquished my rights to the garlic press and nutmeg grinder in the divorce settlement. They will not be replaced.

Just after four o'clock, I collate all the paperwork I've amassed for the new business and leave the apartment.

One of the main attractions of my new home is the location. Situated in a quiet residential street, it's only a fifteen-minute walk from the town centre and train station. I've got a host of pubs, bars, and restaurants on my doorstep, and I can hop on a train and be in London within thirty minutes. It's ideal for meeting potential clients, and for rebuilding a social life.

I set off towards the offices of Gresham Web Marketing, located to the north of the town centre.

Walking rather than driving, I get a better opportunity to absorb my surroundings. My route avoids the town centre itself, and if time were on my side, I'd detour to the High Street to see how much it's changed. The shops will likely be closed by the time I finish my meeting, but it might be an excellent opportunity to vet a few pubs as I seek a new local.

I arrive at my destination; a street-level door with a silver plaque to the side, confirming Gresham Web Marketing Services reside on the first floor.

I'm greeted at the reception desk by a smiley young woman with a prominent nose piercing. She introduces me to Kian — a guy roughly half my age and half my weight.

After I decline coffee, Kian guides me to a meeting room and offers a seat on a bright-red leather sofa.

We sit, and Kian goes through a presentation on a laptop. Most of it goes way over my head, but it's clear I'm dealing with people who know what they're doing. He shows examples of websites they've built for several companies I've heard of, including two small hotel chains.

After a brief conversation about what I'm looking for, Kian takes notes on his phone and confirms my needs aren't complicated, and my delivery timescale is realistic. The whole process takes just forty minutes and, at the end, I receive a limp-wristed handshake and a promise my formal quote will be emailed before lunchtime tomorrow.

I return to the reception area with Kian at my heels. The young woman at the desk is deep in conversation with a middle-aged guy in jeans and a slim-fit checked shirt. He looks up as I cross the carpet and stares at me with a little too much intensity. Unsure how to react, I nod back.

"Sean, this is Wayne," Kian interjects. "The head of the company."

"Oh, right."

Wayne steps into my path and holds out his hand.

"Sorry if this is an odd question," he then says. "Are you the Sean Hardy who attended St Peter's Secondary School?"

"Um, I went to St Peter's, yes."

His face lights up.

"I knew I recognised the name. Do you remember me? Wayne Gresham?"

"I'm afraid I don't remember much about my time at St Peter's. It was a long time ago."

"We were in the same class for music. You played the guitar, right?"

I have the vaguest memory of a kid in my music class called Wayne.

"You used to wear glasses?" I venture.

"That's me."

His handshake is particularly enthusiastic.

"Do you still see anyone from school?" he asks.

"Sadly not. I stayed in Devon after I finished uni. I've just moved back to Guildford."

"That would explain the accent."

"Yeah, kind of," I chuckle.

I can't deny my home counties accent has taken on a slight West Country twang over the years. Whenever I used to visit our hotels in London for meetings, they'd jokingly comment on my Wurzel-like tone. Back in Devon, those born-and-bred in the county claimed I spoke like an Old Etonian. I now have a hybrid accent which is neither pure Devon nor pure Surrey.

"Do you remember Mrs Haywood?" he asks.

"The music teacher? How could I forget."

"She was a monster. I still have nightmares about that woman."

Wayne then relays an anecdote about a damaged trumpet and Mrs Haywood's wrath. He throws in a few names I've long forgotten.

"Still, good times," he says wistfully.

"Are you still in contact with anyone from school?"

"You could say that. I married the head girl, Claire Barker. Remember her?"

I remember her as an overly officious, plump girl with rabid acne and delusions of her own importance.

"God, yeah. She was …"

"Fierce?"

"That's the word I was looking for."

"She still is, mate. Keeps me in check."

Wayne then glances at his watch.

"Listen, Sean. I'm just about to finish up for the day. Do you fancy a quick pint in town? It'd be good to catch up."

Do I fancy a pint with a virtual stranger? I suppose it's better than sitting on my own, and maybe I can haggle a mate's rates deal on the website, even though we were never really mates.

"I'd love to."

"Great. I've got to make a quick phone call, but I can meet you in the King's Head in say, twenty minutes?"

"I'll see you there."

Wayne dashes off to his office, and I trot back down the stairs to the street.

The first full day back in my home town and I've already reconnected with a long-forgotten fellow pupil from St Peter's. I promised myself I wouldn't look back, but maybe that's precisely the place I should be looking if I'm to build a new life here.

Besides, I'm keen to understand why anyone in their right mind married Claire Barker.

5.

I've only been to the King's Head once before. A proper olde-worlde pub with low beams and an inglenook fireplace, it wasn't the kind of place my eighteen-year-old self would have frequented back in the day. Now, it's my idea of the perfect pub.

I head to the bar and order a pint of their guest ale. I've no idea what Wayne drinks but he strikes me as the continental lager type. Although we're the same age, it would be fair to say Wayne has aged far better than I have. I suppose that's down to him working in a creative industry and surrounding himself with youngsters.

I'm halfway through my pint when Wayne wanders in and spots me at the bar.

"What can I get you?" I ask, as he strides over.

"I'll have a Peroni, cheers."

My guess proved accurate. I order accordingly.

"Come on then," I say. "What's your secret?"

"My secret?"

"You're in remarkably good shape for a man in his fifties."

"Ahh, I wish I could take the credit, but it's just good genes."

"You're a lucky man. Some of us haven't aged so gracefully."

It's so slight it's barely noticeable, but his eyes drop to appraise my attire.

"My teenage daughter, Abbey, insists on coming clothes shopping with me. If I were left unsupervised, I'd come home with beige pullovers and comfortable slacks."

"Can I borrow her?"

"Only if you're willing to trawl Top Shop afterwards," he says with a snort of laughter. "And you've got deep pockets."

"Joys of parenthood, eh?"

"Indeed."

Wayne's pint arrives, and we move to a table near the window.

"So, what have you been up to for the last thirty-odd years, mate?" he asks.

"Brief highlights, I met a girl at uni, and we ended up getting married in the mid-nineties. I got a job as head of finance for a hotel chain, and we bought a cottage in a village ten miles from Exeter. That's about it."

We then discuss my new business, and Wayne shares some of his marketing wisdom. He talks enthusiastically about the many ways his company can help. I don't know him well enough to say if he's trying to upsell or he's genuinely passionate about the project.

He closes the subject with a promise to send over a comprehensive marketing proposal in the next few days.

"So, Sean, what brings you back to Guildford?"

"Divorce, I'm afraid."

"Ah, shit. Sorry to hear that."

"It happens."

"You got kids?"

"My ex was more interested in her career than being a mother. I'd have liked kids, but some things just aren't meant to be."

"Never say never. There's still time."

"Right," I cough. "I think my baby-making days are behind me."

"What happened with your marriage?"

I'm a bit taken by the frank nature of his question. Fortunately, I've already considered how I might answer this question.

"We wanted different things," I shrug.

Not strictly true. We both wanted a relationship with a woman.

"Anyway, tell me what you've been up to," I add, keen to move the conversation away from my failed marriage.

"Not much to tell really. I married Claire in '89, and we've been together ever since."

"Is Abbey your only child?"

"Nope, she has an older brother, Ben. He lives in London and works for an investment bank, earning far more money than his old man."

"You seem to be doing pretty well for yourself, running your own business."

"We do okay. It'll never make me rich, but we enjoy a comfortable life. Both the kids are doing well, and we've got a nice house in Wood Street Village."

"Does Claire work?"

"Yep, she's now a headteacher would you believe?"

Yes, I would.

Wayne then grabs his phone and taps the screen. I suspect I'm about to be treated to a montage of family photos. He holds it up to show me the screen.

"The kids, taken at a barbecue last summer."

Two smiling faces look back at me. The kind of disgustingly perfect faces you're likely to see in a Disney movie set in a high school.

"They're good-looking kids," I remark.

"They take after their mother."

He swipes the screen, and the image changes to a middle-aged woman's face. Either the photo is highly filtered, or the woman is drop-dead stunning.

"That's Claire."

"My God," I blurt. "She's changed."

"Just a bit. You should have seen the looks we got when we pitched-up at the school reunion a few years back. It would be no exaggeration to say a few jaws hit the floor."

"I can imagine. You'd never guess it was the same person."

"Claire knew what people used to say behind her back, and maybe some of it she brought on herself, but the stuff about her looks wasn't nice. It spurred her to lose weight and change her image."

I take a sip of ale to mask any signs of guilt on my part.

"Did you make it to the reunion?" Wayne asks. "I don't recall seeing you there."

"I didn't even know there was one."

"Three years ago, to mark the thirty-fifth anniversary of our leaving year. It was all arranged via Facebook."

"That would explain it. I'm one of those oddballs who've managed to live their life without a Facebook account."

"We'll have to address that. There are so many marketing opportunities with social media."

"I'll take your word for that. How did the reunion go?"

"It was good fun, once everyone finished gushing over Claire and telling her how beautiful she looked. What they really wanted to say is they couldn't believe how much that chubby head girl had changed. Ugly ducklings and swans spring to mind."

"In fairness, I think they'd have been equally shocked by how much I've changed, although not in a good way."

"Don't do yourself down, mate," he responds, waving away my self-deprecation. "You should see how badly some of our former school friends have fared. Do you remember Luke Jennings?"

"Popular kid, particularly with the girls?"

"That's him. Thought he was God's gift yet his arrival at the reunion dropped more jaws than Claire's, but for altogether different reasons."

"Why's that?"

"He looked bloody awful, and I mean bloody awful — the kind of bloke who still lives at home with his mum and spends most days in a dark bedroom playing video games, gorging on pizza, and wanking into a sock. He absolutely stunk the hall out."

"Nice imagery," I chuckle.

"I don't mean to speak ill of the guy, but he's a complete loser now. He used to bully Claire something rotten at school, and you should have seen his face when she introduced herself.

He tried acting like they used to be best friends."

"Ha-ha, I bet it was a picture."

"It was so sweet, especially when Claire told him exactly what she thought about his behaviour at school. Poor bloke didn't know what hit him. My wife is not a woman you want to mess with."

"Did he apologise?"

"He did, and to give the bloke credit, he gave Claire the last laugh by confessing he'd failed miserably at life. Who'd have thought it, but once his boyish good looks faded, Luke Jennings had nothing else in his locker. He's now just a sad fuck."

"How the mighty fall."

"Yep, but as shitty as Luke's life turned out, he's in a better place than a handful of former pupils. We had a few sobering moments throughout the evening."

"I'm not with you."

"Statistically, of the few hundred in our year, there was always a good chance some wouldn't have made it to their fifties."

"Ah, right."

"Brian Mountjoy. Remember him?"

"Can't say I do."

"He died in a car accident in Wales in the late nineties."

At my age, you can't help but become acutely aware of your own mortality. That's one reason I'd rather not sit and listen to a list of deceased schoolmates. Nevertheless, Wayne continues.

"And Jennie Furlong. She had a bloody heart attack two days after her fortieth birthday. Congenital heart defect."

"That's awful."

I try to adopt a facial expression which conveys how little I want this morbid roll call to continue, but Wayne is now in his stride.

"Oh, and then there's Gary Pavitt. He was working in New York in 2001."

Wayne looks at me expectedly, like I should understand the

relevance of his statement.

"His office was in the World Trade Centre."

Realisation strikes.

"Fuck. He died on 9/11?"

"Sadly, yes."

"Bloody hell. Poor bugger."

Unsure how many names we still have to cover, I prepare an excuse to leave the table; another toilet break being the most obvious at our age. Hopefully, Wayne will have run out of steam by the time I return. Just as I'm about to offer my apologies, he throws another name at me.

"Of course, there was also Jackie Benton," he says casually. "But you probably knew about her."

The name almost slips past me. It's been so many years since I last heard it, and I spent a long time trying to forget it.

"Eh … what?" I splutter. "Jackie Benton. She's dead?"

"You didn't know?"

I slump back in my seat.

"No, I didn't."

"Did you know her?"

"You could say that. We dated for five years."

Wayne closes his eyes for a moment. I guess he hadn't considered how insensitive it might be to spiel off names of the dead without checking if I knew any of them first.

"I'm so sorry, mate. I honestly thought you'd have heard. It happened years ago."

"When exactly?"

"Christ, now you're asking. Sometime in the eighties, I think."

Punch-drunk, I don't know what to say.

"Poor Jackie," I mumble, still reeling.

Wayne also appears lost for words. He looks at my glass and then escapes the awkwardness by dashing off to buy another round.

I cast my mind back to the last time I saw Jackie Benton. So long ago but it must have been in May 1987, and the day I left for university after the Easter break. At that point, we'd been together for five years. Our relationship had somehow survived the first two years of being apart for long periods, but as I waved goodbye to Jackie from the train, I knew the sternest of tests lay ahead.

I knew it because Carol Shanley entered my life seven months earlier.

Stupidly, I convinced myself Carol and I could be just friends, but as the months passed, our mutual attraction grew stronger. Inevitably, we slept together after a Christmas party. At first, we both agreed it had been a mistake. I felt awful cheating on Jackie, and the guilt proved unbearable.

For the following months I buried myself in my studies and tried to keep away from Carol, but by pure chance we bumped into each other in a pub days before the end of term. We both had too much to drink and ended up spending the night in Carol's bed. I left for home two days later, feeling abysmal. To cheat once was bad enough but to do it twice was unforgivable.

Back in Guildford, I stayed at my family home for the last time. My parents had already put the house on the market in preparation for their move to Bournemouth. I tried to forget all about Carol, and spent most of the Easter break with Jackie, reminding myself why I'd first fallen in love with her, and how much our relationship meant to me.

By the time I boarded that train for Exeter, I thought I'd done enough. As soon as I arrived, I called Carol and told her we couldn't see each other again. Barely a week later, we were back in her bed. She was like a drug I couldn't kick and I fell hopelessly in love.

They say it's not possible to love two people at the same time, but I disagree. Carol was my drug of choice but Jackie was my first love. I thought I'd always love her and she'd be the girl I'd marry.

Although we attended the same school, we'd never said a

single word to one another until one night at a youth disco in town. At the end of the evening, they always played a slow song which split the room in half. All the boys would stand on one side of the hall and the girls the other. Gradually, a few braver lads would cross the great divide and ask a girl to dance. One particular night, as the DJ played Dollar's *Give Me Back My Heart*, I crossed that great divide and asked Jackie if she'd like to dance.

That first dance led to our first kiss, our first date, and for both of us, our first proper relationship. On Jackie's sixteenth birthday, we nervously climbed into my single bed; virgins both. At that moment, I could never have imagined ever wanting sex with anyone other than Jackie — until I did.

Two weeks after I returned to uni, I knew it was unfair on both Carol and Jackie to continue as we were, and by that point, Carol seemed keen to move our relationship forward. I had to decide which girl I wanted in my life: my kind, sweet, first love back in Guildford, or the passionate, driven whirlwind who blew my mind every time we fell into bed. One girl living miles away, or one girl a few streets away?

In mid-May, I called Jackie and told her I'd met someone else.

Being young and stupidly naive, I tried to reassure her she'd find someone new in time, and it would be better to reflect on all the good times we'd enjoyed together rather than dwell on our separation. To this day, I don't think I've heard anyone sob with such heart-wrenching intensity. I couldn't bear it and hung up.

That was our last ever conversation.

In the subsequent weeks and months, I did everything I could to erase her from my memory. Looking back, my efforts were a way to run from the guilt and the shame, or maybe I wanted to ignore the nagging feeling I'd made a mistake. After graduation, I never returned to Guildford, and until now, I've never given much thought to what became of Jackie Benton.

"Here you go, mate."

Wayne places a pint on the table in front of me.

"You okay?" he asks. "You look a bit pale."

"Um, I'm … it's been a manic few days with the move up here and everything. I'm just a bit done in."

"It's not because of what I said, you know, about Jackie Benton?"

"I'm not going to lie — it came as a shock."

"If it helps, I could ask around and see if anyone knows what happened to her? That's assuming you want to know?"

I sip from my glass and ponder Wayne's question.

"Thanks, but as you said, it was a long time ago."

"You sure? It's no trouble."

"I'm sure. There's nothing to be gained from raking over the past."

"Well, if you change your mind, just let me know."

I won't change my mind.

6.

I put the restless night down to the unfamiliar surroundings and the overly-soft mattress.

I'm kidding myself.

I tossed and turned for an age, but no matter where I tried to lead my thoughts, they returned to Jackie.

Visions of her youthful face swirled around my head: that warm smile, her electric-blue eyes, those pearly-pink lips she'd nibble at when concentrating, and her dimpled cheeks. I cursed Wayne for ever mentioning her name, and then I cursed my own mind for posing a question: how could such a perfectly beautiful girl die so young? In the years we were together, I don't recall her suffering anything worse than a cold.

The only conclusion I could draw was an accident — some cruel twist of fate no one could have predicted or prevented. It offered little comfort as my mind stopped posing questions and dwelt upon the last seconds of Jackie's life — the fear in that perfect face when she realised her time was over.

I lie in bed, staring up at the ceiling. I know if I lie here any longer there's a chance my mind might dredge up those awful thoughts once more.

Joints complaining, I get up and pad through to the kitchen, and a game of hunt the cereal ensues. The milk proves easier to find. I switch the radio on and sit at the breakfast bar, chewing through a bowl of fibre-rich mulch with little enthusiasm. While food shopping yesterday, I vowed to improve my diet in the hope of shedding a few pounds. There's sod all I can do about my grizzled features, but if there's ever another school reunion, I don't want to be met by the same astonished gasps Luke Jennings experienced.

The doorbell rings.

I march down the hallway and open the door to a delivery driver with a cluster of boxes at his feet.

"Sean Hardy?"

"Yep."

"Amazon delivery."

"Oh, great."

He bids me a good day and dashes back to his van.

I transfer the boxes to the spare bedroom and begin the unpacking process. Once I've extracted all the parts, I have a small coffee machine and a large pile of landfill.

"Unbelievable," I grumble.

The next box isn't much better, and of the dozen kitchen utensils I ordered, nine of the items come wrapped in an impenetrable layer of hard plastic, including the only pair of scissors I own.

Using a steak knife, I manage to extract the scissors. It then takes me half-an-hour to free the rest of my utensils. The last box is less of a challenge. Inside is a pair of blackout curtains for the bedroom. I remove them from the wrapping and only then do I notice the manufacturer has printed the style name across the top of the packaging; Elaine. Coincidentally, Jackie's middle name.

Seeing the name in inch-high letters summons a memory.

When Jackie and I first started dating, there were a limited number of places we could spend time together due to our lack of money. One of our favourite haunts was a little cafe near the train station. If the weather was bad, we'd sit in that cafe for hours, chatting about everything and nothing.

On one occasion we got on to the subject of marriage. I remember Jackie saying she couldn't wait to marry me, so she could ditch the Benton part of her name — her step-father's surname. She then borrowed a pen from the waitress and practised writing-out the name Jacqueline Elaine Hardy on a napkin, over and over again. Up until that moment, I didn't even know she had a middle name.

I unpack the curtains and swap them with the inadequate pair in the main bedroom. It's only a ten-minute job but long enough for my thoughts to continue their path into the murky past. It's at times like this I wonder if my generation is blessed or cursed in comparison to todays. My memory is sketchy, and we never had the benefit of being able to digitally capture every microsecond of our lives like kids do today. Consequently, I don't possess a single photograph of Jackie Benton. I'm sure there were photographs, but God only knows what happened to them. Lost, I guess, like so many memories.

If I had one, would I want to look at it, knowing how badly I treated her?

Thoughts of the infamous phone call return, and so too does a measure of guilt. How could I have been so cold, so callous? At very least, I should have returned to Guildford and told Jackie to her face. In fairness, I understood that at the time, but I knew the moment I set eyes on her, I'd likely change my mind. Far easier to do it over the phone, knowing I could hang up if I wavered.

Cowardly, really. Jackie deserved so much better.

I wander through to the kitchen to try out my new coffee machine. The resulting beverage has a delicious aroma, but there's a distinct bitterness to it; the metaphor not lost on me.

I'm no longer young, and I can't claim to be stupidly naive. If I've learnt anything over the last six months, it's to confront my emotions. I can't stand the term, but in this instance, perhaps I should have accepted Wayne's offer and sought closure on Jackie's sad demise. The truth has to be preferable to dwelling on a list of macabre possibilities every night.

I decide to call Wayne and grab my phone from the kitchen side. The moment my finger touches the screen, a damning realisation dawns — I'm allowing history to repeat itself. Thirty-three years ago, I took the easy option to spare my feelings. Now I'm about to do the exact same thing. I owe it to Jackie's memory to confirm what tragedy befell my first love — it's not a task to delegate.

I finish my coffee and form a rough plan of action. It's not how I intended to spend my second day back in Guildford, but

I'll never avoid all the Jackie-related regrets unless I add an epilogue to our story.

A deep breath and I confront a list of questions I've never had reason to ask before. How do you establish when and how someone died? And, how do you confirm if they were buried or cremated?

The obvious answer is to ask Google, so I return to my phone screen and stab out my search. A page of results appears, and I tap a few links which lead down blind alleys. At the fourth attempt, I land on an ancestry website which claims to hold the online records for every birth, marriage, and death in the United Kingdom. I take advantage of their free trial and sign-up so I can begin my search. With my one-fingered typing, it's a slow process.

Finally, I get to enter Jackie's full name. The form also requests a year of death, but all I have is Wayne's estimate of 'sometime in the eighties'. With that, I enter 1987 – the year we split up – and 1990. I can't imagine many Jacqueline Elaine Bentons died in that period.

With trepidation mounting, I tap the green search button.

As I anticipated, there's only one result, and I tap the link. Another page loads, with a choice of viewing or downloading the death certificate. I've no desire to keep a memento, so I choose to view the certificate.

The image takes forever to load, but the screen eventually fills with a cream-coloured document; a crest at the top and the fields all completed in scrawled handwriting. The only way to read it is to pinch the screen and zoom in.

The top part of the document only confirms the district and administrative area: Guildford, in the county of Surrey. I scroll down to the next section and unearth the answer to one of my questions. Assuming this is my Jacqueline Elaine Benton, she died on Monday 23rd May 1988 — roughly twelve months after our last conversation. It also confirms she died in Guildford.

I swallow hard and scroll down the document. It lists

Jackie's date of birth as the 12th June 1966. Exactly sixteen years after that date, we celebrated her birthday by consummating our relationship. Beyond all doubt, I now know I'm looking at the administrative end of Jackie's life. She was only twenty-one.

Only one question remains unanswered. I know when Jackie died, but I don't know how she died.

Scrolling on, I learn her occupation: shop assistant. That wasn't her occupation when we split up, but it probably suited her sunny personality better than the mundane office job she had before. Her address is the same house she shared with her parents while we were dating. She didn't have the best relationship with her step-father, but I suppose all teenagers hate their parents at some point, biological or otherwise.

The next section simply states the name of the informant as Derek Benton. Maybe Jackie's mother, Anna, was simply too distraught to deal with all the paperwork.

My eyes drop to the bottom of the screen and three words printed in mottled ink: Cause of death.

The final scroll reveals my answer, and it invokes a gasp. "No!"

Her cause of death was suicide.

I drop the phone on the side but continue to stare at the screen in disbelief. Surely, this must be a mistake?

Jackie was perpetually cheerful — the very last person I'd peg as suicidal. She had this ability to inject colour into the greyest of scenes, to point out the positives when you couldn't see anything but negatives. Jackie Benton loved life and savoured every new day. She was a silver lining kind of girl, her glass always half-full. People like Jackie don't kill themselves. They just don't.

What the hell happened to her in those twelve months? It's a futile question because not long after we split, my parents completed their move to Bournemouth, and I had no reason to return to Guildford. By the time Jackie committed suicide, Carol and I were living together, and I'd secured my first job. Life was good, and I had no interest in what was going on in my home town.

As stunned as I am, there is perhaps a slight sense of relief. If Jackie's suicide had occurred in the days or weeks after we split, many might have assumed the events were connected. To think my actions could have been the catalyst for a young girl taking her own life would be, even now, an awful cross to bear.

However, knowing my telephone call didn't push Jackie over the edge doesn't tell me what did. It's unlikely I'll find the answer online, and that's presuming I want to know.

Still undecided, I pick my phone up. Only two people can answer my question, and there's a reasonable chance neither are alive today. Establishing if they are alive doesn't mean I have to ask the question, but if they've both passed away, I'll likely never know what drove Jackie to suicide.

I search the same website to see if it holds any records of an Anna Benton of Guildford in its database.

There are several records, including an entry for the current electoral roll. Anna May Benton and Derek Edmund Benton both reside at 77 Fir Tree Road, Guildford — the same house I used to visit.

Anna was only a teenager when she gave birth to Jackie, so I'm guessing she's now in her early seventies. Derek was a few years older, but I'm surprised they're both still alive and living at the same address. Then, maybe they couldn't face leaving. Jackie was an only child, and while I can't begin to imagine what it's like to lose a child, in Anna's case, she had the additional pain of no longer being anyone's mother from that terrible day onwards. All the Benton's memories of their one and only daughter remain locked in that house.

I always got on well with Jackie's mum but is it likely she'll even remember my name? If she does, how will she react to a virtual stranger knocking on her door, asking questions about a part of her life she's probably tried hard to forget? Then again, perhaps she's the type who finds comfort in keeping memories alive. Would a chance to chat with her daughter's first boyfriend bring joy or anguish? I don't know, but there is one justifiable reason I need to talk to Anna. If Jackie has a grave locally, the very least I can do is lay some flowers and pay my final respects.

I continue to chew over the possible consequences. At worst, Anna might tell me to fuck off and slam the door in my face. In a way, that would draw a line under my guilt. I would have at least tried.

Not altogether convinced I'm making the right decision; I grab my car keys and leave.

7.

Fir Tree Road is situated in Bellfields; a large council estate to the north of the town. It's a twenty-minute walk from my former family home, but at the time, it felt like walking into a different world. Until I met Jackie, I'd never set foot on the Bellfields Estate.

My world was typically lower middle class: the detached house in a pleasant cul-de-sac, a Ford Granada Ghia on the driveway, a two-week holiday in Spain every year. As kids, we never really wanted for anything; comfortable in our suburban bubble.

Jackie's parents were working class, and proudly so.

Class wasn't an issue for Jackie and me. We were teenagers with more in common than not. In fact, the only time the difference in our family's finances hit home occurred one evening while we were watching television at her house. Halfway through The Chart Show, the television suddenly turned itself off. As I stared at the screen, puzzled, Jackie got up from the sofa and pulled a fifty-pence piece from her pocket. She then pushed the coin into a slot at the back of the set, and it promptly switched itself back on. Even at that age, I knew some families fed a meter for gas and electric, but I had no idea Radio Rentals offered the same payment method for television rental.

From that moment onwards, I always made sure I had a fifty pence piece in my pocket whenever I visited Jackie's house. Not today, though.

It's been so long since the last visit I need the sat-nav's assistance to guide me in.

I reach Fir Tree Road and slow to a crawl. I think the estate was built in the fifties and my overriding memory is one of uniform boxes in dark-brown brick. The same houses are no longer quite so uniform. I'd guess many of them are now privately owned as almost every dwelling is slightly different from its immediate neighbour. Some have been extended, many have sacrificed their front garden for a parking area, and nearly every house has replacement double-glazed windows in varying styles and colours. It's a bit of a mish-mash, really.

As the sat-nav counts down the yards to my destination, a nervousness builds. Part of it, I'm sure, is not knowing what reception I'll receive but I'm also concerned about my reaction should I be invited in. Anna and Derek Benton have had thirty-two years to come to terms with Jackie's suicide. For me, it's been less than an hour.

I pull up to the kerb outside the house. Externally, it doesn't look so different from how I remember it. Thick plastic window frames have replaced the old metal ones, and the front lawn now lies beneath a layer of splintered tarmac. Otherwise, it looks almost the same. The real difference is those living inside.

I clamber out of the car and make my way up a narrow path to the front door which has also changed; more white plastic. I rap the knocker.

Another feature of the estate I recall from my youth is the soundtrack. In the summer, we'd sometimes sit in the back garden, and there was always a constant drone in the air: music, kids playing, men working on their cars, or a mother yelling at their errant offspring. It's much quieter today.

The latch clicks, and the front door slowly opens. The sight of the woman in the hallway steals a breath.

"Mrs Benton?" I gulp.

I asked to confirm, but I already know. The petite frame is the same, although perhaps hunched slightly, and there are still enough similarities this woman shares with Anna Benton, and indeed my former girlfriend. The once gold-blonde hair is now silver but it's a similar length and style. The giveaway, however, is her blue eyes which haven't lost their lustre. Sometimes, I'd look at Anna Benton, and it was like seeing into the future. She would have been in her late thirties when Jackie and I first started dating, but still a fine-looking woman. If our relationship had lasted, I wouldn't have been at all disappointed if Jackie aged as gracefully as her mother.

"Yes, can I help you?"

It's a voice I haven't heard in a long time, and it's almost as unsettling as the optics.

"You probably don't remember me, but I'm Sean Hardy. I used to date Jackie back in the day."

Her eyes narrow, and for a second, I think my premonition about the door slamming shut is about to become a reality. Then, suddenly, the blue eyes light up.

"Sean? It's really you?"

"All eighteen stone of me, I'm afraid."

"My God. I'd never have recognised you in a month of Sundays."

"It has been a while, and Mother Nature has plainly been a lot kinder to you than me."

She smiles, but it fades in a heartbeat.

"Oh, Christ," she then gasps. "If you were hoping to see Jackie, I'm … I'm afraid …"

"I know," I interject in an appropriately solemn tone. "And I'm so sorry. I only found out this morning."

"You know what happened to her?"

"Kind of, and that's why I'm here. I wanted to place some flowers on her grave if that's okay with you?"

"That would be lovely."

"It's the least I can do. Jackie meant an awful lot to me."

So much, I ditched her in a ten-minute phone call.

Anna nods, and then her demeanour abruptly changes.

"Heaven, forgive me. Where are my manners?" she chirps. "Come in, and I'll stick the kettle on."

I amble in behind her, and suddenly I'm seventeen again. Every insignificant feature from the glossed bannisters to the swirly patterns in the artexed ceiling sparks a memory. As I move up the hallway, the flood of emotions is almost overwhelming. It's a relief to find the kitchen is nothing like I remember. It used to be a poky space, but at some point, they've

54

taken a wall down and replaced the old melamine cupboards with fitted pine units.

Anna puts the kettle on and invites me to sit at a circular table while she makes the tea.

"This has changed," I remark, in no great rush to resurrect our previous conversation. "It's really nice."

"It's been like this for years. We bought the place from the council in the mid-nineties and spent a few quid on it."

That would explain why they're still here. Anna seems in good health, so I guess there's been no reason to move.

"How is Mr Benton?"

"He's okay. A few health concerns over the years but nothing too serious."

"That's good to hear. Is he around?"

"No, but he'll be back before lunch I'd guess."

I have no real desire to see Derek again, but it would be rude not to ask after him.

With the cups prepared, Anna joins me at the table while she waits for the kettle to boil.

"I like your accent," she says. "West Country, isn't it?"

"Devon, although in my head I still sound like a true Guildfordian."

"It reminds me of that comedian … what's his name?"

Whenever folk of a certain generation reference accents from the West Country, it's almost a given they'll mention The Wurzels, Pam Ayres, or the comedian, Jethro.

"You're thinking of Jethro."

"That's him. We saw him live once, at The Civic Hall. A very funny man."

"Not had the pleasure myself but I've heard he puts on a good act."

"He does. So, tell me what you've been up to all these years, Sean. You married? Kids?"

"I divorced earlier this year. No kids."

"How long were you married?"

"We celebrated our twenty-fifth anniversary in September last year."

I say celebrated, but Carol wasn't keen on marking the occasion in any significant way. We had dinner out, and I opened a bottle of champagne back home. My wife conveniently developed a migraine after the first glass and went to bed — all part of her deceit, in retrospect.

"That's a long time. I'm sorry to hear it didn't work out."

"Me too, but that's life, I suppose."

"It certainly is," she sighs, getting to her feet.

"Do you take milk and sugar?"

"Black, one sugar please, Mrs Benton."

"It's Anna. I think you're a bit old to be calling me Mrs Benton."

I smile back, and while she pours the tea, I stare out of the patio doors towards a small garden I no longer recognise. Anna returns with two cups on a tray, along with a plate of biscuits. She then silently transfers the plate and the cups to the table.

"Help yourself to a biscuit."

"Thank you."

"She's up at the Mount Cemetery, our Jackie."

From biscuits to her daughter's final resting place in one breath. The abrupt shift in conversation throws me for a moment.

"Right."

"If you head in the main entrance and follow the path to the right, her grave is about seventy yards along. It's in the first row behind the bench so you can't miss it."

"I'll, um, head up there this afternoon."

Anna takes a sip of tea while I pluck a biscuit from the plate.

"You broke her heart, you know?"

The custard cream doesn't make it to my lips. I've been lulled in by all the pleasantries, and now it appears Anna wants to take me on a guilt trip.

"I know," I mumble.

"What happened, Sean? You both seemed so happy together."

I sit back and sigh.

"The truth? I met someone else and fell in love. It wasn't intentional, and if it's any consolation, I hated myself for a long while."

"That's not what I meant."

"Oh?"

"The way you ended it. Was there any need to be so nasty?"

"I wasn't nasty. A bit insensitive perhaps but I swear I never wanted to hurt Jackie … in fact, that's why I told her. I didn't want to string her along."

"She deserved a proper explanation, in person, don't you think?"

"That was wrong, and I hold my hands up. What you have to understand, Anna, is I was a stupid kid with no experience of ending a relationship. Of course, if I could turn back the clock, I'd have … I wouldn't have ended it at all, but we all make mistakes when we're young."

It wasn't an intentional dig, but Anna getting pregnant at seventeen was also pretty stupid, especially as the flaky excuse for a father fucked-off before his daughter could walk.

"I suppose you're right," she replies, looking into her cup. "I don't mean to judge."

"It's okay."

In the ensuing silence, a question begs to be asked. However, I've already got what I came here for, and I can probably live without ever knowing the reason Jackie decided to end her life.

"She wasn't the same girl after that phone call," Anna continues. "I barely recognised her at times."

"I don't know what to say to that."

"You don't have to say anything. I just want you to know what happened."

"I'm not sure that will do either of us much good."

"Why not? Don't you want to know?"

There's the merest hint of indignation in her tone like I have an obvious moral duty to hear her out. Maybe I do.

"If you think it'll help, Anna, I'll listen."

She rests her arms on the table.

"I want you to picture a tree in a meadow, on a bright summer's day."

"Sorry?"

"Just indulge me, Sean."

"Okay."

"Can you see it? The lush green leaves against a vivid blue sky, the ground beneath blanketed with wildflowers of every colour."

I nod.

"Now, picture that same tree in that same meadow, but in winter."

"Err, right."

"The tree is still alive, but it looks dead … just a skeleton of spiky branches framed by a cold, grey sky. There's no colour, no warmth, nothing of the beauty which graced the meadow only months earlier."

Anna delivers each word with such intensity I can almost sense a chill.

"The difference between those two pictures," she continues, "is the difference between the girl you fell in love with and the one who jumped in front of a train."

Six months ago, I walked in on my wife while she was having sex with her best friend — on anyone's scale, a shocking moment. I think Anna's revelation has just topped that moment.

"I … a train?"

"She jumped … she jumped from a bridge near the station."

"I'm lost for words, Anna. I'm so truly sorry."

"That makes two of us," she replies in a hushed voice. "I'm sorry I didn't do more to help my little girl."

"You couldn't have known."

"I knew she was unhappy. After you … let's just say Jackie

didn't take well to single life. Over the months, she became more and more withdrawn and then swung in the opposite direction. She went out every night until the early hours and came home drunk two or three times a week. And when she wasn't drinking, she was smoking weed or hanging around with some unsavoury characters on the estate."

Anna's description sounds nothing like the Jackie I knew.

"Then, she seemed to settle down a bit. She got herself a job in a record shop in The Friary and stopped going out so much. I thought she'd turned a corner until one night in May when she didn't come home at all. I sat in the lounge, waiting for her, and just after six in the morning, the doorbell rang. It was the police. They said ... they said they'd found a body ..."

Her voice breaks up as a single tear rolls down her cheek for possibly the thousandth time, I'd imagine. I reach across the table and squeeze her hand.

"I wish there was something I could say. I feel terrible."

"There's nothing anyone can say, but I didn't invite you in to lay blame or make you feel bad — I just wanted you to know what happened. Jackie was my daughter, and it was my job to protect her. I failed."

"For what it's worth, I think I understand how you feel."

"I doubt that, Sean."

A month after my parents died, I attended a couple of grief counselling sessions. It's unlikely such counselling was widely available in the eighties so perhaps now would be a good time to share my tale of tragedy and some of the coping strategies I learnt.

"Listen, Anna ..."

The kitchen door swings open and a gaunt man stands in the doorway, a carrier bag in his right hand.

Anna gets to her feet.

"That was quick," she says to the man I'm almost certain is Derek Benton. "I wasn't expecting you back until lunchtime."

He looks at Anna, and then at me.

"And you are?" he says.

Growing up, I found that parents tended to fall in to one of two categories. There were those, like mine, who were always friendly and welcoming whenever I arrived home with a friend, sometimes to the point I'd shudder with embarrassment. Then there were a few whose attitude verged on hostile. Derek fell in to the latter category but I put his demeanour down to paternal protection. Jackie wasn't his daughter by blood, but he'd been her father in name since the age of ten.

"Derek," Anna interjects. "Do you remember Sean, Jackie's old boyfriend?"

"You're that kid?" Derek sneers as if he's the adult and I'm still an insecure adolescent.

"I *was* that kid."

"What are you doing here?"

"I moved back to Guildford a few days ago, and I've only just discovered what happened to Jackie."

He puts the carrier bag on the side and slips out of his coat, handing it to Anna.

"You didn't answer my question. What are you doing here?"

"I came to find out if Jackie had a grave. I'd like to lay some flowers."

Derek shuffles over to the table and stands opposite, his hands resting on the back of the chair Anna just vacated.

"What for? Guilty conscience finally caught up with you, has it?"

"Derek, please," Anna pleads. "Sean is our guest."

"He's not my guest. I'd have slammed the bloody door in his face."

He turns his glare back in my direction.

"You've got some front, sunshine, turning up here with your fake sympathy and flowers after you killed our daughter."

My initial instinct is to get up, tell Derek to go fuck himself and leave. The reason I don't follow my instincts is that I'm not willing to accept his crass accusation without setting a few facts straight.

"I didn't kill her. She committed suicide."

"Because of the way you treated her. You might as well have pushed her under that bloody train."

"I don't accept that."

"And I don't give a shit whether you accept it or not — it's the truth. You broke that poor girl's heart, and you drove her to it."

I have sympathy for Anna, but the only feeling I currently have for Derek is a growing sense of annoyance.

"She took her life a whole year after we split up, Derek. A whole year. What the hell were you doing during that time to help her?"

"Don't you dare try and pin the blame on me. It was your fault and yours alone."

"Bullshit."

"It's the truth, and I can prove it."

With no further explanation, he steps across to a dresser and opens one of the drawers. He then begins rummaging through that drawer.

"Derek, don't," Anna says in a low voice. "No good will come of it."

Ignoring his wife, Derek continues his search, and it comes to an end with the removal of a cream-coloured envelope. Opening the flap, he returns to the table.

"Read that," he demands after extracting a piece of paper from the envelope and slapping it down in front of me.

I look up at the twisted face which hasn't changed much in all the years. His hair is all but gone, but the stern features are still present and correct.

"Go on," he urges.

I glance down to the table and the crumpled piece of paper. The left edge is jagged as if ripped from a book. There's nothing familiar about it, apart from the handwriting. It's the exact same handwriting which adorned every Valentine's card I received over a five-year period in the eighties. I scan the first few lines and realise I'm looking at a page from Jackie's diary, dated Monday 11th May 1987 — the day I made that phone call.

THIS IS THE WORST DAY OF MY LIFE!!!

I don't have the energy to write much, and every time I try, I start crying again.

Sean called earlier to say we're finished, and he's seeing someone else. Just writing those words kills me.

I can't think of anything but them together, laughing, joking, kissing, and ... oh God, I want to puke!! I'm on my own in my bedroom, he's in Exeter with her. HER ... the bitch!!!

He promised me he'd be faithful. He swore how much he loved me. It was all lies. The one decent man in my life has turned out to be just like all the others. I hate him ... I HATE THEM ALL!!!

All that talk of getting married one day, buying a little house, having kids together ... more lies! Why are people so cruel? Why is HE so cruel???

THE BASTARD HUNG UP ON ME!!!

He didn't even say sorry ... That's how little I meant to him!

I don't know the right words to say how much pain I'm in. I don't think there are words. It feels like my heart is actually breaking into pieces as I write this. I can't eat, can't sleep, can't function.

I wanna curl up in a ball and pretend none of this is happening but I know I'll wake up, and for a minute I won't remember. Then it'll all come crashing back. It's gonna be like that every day for months, maybe years ... I dunno.

I can't face it. I CAN'T FACE THIS!!!

Why is there no painkiller that works on a broken heart? Why can't I just take a pill that makes everything numb? I want this feeling to go away more than I've wanted anything. ANYTHING!

Now they're playing that new song by OMD on the radio ... Forever Live and Die.

If I have to feel like this, I don't wanna live forever. I really wanna die.

8.

I only half absorbed the words the first time. As little as I want to, I feel compelled to read the diary page a second time.

If anything, it's worse. I can almost hear her saying every sentence while choking back the tears. I can see the anguish on her face; the streaks of eyeliner and the smudged mascara. It's the face of a girl whose boyfriend treated her abysmally.

"See that last line," Derek snaps as he stabs the page with a nicotine-stained finger. "What does it say?"

I don't answer him. Instead, I look up from the table and turn to face Anna.

"I'm so sorry," I croak.

The slightest nod and she bows her head.

Derek then leans in; his face only a few feet from mine.

"I've waited a long time to say this," he spits. "You killed my little girl, and I hope one day you suffer as much as we have."

I drop my eyes back to the page.

"But …"

"From that day on, she was broken, and you broke her."

"I was just a kid."

"Don't give me that!" he sneers, wagging his finger inches from my face. "You were old enough to sleep with her, so you were old enough to take responsibility. The trouble with your kind is you're selfish. Spoilt and selfish."

This is getting out of hand. I'll willingly accept responsibility for the pain I caused, but I'm not going to sit here while an unhinged septuagenarian spits abuse in my face. I stand up, and he withdraws a few feet.

It's clear how much Derek Benton hates me, but I reckon a lot of that hate is born from his inability to do anything more than hurl accusations. Thirty-two years ago, he'd have punched my lights out. In the here and now, he's no longer physically capable.

"Goodbye, Derek."

I splutter a final apology at Anna before darting back along the hallway and out the front door.

This was a bad idea.

Back on the street, I jump in the car and depart the scene with the urgency of a bank robber. I've no idea where I'm heading, but it doesn't matter because my sole aim is to get as far away from Fir Tree Road as possible, as quickly as possible.

After a series of random turns, I reach a stretch of road I vaguely recognise. As my bearings return, I make my way back to the apartment. On arrival, the silence isn't welcome. It doesn't yet feel like home; no sense of sanctuary here.

I stagger towards the kitchen and stop in the doorway. Did I buy any alcohol yesterday? I could murder a shot of whisky, or vodka, or anything to quell the residue shock. Recollecting my journey through the aisles brings disappointment. I settle on strong coffee.

When I began the search for a new home, I ideally wanted a place with a garden. No matter what the season, sitting outside has always proven an effective antidote to a cluttered mind. Alas, the difference in property prices between Devon and Surrey meant choosing a home with a garden, or a home in a central location. Properties with both were way outside my budget.

Now I wish I'd compromised on location.

I sit at the breakfast bar and reflect on my brief visit to Fir Tree Road. I wonder what's being said back at the Benton house. Derek will likely be cursing my name, and Anna almost certainly in tears. In my quest to make amends, I've brought nothing but pain and ill-will.

I should have left them well alone.

Part of me regrets not asking for Derek's phone number before storming out because he should know I didn't walk away unscathed. God, I wish I'd never read that diary page. If God isn't listening, I'd willingly sell my soul to the Devil if he offered to delete the memory.

As it is, neither entity is listening; probably because neither entity exists. The memory remains, and so too does the weight of guilt.

"I'm so sorry, Jackie."

I honestly do feel sorry, but as I reflect on my apology, I begin to question what I'm apologising for. Without a doubt, I messed up that damn phone call, and the very least Jackie deserved was a sincere apology before I hung up. I've seen real and permanent proof of just how badly I hurt her.

Should I feel sorry for the way her life went after we split? No more than Carol should feel sorry for how my life is today, or how it will be next year or the year after. People break up. It's typically painful and messy, and one person doesn't want it. Only six months ago I could have written a diary page which wouldn't have read so differently to Jackie's.

I was an arse, and Jackie deserved better, but what really irks is Derek's allegation. How is it my fault his step-daughter took her own life?

There's no questioning Jackie's mental state when she wrote in her diary, but the date on the page and the date of her suicide were twelve months apart. It makes no sense. Heartbroken as she obviously was, why did it take so long for that closing sentence to become a tragic reality?

Mental health, I know, is a real issue amongst today's young. Back in the eighties, issues like anxiety and depression just weren't as widely acknowledged and if you suffered, you'd likely suffer alone. Better to deal with your own demons than seek help. Different times, I suppose.

Could it be that Jackie's mental health deteriorated right before her parents' eyes and they didn't notice? Did they just put it down to hormones, or the weed she smoked?

As I process my questions, a possible explanation for Derek's behaviour begins to form.

Perhaps now, the Bentons have learnt enough about

depression to realise their daughter was possibly a victim. I can imagine Anna seeing the reports on the news about mental illness and recognising the signs as those Jackie exhibited. Did she discuss it with Derek, and question why they never realised at the time? More likely, Derek being the kind of man he is, he'd have dismissed her concerns. Far simpler to lay the blame at my door.

I can understand why.

A month before my parents were due to depart on their travels, they changed their itinerary. My brother happened to mention he'd been asked to go on a work trip to Cuba and, seeing as my parents had planned to visit Cuba after they'd visited Haiti, they all agreed it was a great opportunity to spend a few days together. If they'd stuck to their original itinerary, they wouldn't have been on that ferry the night it capsized.

I only discovered this a few weeks after their funeral, and before the inquest confirmed who was to blame.

Still raw with grief, I called Stuart and accused him of killing our parents. It's easy to look back now and realise my accusation was ridiculous, but at the time, I desperately needed to channel my rage. It *had* to be someone's fault our parents died that night, and in my head, Stuart was the catalyst. The counselling helped me get beyond all those irrational thoughts.

I suspect Derek never really consolidated his grief, and that's why he wants to blame me.

Perhaps he's partly right. Every action has a consequence and, unlike Stuart innocently asking my parents to change their itinerary, my actions were born of selfishness.

That phone call was not the reason Jackie Benton killed herself, but it certainly set her off on a path to oblivion. If I hadn't called her that night, if I'd waited until I could talk to her face-to-face and maybe told a few white lies to spare her feelings, the diary page wouldn't exist, and I'd have limited the damage.

I couldn't possibly have known that at the time, so why do I feel so awful now?

Whatever is going on back at Fir Tree Road, there's little I can do to change views which have likely cemented over the decades. For my own peace of mind, however, there is something I can do, something I *should* do.

Not that I have much of an appetite, but lunch will have to wait.

I check Google Maps for the location of another cemetery and another florist. The journey is a fraction over a mile. With my ambition of losing weight in mind, I decide to walk. Besides, I could do with some air.

Once I arrive at the florist's, I take my time selecting a suitable spray of flowers. Although Jackie loved roses, the romantic red variety seems inappropriate. I ask the woman at the counter for a combination of pink and yellow. While trimming and tying my order, she points to a display of four-inch cards and asks if I'd like one. I decline. What could I possibly write that would come close to conveying my regret? More to the point, who would ever read it? Certainly not Jackie, that's for sure.

Flowers acquired I continue on my way.

As the name implies, Mount Cemetery sits at the top of a hill. I hadn't factored-in the gradient when I decided to walk, and by the time I reach the gates I'm panting hard. I take a moment to catch my breath and follow Anna's directions. As she suggested, the final resting place of Jacqueline Elaine Benton is relatively straightforward to locate. Managing my reaction is less straightforward.

Below her name, embossed in gold lettering, is the date she came in to the world and the date she left it. She died only weeks before her twenty-second birthday. Two dates: one Jackie had no control over, the other of her choosing.

As I stare at the slab of polished granite, I can't help but wonder how many people have passed by and noted how tragically short Jackie's life was. They didn't know her, though.

They never loved her.

The sight of the grave pains me more than it should. It was hard seeing my parents' grave, but I came to terms with their passing years ago. Chances are, they wouldn't be around today even if they hadn't embarked upon that fateful ferry journey. It's a fact of being fifty-something that you're fortunate if you still have a parent alive; blessed if both are still around.

Even though my parents passed prematurely, they still enjoyed a decent life. They achieved many of their ambitions. Jackie died far too young with a long list of unfulfilled dreams. No fairy-tale wedding, no brood of children, no little house in the suburbs. It was my job to wave the magic wand. Instead, I dashed all her dreams in a brief telephone conversation.

No wonder she went off the rails.

I gently lay the flowers up against the headstone; the vivid pink and yellow petals a stark contrast to the dark granite.

"For what it's worth, Jackie," I whisper. "It turns out I made the wrong choice. I'm sorry it took so long to realise."

There's a laundry list of mistakes I could and should apologise for but what's the point in baring your soul when there's no one listening? Really, what's the point in any of this? It's a much-too-late exercise in easing my conscience. It won't make any difference to the past, and it won't make any difference to Anna or Derek. Whatever personal guilt they're carrying, they'll always believe I played a crucial role in their daughter's downfall. And, even though we hold differing views on my accountability, it doesn't make them wrong.

I sit down on the bench; staring glassy-eyed at Jackie's headstone.

It's true to say I've suffered over the last six months. I've been through the emotional wringer and somehow come out the other side, but the circumstances were different — I was the innocent party. Now, I get to experience the burden of guilt. I don't like it, and I take no comfort in knowing Carol might have felt the same way. Then again, I don't think she had any regrets, and therefore she probably didn't carry much guilt either.

To distract from the negative thoughts, I consider what Jackie would make of the forlorn, self-pitying figure slumped on a bench by her headstone.

I don't think she'd like him much. Jackie wanted everyone to share in her sunny optimism.

When we could afford it, we used to take in a film at the Odeon cinema in Guildford. I noticed yesterday it's no longer there. The guy who worked in the ticket office was a right miserable bugger, and on every visit, he'd take our money and slap the tickets down without a please or thank you.

On one visit, the bloke in the ticket office processed our transaction in his usual grumpy manner. Jackie then went to the confectionery counter and bought a bag of Opal Fruits — Starburst these days. She then returned to the ticket desk and opened the bag. One by one, she laid the bright coloured sweets out in a grid while the sour-faced bloke watched on.

"These are for you," she said, placing the last of the chewy sweets on the counter.

He stared at her, puzzled.

"We all need some colour in our lives," Jackie continued. "So, these will give you a burst of colour every day for the next few weeks."

Unbelievably, the bloke cracked a smile and even said thank you.

The next time we visited the cinema, he remembered Jackie. Not only did he smile, but he gave her a free ticket.

If she were here now, I think she'd offer me an entire bag of Opal Fruits. To my surprise, that thought prompts a smile. Then again, Jackie always made me smile, even when I didn't much feel like it.

I realise I've been dwelling on her memory in a way she wouldn't have wanted. Knowing Jackie, she'd want people to bask in her light, not sulk in the shadows of regret. I can't switch off the guilt, but I can temper it by celebrating all the fond memories Jackie left behind.

If I can just forget that bloody page in her diary, I might just be able to do that.

9.

I decided a walk around Guildford town centre would be a good place to rekindle fonder memories of Jackie. When we weren't in my bedroom or hers, we'd spent most of our time wandering around the shops, window shopping items we couldn't afford but one day might. We'd sit in cafes and make a cup of tea or glass of Coke last two hours. In the summer we'd take a blanket and lie for hours on the grassy banks of the River Wey or hunker down in the grounds of Guildford Castle.

We didn't have much, but we had each other. For one of us, that was more than enough.

I cross the river bridge, which leads to the lower part of the High Street. Before the shopping centre opened in 1980, this was the centre of Guildford's retail experience. The High Street itself is a wide, cobbled road with a modest incline; sometimes treacherous in winter months.

As I wander, I struggle to remember what was where. The banks and building societies still occupy the same buildings, including the branch I opened my first ever bank account. Back then, the name above the door read Abbey National. Now, it's Santander. There are also a number of retail names that didn't exist when I last walked up this street with no money to spend, along with the usual established names you'd likely find in any town centre.

Halfway up, all the high-end fashion retailers are clustered together. They're not the kind of shops I frequent, but I've already passed a branch of Marks & Spencer, so my limited clothing needs are covered.

The House of Fraser department store is still going, although in my day it was called Army & Navy. Mobile phone shops surround it. As hard as I try, I can't remember what businesses were here before the likes of Vodafone and EE, but there were at least six of them. Maybe, like so many retailers, they offered products the internet rendered obsolete. No one nips to

Blockbusters to hire a video, nor do we flock to record stores to buy whatever single is number one in the charts.

There was also a branch of Currys Electrical somewhere on the High Street. I remember it because it's where I used to buy blank C90 cassettes to record the top-40. That shop has gone too — they've probably relocated to larger, cheaper premises on a retail park somewhere.

I reach the Tunsgate Arch with its grand pillars of Portland stone. I think Dad told me it was once a corn market but, as far back as the First World War, and as long as I've been on this planet, it's only served as a thoroughfare from the High Street to the back roads of Guildford. I do remember Jackie and I sheltering here if we were ever caught in the rain. I think we might have even stolen the odd kiss or two, hidden away from the passing shoppers.

Crossing the street, I step beyond the tall pillars. Out of the sun, it's markedly cooler. So cool, in fact, a shiver arrives. I suspect it's more to do with the sudden flood of memories than the temperature. I don't know what it is about really old buildings, but you can almost sense the history oozing from the masonry. In my case, that history only stretches back three-and-a-half decades, but it's no less significant, no less poignant.

Stood here now, I can picture two teenagers huddled together in the corner; their arms wrapped tightly around one another as they seek shelter from a sudden downpour. The girl, in a pale pink coat, is staring up in to the boy's eyes and then, using the thumb of her right hand, she wipes a droplet of rain from his cheek. He gently takes her hand and kisses it. Even if the rain were to last all afternoon, they appear happy right where they are.

I breathe a melancholy sigh and step back into the sunshine via the archway at the rear. Quieter than the High Street, Tunsgate is roughly a hundred yards long with some kind of major construction project underway on the right, and a row of independent shops on the left. This isn't a part of town I ever had cause to visit so the shops could have been here for decades.

I walk on and stop when I reach a junction. Across the road, an area of lawn rolls down towards a gate and beyond that gate is a place Jackie and I spent many a happy hour — the grounds of Guildford Castle.

I cross the street and approach the main gate.

To call Guildford Castle a castle is a stretch. All that remains of the Norman structure is a squat tower, the height of a three-storey building. However, the parkland which surrounds the tower always felt like an enchanted garden with a mix of trees and tall hedges, narrow winding paths, and quiet corners to hide away in. Some parts were so secluded you could almost forget you were in the middle of a bustling town. It was Jackie's favourite place to spend time, and of all the time we did spend here, there was one spot she particularly adored.

If I can remember where it is, that's the spot I'd like to revisit.

I follow the circular path around the tower and cut through a gap in what remains of a stone wall. Glancing left and right, I spot a trio of steps leading down to another path. I plod down the steps and walk another twenty yards alongside a privet hedge. I don't know if I'm heading the right way, but it feels familiar.

The path and the hedge both end abruptly, but beyond the last few feet of hedge, there's a stone bench recessed in what was probably the outer wall of a building nine-hundred years ago. Only five feet across and carved from the same stone as the wall itself, the bench is just big enough for two people. Today, and for the first time, I'm here on my own.

The sheltered nook has an air of reverence, and for a minute, I can't convince myself it's a good idea to sit down. This was *our* little hideaway, and it feels wrong being here without Jackie.

I'm being stupid, I concede.

The very reason I'm here is to remember all the special moments we shared in this spot. The least I can do is sit my fat arse down and invest ten minutes reminiscing about those moments.

I slowly take a seat in the centre of the bench. The last time my buttocks rested on the cold stone, I was a hell of a lot younger and a hell of a lot slimmer. I also had a thick blanket to sit on, courtesy of an ever-thoughtful girlfriend.

The reminiscing proceeds without a blanket to sit on, or a girlfriend by my side to offer an occasional hug. It proves a bittersweet experience.

Ten minutes turns into twenty, and with some reluctance, I get to my feet. I know I'll come back again. I owe it to Jackie to keep her memory alive.

As luck would have it, the castle is only a few seconds walk from the King's Head — the pub I met Wayne yesterday evening. It feels like a fitting venue to raise a glass to Jackie. And frankly, I need a drink after the day I've had thus far.

Precisely one minute later, I push open the door.

The King's Head is much quieter than yesterday; unsurprising as it's post-lunch on a Wednesday afternoon. Fortunately, that means I can sit at the bar. The first step in establishing yourself as a local is to claim a stool and swap small talk with the bar staff. I take my place and order a pint.

The barman is young and shows no interest in small talk, even when I jokingly remark about a pint costing more than a gallon of petrol. The youth of today.

One reason I think this pub could be my local is the volume of the background music. I know some pubs choose not to play any music at all, but the constant thrum of undiluted chatter gets under my skin. Conversely, I detest pubs where the music blares so loudly you can barely hear yourself think.

The King's Head has struck the right balance as Sinéad O'Connor launches in to the chorus of *Nothing Compares 2 U*. From memory, *Now 18*, track 7.

It feels like an appropriate moment to raise my glass.

"To you, Jackie Benton," I whisper.

I'm three-quarters through my pint when an old boy

approaches the bar. Smartly dressed in a navy cardigan, checked shirt, and corduroy trousers, he addresses the barman as Tom and requests a pint of Guinness. As the barman tugs at the pump, he asks the old boy if he's having a good day, and drops his name at the end: Leonard.

The second step in establishing yourself as a local is to converse with other locals. Clearly, Leonard is such a stalwart of this establishment he's on first name terms with the chippy young barman. Leonard pays for his drink, and I order my second, nodding politely at my fellow bar dweller.

Tom requests payment, and I hand over a five-pound note. It's a critical moment; a conversation starter. I glance at Leonard and shake my head.

"First time I bought a pint, it cost ninety pence," I sigh. How times have changed, eh?"

"Not necessarily for the better," he replies with a smile.

There's a moment of silence, and then Leonard continues the theme of our conversation.

"I'd imagine beer is a bit cheaper back home," he says. "That's a Devon accent if I'm not mistaken."

"Well spotted, although Devon is no longer home. Never was, really."

"No? Where you from then?"

"Guildford, actually. I moved down to Exeter when a pint cost ninety pence, but now I'm back, and it's five bloody quid."

Leonard chuckles and adjusts his position on the stool, so he's facing me. Step two.

"How did you place my accent?" I ask. "Most folk think everyone living west of Wiltshire speak with the same accent."

"My wife. She was a Torquay girl."

"Ahh, I see. That would make us sworn enemies then."

"You're probably right although my Mary didn't have any enemies. Too big a heart."

Twice now he's referenced his wife in the past tense, suggesting Leonard is a widower. It's not a question you ask a stranger.

"Your Mary, how long did she live in Torquay?"

"The first nineteen years of her life. I met her when we were both eighteen, and we married a year later."

"What were you doing down in Torquay? You sound local."

"Seems a lifetime ago now but my aunt used to run a boarding house down there. After my uncle died, she needed a hand around the place, you know, keeping up with the maintenance and the like, and I needed a job. So, in April 1961, I packed my bags and jumped on a train. Three weeks after I arrived, I wandered into an ice cream parlour for a rum and raisin cornet, and there she was, behind the counter — can still remember the moment like it was yesterday."

"And you ended up back in Guildford?"

"Wasn't much work down there in the low season, so we made a life for ourselves here. Fifty-six years we were married … lost her eighteen months ago."

"I'm sorry to hear that."

"Thank you," he replies in a low voice.

Needing to fill the ensuing silence, I offer a handshake.

"I'm Sean, by the way."

"Leonard Crosby," he replies, firmly shaking my hand. "And thank you for saying hello. It isn't much fun drinking on your own."

"No, but better than sitting at home alone, staring at the walls."

He raises his glass.

"Amen to that."

We continue chatting, and Leonard tells me he used to be a police detective here in Guildford. Patently a job he loved; he wasn't so keen on the early retirement age. Besides the difference in careers, my new drinking buddy and I have a lot in common. We're both the uncomfortable side of fifty, living alone, and have memories of life in Devon. Leonard only lived there briefly, but he and Mary would visit three or four times a year to see family. I discover they had a son, John, who lives with his wife in Newcastle, and a daughter, Susie, who lives twenty miles away near Bracknell but pops over to see him every week. Despite those weekly visits, it's clear Leonard is lonely.

It's a conclusion which worries me as much as it saddens me. I learn he's twenty-three years my senior and I can't help but think I'm looking at my future self — spending every afternoon in a backstreet pub in the hope of a few minutes conversation with a stranger. At least Leonard enjoyed a long and happy marriage, and the chance to see his grandchildren growing up.

Who will I have in my life when I'm Leonard's age?

More than ever, I rue that decision I made back in 1987. If I'd stayed away from Carol, I might now be celebrating a milestone marriage anniversary with Jackie. It's almost certain we'd have had children and maybe even a couple of grandkids by now. I wouldn't be sharing my Wednesday afternoon with a widower; getting mildly steamed.

The bar becomes busier and, as I order our sixth round of drinks, I realise most of the newcomers are in office attire. Without realising the time, I've been supping ale with Leonard for more than three hours. Still, there was bugger all in my diary, and I've enjoyed Leonard's company. I think he's enjoyed mine, too.

We continue nattering away over what turns out to be our last pint. By his own admission, Leonard can't handle his ale like he used to. Neither can I. Just after six o'clock a taxi driver pokes his head around the door and calls Leonard's name. We exchange phone numbers and agree to meet up again next week.

I consider booking my own taxi, but a walk might sober me up a touch. There is one place I want to visit first, though. Revisit, more accurately.

I'm not sure how but three pints earlier, Leonard and I got on to the subject of cemeteries, and it turns out Mary's grave is only a few hundred yards from my parents. Every Monday afternoon,

Leonard visits that grave with a miniature bottle of Navy Rum and a shot glass in his pocket. He then pours himself a nip and toasts his wife goodnight. I thought it an odd gesture until he explained he and his wife would share a shot of rum every night before bed — a ritual they'd maintained every year of their long marriage.

My emotions no doubt heightened by alcohol, I think it would be fitting to pay a similar tribute to Jackie, although not with Navy Rum.

I summon Tom and order a bottle of sweet cider to take away. On unsteady legs, I then make my way back up the hill towards the castle. The gate still open, I follow the path back to the steps, along the privet hedge, and back to our nook.

The sun has shifted position, so the scene isn't exactly as I left it, the shadows now longer and the earlier breeze has faded. I sit down on the stone bench and use the edge to prize the lid from my bottle of cider. Roughly thirty-eight years ago, Jackie and I first got drunk together in this spot, courtesy of a cheap, two-litre bottle of sweet cider. Merrydown, if memory serves.

At the time, our only source of portable music was a battery-operated radio; a Christmas present from my parents. It must have been a Sunday afternoon because the start of the weekly chart rundown on Radio One coincided with our last few sips of cider. I think Simon Bates was the presenter.

Keen to recreate the scene as sympathetically as possible, I open the Spotify app on my phone and find a playlist for that same year. It begins with *Truly*, by Lionel Richie.

I take my first sip of cider; the intense sweetness a stark contrast to the ale I've been guzzling all afternoon. Jackie didn't really like the taste of alcohol, and sweet cider was the only drink she was willing to try as we discussed the options. Being only sixteen at the time, I had to beg my brother to buy it. Still, Jackie liked it enough to knock back her share of the two-litre bottle. By early evening we were more than a little tipsy.

One by one, distant memories of that afternoon cascade.

At one point, I remember we sang along to a Yazoo number riding high in the charts that week. Which one was it? I thumb the screen searching the playlist and find what I'm looking for halfway down — *Only You*.

I tap the screen and a tinny interpretation of Alison Moyet's voice trills from the phone speakers. In fairness, they're slightly better than the single speaker on my old portable radio.

Placing the phone on the bench, I turn and put my feet up, my back resting against the inside wall of the nook. It's not wide enough I can stretch my legs out fully but more comfortable than perching on the edge.

I close my eyes and take another sip of cider.

I'm in the same spot with the same taste on my lips, the same music in my ears, the same sense of tranquillity. It's almost a perfect recreation of our afternoon. Almost, but not quite.

The reason I can remember it so vividly is not because of the cider or the music or even the location — it's because I shared it with Jackie. My first love; the girl I should have continued to love, and would almost certainly still love today.

If only.

Having expunged Jackie from my life, I was able to treat my love for her like an unwanted family heirloom. I put it in a box and dumped it in a dusty corner of the attic where it would stay for decades; out of sight, out of mind. Coming back and discovering the awful truth has ripped that box open. They say first love is eternal and maybe they're right.

I loved Carol. I'm sure of it. I must have loved her enough because when she left I tried telling myself she might come back, and I still recall the pain I felt over the long weeks. Granted, it was never likely, but when you're at rock bottom, you'll seize even the thinnest strand of hope.

If Jackie were still alive today, living here in our home town, I wonder if there would be a similar strand of hope? I wonder what she'd think if she heard Sean Hardy had moved back? Who knows, maybe she might have tracked me down, and perhaps we might have met up for a drink. We might even have rekindled our relationship.

Sadly, I'll never know what might have been — then, or now.

That damning thought hurts far more than it should. Far more, if I'm honest, than discovering Carol's infidelity.

What is wrong with me? I'm fifty-four years of age and pining like a lovesick teenager. I had my chance of happiness with Jackie, and I squandered it — a long, long time ago. Doesn't mean I can't fantasise, though, or wish life hadn't panned out differently for both of us.

I take another sip of cider as Alison Moyet winds down; her voice replaced by birdsong and the faint sound of Guildford shutting down for the day.

The alcohol and the abysmal night's sleep make their presence felt. I put the bottle down and let my mind drift further away from the shitty reality, which won't have changed when I get up and leave this place.

In that surreal space between sleep and consciousness, a face forms. I'm looking into electric-blue eyes, while pearly-pink lips form a smile. Speech feels like too much effort, but in my head, I utter six words: I wish you were here, Jackie.

The birdsong fades as I slip away. Sleep arrives.

10.

"Oi!" a voice bellows.

I dismiss it as my own creation as I drift in a dream world.

"Oi! You!"

Perhaps not.

One by one, my senses come online. The last of those senses is sight, and I squint up at a silhouette.

"You're not supposed to be here," the silhouette says.

Seconds pass as I try to ascertain where I am and why I'm not supposed to be here. The stone beneath my buttocks triggers a succession of hazy memories. I'm still in the nook.

"Bloody hell," I groan, while easing my leaden legs off the bench. "What time is it?"

The silhouette checks his watch.

"Eight-fifty."

Christ, I've been asleep for over two hours, and the castle grounds must have a closing time which has already passed. That might explain why I'm not supposed to be here.

As I shift position, the privet hedge blocks out the sun and the silhouette transforms into a stern-faced man roughly my age, wearing a utilitarian brown uniform. Best guess is he's the castle warden or groundskeeper.

"I'm sorry," I rasp. "I had a few drinks and must have dozed off."

"You should know better at your age," he scolds.

He checks his watch again; more a sign of impatience than a time check as he only looked at it seconds ago.

"Alright, alright. I'm going."

"Be quick about it, and don't let me find you kipping down here again."

I consider pointing out he's an overly officious dick but think better of it. I just want to get back to the apartment and sleep.

He marches away as I assess my various aches and pains. I feel horrendous. The fundamental problem with afternoon drinking is the same-day hangover, and this one is a humdinger. Sleeping on a solid stone bed hasn't helped.

I gingerly stand up and pat my pockets to check I've got everything. Keys: present. Wallet: present. Phone: not present.

Frantically, I search every corner of the nook and the lawn in front. Then, I think back to the last time I had it in my hand.

"Ahh, bugger."

I distinctly recall resting my phone on the bench while listening to music. After I drifted off, some toe rag must have passed by and helped themselves. Fortunately, I'm due a handset upgrade, but it still irks. At least I've still got my wallet, I suppose.

Agitation trumped by tiredness; I stretch out the worst of the stiffness from my limbs. I then stagger back towards the hedge and the path beyond.

As I pass through the main gate, I come to a stop. Now the worst of the post-slumber grogginess has passed, something doesn't feel right, and it isn't just the splitting headache. I check my watch. At eight-fifty on a May evening, dusk should be setting in. If anything, the sun appears to be creeping higher in the cloudless blue sky.

There is an obvious explanation.

I don't think I fell asleep for just a couple of hours — I think I spent the whole night snoring away in the nook and it's now eight-fifty in the bloody morning. No wonder that bloke was so annoyed with me. He must have thought I was a drunken vagrant dossing down in his park overnight.

In fairness, I probably smell like a drunken vagrant. I also have the full bladder to match.

Unsurprisingly for a man in his fifties, I've woken up in dire need of a piss. My apartment is at least a fifteen-minute walk away, and I don't think I'll make it. I've suffered quite enough humiliation this morning without being caught relieving myself in an alleyway.

The town centre, however, is just a minute away and I recall passing a branch of Starbucks at the bottom of the High Street yesterday. I can use their facilities and get a much-needed injection of caffeine at the same time.

Plan set, I amble down the hill towards the King's Head. There, I turn right into Quarry Street; a narrow, one-way lane which leads out to the lower part of the High Street opposite Starbucks.

As I walk, the same sense of unease I felt by the castle gate returns. I can't put my finger on it, but it's not unlike visiting a motorway service station — a sense of not being anywhere other than between two places.

I pass the church, and two cars parked tight to the kerb. Bizarrely, both are modern classics, the like I haven't seen in years other than in motoring shows on television. The first is a silver VW Golf, possibly a Mark Two, and the second a dusty blue Ford Sierra. It's a shame I'm so desperate to relieve myself as I wouldn't mind taking a few minutes to admire the remarkably pristine cars.

I emerge from Quarry Street and look across the road, expecting to see Starbucks straight ahead of me.

It's not there.

Confused, I turn right and look back up the High Street in case I've got my bearings wrong. I haven't, and I look back to where Starbucks should be. I'm almost positive it was situated at the entrance to White Lion Walk; a precinct-style arcade of shops.

In Starbuck's place is a branch of Next with clothed mannequins in the window.

Still unwilling to believe my own eyes, I look down the High Street expecting to see Starbucks at least nearby. It's not beyond the realms of possibility I've simply misremembered the location.

There are no obvious signs, so I plod further down the street until I catch sight of a shop window with a dozen or so domestic appliances beyond the glass. I have no recollection of passing an electrical goods store when I wandered up the High Street yesterday. It's puzzling I missed it, but as I look up the name on the fascia defies belief.

I stare open-mouthed at the sign. It reads, Currys.

"What the …"

This wasn't here yesterday. I know I'm not mistaken because I would have seen the massive posters in the window, and questioned why they all feature obsolete electrical goods.

I edge a few feet closer and study the nearest poster promoting a range of television sets. They're not flat-screen, high definition, smart televisions like the one gracing my lounge back in the apartment, but boxy sets similar to the one I watched as a child.

Is this a promotional stunt? Are Currys celebrating the anniversary of their first branch opening by recreating a pop-up facsimile?

I step right up to the window. My eyes are drawn to the left-hand wall behind a beige fridge-freezer. There are three shelves, each lined with a number of black cube-shaped hi-fi units. Every one of them has at least one cassette deck, and most have a record player on top. Surely, they're dummy replicas like the display phones they use in mobile phone shops. The only other explanation is that Currys unearthed a cache of forgotten stock in the corner of their warehouse.

I'm curious enough to enter. Perhaps they'll let me use their retro toilet.

I make straight for the shelves of mock hi-fis. On closer inspection, they certainly look like the real deal, and when I press the tape eject button on a Saisho model, it eases opens.

"Can I help you, Sir?"

I turn to face a twenty-something guy in a pale-blue shirt. His badge displays the name Dean.

"Two questions: are these originals, and can I use your toilet?"

"Yes, and yes."

He beckons me towards the back of the store and through a door.

"There you go," he says, pointing to a door halfway along a corridor. "I'll wait here."

I thank him and dash off to answer the now desperate call of nature. God knows how I've kept it in, but many pints of ale are expelled.

"You're a life-saver," I say, returning to the corridor.

"No problem. So, you're interested in a hi-fi, are you, Sir?"

I don't want to appear rude after he let me use their facilities, and I'm admittedly interested in how they collated such an extensive range of obsolete products.

"I might be in the market for a bit of old-school nostalgia, yes."

"Right, um, shall we go and look at some options?"

I smile politely and follow Dean back to the shelves.

"What kind of budget do you have?" he asks.

I pick a figure at random.

"Two hundred."

"And what features are you looking for?"

"You tell me. What features do I need?"

He points to a unit just shy of two-hundred quid.

"This one is a popular model. It's got a compact disc player, double tape-deck, graphic equaliser, Dolby Sound."

"But not Bluetooth connectivity?" I chuckle.

Dean doesn't share my mirth and returns a blank stare.

"What's Bluetooth?"

"Are you kidding me?"

"No. I've never heard of it."

"Ahh, I get you. This is all part of the retro experience, right?"

"I'm not with you."

"This place. I have to say I'm impressed you got it up and running in a day."

"Sir, as far as I know, this branch was opened several years ago."

"Of course, it was," I reply with a wink.

"Um, so, are you looking to buy a hi-fi, or not?"

"To be honest with you, Dean, I was actually looking for Starbucks. I'm desperate for a double espresso."

"Starbucks?"

"Yes, and if you can drop the act for a moment and tell me where it is, I'd be grateful."

"Listen, the only Starbuck I've ever heard of is Lieutenant Starbuck from Battlestar Galactica."

"I knew I'd heard the name before. Seriously, though, where is Starbucks?"

Dean's expression hardens.

"I don't know, and unless you're looking to make a purchase today, Sir, I can't help you."

I roll my eyes and leave.

Coffee really isn't my top priority now, but I'm perplexed why my memory is so skewed.

Still convinced Starbucks must be close by, I scan the shops on the opposite side of the street. For the second time in ten minutes, my mouth bobs open when my eyes fix on a building society. Yesterday, the sign above the door read Santander. Today, it's Abbey National.

I'm no longer perplexed — I'm approaching a state of what-the-fuckery?

I stagger across the cobbles and push open the door. Immediately, I'm struck by how little it has changed since the last time I had reason to be here, many decades ago. There's just one elderly woman in the queue, so I stand behind her; intent on asking what the hell is going on with their signage.

A young mother with a pram departs, and the elderly woman takes her place, handing the teller a red passbook. My attention shifts to a poster on the wall: *Our Spring Mortgage Deal — 13.99% Fixed for Three Years.*

I'm stunned enough to ponder a question: what kind of

moron would sign up for a deal like that? I did consider getting a small mortgage before I bought the apartment, and most of the fixed-term deals were at three or four per cent. Even customers with the poorest credit rating would baulk at such an outrageously expensive mortgage.

The elderly woman departs, and I take her place at the counter. The female teller greets me with a smile.

"Good morning."

"Uh, yes, good morning."

"What can I do for you today?"

"I'd like to know what's going on with the signs."

"What signs?"

"Outside, in here. Why do they all say Abbey National?"

"Because this is Abbey National, Sir. What else would they say?"

"Santander."

She appears confused.

"I have an account with you," I declare. "And I haven't seen the name Abbey National on a statement for years."

"Are you sure you've got the right building society?"

"Yes, I'm sure. I remember opening my account in this very branch."

"When?"

"I don't know exactly. The mid-eighties at a guess."

"Do you know your account number?"

I'm not in the mood for this, but I'm a slave to my own curiosity.

I quote the eight digits of my account number as the teller taps a keyboard.

"Can you confirm your name?"

"Sean Hardy."

"And your date of birth, Mr Hardy?"

"9th March 1966."

She glares at the screen, looks up at me, and then back at the screen.

"You're twenty-two?" she snorts.

"Don't be ridiculous. I'm fifty-four."

"I'm sorry, Sir, but I don't think we're talking about the same account unless there's been some kind of computer glitch."

Frustrated, I pull the debit card from my wallet and slide it across the counter.

"There," I sigh. "My debit card, and as you can see it clearly says Santander."

She picks it up, takes one look, frowns, and slides it back across the counter.

"Is this some kind of prank?" she asks.

"I beg your pardon?"

"Firstly, we have no connection to any financial institution by the name of Santander, and secondly, your cash card states it's valid from 02/19 to 02/22."

"Your point being?"

"My point being, it's 1988."

"Very funny."

"I'm not laughing, Sir. Either this is a prank, or a hapless attempt at fraud. Either way, I suggest you leave before I call security."

"I'm not going anywhere. I demand to see the manager."

"He's busy at the moment. Please leave."

Behind me, someone tuts. I turn around. There are now three customers in the queue, headed by a bloke in a pinstripe suit.

"Are you going to be much longer?" he asks, checking his watch. "Some of us have work to do."

"What's today's date?" I ask him.

"If I tell you, will you hurry up and complete your business?"

"Whatever."

"It's Friday 13th May," he sighs.

"No, it's … Thursday, 14th May. I know because they're coming to install my broadband today."

"You're mistaken. It's my son's eleventh birthday, so I know what bloody day it is."

"Clearly, you don't. It's Thursday …"

A security guard appears at my shoulder and clears his throat.

"You need to leave, Sir."

"I'm not leaving until someone tells me what the fuck is going on here."

"No need for that language. Now, I'll ask you one final time, and then I'll have no choice but to remove you from the premises forcibly."

Fitter and possibly two decades younger, I fear he's more than capable of fulfilling his threat.

"Fine," I snap. "But I'll be closing my account and emailing your CEO."

With the guard's hand on my elbow, I'm escorted out to the pavement.

"Have a nice day, Sir."

Considering the start, I think it's unlikely. I'm hungover, tired, and seemingly, losing my mind. As I watch the security guard return to the branch, a woman brushes past me.

"Excuse me," I call after her.

She turns around.

"Can you tell me today's date, please?"

"13th May."

"And the day?"

"Friday."

She continues on her way. I stop another woman coming from the opposite direction and ask her the same question. I receive the same answer, and on the third, fourth, fifth, sixth, and seventh time of asking random strangers. I elect to re-frame the question and try again.

A pension-age couple approach.

"Excuse me. Do you have a moment?"

The couple confirm they do.

"I'm conducting market research about political awareness.

Would you mind answering a couple of brief questions?"

They nod in agreement.

"Do you know when the last General Election was held?"

"Last year," the husband replies.

"And who won?"

"The Conservatives."

So far, their answers tally with reality.

"And who is the current Prime Minister."

"Maggie Thatcher."

"Pardon?"

"Margaret Thatcher," the wife loudly states, as if I'm deaf.

"Right. Thanks for your time."

Just my luck to ask a couple suffering from early-onset dementia. I scan the pavement for another candidate and over a ten-minute period, I ask the same three questions to nine different people. They all return the same answers.

What is wrong with these idiots?

It could be because I'm dehydrated but a sudden bout of nausea kicks-in. Light-headed, I sit down on the kerb. From my vantage point, I watch dozens of people pass by. Dozens become hundreds until my surveillance highlights a subtle anomaly — I haven't seen a single person using a mobile phone. Nobody checking directions or sending a message or taking a selfie or scrolling through a playlist.

"What the hell is this?" I mumble.

Have I woken-up in a version of *The Truman Show*? Someone's audacious idea of a psychological experiment?

A more likely explanation is I'm suffering a mental breakdown. The last six months had already taken their toll before I discovered Jackie's fate. Is it any wonder my brain is mashed?

Why, though, would it create *this*?

11.

The nausea finally passes.

I need to stay calm. Clearly, I am not in 1988, but I'm not where I should be.

Am I still in Guildford?

It would explain why everything looks so different from yesterday, but it doesn't explain why no one is using a mobile phone, why there's a branch of Currys selling thirty-year-old stock, or why my building society has rebranded overnight.

Then, there's the mass delusion of this town's inhabitants. That's even harder to explain.

I think back to the moment I woke up in the nook. I recall the conversation with the groundskeeper, and then I made my way back through the park, down the hill past the King's Head, and along Quarry Street.

This is definitely Guildford. That much I must accept.

It's a start.

Next, I need to bring some order to my thoughts.

For my entire career, I've worked through problems in a methodical manner. I like numbers because they're not open to interpretation — two plus two will always equal four no matter what. I simply need to apply the same systematic thought process to my current predicament. If I am experiencing a breakdown, surely I'll snap out of it at some point.

For now, though, I need to focus on psychology rather than maths.

On a management training course a few years back, we were introduced to Abraham Maslow's hierarchy of needs; essentially a list of our needs as humans, organised into a pyramid with the most basic needs at the base. The course leader took our group through a PowerPoint presentation to demonstrate how each level of Maslow's pyramid might be relevant in the workplace, specifically with staff management.

It was incredibly dull but perhaps useful in this ridiculous construct my mind has created.

I'm light-headed because I'm dehydrated, and I haven't eaten since yesterday lunchtime. Therefore, my basic needs are food and fluids, and after that, shelter.

It's a simple enough plan. I'll head back up the High Street and stop at the first place I can buy food and drink, consume it, and then make my way home. Act normal, and perhaps normal will return.

I clamber to my feet, my backside numb and head throbbing. How can an illusion hurt so much?

A few deep breaths and I take the first cautious steps forward, gradually breaking into a stride. That stride falters every dozen yards as I pass one now-defunct retail name after another: Freeman, Hardy, and Willis, Ratners Jewellers, Timothy Whites, Bradford & Bingley, and Trueform Shoes. Halfway up the High Street, I stop outside Kinch & Lack — the school uniform shop I visited with Mum every August. I remember her being quite upset when she heard they closed for good in 1991. And yet, that shop is seemingly open for business.

Further on, House of Fraser is Army & Navy once again and opposite, the sign above Clarke's shoe shop now reads John Farmer.

How the hell can anyone's imagination fashion such detail in an illusion? I'd all but forgotten many of these shops, and I'd be hard-pressed to recall their exact location on the High Street or how the exteriors looked.

Across the street, just past the Tunsgate Arch, the sight of one particular establishment halts my stride again. The view triggers so many fond memories I'm compelled to take a closer look.

La Boulangerie was, but still is in my illusion, an independent bakery. Jackie and I used to pop in regularly on the way to the castle grounds. They made the most delicious cheese straws and, if we had enough money, we'd buy a dozen along with an iced bun or a slice of caramel-topped shortbread.

Yesterday, you wouldn't have been able to buy any of their baked goods as La Boulangerie wasn't here. I distinctly remember feeling more than a touch disappointed about that.

I open the door and step inside.

Taking a moment to soak in the nostalgic ambience, I stare longingly at the cakes and pastries displayed in the glass-fronted counter. If I'm dead — which I've not yet discounted — this is surely heaven. It's without doubt unnervingly real.

"Can I help?" a woman behind the counter asks.

"Um, four cheese straws and a can of Coke, please."

The straws are tonged into a paper bag and placed on the counter with the can of Coke.

"That's one pound exactly, please."

I take a ten-pound note from my wallet and place it on the counter.

"Sorry, I don't have any change."

The assistant picks up the note, examines both sides, and then places it back on the counter.

"Nice try," she says. "But I'm afraid we don't accept pretend money."

"Eh? It's a ten-pound note."

"No, it's too small and not even made of paper."

To prove her point, she pings the till open and extracts a tan-coloured note.

"See?" she says, laying it next to mine.

"This is a joke," I groan. "An awful, awful joke."

"Are you going to pay for your goods?"

"Do you take cards?"

"For a pound? No."

It's irrelevant anyway. My debit card won't be valid for decades, apparently.

I apologise and skulk out the door.

Having failed to fulfil one of the most basic needs on Maslow's pyramid, only two options remain: a spot of shoplifting or I return home. The first option can remain a last resort for now, but my concerns are now mounting about what I might find at home. Perhaps the apartment represents a metaphoric way back to reality, but it could also be just another building, and in this composite of 1988, I won't live there.

What the fuck do I do then? Homeless, no money, and trapped in a delusion.

"None of this is real," I mumble under my breath, as I pass under the Tunsgate Arch. "Whatever you do, it doesn't matter."

As mantras go, it's a tough one to buy in to.

My progress back to the apartment is slow as I scour every detail of every street, hoping to find a thread which might unravel this nonsense. No one's imagination is so vivid they can perfectly recreate entire streets from thirty-plus-year-old memories. There must be blanks, and if I can find one, it might lead me back where I'm supposed to be.

I see dozens of cars as I walk, some driving past and others parked up along the streets. Those cars include VW Jettas, Ford Escorts, Mini-Metros, Vauxhall Cavaliers, Austin Maestros, and even a couple of Ford Capris. Not one single car built after 1988, nor a bus, lorry, or van.

By the time I turn into Harvey Road, I still haven't found that elusive thread.

The building which houses my apartment comes in to view, and my heart sinks. There's no Mercedes in the parking bay outside because there's no parking bay outside.

That is just the first of many differences between the property I left yesterday and the one before me. There's the colour for starters. Yesterday, the building was rendered white, and today it's bare brick. Yesterday, red clay tiles lined the roof, but today those tiles are grey slate.

Most telling though is the building itself. The estate agent told me it was formerly one house, presumably with one front door. I don't know when it was converted into two apartments, but the developers installed a second door for the upstairs apartment. That door is no longer there, which suggests the conversion is yet to happen.

Why have I made myself homeless in my own illusion? More to the point, where do I go from here?

I sit down on the pavement and lean up against the brick wall of a home no longer mine.

The only way to plan is to know what I'm dealing with. I need to take stock.

This is not the product of a mind in sleep, that's for sure. Could I be in a coma? I've read reports of patients who've woken up and relayed stories of hallucinogenic dreams while hooked up to a life-support machine. Are those dreams likely to be any more realistic than those experienced in regular sleep?

I brush my hand across a paving slab. There's a degree of warmth from the mid-morning sun as my palm scrapes across the coarse surface. The sensation is no less real than I'd expect if I'd done it yesterday or the day before.

That is disconcerting because it means I'm actually here, wherever here is. How I leave is another question.

Should I kill myself? If I'm dead, surely I'll return to where I'm supposed to be?

If my day wasn't already insane enough, I contemplate methods of ending my own life. Drowning in the River Wey holds no appeal, and neither does throwing myself in front of a bus or a train. It wouldn't be fair to inflict the trauma on an innocent driver. Besides, what if I get it wrong and lose an arm or leg but survive? One of the few things I do know is I can feel pain.

A thought suddenly punches me between the eyes.

"Suicide," I gasp. "Shit."

According to most of the apparitions I've spoken to, today is Friday 13th May 1988. Jackie Benton committed suicide on Monday 23rd May 1988 — ten days from now.

The realisation adds credence to my breakdown theory. The guilt I experienced after reading Jackie's diary page has manifested itself in a living nightmare; one so convincing I can no longer tell fact from fantasy. I've created a perfect psychosis to cope with that guilt.

In a situation lacking any sense, at least there's some rationale to my theory. The question is: how do I escape? A man in prison knows which prison he's in, and the date his sentence will end. I'm trapped in a prison of my own making, and logically, my sentence should end in ten days when Jackie takes her own life. On that day, will I be released from this place or will that be the end for me?

My mind forms a vision of an eighteen-stone male body lying inert in an intensive care bed. Earlier, a passer-by found that male slumped unconscious in a nook at Guildford Castle. Paramedics soon arrive on the scene, and they rush the male to Surrey County Hospital. On arrival, he slips into a coma; his body unresponsive but his mind working overtime.

Strangely, the vision doesn't fill me with the fear I would have expected. Fear is often born from not knowing, which is why nervous flyers are encouraged to understand the science behind aircraft flight. I now understand why my mind has created this world — my guilt needs an outlet, and I've created one so real I'm currently living in my own role-playing game with a clear goal: to stop Jackie killing herself. That is how I presumably escape the coma.

I lean my head back against the wall and close my eyes. The panic and the hopelessness remain, but the intensity drifts towards manageable. I've felt both before, and not so long ago. During my separation from Carol, the pain only eased once I finally accepted the situation. That allowed me to move forward and plan the rest of my life. The acceptance and associated distractions helped me get through some of the toughest days of my life, and I'd be a fool to ignore the lesson.

My energy levels returning, I get up and slap my parched lips together. This might not be real, but my thirst certainly is. Maybe, back in that hospital bed, I'm equally dehydrated, which is why finding something to drink is my number one priority.

I set off back towards the town centre.

As I walk, the switch in mindset casts my new world in a different light. Looking at it before, through the prism of denial, I couldn't appreciate what I was seeing. On the return leg, acceptance has changed my perspective, although once you look beyond the superficial, the changes are minimal. The sky is still blue, the front lawns still green, and the grey tarmac roads still scarred with potholes.

The devil, as they say, is in the detail.

On my earlier walk up the High Street, I paid no attention to the way people dressed. Now, as I pass a student-age couple, I can understand why.

Over recent years, I've been to several eighties-themed parties where the host enforced a dress code appropriate to the era. Any youngsters at those parties might be forgiven for thinking every man who lived through the eighties dressed like Adam Ant, or George Michael in his Wham days, while every woman religiously copied Madonna's style. Throw in a few white t-shirts with slogans, some neon-coloured accessories, a bit of lace, and that was the sum interpretation of eighties fashion.

After leaving uni, I rotated through three similar outfits: a charcoal grey suit for work, jogging pants and sweatshirt around the flat, and stonewashed jeans with a baggy sweater — usually in teal, lemon yellow, or rust-red — whenever I went out. I never once wore a 'Frankie Says Relax' t-shirt or pink fingerless gloves, and neither are the student-age couple. They're both wearing branded trainers and tracksuit-style tops you'd likely see in any modern-day clothing store, but the difference is their jeans which are a baggier cut than the painted-on style kids wear today.

The hairstyles, too, are of their time. Overly coiffed hair is one aspect of eighties fashion that did permeate most of the decade, but the trend faded towards the late eighties when common sense finally prevailed. Sadly, I lost my mullet-growing abilities fifteen years ago. I do miss it.

With Abraham Maslow screaming in my ear, I reach the High Street. Earlier, I theorised shoplifting might be an option but, now I'm outside WHSmiths, I'm not so sure I can do it, as thirsty as I am. I'd like to say my reluctance is down to a robust set of morals, but really, I'm just afraid of being caught.

Why though?

This isn't real, so what's the worst that could happen? I get caught by an imaginary store detective, and he calls the imaginary police? I get arrested and sent to an imaginary court where I'm ordered to pay an imaginary fine?

I push open the door and make straight for the drinks chiller where I grab a random can. After a quick scan of the aisles, I turn around and make for the door, plucking a bag of crisps from a shelf as I pass. With a final furtive glance over both shoulders, I push the door open and stride away.

Forty yards on, I duck down a narrow passageway to inspect my ill-gotten gains. In my haste, I snatched a can of Top Deck shandy and a packet of Golden Wonder cheese and onion crisps. I hate cheese and onion, but they usually come in a blue bag. Not here, they don't.

At some point in the past, or the future, crisp manufacturers decided to mess with our heads and swap the colour scheme with salt and vinegar. I've just fallen foul of their mischief-making, but I'm too hungry to care.

I swig large gulps of shandy to wash away the foulness of the cheese and onion. I suspect it's a self-inflicted punishment for shoplifting — why else would I end up with my least favourite flavour of crisps? On the upside, I haven't enjoyed a can of pop so much in years.

Loitering in the passageway, still hungry and still thirsty, I consider making a return run. I conclude it's a ridiculously short-term strategy. I can't live on stolen snacks and fizz for ten days, so I need a sustainable source of provisions. I also need somewhere to stay.

Inevitably my thoughts turn to money, and how useless the notes in my wallet are. I need to think long and hard about my options and, while I'm at it, I also need to formulate a plan for the reason I'm suffering this world. Somewhere not too far from here, Jackie Benton is alive. I have just ten days to befriend her, gain her trust, and then miraculously talk her out of committing suicide; a task I'm woefully ill-qualified to perform.

Christ alone knows what will happen if I fail, but she must be the reason I'm here, which leads me to believe her survival is critical for mine. Nothing else makes any sense.

Out on the High Street, a busker is in the process of murdering Ralph McTell's *Streets of London*. It's my cue to leave and to find somewhere quiet I can sit and think.

12.

The grounds of Guildford Castle are the ideal location for my planning. It's only a minute away, and it should be suitably quiet. There is another reason behind my choice of venue. It had occurred to me I was in the nook when sanity slipped away, and it's also the place where the insanity began. It is ground zero for this headfuck.

I make my way through the main gate and hurry along the path. Fortunately, there's no sign of my uniformed nemesis as I skirt along the privet hedge. The view beyond is the same as it was earlier and the same as it will be in thirty-two years' time.

With some trepidation, I cross the small area of lawn and take my place on the stone bench.

Nothing happens. I put my feet up and assume the same position I adopted when listening to music and sipping sweet cider. Still, nothing happens.

Frustrated, I swing my legs off the bench and sit forward, head in hands.

In this game, it seems the only way to end it is to complete it. There is no magic portal or hidden doorway back to reality.

I must plan.

The tranquil setting is a boon to my thinking, and after a few minutes of silent contemplation, I conclude my quest has two parts. Putting myself in Jackie's shoes, would I accept advice from a complete stranger, particularly when that advice relates to a subject as sensitive as suicide? No, I wouldn't; no one would. Therefore, there will be no quick fix. I'll likely need every one of the ten available days to save Jackie from herself, but I'll be of no help if I'm living like a hobo.

I need to get my hands on some cash — enough for a hotel stay, two meals a day, and possibly a change or two of clothes.

This kind of challenge shouldn't be beyond me as I've spent much of my career performing financial miracles with limited resources. All that's required is a little creative thinking and an actionable plan.

I make a mental list of the traditional methods used to generate cash: beg, borrow, steal, or earn. Getting a job would be too impractical a task as I'm of no fixed abode and the process would likely take weeks, even if I had somewhere to stay. I could steal money, but where from, and how? I'm no bank robber, and the thought of mugging someone in a dark alley doesn't sit right, even if that someone is an illusion. Borrowing is fraught with complications too numerous to contemplate.

Those options discounted, I'm left with one: beg.

Live Aid happened in the eighties, so I suppose there is a degree of charity in this era, but realistically, how much does a beggar make in one day? I doubt I'd scrape enough together to eat, let alone pay for a hotel room.

"Think, Sean. Think."

Taking long, slow breaths, I close my eyes and concentrate. In a swirl of random thoughts, I can sense the presence of an embryonic idea, but it isn't evolving. Some part of it is missing.

"Live Aid," I mumble.

My strategy begins to pay dividends as several vague notions cluster together.

Back in 1984, Bob Geldof had an idea to raise money for the starving in Africa. It started as a charity single and culminated in a ludicrously ambitious concert at Wembley Stadium in 1985. From what I remember, 72,000 people clambered for tickets to a once-in-a-lifetime event. I'm sure the majority of those who attended were pleased to support Geldof's cause, but I suspect most just wanted to see the likes of Queen, Bowie, U2, et al.

Those artists never begged for money. They performed for money, much like the god-awful busker I heard on the High Street.

I can play the guitar, I can hold a tune, and I've performed in countless pubs and clubs over the years. Why beg for pennies when I could busk for pounds?

As the idea evolves, an obvious issue comes to the fore — I

don't have a guitar. But I do know there's a guy currently dying on his arse nearby who does.

I jump off the bench and hurry back through the castle grounds, praying all the way the busker hasn't given up yet.

Cutting through Tunsgate, I catch a distant voice crooning the chorus of *Fly Me To The Moon*. The voice is so off-key, Dean Martin is probably spinning in his grave, assuming he's dead in 1988. I don't know.

I pound the pavement to the corner of Market Street where the busker is performing. Thin, shabbily dressed, and with a mane of long, greasy hair, he has the look of a malnourished drug addict.

I'd rather not interrupt him mid-wail, so I approach slowly and peek into his guitar case which is open on the floor for passers-by to toss in donations. It's no surprise to see just a few coppers and the odd silver coin — a couple of quid at best. If I had money, I'd gladly pay him to stop singing.

Eventually, he does, and I seize the opportunity.

"How's it going?" I ask.

"It's Friday. Slow."

He plucks a packet of cigarettes from his pocket and lights one up.

"How much do you usually make in a day?"

"None of your business, mate."

I throw an exaggerated glance towards his scattering of coins.

"Actually, it is," I reply. "I've got a proposition for you."

"Oh yeah, What's that?"

"How do you fancy putting your feet up for the afternoon while I perform in your place? I'll give you twenty per cent of everything I take."

He snorts a stream of smoke through his nostrils.

"Why would I do that when I can carry on and earn one hundred per cent?"

"No offence, my friend, but you're tone-deaf. I reckon I

could earn ten times what you usually make so you'll double your money without singing a single note."

"If you're so bloody good, buy your own guitar and try. You'll see how hard it is."

Detecting a hint of aggression in his tone, I change tack.

"I can't. I'm homeless, penniless, and a long way from home. If I don't earn some money today, I'll be sleeping on a bench with an empty stomach tonight."

My plea appears to pay off as the hard lines on his face soften.

"I'll give you a one-song trial," he concedes. "Show me how good you are, and then I'll decide."

"Deal."

I hold out my hand and introduce myself.

"I'm Jimmy," he sniffs, before wiping his nose on a sleeve.

He then hands the guitar over. I can instantly tell it's a cheap, mass-produced model more suited to school music lessons. It'll have to do. I slip the strap over my shoulder and check the tuning.

I haven't had appetite or reason to pick up a guitar since the last Busted Flush gig, nine months ago. Even so, it's like slipping on a pair of well-worn shoes. I now have an audition; I just need a suitable song to perform.

Over the years, I've endured some tough gigs. Sometimes the crowd would rather watch the football or natter than listen to a band of middle-aged blokes doing cover versions. For such occasions, we'd bring out the big guns — a set list of tracks which never failed to get the room rocking. I think back to the list and work through the options. After weeding out the songs yet to be written, I settle on one still reasonably current in 1988 and ideal for one man and a guitar.

Being in a band offers some measure of collective protection against an unappreciative audience. I don't have that luxury today, or an audience for that matter. However, who cares if I make a fool of myself? It's not as though I'll ever see any of these people again because they're not real.

I step in front of the guitar case and strum a few chords to warm up. My mouth was already dry before, but now it's virtually arid. A couple of coughs help.

With only one chance to prove myself to Jimmy, I need to gather at least a handful of people before I sing a single note. Being that humans are curious by nature, if a few people stop to watch, others will quickly join them.

I clear my throat.

"Ladies and gentleman," I holler. "Anyone a George Michael fan?"

Several heads turn in my direction, and a few people slow their stride.

"Come on. Who loves George Michael?"

Two young women in office attire stop and edge closer. They're curious, but not yet committed, so I strum the immortal opening chords to *Faith*. Curiosity piqued, they move a few steps closer.

"Who wants to hear the best George Michael impersonation outside of London?"

Slowly, but surely, the two young women are joined by a dozen others. It's enough.

Calling my rendition of *Faith* an impersonation would be a stretch, but I know the guitar part note for note. If George himself were to pitch up and join me, I doubt he'd play it any better. It's odd to think that I've imprisoned myself in a time where it's still possible to duet with George Michael. Sadly, no longer the case in reality.

I begin.

The difference between Jimmy's busking and mine is the difference between a jukebox and a live performance. If I learnt anything from all the gigging, it's that you've got to engage with an audience, no matter how small and unenthusiastic they are. If you don't, you're just background noise.

Rather than stand behind the guitar case, I strut around the cobbles and attempt to emulate George's hip-swinging. His hips were twenty-four, mine are fifty-four. Despite my improvised dad dancing, the crowd continues to grow and, two-minutes in, I have an audience most acts at Covent Garden would welcome. I encourage them to sing the chorus with me.

I reach the end and bow to a surprisingly decent round of applause, almost forgetting the point of my performance.

"If you enjoyed the song, please donate generously to my dinner fund," I call out, waving towards the guitar case.

A good number of the crowd step forward and toss coins into the case while I shoot black looks at those who peel away without paying for their lunchtime entertainment. A few backtrack and begrudgingly add to my coffers.

Once the donations have dried up, I check the balance.

"Just over eight quid," I smile at Jimmy.

"Credit where it's due," he replies. "The gigs yours but I want thirty per cent."

"Twenty-five."

"Fair enough. I'll come back at four."

He bends over and snatches two pound coins from the case.

"Beer money," he says. "I'll be in the Three Pigeons if you dry up earlier than four."

Last night, two quid wouldn't have covered half a pint of the cheapest lager in the King's Head, but here, it probably will buy Jimmy a couple of pints — not too far from the point I made to Leonard. I wonder if this is my subconscious mind at play, actualising a memory.

Again, it fits with my theory.

Jimmy strolls away, and I turn my thoughts to the next performance. With a few of the crowd still milling around, I need to keep the momentum going and choose wisely from my set list.

"Who fancies some Bon Jovi?"

A few murmurs of agreement and the odd cheer are answer enough. I clear my throat and launch into *Livin' On A Prayer* —

a challenge on an acoustic guitar. After that, it's *Summer of '69* followed by Wham's *I'm Your Man*.

The crowd remains a consistent size, and the donations plentiful after each performance. However, by the twelfth song, my throat is starting to suffer, and I'm running low on material. At one point, without thinking, I strummed the opening to *Wonderwall*. Little did they know it but my select audience got a sneak preview of Oasis' biggest hit, at least six years before Noel Gallagher even thought about writing it.

Just after two o'clock, I concede defeat and take a break.

I squat down to count my earnings and, as I do, a pair of polished black boots appear next to the case.

"By rights, I should confiscate that," a stern voice chides.

I look up, in to the face of a policeman.

"You know busking is illegal?"

I stand up.

"Honestly, officer, no. I didn't. Sorry."

"The only reason I'm going to let you off with a warning is that I happen to like *Town Called Malice*. You're no Paul Weller, but it wasn't a bad effort."

"Thanks, I think."

In his early forties, the officer appears experienced enough to apply some common sense to his duties. Either that or I'm not worth the paperwork.

"You're welcome," he says with a thin smile. "Now, finish counting your money and be on your way."

I'm tempted to ask if he knows Leonard Crosby but think better of it. He'd likely ask questions near-impossible to answer; like how I met Leonard. Technically, I haven't met him yet.

The policeman strides away, and I continue counting my earnings. I've made £34.72. It's a decent amount in any era, but now I've been warned busking is illegal, how do I avoid being arrested? The consequences are irrelevant on almost every level, except that of completing my quest to save Jackie.

I need to come up with a plan-B.

For now, though, at least I've got some money so I won't starve. I gather up the coins and put them in my pocket, and the guitar back in its case.

The Three Pigeons is at the top of the High Street, and like the King's Head, it wasn't a pub I frequented in my youth. Friends warned me it attracted some of the less-savoury drinkers in Guildford.

I enter. Jimmy is at the bar, looking right at home.

"Here so soon?" he says as I approach. "What happened?"

"A warning from the local constabulary."

"Ahh, shit. I should have warned you they're on the prowl most days. Nothing better to do, the bastards."

"The law is the law. Anyway, I didn't do too badly."

I delve into my pocket and hand over £8.68 in loose change.

"How much did you take then?" Jimmy asks in a suspicious tone.

"£34.72, and I've just given you twenty-five per cent."

Judging by his lack of a response and strained expression, I'd guess he's doing the maths. A few decades from now he'll be able to whip out a mobile phone and check my sums within seconds, but here, he must rely on good old-fashioned mental arithmetic. I suspect it's not Jimmy's strong point.

"Sounds about right," he finally concedes.

"It is right."

"You gonna buy me a pint then, to say thank you for the loan of the guitar?"

"I've already paid you."

"Alright, stay and have a beer with me then. We'll go Dutch."

I'm tempted by the prospect of a pint, although not necessarily one consumed in Jimmy's company, but drinking on an empty stomach got me into this mess. Besides, I need to watch every penny, no matter how cheap the beer might be.

"I'd love to stay," I lie. "But I need to sort out somewhere to stay tonight."

"Fair enough," he shrugs. "Where have you tried?"

"Nowhere yet. Any suggestions for cheap accommodation?"

He scratches his chin and ponders.

"There's a place on Ludlow Road, the opposite side of the train station. It ain't The Ritz, but they'll let you have a room for a tenner."

"That sounds ideal. What number is it?"

"Seventy-four. Speak to Ray."

"Thanks, Jimmy."

"Anytime, and if you want to borrow the guitar again, you'll usually find me in here."

"Noted."

I leave him to his near-empty glass and set off back down the High Street. I come to an abrupt halt halfway down, right outside another apparition from my past.

My priorities change.

13.

The lure of a Wimpy restaurant proves too strong, and before I know it, I'm on the opposite side of the glass door.

I'm not sure when I last entered a Wimpy, but it was probably with Jackie, and it was almost certainly this branch. It was a rare treat, and we'd usually have just a milkshake, but if I had a few quid spare, I'd treat us both to a Brown Derby: a freshly cooked doughnut topped with whipped ice cream, chopped nuts, and chocolate sauce.

Unlike McDonald's and all the other American fast-food joints, Wimpy provide table service. I order a burger with fries, a Coke, and a Brown Derby.

I demolish the entire meal in minutes and then rue not savouring the Brown Derby. Stupid, as the taste is only a figment of my own fractured memories.

I leave with a full belly and my promise of healthier eating in tatters, not that it matters here in Comaland: the name I attached to this unreal place, my interpretation of Guildford in 1988.

Ludlow Road is a good ten-minute walk from the town centre, and an opportunity to consider what my financial plan-B might be now my short-lived busking career has been curtailed. As hard as I try to focus on that plan, my mind would rather dwell on Jackie. Having just eaten a meal in the same booth she used to favour, it's hardly surprising. Now, without a plate of food to distract me, memories of her face have reignited in my mind's eye. Unlike the visions I had yesterday, this one is currently living across town, looking more or less like my memories.

I, for better or for worse, look nothing like my younger self.

My mind then turns to that dichotomy, and if there's any chance Jackie might recognise the fifty-four-year-old me. It's another absurd question as she knows I'm currently in my early twenties and living in Exeter. I also inherited my mother's looks, so there aren't any obvious similarities to my father, either. He still had a full head of hair in his early fifties. Then there's my voice. People's voices tend to change as they age, and mine has the addition of a Devonian twang. It's virtually incomparable to the voice Jackie once knew.

Knowing Jackie won't recognise me is both a blessing and a curse. She won't recognise me because I'm a comparatively old man, but my age also makes it unlikely she'll want anything to do with me. It's hard to think of any scenario where a fat, middle-aged man would attempt to befriend a young woman without his motives being called into question. I need to think long and hard how I overcome that problem, otherwise, the next conversation I have with a police officer won't be so cordial.

I reach the Farnham Road bridge which crosses the railway tracks, some hundred yards from Guildford station. It's a bridge I've crossed without thought hundreds of times in the past.

Not today.

Anna said Jackie jumped from a bridge near the station. This is the only bridge near the station I know of and the most likely contender, which means I'm only feet away from where Jackie ended her life.

The thought alone is enough to summon a cold dread; not so different from seeing my parent's headstone for the first time.

Shock seizes my legs momentarily, but I don't want to spend a second longer than necessary on this bridge. I move as fast as I can and don't stop until the bridge is behind me and the road ahead begins to climb sharply.

The burning sensation in my calves proves a welcome distraction from the shock. Not wanting to think about Jackie's suicide, I return my thoughts to the pre-bridge problem; that of connecting with my one-time girlfriend.

I play out some scenarios in my head, but the more I visualise the first conversation with Jackie, the more uncomfortable I feel. This is the girl I lost my virginity to, a girl I loved, and a girl I've seen naked hundreds of times. That may have been a lifetime ago, but the memories remain. How on earth do I adopt a paternal role while keeping those memories at bay?

Yesterday, I'd have given anything for a chat with Jackie Benton. Today, the prospect terrifies me.

Ludlow Road comes into view, and I cross to the opposite pavement.

On entering the road, the first house I pass is in a state. Probably a hundred years old; I reckon it hasn't seen a tradesman of any kind since the days of black and white television. There's no number on the door but being the first house on the road, it must be number one. I continue, and the second house does have a number displayed on the door: seventy-two. The next house is seventy.

"Ahh, bugger."

I turn around and return to the first house.

Why in God's name did I imagine-up a seedy character like Jimmy, and then follow his recommendation to this shithole? Is this a form of self-flagellation; punishment to offset my guilt?

There must be a reason I'm here, and whatever it is, I dreamt it up. For that reason alone, I should play along.

Reluctantly, I plod up the weed-ridden path and knock on the door. The bloke who eventually opens it could be Jimmy's much fatter, older brother; the same unwashed, dishevelled look about him.

"Yeah?"

"I'm looking for Ray."

"And you are?"

"I'm Sean. I'm told you rent rooms?"

"Who told you that?"

"Jimmy. I've just left him in the Three Pigeons."

"You want a room for an hour or the whole night?"

"Why would I want a room for just an hour? I need a room for the night."

"It's ten quid, cash up front. You need to be out by nine in the morning."

"Fine. And presumably, you are Ray?"

He nods, and then beckons me into the hallway but not before furtively glancing up and down the street.

Trying to ignore the stench of damp and body odour, I count out ten quid in shrapnel and hand it over. Ray pockets the coins and leads me up a flight of stairs to a landing. There are four doors, all shut, and another staircase.

"Bathroom is in there," he grunts, as we pass one of the doors.

Ray then wheezes up the second set of stairs to another landing in the eaves with two doors opposite each other. He unlocks the door on his right and enters the room. I follow.

"Today's your lucky day," he says, handing me a key.

"Is it?"

"Yeah, it's a Friday. I change the bed linen every Friday."

I devised some extreme penny-pinching policies over the years, but even my previous employers would have drawn the line at changing the beds just once a week.

"Nice. What a shame The Hilton had rooms last night."

"We were full last night," he replies, missing my sarcasm.

With a reminder I'm to be out by nine tomorrow, Ray leaves me to it.

Despite the recently laundered linen, the room isn't much better than a squat. The furniture, what little there is, appears recently plundered from a skip and the wallpaper is peeling like a redhead on a two-week beach holiday. The stench of body odour left with Ray but the dank hum remains.

Grim doesn't quite cover it.

With nothing to unpack and the wardrobe close to collapse anyway, I flop down on the bed. Like everything else in the room, it's unfit for purpose, and I can feel the base struts through the thin mattress. It is, however, marginally more comfortable than a stone bench.

"Beggars can't be choosers," I mumble.

Out of morbid curiosity, I open the top drawer of the bedside table. There's no bible but a lot of dust. The next drawer provides evidence of how infrequently the rooms are cleaned. Along with half a packet of Extra Strong Mints, there's a week-old copy of the Sporting Life newspaper. The third contains a single sock, which at some point in its life was probably black. Now it's a shade of mottled grey.

I shudder and slam the drawer shut.

The room might be cheap, but there's no way I'm willing to stay here more than one night, and that's assuming I make it that far. I need to focus on that plan-B and fast.

I close my eyes and concentrate.

Only minutes later, my thoughts are interrupted by footsteps on the stairs. Those footsteps are followed by hushed voices outside my room: one male, one female.

I hear a door open and close, and then just a few sporadically murmured words. Presumably, Ray has just checked-in a couple more suckers to the guest house from hell. Silence returns and I close my eyes again.

The silence doesn't last.

It begins with a repeated thud against the adjoining wall, which builds into a steady rhythm.

Thud. Thud. Thud.

This continues for a minute; the thuds spaced with metronome precision. Then, the frequency increases.

"Oh, yeah. That's perfect," the woman groans.

A series of enthusiastic grunts then accompany the thuds. Either the new guests are repairing the furniture with a lump hammer, or they're having sex.

Great.

I try to block it out but the thumping intensifies, with the woman yelling increasingly graphic instructions.

"Smash me harder, dirty boy!"

"Please don't," I groan, looking up to the cracked ceiling.

It goes on and on and on. I'm about to get up and bang on the wall when the woman yells another instruction I don't quite catch. It does the trick, and suddenly the man's grunts erupt into a protracted howl.

"Geronimo!"

All is quiet again. The door then opens and the sound of footsteps trail back down the stairs. Relief washes over me.

It's short-lived.

Ten minutes later, another couple are raucously shagging next door. It then dawns on me why Ray asked if I wanted the room for just an hour. I'm lodging in a one-star knocking shop.

This time I do get up and leave.

I wander aimlessly with no clue how to fill the time before I'm tired enough to sleep through the Ludlow Road fuckfest. I've got barely a tenner to my name, nowhere to go, and no one to share my time with.

Without any forethought, I end up traipsing in a northerly direction away from the town centre. With the working day almost over, it'll soon be swarming with office and shop staff as they begin their Friday evening revelry in the pubs and bars. It's the last place I want to be, apart from here.

An hour into my aimless walk, the novelty of my surroundings has well and truly worn off. In many respects, it's like looking through an old photo album of distant friends and family members you haven't seen in years. Perhaps if I'd lived in Guildford all my life, the reset would be a much starker experience, but I'm merely passing through streets no different to how they were in my teenage years. Everything is pretty much as I remember, which is no great surprise considering the circumstances.

I pass a pub with a couple of rickety benches outside. Needing a sit down, I nip in and order half of bitter, and while away almost an hour on one of the benches. No one approaches me or even seems to notice I'm there. It suits me. I'm content wallowing in my own thoughts.

It's still light, so I press on, eventually reaching the fringes of Bellfields Estate. At no point did I consciously plan to end up here but if I continue for another six or seven minutes, I'll reach Fir Tree Road — home to the Bentons.

I come to a stop and lean up against a wall. Do I continue, and if so, why? Unless I'm prepared to knock on the door and somehow talk my way inside the house, what's the point? Acting on impulse rarely works in my experience and any attempt to interact with the Bentons, particularly Jackie, would be futile as it stands. Careful planning is required, and that involves dealing with my immediate problems first.

I turn around and set off in a different direction.

By the time I reach Ludlow Road, it's nearly dark, and I'm exhausted — the whole purpose of my marathon stroll. I wearily plod up both flights of stairs to the room and crash on the bed, fully dressed in case I'm eaten alive by bed bugs. Besides the odd car passing outside, it's quiet. Then again, they could hold an orgy in the adjoining room, and I think I'd sleep through it.

I close my eyes and wait for sleep to come.

Long minutes pass and the blissful slumber I anticipated fails to materialise; my mind not willing to cooperate. It wants to dwell on a young woman across town and what she's currently going through.

Is she currently planning her suicide; weighing up the pros and cons of possible methods like I did outside the house in Harvey Road? I was thinking hypothetically, and if it came to it, there's no way I could take my own life, but Jackie has every intention of killing herself, and she will succeed.

How far must you fall to think that way?

Even in my darkest days post-Carol, the prospect of ending it all never came close to my thinking. All that pain I suffered, I was convinced no human could feel any worse, but I kept faith one day I'd feel a fraction better, and maybe the day after that, a fraction better still. I maintained hope, but Jackie's reserves must now be running close to empty. In ten days, she'll be clean out of hope.

Where do I fit in her descent into despair?

I've tried hard not to think about it, but the words from her diary page return to focus. Is Jackie still cursing the day we first met? Perhaps I'm not even in her thoughts. There's no way of knowing, and that just keeps the guilt simmering.

I sit up and turn on the bedside lamp. Instinctively, I reach into my pocket for a mobile phone that isn't there. I can't watch a video or listen to music or anything else which might drag my thoughts in a different direction.

Desperate for an alternative, I open the drawer in the bedside table and pull out the copy of Sporting Life. Their news is six days old today, but beyond Comaland it's decades out of date and of little interest. I flick through the pages, scanning the headlines for anything worth reading.

On page eight, I stop to read an article about the FA Cup, and the rank underdogs in this year's final, Wimbledon.

The article paints a picture of a David versus Goliath battle. Wimbledon clambered up the football pyramid from non-league, utilising a team of former scaffolders, plumbers, and assorted footballing misfits. Collectively known as the Crazy Gang, the article implies it's a minor miracle Wimbledon are even in the final but they stand little chance against this year's Division One champions, Liverpool.

Whoever penned the article, they'll eat their words when Wimbledon do lift the FA Cup, creating one of the biggest upsets in modern-day football. I watched that final in the pub with Carol and some Scouse friends from our uni days. They were so confident Liverpool would win, they bet us the cost of dinner. I can still picture the look of horror on their faces as we ordered the most expensive …

A mental lightbulb pings on, illuminating an idea so obvious I can't believe it hasn't already crossed my mind.

"Please be right," I plead, frantically turning pages to confirm the date on the front again: Saturday 7th May 1988. That's six days ago.

I re-read the article. It specifically refers to the match taking place next Saturday.

"Sweet Jesus!"

The FA Cup final is tomorrow, and I know the result.

Jumping off the bed, I pace up and down the sticky carpet; partly to quell my excitement and partly to work out how I can monetise this information. Besides a few friendly wagers with friends, I've never placed a bet in my life.

I take a moment to calm myself. I might not understand betting, but I do understand odds, and the odds for one team to win over another in a two-horse race are unlikely to be generous. I might double or triple my stake but with only a tenner to bet, the winnings won't fund a ten-day stay in Comaland.

For the first time in my life, I regret not being a gambler.

I do know it's possible to bet on which team scores first, who scores that goal, and the final score. Individually, the odds aren't long enough to make a serious return, but if I can find a bookie willing to accept an accumulation of those bets, I might be able to multiply my stake many, many times over.

If only I could remember who scored that first and only goal.

I know he scored it in the first half as we teased our friends about it at the bar at half-time. What was his name, though? Larry something? No, I can't recall any professional footballer named Larry. Lenny? No, that's not it either.

Experience tells me the most effective way to retrieve a lost memory is to stop thinking about it. I venture from my room to the bathroom on the first floor, and the name Lawrie suddenly pops into my head while I'm washing my hands.

"Lawrie Sanchez," I murmur, smiling to myself in the cracked mirror.

I return to my room.

At three o'clock tomorrow, a football match will kick off, and I already know the result. Thanks to a chance read of a discarded newspaper, I stand to make a tidy sum on a dead cert bet.

Perhaps my choice of lodging wasn't such a terrible idea

after all.

14.

Things I thought I'd never do in my life.

One: stay in a guest house that doubles as a knocking shop.

Two: get up at the crack of dawn and scavenge for food in the kitchen of said guest house.

Three: breakfast on a sandwich of prawn cocktail crisps.

Four: dress in soiled clothes after an ice-cold shower.

I hand over my room key at half-eight. Ray doesn't ask for my feedback on the room or the facilities. Just as well.

As I leave Ludlow Road, my breakfast repeats on me. I'd rather not be reminded of the culinary abomination but, needing to save every penny for today's bet, I had little option. As it stands, I'll be skint until five o'clock this afternoon.

Before I fell asleep last night, I devised a plan to fill at least a few hours before I can collect my winnings. Obviously, I need to locate a bookmaker first and place a bet at the longest odds I can get.

Once the bet is secured, I need to find somewhere to stay. A decent hotel is out of the question as, allowing for inflation, it's likely to cost at least forty quid a night. That leaves me with only a few options for accommodation and limited search resources. Without the internet, I'll be relying on cards in newsagent windows and classified ads in the local newspaper.

Then, I need to establish Jackie's place of work.

As I tossed and turned in my God-awful bed last night, a memory of the conversation with Anna returned. I'm sure she mentioned Jackie had a job in a record store in The Friary Shopping Centre. I've no intention of interacting with my former girlfriend yet, but I would like to see her. Hopefully, it'll take the edge off the weirdness when I eventually do introduce myself. A subtle reconnoitre before the real battle commences.

The town centre is slowly coming alive as I pass the Friary Shopping Centre. It's unlikely I'll find a bookmaker in there, and I don't recall seeing one on the High Street. Instead, I wander up North Street which runs parallel to the High Street. It lacks the charm of its prettier sister; some of the buildings constructed in the sixties and seventies. It also forms part of the town centre's confusing one-way system, so it's usually busy with traffic.

I cover a few hundred yards of pavement, continually checking both sides of the street for bookmakers. Then, I pass the infamous Horse & Groom; one of two Guildford pubs bombed by the IRA back in 1974. I was only a kid when it happened, so it passed me by, but the investigation continued for years, and occasionally a photo of the bombed-out Horse & Groom would feature in the national press. I might be wrong, but I think the four men who were convicted, and are currently in prison, will have their sentences quashed a year from now; if now is now, which is unlikely.

Turning back to my side of the street, I pass Guildford Library. Seeing it, I alter my plans. I'm sure they have copies of the local newspaper, and I'll be able to sit down in relative comfort to browse the ads. It's a better solution than the one I planned — loitering with intent in WHSmiths.

I reach the end of North Street where it merges into the top part of the High Street. Scanning the road ahead, I can't see any sign of a bookmaker. Without Google Maps at my disposal the next best option is to ask someone. I wait until a man roughly my age passes by.

"Excuse me. I'm trying to find a bookmaker. Do you know if there's one nearby?"

"There's a William Hill in Swan Lane."

"Great. And where is Swan Lane?"

He nods back down North Street.

"Second left."

"Thanks."

I retrace my steps and follow the directions. True enough, I find what I'm looking for and enter. I'm surprised how busy it is, considering it's only just opened for the day. It is a Cup Final

Saturday, I suppose, and with no online gambling, how else do you place a bet?

I join a queue which moves quickly enough. One of the positions becomes available and a woman – styled like a lead singer in an early-eighties soft rock band – beckons me to the counter.

"Hi, I'd like to place a bet on the FA Cup Final, but not just the winner."

"No problem. What did you want to bet on?"

"The first goal scorer and the final score."

I confirm that goal scorer's name and my prediction for the final score. She taps away at a calculator.

"We can offer you 40/1."

"Perfect. I'll take that, thanks."

I leave with a betting slip and the knowledge I'll be returning at the end of the day to collect £400, plus my original stake.

The next item on my to-do list is accommodation. I traipse back up North Street to the library.

A particularly chirpy librarian confirms they do indeed keep copies of the local paper in the reference section, and she even provides a scrap of paper and a pen.

I find the latest edition of the Guildford News & Mail and sit down to read it. For the first time since this madness began, there is some semblance of normality. I'd occasionally visit the library in Exeter while Carol trawled the shops. I'd happily while away a few hours nosing through non-fiction books and perusing a local paper I really should have purchased. Here in Comaland, all that's missing is a plastic cup of water from the cooler, and my sanity.

I leaf through to the classified section, and rooms to rent.

My initial optimism ebbs and flows over the first column of adverts. The rates appear well within my budget, ranging from thirty to fifty pounds per week. However, every advert ends with the same instruction: for more information, please call the following number.

Folk often remark how life used to be so much simpler in the past, and in many ways they're right. However, what those folk forget is that certain tasks were also a massive pain in the arse before we had the internet. Progress is so gradual, we don't notice the incremental ways our lives change because of technology.

Here and now, I realise just how much I took my smartphone for granted.

A few months ago, my search for a new home began on an app. There, I was able to filter my search in a number of ways and study swathes of information on any given property: virtual tours, floor plans, scores of photographs, and the view from the street. I could then reference crime statistics for the area, check the distance to all the local amenities, view historical property prices for the road, and distances to train stations and motorway links — all while slumped on the sofa at home.

Now, all I have is a few lines of text to go on, and a phone number I can't call until I collect my winnings later. Even then, I'll need to load up on ten-pence pieces and visit a phone box.

This is the not-so-good of the good old days.

I start jotting down the phone numbers together with the respective room rates, excluding those at the lowest end of the scale. I'm not expecting to find a palace, but equally, I don't want to stay in another shithole like the one I spent last night in.

I'm on to my eighth number when a particular ad catches my eye. Unlike all the others, it mentions an address and says callers are welcome. It's only forty quid per week, or fifty if the tenant wants evening meals included.

I scribble the address down.

I'm not familiar with the road but, fortunately, I'm only ten feet from a shelf of Ordnance Survey maps. I consult the Guildford edition.

It turns out that Cline Road is only a five-minute walk from Harvey Road, where I currently don't live. I decide to head straight there; the mention of home-cooked evening meals as good an incentive as any. Besides, I've still got seven hours to kill, and if there's anything I can do to delay my first encounter with Jackie, I'm game.

I use the walk to devise a back-story for my prospective landlord. It makes no sense telling them my stay is likely to be brief — it's not as though I'll be around to face the consequences of a breach of contract. My accent suggests I'm not local so I'll say I've just moved here to start a new job. It's not so far removed from the truth.

Fifteen minutes later — as I wander along Cline Road — I'm hoping someone is home and I haven't had a wasted journey. The house I'm looking for is at the very end of the road; a pleasant-looking 1930s semi-detached with a manicured front lawn and garage at the side.

Keeping my fingers crossed, I ring the doorbell.

After a long moment's wait, a woman with a bob of silvery hair and spectacles opens it. She's dressed ultra-conservatively in a mushroom-coloured skirt and matching cardigan, partially hidden behind a pinny.

"Good morning," she says brightly.

"Morning, I'm here about the room advertised in the paper."

"Oh, you've caught me at a slightly inopportune moment. I'm just finishing up a batch of pastry."

"Would you like me to come back later?"

"No, if you don't mind taking the house as you find it?"

"Happy to. I assume the room is still available?"

She wipes her right hand on the pinny and offers it to me.

"Yes, it is, and I'm Mrs Butterworth."

Just as I'm about to reply with my name, the consequences cross my mind. Jackie won't appreciate a man with the exact same name as her cheating boyfriend trying to befriend her, so perhaps it would be sensible to start as I mean to go on. I decide to use a different surname.

"Sean Brown. It's a pleasure to meet you."

She invites me into the hallway and, on first impressions, the house couldn't be any more different from the one in Ludlow Road. The decor is slightly dated, even by eighties standards, but it's otherwise impeccable — so much so, I offer to take my shoes off.

"If you wouldn't mind. I only had the carpet laid last year."

Hoping my socks aren't too pungent, I slip off my shoes and place them on the doormat.

"You're not local," Mrs Butterworth remarks.

"Originally from Guildford but I've lived in Devon most of my adult life."

"And what brings you back here, Mr Brown?"

I get the impression Mrs Butterworth is a stickler for old-fashioned etiquette, so I don't suggest using my first name.

"I've just secured a new job which is why I'm in the market for somewhere to stay."

"Shall we start by showing you the room, then?"

"Sounds good."

Mrs Butterworth leads me up the stairs to the landing and opens the third door along. She then enters and beckons me in.

"This is the room," she announces, stating the obvious.

I take a few seconds to absorb the details, and it reminds me a little of the lounge in the house I grew up in: a bit chintzy but ever so homely. The furniture is the same kind of walnut veneer as Dad's cherished drinks cabinet and the swirly patterns in the wallpaper are broken up by a couple of landscape paintings and a window overlooking the rear garden. The carpet is so thick it's like walking on sand.

"What do you think?" she asks.

"It's perfect."

"Does that mean you're interested in taking it?"

"Definitely."

"Good. Shall we retire to the lounge and discuss the finer details?"

"That would be great."

The lounge in question is *exactly* like that of my former

family home. I'm invited to take a seat in an armchair.

"If you give me a minute, I'll make us a cup of tea."

"Lovely. Thank you."

The minute turns to five as I sit and listen to the ticking of a carriage clock on the mantelpiece. By the time Mrs Butterworth returns with a tray, I'm close to nodding off.

"Here we are."

I expected a cup and saucer, but the tray is laden with a full china tea-set. Of most interest is the plate of biscuits.

"One lump or two?"

"Two, please."

Using a pair of silver tongs, Mrs Butterworth transfers two sugar cubes from a bowl to a cup. She then pours the tea, and I'm encouraged to help myself to biscuits. Four seems a reasonable amount.

"You have quite the sweet tooth, Mr Brown," she observes.

"I'm afraid so."

"Nothing to be afraid of. I'm a keen baker and rather partial to sampling my own wares."

Maybe this isn't hell after all — a lovely room with baked goods on demand.

Beverages and biscuits sorted, Mrs Butterworth spends fifty minutes outlining the extensive house rules, and then I'm asked a series of questions about my situation. At one point, I feared she might ask for references, which would have proven problematic, but instead, she stresses how good a judge of character she is.

The inquisition complete, I'm finally deemed worthy of a room in Chez Butterworth.

"Shall we try a four-week trial?" she then suggests. "See how we all rub along together."

"That's fine with me. Can I ask who the 'we' are?"

"I've only one other tenant at the moment. Young Jeremy has been here for six months, but you're unlikely to hear a peep from him. He's quite a shy boy but an intelligent one when he's minded to chat."

It's of no consequence to me if young Jeremy is shy or not, as I won't be here long enough to get fully acquainted. There's no mention of a Mr Butterworth, though. I don't enquire.

"I'm sure we'll get along just fine."

"As am I, so if you're willing to commit, the room is yours. You can move in whenever you're ready, subject to the first week's rent being paid in advance, and a fifty-pound deposit."

I hadn't thought this far ahead and need to improvise an excuse.

"I'd love to move in this minute, Mrs Butterworth, but there's a minor cashflow issue I need to resolve first. I'm due to pick up some cash late afternoon today, so if you're willing to hold the room until half-five, I'll happily pay the week in advance and the deposit."

"Very well, but only until half-five, mind."

"Thank you."

She nods and takes a sip of tea.

"Do you have much in the way of possessions?"

"Um, not really. Most of what I own is in storage, so I'm travelling light."

So light, I'm wearing everything I own in Comaland.

"That'll make life easier, I suppose. Will you require dinner today? It's homemade quiche with Jersey Royals and baby carrots."

"I'd love dinner. Thank you."

Our business complete, Mrs Butterworth leads me back to the hallway. I snatch another chocolate digestive on the way and slip it into my pocket.

"I'll expect you around five-thirty, then?"

"Yes, definitely. And thanks for allowing me to stay. It's a real weight off my mind."

We say goodbye, and I make my way back up Cline road, nibbling on the digestive.

Two tasks down; one to go.

Alas, that task is the one I've been dreading but with only nine days before Jackie's date with a dreadful destiny, I can't afford to dither around.

Next stop, The Friary Shopping Centre.

15.

On the whole, I think Governments should interfere in our lives as little as possible. However, at some point, a bod in Westminster must have suggested smoking in shopping centres and other public spaces wasn't good for the nation's health.

As I enter The Friary Shopping Centre, that suggestion is yet to be implemented, and there's no smoking ban in force. I should congratulate my imagination for recalling such detail.

I've never smoked before, but I understand nicotine helps relieve stress. Maybe now would be a good time to start.

My memory isn't what it was, but I spent many a happy hour browsing the stock in Guildford's record stores, so I know there are two in The Friary: Subway, and Our Price. Ironically, I can't remember if there are any in Exeter, despite visiting the city centre countless times. Alas, I suspect I can't remember because there are so few around these days.

As it's nearest, I decide to visit Our Price first and, with every passing yard, my heart rate increases. I slow my pace, but it makes little difference, other than prolonging the inevitable. If it weren't for the Jackie factor, it would be a remarkably nostalgic stroll, but I'm far too anxious to appreciate the retro retail experience.

The bright red facade comes into view. At the same moment, a thought occurs.

I'm confident this illusion is grounded in latent guilt for my part in Jackie's descent into depression. Would a simple apology banish that guilt? It might not make any difference to Jackie because I'm just some random, middle-aged man, but if I say the words to her face, it might just trigger my release from Comaland.

Surely, it's worth a shot.

Thirty yards. Twenty yards. Ten yards.

My focus remains steadfastly fixed on the entrance but a poster in the window, advertising a certain compilation album, snags my attention momentarily: *Now That's What I Call Music 11*.

To calm the growing anxiety, I recite the track list in my head. *Always On My Mind* by Pet Shop Boys, *Heaven Is A Place On Earth* by Belinda Carlisle, *Get Outta My Dreams, Get Into My Car* by Billy Ocean, *Say It Again* by Jermaine Stewart.

I'm suddenly in the shop and struggling to breathe. Refuge comes from a similar experience.

Seven years ago, I had a worrying health issue and went to see my GP. He took a blood sample, and some days later, I turned up early at the surgery for the results. I then paced up and down the waiting room, getting myself in a real state before I realised why they have magazines in waiting rooms. I couldn't say what I read, but I know it helped ease my apprehension. It turned out I only had a mild iron deficiency.

I stumble towards a rack of vinyl and snatch the first album my hand touches, which happens to be *Push* by Bros. I've never understood their appeal, but then I've never been a fourteen-year-old girl. I slide it back into the rack before anyone sees me, and replace it with Morrisey's *Viva Hate*. Just my luck to choose an album with so little text on the cover; the rear of the sleeve just the track list over a backdrop of grey clouds.

I try another album.

By the sixth album cover, I dare to look up from the rack. It's just a glance but long enough to establish how busy the store is, but then it is Saturday.

I risk another, more prolonged glance in the direction of the counter, but I can't see much beyond the throng of shoppers. The last traces of anxiety ease and I concede this is no time to be fannying around as I don't even know if Jackie works here, and I won't be going home unless I find her.

The aisle I'm in runs parallel to the counter, so I follow the racks to the far end of the store and turn right. From my new vantage point, I'm both relieved and disappointed to see two young guys serving.

I approach one of the young men; his floppy blond hair parted in the centre.

"Hi, I was wondering if Jackie Benton works here?"

"Why?"

"I, err, she's my niece, and I wanted to treat her to lunch. I know she works in a record shop, but I wasn't sure which one."

"Right shop, mate, but she's already gone out for lunch. Be back in about half-an-hour."

"Right, thanks."

I amble away, having at least confirmed where to find Jackie.

Standing outside, I'm unsure what to do next. An empty bench offers an option, so I make my way over and sit down. It's close enough I can watch the steady flow of people entering Our Price. As my feet are killing me and Jackie is unlikely to return just yet, the bench is as good as place as any to loiter.

I sit, and I wait, and if I close my eyes and try hard enough, I can pretend I'm not really here. The sound of this shopping centre is no different to the one I last visited: the constant drone of a hundred conversations, interspersed with laughter, and the occasional shriek of boisterous teens. The illusion is shattered when someone stubs out a cigarette in an ashtray a few feet from the bench. Then, a voice booms from the public address system.

"Would the owner of a blue Austin Allegro, registration PKR 642W, please return to your vehicle. Your lights are on."

I feel sorry for the owner. Not because he or she might return to a flat battery, but because they own a 1981 Austin Allegro. One of my uni tutors had one, and he never stopped complaining about it.

I've no idea how many people pass through The Friary on a typical Saturday lunchtime, but it's a lot; far more than the world I inhabit. The concourse is positively heaving, which makes it near impossible to identify one individual, particularly when that individual is only a shade over five feet tall and likely different from the girl I remember.

Nevertheless, I continue to scan the sea of faces passing Our

Price. Dozens of shoppers leave, and dozens enter. Not one of them is Jackie. A few times, I catch a fleeting glimpse of a blonde-haired girl with a similar frame, and my heart skips a beat. Each time, a closer look brings disappointment.

Then, I do spot a face I recognise, but it's not Jackie's.

"Bloody hell," I murmur.

Dressed in jeans and a brown leather jacket, Derek Benton strides purposefully towards Our Price. I lose him in the crowd for a second but catch him again just as he's entering the store. Unlike the seventy-something Derek Benton who verbally assaulted me in his kitchen, this is the version who intimidated me as a kid; the Derek Benton who thought I was an entitled brat.

Perhaps he's agreed to meet Jackie for lunch. If so, he's late and likely to be disappointed.

I get up and edge through the crowd towards the entrance to Our Price. There, I lean up against a pillar so I have a clear view of everyone entering and leaving the store.

I've only been at my post for a matter of seconds when Derek re-appears. He stops dead, checks his watch, and looks up and down the concourse. Only ten feet away, our eyes meet for less than a fraction of a second before he frowns, mutters something under his breath, and strides off into the crowd.

It was hardly a meeting but a stark reminder of how much I didn't like Derek; the pot of long-forgotten negative emotions given a thorough stir.

As I try to shake off the uncomfortable feeling another one arrives, courtesy of my bladder and the two cups of tea I drank with Mrs Butterworth. The timing isn't great, but if I'm quick, hopefully, I won't miss Jackie. I look up to the left where a sign hangs from the ceiling thirty yards away, offering directions to the toilets. Unable to quite read it, I push away from the pillar and move a few feet forward. My unexpected advance lands me directly in someone else's path, and we bump into one another.

"Damn, I'm sorry," I splutter, turning to face the unfortunate soul who collided with my eighteen stone of immovable bulk.

"It's okay," the young woman says flatly.

It's not okay. It's a million miles from okay. I freeze.

"I'm … I'm sorry," I repeat.

"Honestly, I'm fine."

The blonde-haired girl looks up at me.

"You alright, though?" she asks. "You look like you've seen a ghost.

My thoughts are so scrambled, all I can do is nod.

"Are you sure?"

"No, I'm … um, fine. For a second you reminded me of someone, that's all."

Beneath her denim jacket, she's wearing a red polo shirt with a badge on the chest. In large capital letters, it confirms what I'm already sure of — I'm looking at Jackie Benton.

Without another word, she hurries towards the store and disappears inside. I can't move, can't think, can barely breathe.

Real or otherwise, I've just spoken to Jackie Benton. Jackie bloody Benton. Fortunately, my concern there might be some flicker of recognition in her eyes proved unwarranted. To Jackie, I'm merely a random stranger. A clumsy random stranger.

I compare the two faces: the one freshly implanted in my mind and the one I've kept in the deepest recesses of my memory all these years. Her hair is different now, shorter and choppier, and the makeup palette has lost a few of the brighter shades she once favoured. The pretty girl I said goodbye to at the train station decades ago has evolved into a stunning young woman, except it wasn't decades ago — it was only last year.

My head begins to throb as dozens of thoughts randomly collide like bumper cars.

I imagined seeing Jackie's face would be disconcerting enough, but I hadn't considered how I'd react to hearing her voice. It's not that hard to remember a face when it was part of your life for so long, but the sound of her voice faded away as the years passed. Hearing it again is akin to a song you haven't heard since childhood suddenly playing on the radio, reopening a trove of associated memories.

I replay our brief conversation over and over again, focusing on every syllable and every slight change in her expression. Hardly sufficient time to draw any real conclusion but she didn't strike me as overly sullen. Either she's putting on a front, or I happened to catch her during a brief period of respite from her depressed state. Perhaps that's how depression works; the black clouds occasionally break and allow sunlight to burst through. Those clouds will gather again, I know.

Beyond Jackie's state of mind, it's clear my apology achieved nothing. That would have been too easy. Somehow, seeing her in the flesh has changed my perspective, and this no longer feels like a game. The jolt I felt as I bumped into Jackie, and the flutter in my chest when I looked into her eyes, no illusion.

I must save her, and whatever happens to me, happens.

That said, what do I do next?

An old workplace mantra springs to mind: fail to prepare, prepare to fail. It might be pseudo-advice but there's some substance to it.

I set off back to the library.

The pavements on North Street are as crowded as the concourse in The Friary, and I cut through the dawdling shoppers with purpose. As I see it, I've got one chance to ingratiate myself into Jackie's life, and if I blow it, it's game over. I need to gain her trust and work out what's going on in her head. Maybe then I can get her help, and we can both return to normality.

As challenges go, it's as tough as any I've faced in my career, if not my life. How the hell does a man my age befriend a twenty-one-year-old woman?

Back in the library, I ask the librarian for a pen and a wad of scrap paper for note-taking. She obliges, and I return to the same table I occupied earlier.

The planning begins with a list of Jackie's general traits. It peters out after two entries: she loved music and writing. Should I be so surprised it's bloody difficult recounting facts from so long ago? Back in the days before Carol met Vicky, when we were happyish, she'd occasionally recall an anecdote about our wedding day as if it had happened the week before. I could barely remember my best man's name, let alone Carol's Aunt Christine getting wasted on Asti Spumante and falling asleep in the toilets.

I continue staring at a near-blank piece of paper.

"Think," I mutter.

As time passes and the pen remains redundant, I realise I'm going about this the wrong way. You can't define a person by merely listing their traits; one reason I'd never use a dating website.

I start with a fresh piece of paper, but rather than write a list I conduct a brain dump; the source of inspiration being our first proper weekend away as a couple.

We were in college, so money was tight, but we managed to book a room in a crummy hotel near Waterloo. The great thing about London is there's plenty to do even if you're skint. We enjoyed a leisurely stroll along the banks of the River Thames, lunched on Lemonade Sparkle ice lollies in Hyde Park, watched the changing of the guard at Buckingham Palace, and fed the pigeons in Trafalgar Square.

Everything anyone would want to know about Jackie Benton could have been gleaned in that weekend. The wonderment in her eyes when we first stepped onto Waterloo Bridge as the Houses of Parliament and Big Ben came into view. Her excitement when she thought she saw the Queen in one of the windows at Buckingham Palace. The way she laughed when a pigeon shat on some po-faced guy in a suit near Trafalgar Square.

In particular, I remember our first evening. We stumbled upon a backstreet pub not far from our hotel and the sound of some band belting out punk-inspired tunes lured us in. Jackie remained mesmerised throughout their entire set. Afterward, she confessed she'd never seen a band play live before. It was like an awakening, and we saw a lot of live music in the all-too-short time before the infamous phone call.

I might not remember much about my wedding, but my weekend with Jackie I remember every smile, every pout, every snigger, every gasp, every sigh, every tiny quirk my beautiful girlfriend possessed.

For this exercise, it's all I need.

Six pages of notes later, I have enough material. I also have a seed of an idea for a cover story, but for it to sound convincing, I need to conduct as much research as I can cram into three hours. I dart over to the non-fiction section and scan the shelves. The three books I pluck will hopefully furnish enough factual matter to beef up my plot.

I leave the library at four o'clock and stride back down North Street towards The Friary, ready as I'll ever be to take my one shot.

16.

Halfway down North Street, I'm beginning to wonder where everyone has gone; the pavements near-empty compared to this morning.

Then I remember.

It's FA Cup final day, in a time when everyone would religiously congregate around their television set at home to watch. When I had Sky TV, rarely a day went by when there wasn't a live game somewhere in the world beamed to my television. In this era, live football is a rare treat.

I reach the doors of an equally quiet shopping centre and make my way back towards Our Price. For my plan to work, I need to suppress my nerves and hope luck plays its part. Any cock-ups and I'll no longer be just a random stranger Jackie bumped into — I'll be a creepy pest with an unhealthy interest in young women.

Returning to the same rack of albums I perused earlier, I check who's serving: Jackie and the kid with the floppy hair. So far, so good. It also helps the store is nearly empty.

I move closer to the counter and stop at a bargain bin of cassettes. It's the ideal cover as I wait for the right moment.

With one eye on the counter, I sift through the bin and casually inspect albums by artists I've never heard of.

A tall youth in a baseball cap approaches the counter and hands an album to the kid with floppy hair. I make my move and step towards the till, where Jackie awaits the next customer.

"Hello again," I say with mock surprise.

"Oh, hi," she replies, expressionless.

"I'm not stalking you, I promise."

Is stalking a thing in the eighties? Jackie appears nonplussed by my reappearance.

"I'm wondering if you can help me with some advice?"

"Okay."

I swallow and brace myself for the bullshit impact.

"My name is Sean, and I've just started working for the NME."

"The NME," she blurts. "As in, The New Musical Express?"

"That's the one. I'm a music journalist."

For the briefest of moments, there's a flash of excitement in her features, but she quickly swit **vocalist** ches it off, as if it might be deeply uncool.

"Nice work if you can get it," she says with a nonchalant shrug. "I don't suppose you fancy swapping jobs?"

Once Jackie left college, she hoped to do a journalism course at uni, but her A-level grades weren't good enough, and she ended up working as an office junior for a newspaper with more adverts than news. Somewhere along the line, she obviously lost that job which is why she's now working in Our Price — possibly because of my actions. It might have only been a pipe dream, but I do recall she fancied the idea of working for the NME; the de-facto newspaper for music aficionados.

"I wouldn't mind working in a record store," I reply with a chuckle. "But I don't think my wife would approve of the wage packet."

Mentioning a wife so soon in the conversation will hopefully demonstrate I'm a happily married man and not some lecherous perv. As it is, I'm neither.

"No, the pay isn't great. What is it you wanted to know?"

"Ah, yes. I've only just started in this role, and as you can probably tell from my accent, I'm not local. I was hoping to get some insight into the Guildford music scene, and some of my best tips in the past have come courtesy of folk working in record stores."

"Right, you're looking for info on gigs?"

"Exactly. I just need a handle on where the best venues are, and if there's anyone playing tonight?"

"Might be."

She shoots me a look I don't think I've ever seen before. Not quite suspicious but definitely guarded.

"Might be, or is?"

"The Britannia, down by the river. They have live music most Saturdays."

"Thanks. I appreciate the tip. Anywhere else?"

"You said you're a journalist, right?"

"Yes."

"Do some investigation, then," she huffs. "I'm paid to sell records."

Her attitude is so far removed from the easy-going girl I once knew, but her mother did imply Jackie's attitude had hardened. I have an idea which should soften it.

"Do you listen to a lot of live music locally?"

"A fair bit. Why?"

"Maybe you can help me then."

"With what?"

"I could do with a guide, just for a week or so while I find my feet."

"No offence, but I don't want to trawl around the pubs and clubs with a middle-aged man in tow."

"Ah, that's a shame. I had some concert tickets going spare, as a thank you."

"Tickets for what?"

"They're probably of no interest to you but Gary Numan. He's playing at the Civic Hall in September."

There's no angsty retort this time.

The first album Jackie Benton ever bought was Gary Numan's, *The Pleasure Principle*. She was fourteen at the time and purchased it from Woolworths with a record token received on her birthday. Some years later, she admitted to me the only reason it appealed was the photo of Numan on the cover. Admittedly, it made him look impossibly beautiful.

Despite her shallow reasoning for buying his album, Jackie became a Gary Numan superfan and, to the best of my knowledge, she's never seen him play live.

"His Metal Rhythm tour?" she asks, her tone mellower.

"Yep, but I'm not sure they're worth the damage to your street cred. I'll nip over to Subway Records and see if anyone there is interested. Thanks for your help."

It's time to see if my gamble has paid off; a straight bet between Jackie's desire to see Gary Numan, and her pride. I turn to walk away.

"Wait."

"Yes?"

"Okay, I'll do it. I'll show you around."

"You will?"

"Yes, but there are conditions."

"I'm listening."

"You buy the drinks."

"Fair enough."

"And no funny business. If you start acting pervy the deal is off, and you'll get a kick in the nuts for your trouble."

"You've no worries on that front, Jackie. I'm a …"

"Wait," she snaps. "How do you know my name?"

I nod towards her chest.

"It says on your badge."

"Err, right."

I shake my head and continue with my pre-prepared white lies which should offer her sufficient peace of mind.

"I'm a happily married man with a daughter roughly your age. Trust me; I'm the last person likely to try anything on."

It's the truth, in part.

"Alright. I'll meet you outside The Britannia tonight at eight. Do you know where it is?"

I do.

"I'm sure I'll find it. See you later."

Out on the concourse, a flood of emotions washes over me. I'd imagine they're similar to those Lawrie Sanchez must have experienced earlier: relief, elation, and finally, nervous dread. I might have netted the first goal, but there's an awful lot of the match still to play.

With time to kill, I take a slow walk back to the High Street and watch the last twenty minutes of the FA Cup final on a television in Currys' window. I'm joined by several blokes who would rather be at home. When the match ends, they're all stunned Wimbledon won. I'm not, and head off to collect my winnings.

The cashier in William Hill accepts my slip and hands over the cash without comment. In her job, she must see hundreds of punters defy the odds so my 40/1 bet can't be that remarkable. If only she knew.

Finally, I have a pocket full of eighties cash and somewhere to go. The first stop is Boots where I grab some basic toiletries, and then Marks & Spencer where I rush to buy socks and pants, two pairs of jeans, and a couple of sweaters before they close. Turns out clothes shopping is just as uninteresting in Comaland as it is in real life.

Carrier bags in hand, I guzzle a celebratory can of Lilt on the way back to Cline Road.

The jubilation is, however, short-lived when my thoughts turn to meeting Jackie later. I've got a foot in the door, but that was the easy part. I can only plan so much, and there's no telling if Jackie will open up to me, or when. I've got so little time to work with. I suppose I could tell her the truth — I'm the middle-aged incarnation of her first boyfriend, and I'm currently experiencing a hallucinogenic trip back in time, tasked with preventing her suicide.

Maybe not.

I ring the doorbell precisely one minute later than I predicted. Mrs Butterworth answers, her pinny still in place.

"I wasn't sure if you'd come back," she says. "Some people aren't keen on my house rules, but they're not blessed with either the good manners or spine to say as much."

"No complaints from me," I reply. "And besides, I'm rather partial to homemade quiche."

The faintest hint of a smile reaches her mouth.

We return to the lounge where I'm relieved of one-hundred pounds and reminded another fifty is due next Saturday. Setting that aside, and after my brief shopping expedition, that leaves me with a shade over two hundred to last however long I'm stuck here.

"Dinner will be ready in twenty minutes," Mrs Butterworth says. "Time enough for you to unpack your bags."

I concur and head up to my bedroom. It takes three minutes.

Not wanting to get under Mrs Butterworth's feet, I use the rest of my time to inspect the room properly. The furnishings and decor might be a bit dated, but there's not a trace of dust anywhere. I test the bed by flopping down on my back. It's firm but not overly so — just how I like it. Given how quiet it is, I could easily fall asleep, but I don't want to get off on the wrong foot by being late for dinner.

The sound of a door opening on the landing breaks the silence. It's followed by slight footsteps and another door opening and closing. I presume it's my fellow tenant, Jeremy. A minute later, I hear the toilet flush and the taps running before the same slight footsteps pad down the stairs.

If he's heading down for dinner, I might as well say hello. I change my socks before heading down to the kitchen.

When I arrive, Mrs Butterworth is at the hob, but Jeremy is nowhere to be seen.

"Is there anything I can do?" I ask, keen to make a good impression on my landlady.

"Jeremy is laying the table in the dining room, so everything is under control, thank you."

"If you're sure?"

"Yes, yes. Why don't you go and introduce yourself? The dining room is the first door on the right."

I'm patently not needed here, so I do as I'm told.

I enter the dining room to find a young man laying out the cutlery. With mousy-brown hair neatly parted at the side and dressed in corduroy trousers and a plaid shirt, he has the look of a student dressed in his dad's clothes.

"You must be Jeremy," I say with a smile. "I'm Sean."

"Hello," he squeaks, barely lifting his eyes from the table.

Mrs Butterworth did say he was shy, so it looks like the onus is on me to spark the conversation.

"Where should I sit?" I ask. "I don't want to steal someone's seat at my first dinner."

"Here's fine," he replies, gesturing to the place he's setting.

I cross the carpet and offer my hand.

"It's nice to meet you, Jeremy. How long have you lived at Cline Road?"

"Six months or so," he replies with a hesitant handshake.

I sit down.

"Did you watch the Cup Final?" I ask.

"No."

This lad is hard work.

"You're not a football fan?"

"Not really."

He picks up a spoon and turns it over in his hand, placing it down a fraction of an inch to the left of where it was.

"Have you always lived in Guildford, Jeremy?"

"No."

Mercifully, Mrs Butterworth enters the room, carrying a ceramic bowl full of Jersey Royal potatoes.

"Are you two suitably acquainted?" she asks. "If so, could you fetch a jug of water please, Jeremy?"

He scoots away, her question unanswered.

"He's a lovely young man," she whispers. "So polite and helpful."

"Indeed."

But not big on chat, apparently.

After two additional trips to the kitchen, Mrs Butterworth serves dinner. It's all a bit formal for a Saturday, but the food itself is delicious. The conversation is minimal, although I do manage to extract a few snippets of information from Jeremy.

He's twenty-two and originally from Maidstone in Kent where his parents still live. Having secured a first-class degree at the University of Kent, he now works in biochemistry at the Research Park.

I do wonder what life has in store for Jeremy. Apart from his crippling shyness, he appears so disconnected from what interests most youngsters. He doesn't listen to pop music, watch movies, or enjoy any sports. And, although I'm not in any position to criticise, I reckon his mum still buys his clothes.

Our plates cleared, Mrs Butterworth takes them out to the kitchen and returns with another homemade creation: a raspberry Pavlova. I've eaten in many Michelin-starred restaurants in my time, but I don't think I've enjoyed a meal quite so much. My repeated offer to help with the washing-up is declined, so I skip up to the bathroom for a quick shower.

With no hair to style, it doesn't take long to get ready. I stand in front of the mirror in my new clothes and sigh. Rather than a journalist for one of the coolest music newspapers on the planet, I look more like a middle-aged geography teacher. On the flip side, I know more about up-and-coming music acts than any journalist alive because, outside of Comaland, most of those acts have already come and gone.

Feeling a bit like a teenager I traipse down to the lounge to ask for a key and to confirm I won't be home late. Mrs Butterworth is watching Dad's Army on her antiquated television set.

"I'm just meeting up with an old work colleague," I tell her. "I'll be back before eleven."

"Jeremy and I are usually in bed by ten, so please try not to make any noise."

I try to dismiss the picture of them in bed together — a truly haunting vision.

"I'll be quiet as a mouse."

She hands over a front door key, and I leave her to Captain Mainwaring and Private Pike.

With little faith in eighties antiperspirant, I trudge slowly towards town; the anxiety building with every step. I'm nervous about spending more than a minute in Jackie's company, but also because I have no idea how the evening will play out. This version of Jackie isn't the one I knew, and that makes her unpredictable. I only hope once I scratch beneath her hardened exterior enough of my first girlfriend remains.

I cross the river bridge, and The Britannia comes in to view across a car park. This is a pub I visited in my youth, so I'm hoping there won't be any surprises.

The front is exactly how I remember it: eight rickety picnic benches, each with a weather-beaten parasol above. Every one of the tables is occupied. Jackie isn't due for another ten minutes, which means I've time to nip inside and neck a swift pint before she arrives. And by God, do I need one.

It's already crowded and after a fight to grab the barman's attention, I order a pint of Old Thumper. He asks if I want anything else and I almost order a sweet cider for Jackie. That would be a mistake, but it is a timely reminder I need to be on guard. Jackie and I are strangers.

I wander back outside and lean up against the wall, hoping to blend in with the brickwork. The clientele is young, and I can see why Jackie wasn't keen on being seen with me. Even taking in to account the late-eighties fashion, the crowd are cooler than I ever was, and significantly cooler than I am now.

I'm halfway through my pint when eight o'clock rolls around. A minute later, I spot a young woman sauntering across the car park in the direction of the pub. At first, I dismiss the sighting as the young woman doesn't look a lot like Jackie, but as she gets nearer, I do a cartoonish double-take.

My former girlfriend shopped in places like Chelsea Girl and Miss Selfridge, and rarely strayed from conventional High Street fashion. The young woman approaching is sporting a black miniskirt over fishnet tights, together with a pair of red Dr Marten boots and matching leather jacket. Her blonde hair is more an explosion than a style.

She spots me, bows her head, and continues in my direction. Hands dug deeply into her jacket pockets, she takes a furtive glance around.

"Alright," she mumbles.

"Evening, Jackie."

17.

It was quite fortunate I met Jackie at that youth disco all those years ago. A few weeks before our first dance, I somehow enticed another girl to dance with me. I don't think I fancied her that much but teenage hormones being what they are, I wasn't going to pass on the chance of a possible snog. As the song ended, the lights came on to signify the end of our evening. I was about to ask the girl for her number when someone hollered my name. I turned to see my dad stood in the doorway, dressed in khaki shorts, a hideous Hawaiian shirt, ankle socks, and sandals, waving like a demented auctioneer to grab my attention; I could have died. I never did get that girl's number, but on the way home, Dad commented I had a face like a slapped arse.

That term would now accurately describe Jackie's face.

"Can I get you a drink?"

"Cinzano and lemonade."

"Ice?"

"No."

"Are you coming in with me or waiting out here?"

"I'll wait here."

For a girl who never liked the taste of alcohol, Cinzano is an interesting choice. I return to the bar and after another battle to be served, plod back outside. Jackie is in conversation with some scruffy lad in ripped jeans and a black denim shirt.

"One Cinzano and lemonade," I confirm, handing her the glass.

She takes it and mumbles a half-hearted thank you. The lad looks me up and down but says nothing.

"Have I interrupted something?" I ask.

Faced with no option but to make an introduction, Jackie waves a hand in my direction.

"Gary, this is Sean. He works for the NME. Sean, this is Gary."

I receive a nod and a grunt rather than a handshake.

"What kind of music do you write about?" Gary then asks. "Folk, or country and western?"

"Why those genres?"

"Dunno, your accent and your age, I guess. How old are you, mate? Sixty?"

He laughs at his own witticism while Jackie forces an embarrassed smile.

"Fifty-four, since you ask. How old are you, Gary?"

"Twenty-eight."

"And what do you do for a living?"

"Bit of this, and a bit of that."

"Pay well?"

"I do alright."

"I can tell," I reply, nodding towards the digital watch on his wrist. "That Timex must have set you back at least a tenner."

Ignoring my barb, he turns to Jackie.

"I'll catch up with you later, babe. Have fun with Val Doonican."

He swaggers away, blanking me in the process.

"Gary a friend?" I enquire as Jackie knocks back her Cinzano.

"Kind of."

"What exactly does he do for a living?"

"No idea, and don't much care. I'm not looking to marry the bloke."

Her tone hints they might be more than just friends, but I'd rather not know.

"What time does the band start?"

"Whenever they feel like starting."

"Right."

The aversion to eye contact continues. It's beyond awkward.

"What kind of music are you into, Jackie, apart from Gary Numan?"

"All sorts," she shrugs. "I quite like some of the current dance acts."

I leap on the opportunity to create conversation.

"You're in luck as there's a ton of new dance acts coming down the line. Any time now, acid house will explode. Then, there's new forms of dance music on the way: techno, garage, and trance."

I know precisely nothing about techno, garage, or trance, but I need to sound convincing if I'm to break down the barriers.

"You know your stuff," she concedes. "You ever been to a rave?"

"A few?"

"Really? Where?"

I reply with a random list of towns. It makes no odds what I say as, without the internet, there's no way Jackie can check I'm telling the truth. The only pro of the pre-internet age I can see.

"Did you do drugs?"

Sticking as close to the truth as possible, I tell her I've only smoked weed. I don't tell her it was many decades ago, while at uni.

"You've never taken acid?"

"No, because it's quite hard reporting on an event when you're off your face. Besides, that shit can kill you."

"It can't."

"I've seen several reports of kids younger than you who've died after taking acid."

"Life's full of risks," she shrugs. "And you're only young once."

In her case, she'll remain perpetually twenty-one according to her death certificate.

"True, but there's plenty of good stuff to look forward to as you get older."

"Like what? Saggy tits and living with some no-mark husband who likes to get handsy whenever the mood takes him. No, thanks."

Her cynicism jars. What the bloody hell happened to the bubbly optimist?

"I don't want to sound like a preachy old fart, Jackie, but your life can be whatever you want it to be."

"If you say so."

The awkward silence returns; my first effort at stoking optimism falling flat. There are a thousand different subjects I could discuss with Jackie, and just as many questions I'd love to ask her, but they're almost all off-limits, except one.

"I take it you're a big Gary Numan fan?"

"Massive."

"Got all his albums?"

"Every one of them."

"Which is your favourite?"

The slight easing of her taut features is a good sign.

"That's a hard question to answer. They're all incredible."

"Okay, which one did you listen to first?"

I already know the answer.

"*The Pleasure Principle.*"

"Good place to start. What's your favourite track?"

"*Complex.*"

"Yeah, great tune. It's probably my second favourite, after *Conversation.*"

She played the album to me so many times; I know every track by heart.

"Right."

The conversation peters out. Jackie then holds out an empty glass in my direction.

"Same again."

"Same again, *please.*"

She rolls her eyes.

"Please."

Just as I shift my feet, a few familiar words boom from inside the pub.

"Testing. One, two. Testing. One, two."

I turn to Jackie.

"Sounds like they're about to start. Shall we go in?"

"If we must."

She remains three paces behind me all the way to the bar and then loiters six feet away, so no one will assume we're together. Most of the crowd have already moved towards the back of the room where a four-piece band are completing their warm-up.

The barman places our drinks down, and I pay the two quid bill. I grab my pint but leave the Cinzano and lemonade where it is. If Jackie is so keen to keep her distance, she won't appreciate me handing her a drink. Then, like a dog snatching at fallen scraps beneath a dining table, she swoops in and grabs the glass before returning to her position.

I've never felt so uncomfortable.

"What are they called?" I ask across the void. "The band."

"Rhubarb Blue," she mumbles, again avoiding eye contact.

To my relief, they begin their set. Seeing as I'm supposed to be a music journalist, I should try to appear interested.

With my pint in hand, I move towards the crowd and lean up against the wall to the side. For a pub, the room is a decent size, yet the sixty or seventy-strong crowd, standing shoulder to shoulder in front of the stage, make it feel much smaller. It's not too dissimilar to some of the venues I've played although our audiences were older and less enthusiastic. Also, we never played in a fog of cigarette smoke.

If I had any expectations about the band we're here to see, they were probably low, so I'm pleasantly surprised when my right foot begins tapping. It's clear from their stage presence Rhubarb Blue have been gigging a while, and the opening track is a catchy number, their sound somewhere between Big Country and Prefab Sprout.

Twenty feet away, Jackie watches on from the bar. Seemingly disinterested in the music, she gulps back her drink and orders another one. My Jackie was never a big drinker, and three glasses of Cinzano and lemonade would have transported her to the fringes of drunkenness. This Jackie has a greater appetite and tolerance for alcohol. If there's any upside, perhaps she'll be less guarded with a few drinks inside her. Hopefully, less standoffish.

Sipping at my pint, I pay more attention to the band than my reluctant guest. The next four tracks are a mixed bag, and the last doesn't go down too well with the crowd; a slow, melancholy tune called *Window to My Heart*. In an attempt to reengage, they move on to an upbeat cover of Curiosity Killed The Cat's hit, *Down To Earth*.

It's a song I've heard more times than I care to remember. I glance over to the bar to check if it's quiet enough I can get another pint before the next track starts. Jackie is still there, but she's no longer alone; joined by her cocky turd of a friend, Gary.

Standing only inches apart, his hand is on her arm, and they're deep in conversation. Across my fifty-four years, there aren't many people I've taken an instant dislike to, but Gary is one of them.

He leans in and whispers something in Jackie's ear, and she responds by sliding her hands around his waist. Before I know it, they're engaged in a deep, hungry kiss.

My stomach turns but, like a rubbernecker passing a crash scene, I can't fight the compulsion to watch.

In the months after I ended our relationship, I couldn't stop thinking about Jackie with someone other than me. Occasionally, I'd imagine her kissing him and, although I had no right to be jealous, it provoked pangs of envy. Then, I'd imagine her rolling around naked in bed with some lad. It proved too much and, on reflection, it was the reason I had to block her out of my mind completely, the jealousy too acute.

The scene I'm now witnessing is the worst kind of punishment — it must be. I suppressed the thoughts of Jackie and another man for so long, my broken mind can no longer keep those thoughts bottled up. This is what I deserve for the way I treated her. This is my penance.

They finally break, and Gary slaps her on the backside. He then grabs his pint from the bar and disappears into the crowd.

What a gentleman.

I don't know what to do because I have no right to do anything. I certainly have no right feeling the way I currently feel. Putting aside how I once felt about Jackie, should she be involved with a lad like Gary? If my imaginary daughter brought Gary home, I'd kick his arse out and ban the good-for-nothing oik from ever darkening our door again.

The shock of seeing my first love groped by another man still lingers, and I need a drink more than ever. I make my way over to the bar.

"What do you think of the band?" I ask casually.

"Not much."

"So, apart from The Britannia, where else can I find live music?"

"There's The Star in Quarry Street, and Pews Bar on Chapel Street."

"Right, thanks."

I order another pint, and Jackie slides her empty glass in front of me.

"That'll be your fourth or fifth?"

"I'm not counting."

"You're planning to make a night of it?"

"Yep, as long as you're buying."

The barman delivers my pint, and I order another Cinzano and lemonade for Jackie. The timing is perfect as the band announce they're taking a short break. The crowd flock in our direction.

"Shall we go stand over there?" I ask Jackie, pointing towards my previous position near the side wall. "We're in the way here."

"I'll meet you over there. I need the loo."

She saunters away, leaving her drink on the bar.

When Jackie returns, the conversation is just as stilted, until she asks about the concert tickets and when she can have them. I blag an excuse about the promoter sending them next week, once

I've settled in my new office.

The band begins the second half of their set, and it's too noisy for chat. We watch them play two numbers with Jackie standing a few feet away. She then shouts in my ear that Rhubarb Blue are shite and her glass is empty, and she promptly returns to the bar.

I check my watch. I've been here well over an hour, and all I've learnt about Jackie is that she's shed many of her redeeming qualities over the last twelve months. I can't say I'm a fan of this version, although I don't see any obvious signs of depression either. Yes, she's a bit surly, but that's not an unusual trait in kids her age — I studied with more than a few moody buggers at uni. They shouldn't have listened to The Smiths so much, in my opinion.

Maybe I need to subtly broach the subject of mental health and gauge her reaction.

As I ponder how, I notice Gary crossing the room. He makes straight for Jackie, and they talk for a minute before he shouts an order at the barman. Two drinks are duly served. I slip into over-protective father mode; keeping one eye on the bar and the other on the stage. Whenever it looks like the young couple are about to get intimate, my head snaps towards Rhubarb Blue's lead vocalist.

The glancing left and right continues for ten minutes until the mood at the bar changes. I can't hear what they're saying but the scowl on Jackie's face suggests they're having a lover's tiff. Gary waves his right arm around, pointing in random directions before he slaps his hand down hard on the bar. Jackie responds with some aggressive finger-pointing, and the barman takes an interest, watching the argument unfold as he restocks a fridge.

The situation then escalates as Gary's expression grows darker, and he suddenly grabs Jackie's wrist. She attempts to shake it off but to no avail. As the two wrestle, I can no longer stand by and watch. I march over.

"Everything alright here?" I ask.

"Piss off, granddad," Gary spits, his hand still locked around Jackie's wrist.

"He's just leaving," she says defiantly. "Aren't you, Gary."

"I ain't going nowhere till you tell me what you said."

"You'll be waiting all night then."

His knuckles whiten, and Jackie hisses at the increased pressure.

"Tell me, bitch!"

I have to intervene.

"Let go of her," I demand.

"Or what?"

Any time I've ever come close to trouble, a stern glare is usually enough to ward off any aggressor. Standing a few inches over six feet, I'm no fighter, but I do possess the features of a nightclub bouncer, albeit an overweight bouncer in the twilight of his career.

"Do you really want to find out?" I growl, taking two steps forward.

Gary appraises his options. If we were boxers, he'd barely scrape in as a welterweight while I'd comfortably sit in the heavyweight class. He might be younger and fitter, but if I caught him with a punch, it'd likely be enough to floor him.

He lets go of Jackie's wrist and barges past me; his weight insufficient to make any impact. I watch him all the way to the door.

"What did you do that for?"

I turn to Jackie, expecting gratitude. Her irritation levels appear unchanged.

"He was hurting you. That's not on where I come from."

"I don't need you or any man fighting my battles, thanks."

"Sorry, I didn't mean to interfere, but …"

"Men are only good for two things," she snaps. "Buying drinks and mowing the lawn."

"A bit harsh. We're not all like Gary."

"Yeah, right."

She snatches her glass from the bar and downs the contents.

"I'm going."

Jackie then reaches into her handbag and pulls out a notepad and pen. After scribbling something down, she thrusts a piece of paper in my direction.

"What's this?"

"My address. I'll expect those tickets within the next ten days."

"Hold on. I, um …"

"I did what you asked, and now I'm going home."

"The band haven't finished yet."

"So?"

"Don't you want another drink?"

"No, and I don't want to do this again."

I can feel her slipping away, and that can't be good.

"Jackie, wait. Please."

"What?"

"Can I walk you to the taxi rank?"

"Like I said: I don't need a man to look after me."

She storms away.

18.

Three sharp knocks on my bedroom door.

"Sean, are you awake?"

I've been awake most of the night; tossing and turning.

"Yes, Mrs Butterworth," I croak.

"Would you like breakfast? I'm preparing eggs and bacon."

"That'd be lovely, thanks."

"Fifteen minutes."

"Okay."

I squint at my watch. I don't want to be awake at eight o'clock on a Sunday morning any more than I want to be in this room, in this nightmare. A couple of slaps to my cheek confirm the nightmare is still ongoing. It's such an accurate recreation of reality I even have to suffer the usual aches, pains, and stiffness as I clamber out of bed.

Dressed in just a pair of boxer shorts, I check the coast is clear and waddle across the landing to the bathroom.

Bladder emptied, teeth brushed, face washed, and dressed, I follow the enticing aroma of bacon down the stairs. It leads me to the kitchen, where I bid Mrs Butterworth a good morning.

"I think we can dispense with the formalities now you're living here. You may call me Sylvia."

"Will do, and thank you. I wasn't expecting breakfast."

"You're welcome, but it's only at weekends, mind. I like to have a good breakfast before church."

"Is there anything you'd like me to do?"

"Just sit yourself down in the dining room."

I leave Sylvia to her frying pan and wander through to the dining room. Jeremy is already sitting stiffly at the table, dressed in a grey lambswool cardigan over a white shirt.

"Morning, Jeremy."

"Good morning."

"Are you off to church too?"

"No."

"Oh."

I sit down opposite. Once again, I find myself in the company of a youngster who doesn't want to engage, albeit for different reasons.

"Anything exciting planned for the day?" I ask.

"I'll be reading a novel until lunchtime. I might go for a walk this afternoon."

It seems he is capable of speaking in sentences.

"What novel are you reading?"

"*The Currents of Space* by Isaac Asimov."

"The sci-fi author, right?"

"Correct."

Now I've revealed the sum total of my Asimov knowledge there's not much else I can add to the conversation.

"Do you listen to much music?"

He shakes his head.

"You don't have a favourite artist, favourite album?"

"My parents frowned upon popular music. They considered it a negative influence."

"What? All of it?"

"All popular music, yes."

"Bloody hell."

"Language," Sylvia coughs, as she bustles in.

"Sorry."

Breakfast served, we eat in near silence; just the chinking of stainless steel on china and the odd remark from Sylvia. Once again, I offer to wash-up and once again she declines my offer. In Sylvia's experience, men are good at tinkering with all things mechanical but hopeless at domestic duties. Her comment on the inadequacies of men is an unwelcome reminder of Jackie and her even lower opinion of my kind. So far this morning, I've kept her on the periphery of my thoughts.

I know I'm postponing the inevitable.

With Sylvia busy clearing the kitchen and Jeremy reading in the lounge, I retire to my bedroom. I need to consider my next move, if there's even another move to make.

Lying on the bed, I stare up at the ceiling and replay last night's events in my head. From beginning to end, there are no positive highlights.

I knew it would be a challenge connecting with Jackie, but I grossly underestimated that challenge — I might as well have met up with a completely different girl.

Did I really inflict so much damage she now harbours a deep mistrust of men? It's not beyond the realms of possibility, I suppose. What is it they say about a woman scorned?

I think back to her diary page, and the words ingrained in my memory like an epitaph on a headstone: *the one decent man in my life has turned out to be just like all the others. I hate him ... I hate them all.*

It's not hard to understand why she'd feel that way.

We rarely talked about her absent father because, even as a naive teenager, I could tell how much it still hurt, and the resentment Jackie felt towards him. I never did and never will understand that arsehole's thinking, but I got to hear about the consequences. Before Anna met Derek, she and her young daughter lived a hand-to-mouth existence. Jackie told me her first school shoes were from a jumble sale, and her packed lunch usually consisted of a cheese sandwich and a single digestive biscuit; Anna too proud to accept the charity of free school meals.

Then, Jackie met me, and slowly she regained her faith in men, even if the man in question was just a lad. She built upon that faith for a shade over five years, until I smashed it to pieces in one brief phone call.

Now, I've seen first-hand the damage I caused. Along with her feckless father, I helped to create this bitter, hate-filled version of Jackie Benton. Worse still, I blew my only chance to make amends.

Consequently, Jackie will soon take her own life.

"Not strictly true," I mumble.

Jackie took her own life, past tense, but now I must accept my share of the liability. Only now do I understand how Anna felt as she confessed her guilt to me in their kitchen. I can even understand why Derek shoved that diary page in my face. Who wouldn't want to lighten such a weight of guilt, given the chance?

We all failed Jackie, and this is my sentence — a ringside seat to watch the tragedy unfold, knowing there's nothing I can do to stop it.

The silence becomes too much. I get up and, without thinking, pat my pockets. There's no phone and no means to distract my thoughts.

There is, however, another way I could distract myself.

"Of course."

It never ceases to amaze me how the human mind works, or my mind at least. You just feed in the information and let it stew for a while. I've been thinking about that infamous diary page, and Anna's guilt, and Jackie's understandable lack of faith in men — all interconnecting points on a path to one solution.

I thump down the stairs to the lounge.

"Has Sylvia left for church yet?"

"You just missed her," Jeremy replies over his book.

"I don't suppose you have any writing paper I could borrow?"

"I'm afraid not."

"Bugger. I need to get a letter to someone urgently."

"There's no post today."

"I know. I intended to deliver it by hand this morning."

"You could, um, use the word processor on my computer ... if you like?"

"Even better. My handwriting is appalling."

He slides a bookmark into place and stands.

"It's up in my room."

I follow Jeremy up the stairs to a bedroom slightly larger than mine. A well-stocked bookcase dominates the back wall, but on a desk near the window is a pale-grey computer.

"Is that an Acorn?"

"It is," he replies with an undercurrent of pride in his tone. "The A3000, with 1 megabyte of RAM."

"A whole megabyte, eh? Impressive."

That's a mere 7,999 megabytes less than my mobile phone. It's like comparing the performance of a Ferrari with a horse and cart; the Ferrari being the size of a matchbox.

"Do you know much about computers?" Jeremy asks.

"A bit, but I'm a used to an operating system that … isn't very popular at the moment."

"I use computers every day in the lab."

"Best I let an expert show me how to use this one then."

For the first time since we met, and possibly the first time in his adult life, Jeremy's lips curl into a slight smile. He sits at the desk and boots up the computer. The screen — another grey box — flickers in to life.

"This is a mouse," he then states, tapping a rectangular box with square buttons on top. "You use it to navigate the cursor around the screen and select certain options."

"Fancy."

"I used to have a BBC Microcomputer, but this machine is in a completely different league."

"More of an Atari man myself. I wasted way too much time playing Frogger."

"I wasn't allowed to play games," he replies with a sigh. "My computer was purely for educational purposes."

Christ, what kind of teenage life did this lad lead? No pop music and no computer games. I don't ask, but I'm willing to bet his parents never had a television set, let alone a VHS video recorder.

He taps the mouse a few times, and a clunky word processor loads up, the cursor blinking in readiness.

"All set," he says, vacating the fold-up chair.

"Thanks, Jeremy. I appreciate this."

"Let me know when you're done, and I'll come back up and print off your letter."

"Will do."

I'm left alone.

Faced with a blank screen, I should probably consider what I'm going to write. It's clear Jackie has serious trust issues, and I don't have time to change her low opinion of men before the fateful day arrives. However, she does trust her mother. If I can anonymously warn Anna about Jackie's mental state, and my concerns she might be at risk of committing suicide, she'll surely intervene. When we talked, Anna admitted her daughter's behaviour had significantly changed so it shouldn't come as a complete surprise.

How do I say it, though, without sounding like a crackpot?

It's just as well I'm not using a pen and paper as, for the next half-hour, the delete button receives a lot of attention. I finally settle on a suitable tone and enforce a limit of just two paragraphs. Anna doesn't need to hear my opinion; she needs to know the cold hard facts. I confirm I'm a close friend and genuinely concerned about Jackie's state of mind. In the second paragraph, I embellish the truth by mentioning a recent conversation with Jackie, in which she referenced suicide as a way to solve all her problems.

I end the letter with a warning — it is imperative Jackie receives professional help immediately — and sign off as a concerned friend.

Putting myself in Anna's shoes, I read the short letter three times. Clear, concise; the message unambiguous. If I received such a letter, I'd definitely act upon it. I only hope Anna is true to her word and grasps this final chance to save her daughter.

I call down the stairs, and Jeremy returns.

"All done?"

"Yes, thanks. I just need to print it off."

He turns on the printer and nudges the mouse around the mat, clicking it several times.

"It'll take a few minutes to print."

"Right."

"Do you want to save the letter?"

"No, thanks."

He taps a couple of keys and remains in the chair. The printer — with a lumbering daisy wheel mechanism if I'm not mistaken — springs into action, rendering every line one character at a time like a mechanical typewriter.

I attempt small talk while we wait.

"What do you get up to when you're not reading or walking? You must have hobbies?"

"Yes, reading and walking."

"I mean, don't you have any other interests?"

"My work."

"That doesn't count. I'm talking about the kind of things most lads your age do."

He scratches his head.

"Do you go to the pub much?" I add. "Or the cinema?"

"No."

"Are you telling me you spend all your free time either reading, walking, or chatting to Sylvia over shepherd's pie?"

He shuffles uncomfortably in the chair and nods.

"Take it from me, Jeremy — you're only young once. You should be out with your mates, enjoying yourself."

"I know," he replies in a low voice, staring down at the keyboard. "But I don't really have any friends."

It would require a heart of stone not to be saddened by such an admission.

"No one?"

He shakes his head.

It suddenly strikes me that in 1988, when you were alone, you really were alone. Back in reality, even the most socially awkward kids can find kindred spirits online. For all its ills, the internet allows people like Jeremy to connect, to make friends, and to do whatever nerdy types do together. If this were my today, he'd likely be spending his free time chatting to like-minded souls all around the world while defeating dragons and wooing busty maidens in some virtual fantasy land. It's not a world I understand, but surely online friends are better than non-existent friends.

I put my hand on his shoulder.

"Well, for what it's worth, you have a friend now."

He looks up and finds a half-smile.

The printer falls silent. Jeremy leans over and tears away a length of perforated paper imprinted with my words.

"Do you need an envelope?"

"If you've got one, please. Oh, and a pen."

He opens a drawer and hands over a plain white envelope and a biro. I fold the letter, slip it into the envelope, and scrawl Anna Benton's name on the front.

My task complete, I should be on my way, but Jeremy's doleful face won't allow me to leave just yet.

"If you fancy it, we could go to a record store this afternoon, and I'll help you start your voyage in to popular music. The first album is on me."

"That's very nice of you, but it's Sunday."

"Why is that a problem?"

"The shops are shut."

"Uh ... yes, of course they are."

What the hell did I do with my Sundays in 1988? One vague recollection from my teenage years comes to mind.

"Have you got a radio?"

"No, but Sylvia has one in the kitchen. Why?"

"Do you ever listen to the charts?"

"What charts?"

"The music charts. The top-40."

"Never."

"It's on at five o'clock. Why don't we borrow Sylvia's radio and listen in?"

"But I don't know anything about popular music."

"Yes, and at one point you didn't know anything about computers. Think of it as an educational exercise; the first syllabus in being a typical young lad."

"Right, yes. Okay."

"Great. I'm just popping out, but I'll be back well before five."

His doleful expression fades, and I leave him to turn off his pre-internet computer.

After putting on my shoes, I leave the house to find today is one of those days with no weather: not warm but not cold, not bright but not dull.

As I stroll along Cline Road, I question what in God's name is wrong with me. I'm now so invested in this illusion, I've created a fictional figure I feel sorry for, and I'm going out of my way to help. What does it matter if Jeremy is a sad, lonely young man as he's only a figment of my imagination? Why do any of them matter? Jackie, Anna, Derek, Jeremy, Sylvia … they're no more real than the characters in a film, and I've never left a cinema feeling guilty because the protagonist didn't get his just reward or the antagonist came out on top.

I shouldn't care, so why am I following my gut rather than my head; wandering halfway across town to deliver a letter which has no realistic chance of changing what has already happened?

This is not me.

I built a successful career thinking rationally, logically. Two plus two has always equalled four yet here it could be three or five or ninety-bloody-nine. I don't understand what's happened to my usually pragmatic mind, my sound judgement.

And yet, my legs keep moving as my now unreliable mind navigates.

This trip better be worthwhile because I'm not sure how much more of this I can take.

19.

I turn into Fir Tree Road and check my watch. It's nearly eleven o'clock.

If I wished, I could calculate precisely how many hours have elapsed since I drove along this road in my shiny Mercedes. I know it's less than one hundred, but close to three-hundred thousand hours have passed since I last walked along this version of Fir Tree Road.

The front gardens are still front gardens. Almost every window still contains a weathered steel frame. There are no extensions.

Perhaps more telling are the cars lined up along the kerb. Far fewer in number, and far older in relative terms. Outside of Comaland, I left a world where almost anyone could afford a new car thanks to the myriad of finance options available. Granted, most never own the car but irrespective of social class, we're all able to watch a hunk of metal depreciate on our driveway for a few hundred quid a month.

Here, it's a graveyard of second-hand bangers where the Ford Capri is still cool, and a ten-year-old Vauxhall Cavalier is an object of envy.

In the distance, I catch my first sight of the Benton residence, exactly how I remember it. Even Derek's rusty old Morris Marina is parked outside.

I cross the street and slow my pace. I'm hoping Jackie isn't in, or still in bed. The last thing I want is a doorstep confrontation after she made it clear last night our paths would never cross again. If she kicks off, it'll likely attract unwelcome attention from Derek or Anna.

No, the plan is simple: walk up to the front door, deliver the letter, and be away before anyone notices me.

I reach the path.

Keeping my head down, I hustle up to the front door with the letter in my right hand and pull the letterbox flap open with my left. Rather than an open gap, I'm reminded of my days as a newspaper boy and the kind of letterbox I despised, with two sets of stiff bristles acting as a draft excluder. Too many times, customers complained because their News of The World landed on the doormat in a crumpled state. They should have thought about that before installing an impenetrable set of bristles.

Knowing a thin letter won't have the sufficient stiffness to make it through, I ease the bristles apart with my left hand; the spring-loaded flap resting on my wrist. I'm just about to insert the letter when I hear a muffled shriek from somewhere in the house.

I freeze.

A raised voice follows the shriek. Presumably, it's Derek doing the yelling, but I can't make out what he's saying. Have I caught Mr and Mrs Benton in the midst of a domestic?

Another shriek, followed by a flurry of words partly shouted, partly screamed. The second voice is female, adding weight to my theory the Bentons are arguing.

I need to act while they're distracted. Sliding the letter past the bristles, I slowly allow the spring-loaded flap to close rather than snap shut and alert the Bentons to my presence. Suddenly, a female voice screeches two distinct words.

"Fuck you!"

Heavy footsteps thump down the stairs. Someone is heading towards the hallway, and they'll almost certainly see my bulky silhouette beyond the frosted glass.

I quickly slide my hand away from the letterbox flap. I glance left and right, but there's no cover. Whoever opens the front door is bound to see me waddling away.

Then I remember — the side passageway.

Whenever Jackie forgot her front door key, we'd use the back door, which was actually at the side of the house, accessed via a narrow passageway fifteen feet to the right of where I'm currently standing.

I duck down and skulk past the lounge window towards the

passageway. The second I lean up against the damp brickwork, out of sight, the front door opens and slams shut. It's closed with such force, the glass rattles in the frame.

I risk a peek around the corner.

Jackie storms down the path and turns left. If she happens to turn her head ninety degrees, she can't fail to spot the eighteen stone bloke hiding in her parents' side passage.

Just as she draws level with my position, Jackie raises a hand to wipe her eyes on the sleeve of her coat. It's followed by a sniffle. Last night her mood switched between irritated, embarrassed, and angry. This morning she appears genuinely upset.

"Jackie!" a voice bellows to my right. "Get back here now. I ain't finished with you."

Derek.

Rather than reply, Jackie dons a set of headphones and marches on defiantly. I glance towards the front path where Derek is standing with his hands on his hips. Rather than chase after her, he cusses and slopes back up the path. The glass in the front door clatters again.

Finally, I'm able to breathe.

To avoid passing the lounge window, I edge along the waist-high boundary fence and climb over it.

Now what?

As I consider my options a young woman approaches, pushing a buggy. She slows down, and I step to the side so she can pass. We swap smiles, and she continues on her way. I happen to look back up the pavement at the exact moment the young woman decides to cross the road. Just as she's about to dip the front wheels of the buggy over the pavement edge, a car comes tearing up the road at speed. The young woman stops and yells a few angry words at the driver. Pointless, as the car is already screaming towards the junction fifty yards away.

She looks back at me and, placing a hand on her chest, puffs a long breath. She then mouths a thank you before crossing the road.

It takes a few seconds to realise why the young woman thanked me. If I hadn't been standing here and delayed her journey by a couple of seconds, she and her toddler would have been halfway across the road when that boy racer appeared.

One brief and seemingly innocuous interaction might have just saved two lives.

Every action has a consequence.

"Bloody hell."

My mind races as I dwell on the consequences of messing with Jackie's life. Even our brief encounter outside Our Price could have changed her timeline in some way, and yet I spent a significant chunk of time with her at The Britannia. If I hadn't intervened when she argued with Gary, would they have kissed and made up, and gone back to his place? Would Jackie still be there this morning? I'll never know, but what if my interference has already altered Jackie's plans to end her own life?

Again, I think back to my conversation with Anna. Jackie had got her life back together, but last night she stormed off in a rotten mood because I interfered. Did she revert to her old ways and go on to another pub or club, and continue drinking late in to the night? Did she arrive home, drunk and angry, and start an argument with her parents? That would explain this morning's heated exchange with Derek.

For all I know, Jackie could be heading towards a bridge over the railway tracks this very moment; angry with me, with Gary, with Derek, with life.

I need to follow her.

I'm not built for speed, but my strides must be thirty per cent longer than Jackie's and Fir Tree Road is at least five-hundred yards long. Within the first one hundred of those yards, I'm already panting like a post-marathon pug.

I finally spot Jackie on the opposite pavement, sixty yards ahead. With her hands in her pockets, she's not moving with any great urgency, and I close the gap between us to thirty yards by the time she reaches the junction. It's as close as I dare get.

Fortunately, she then takes a route along a busy stretch of road with several lanes running in each direction. By remaining on the opposite pavement and maintaining enough distance, I can follow her with minimal chance of being spotted. When the road narrows to two lanes, there's still plenty of traffic for cover, even on a Sunday morning.

The road, I realise, is Stoke Road and it leads to the town centre. Having learnt the shops are shut today, what reason could Jackie have for going into town? That question spikes concern.

As the pursuit continues, my legs become increasingly weary; the road so much longer than it ever seemed in a car. With immense relief, we reach the end. Jackie slows to a standstill, and I bend down to tie a shoelace which doesn't need tying, just in case she should turn around.

There are two routes open to her. She can bear right on to North Street, which leads to the shopping centre and the railway station beyond, or she can branch left towards the High Street.

She takes the second option towards the High Street.

I'm relieved but also perplexed. Unless Jackie intends to spend her morning window shopping, there's no obvious reason to head that way.

With no traffic and very few pedestrians around, I need to hang back even further. Jackie then crosses the cobbles to the left-hand pavement. She passes La Boulangerie, where I failed to acquire cheese straws, and then skips up the steps into Tunsgate Arch.

Her route matches the one I took two days ago. Could it be she's heading to the same destination?

I follow her along Tunsgate to the junction where she crosses the road towards an expanse of lawn. I stop and watch her approach the gate to the grounds of Guildford Castle. The second she passes through that gate, I know precisely where Jackie is heading — the nook.

We spent a lot of time together in the nook, but it was Jackie who first discovered it, and she'd sometimes visit on her own whenever she needed a spell of quiet time to reflect. Unlike me, Jackie possessed a spiritual side, and she believed the castle grounds radiated positive energy. That positive energy didn't help with her A-level grades, but the nook did provide a haven to contemplate her future in the days afterwards. Shame I buggered that future up.

With no great urgency, I cross the road and enter the castle grounds. There are several benches dotted around, and I flop down on the nearest one, grateful for the chance to rest my legs and consider what, if anything, I do next.

Jackie's decision to visit the nook suggests she's not about to throw herself off a railway bridge, yet — it suggests she's got a lot on her mind. Most kids her age have close friends to chat through their problems with. Unfortunately for Jackie, we were so besotted with one another throughout the last year of school, and our two years of college, we both missed out on the social scene our single friends were enjoying, and those friends slowly drifted away. Neither of us cared much as we had each other, and that was enough. Jackie was my best friend, and I was hers.

Then I found a new best friend in Carol.

I wonder if Jackie's visit to the nook is because she no longer has anyone to turn to; certainly no one close. Loneliness, as I discovered in recent months, is a shit-awful place to be. At times I felt like a dying star; gravity sucking in every atom of hope and crushing it. If it weren't for the decision to make radical changes to my life, I'd still be wallowing in a pit of despair back in Devon. Who knows how my life might have turned out if I'd stayed in that pit?

The difference between my situation and Jackie's is that I had options. I had money, a lifetime of work experience, and mobility. What does Jackie have? A job as a sales assistant in a record shop, a bedroom in a council house, and a bucket load of resentment for the men who've let her down. The one thing she and most of her generation don't have is a certain future.

People forget the eighties were a shockingly bad decade for young people. No one looks back and fondly remembers the high unemployment, high inflation, high interest rates, the deep recession, or the years of austerity. The markets might be booming now, but there's a bust around the corner, along with another recession.

Perhaps Jackie is in a pit of her own. Could this be the beginning of the end; the moment she first contemplates her way out?

I don't know what to do. Can I rely solely on my anonymous letter to Anna?

Part of me wants to get up and follow the path to the nook. I want to talk to Jackie and tell her everything will be okay. If I thought for one second she might believe me, I'd tell her the truth.

I spend the next ten minutes playing out that scenario in my mind. There are facts I could relay; things about Jackie only Sean Hardy would know. On their own, they're barely evidence, let alone proof. Knowing Jackie kept a diary, her logical conclusion would be that I, or young Sean, also kept a diary and that's where I gleaned my information. I never kept one, but she doesn't know that.

Whichever way I look at it, there's no reason on earth Jackie would accept my explanation. I bloody well wouldn't. I'm a fifty-four-year-old man, and in Comaland, Sean Hardy is twenty-two. That is all the proof she needs.

The truth won't help and on reflection, joining her in the nook would also be a bad idea. So few people know about it she'd assume I followed her there. I can imagine her freaking out if I suddenly appear.

I close my eyes and focus on the birdsong and the scent of spring. If I allow my mind to drift, maybe it'll throw up another solution. I'm clean out of ideas and, with nowhere better to be, this is as good a place as any to ponder.

The peaceful setting, however, is also conducive to sleep and

I've had precious little of it recently. I let my head loll back and count every slow rise and fall of my chest as I breathe deeply. Maybe a twenty-minute nap will help clear my mind and boost my energy.

I slip further and further and further until I nod off.

I'm then rudely awoken.

"Sean!"

My eyes blink open.

"What the hell are you doing here?"

"Um … hello, Jackie."

20.

Jackie's face hasn't altered much since last night as it's still etched with a scowl. The main difference is her puffy eyes and lack of makeup.

"Well?" she snaps.

"Well, what?"

I sit up.

"What are you doing here?"

Having summarily failed to connect with her last night, I've nothing to lose by changing tack and fighting indignation with indignation, and perhaps a slither of sarcasm.

"Sitting on a bench in a public park. What are you doing here?"

"None of your business."

"Are you following me, Jackie?"

"Eh? No, of course not."

"I'm flattered, honestly, but I'm far too old for you. It'll never work."

"In your dreams, mate," she snorts.

"Perhaps," I respond with a wry smile. "But I suspect it would be more a nightmare, don't you?"

Her scowl eases a touch.

There's a moment of silence as Jackie looks in the direction of the gate. Without a crowd of her peers watching on in judgement, she doesn't appear quite so standoffish. Maybe the only chance I had last night wasn't the only chance after all. I need to choose my next words with extreme caution if I'm to exploit it rather than blow it.

"In answer to your question, I found this place a few days ago, and I like it here. It has a certain energy."

"You think?"

"I do, but most people would dismiss it as mumbo-jumbo. Not everyone is in tune with their spiritual side."

Her eyes widen a fraction.

"I am," she blurts.

"You're what?"

"In tune with my spiritual side."

"That's odd because last night you seemed more in tune with your aggressive side."

"I was pissed off," she shrugs.

"With?"

"Everything."

"And everyone. Me included."

"I'm not going to apologise for standing up for myself. When I said I don't need a man fighting my battles, I meant it."

I raise my hands, palms forward.

"I wouldn't expect you to apologise. In fact, I admire your stance. Girl power, and all that."

"What the hell is girl power?"

"Um, nothing. It's just good to see a young woman sticking up for herself."

She looks towards her trainers.

"Thanks."

We're actually having a conversation, although it's not exactly flowing. I need to up the ante. No, I need to go all-in before she walks away.

"I'm glad I bumped into you, though."

"Why's that?"

"I felt guilty. I might have told you a small white lie."

"About?"

"My marital situation. The truth is, my wife left me a few months ago because she met someone else."

It's a bold and risky attempt at empathy, but hopefully it'll shift Jackie's view of me from a fat old bloke she has nothing in common with, to a fellow victim of infidelity.

"Sorry. That sucks."

"Do you want to know the worst part? I found her in bed with a woman."

"No way! Are you kidding?"

"I wish I was."

"My God, that's awful … wait, why are you telling me?"

It's an excellent question.

"Honestly? I don't know. I suppose it's a test."

"In what way is it a test?"

"To see how far I've come. A few months back, every time that image popped into my head, I felt physically sick. The last thing I wanted to do was talk about it, but that's not healthy. Acceptance is an important part of the healing process — it's the only way to move on."

"Is that why you moved here?"

"Yep, for a fresh start. The accent is a giveaway, eh?"

"A bit. Where are you from?"

Sticking close to the truth appears to be paying dividends, but I don't want to risk irking Jackie by telling her I'm from the same city where her former boyfriend and his girlfriend set up home together.

"Cornwall."

"Bet you love a pasty."

"Look at me. Can't you tell?"

At last, a smile. For a fleeting second, I get to see the Jackie I once knew.

It quickly fades, and she looks towards the gate again. We've reached the end of our chat; the brief connection about to be broken.

"Anyway," she puffs. "I should get going."

"Don't suppose you fancy a quick coffee before you head off? My treat."

"I don't like coffee, and besides, all the cafes are closed."

"Oh, right, of course. I used to live by the sea, so there was always a cafe open, even on a Sunday."

"Something you'll have to get used to — no cafes open on a Sunday here. No sticks of rock or candy floss either."

"Sadly not."

Desperately, I scour my mind for a relevant subject which

might keep the conversation going.

"I, err …"

"See you around."

She turns away and takes four steps. If I don't say something, anything, Jackie's life will rest solely on an anonymous letter to Anna — too high a risk.

"Jackie," I call after her.

She stops and turns around.

"What?"

"Sorry, there was something else."

"Go on," she sighs. "What now?"

"Well, it's, um … I could do with some advice."

"Advice? From me?"

"Yes."

"On what?"

"Who … err, where would a lad your age meet people, locally?"

"What do you mean?"

I'm not sure I know myself. Further improvisation is required.

"The house I'm staying at, this young lad is renting a room, and I get the impression he's a bit lonely. I thought you might know where he could make some friends. I'm just trying to help."

"No offence, but he probably doesn't want your help."

"What makes you say that?"

"Most boys my age would think it's a bit lame even admitting they're lonely."

"True, but Jeremy isn't typical of most boys your age. I don't know him that well, but he's the quiet and considerate type."

"Boring, you mean?"

"If by boring, you mean sensible, reliable, and honest, then yes. He's nothing like that Gary character you were with last night."

"You didn't like Gary much, did you?"

"Not really. Do you?"

"He serves a purpose."

I'd rather not know what that purpose is.

"All I'm asking, Jackie, is if you know where Jeremy might make a few friends. If you don't know or don't care, that's fine — don't let me keep you."

The purpose of my remark was to test how much of the old Jackie remains. She was a natural carer; the kind of girl who'd regularly call in on old folk in her neighbourhood for a cuppa and a chat.

"What's his surname?" she asks, her tone unreadable.

"I don't know. Why?"

"Just wondered if he went to my school."

"No, he's from Kent. He doesn't know a soul in Guildford."

Behind her blue eyes, I sense there's a battle going on between old Jackie and new Jackie. The problem with being a caring type is one day, inevitably, someone mistreats you, and you stop caring yourself. In Jackie's case, I was that someone.

"What's he in to?" she asks. "Music? Films? Clubs?"

"Err, I think he's open-minded."

"That doesn't help."

"Oh, err … why don't you meet him, and he can tell you."

I'm not sure how we got here, but it's not the worst idea in the world.

"Alright," she replies with a tired sigh. "But you'd better make it clear it's in no way a date. I don't want him getting the wrong idea."

"Well, I could come along too … it'd be less awkward. Just a few drinks."

"I suppose. Are you buying?"

"Only if you don't knock back Cinzano like it's water."

"As I said, I was pissed off last night, and I just wanted to get wasted. I'm not an alcoholic."

"I hear you."

"Good."

"So, how about tomorrow evening?"

"Nothing else in my diary."

"Shall we say The King's Head, at half-seven?"

"Why there? It's full of sad old men."

"It may have escaped your attention, Jackie, but I'm a sad old man. I like it there."

"Fine. I'll be there at half-seven."

"Thanks. I do appreciate it."

She nods, and this time makes her escape. I watch her all the way to the gate, hoping her body language might offer a clue to her mood. It doesn't.

I slump back on the bench and reflect.

Flying by the seat of my pants, I've somehow managed to orchestrate another evening with Jackie. If I'd pre-planned it, I'd now be basking in the glow of self-congratulation. However, now is not the time to be smug. Now is the time to work out how the hell I sell this idea to Jeremy. If I can't get him on board, my improvisation will have been for nothing.

With time against me, I get up and head back to Cline Road.

It's past two o'clock by the time I open the front door to a mouth-watering aroma.

"Oh, there you are," Sylvia says, as she emerges from the kitchen. "I'm afraid we couldn't wait."

"Sorry? Wait for what?"

"Sunday lunch."

The dots connect. The aroma is roast beef and vegetables.

"My apologies. I didn't know what time you had lunch."

"Like most people, Sean — at lunchtime."

"No, I meant I didn't know if you had Sunday lunch or Sunday dinner."

"You're forgiven. I should have mentioned it this morning, but it slipped my mind."

"Oh well. My loss."

I offer my best impression of a forlorn Oliver Twist.

"I saved you a plate. It's in the microwave."

"You're a star. Thank you."

"Would you like me to show you how it works?"

"The microwave? I think I'll be okay."

"Very well. I'll be in the garden if you need me. The borders need attention."

"Okay. Is Jeremy in his room?"

"No, he's gone out for his Sunday afternoon stroll."

"How long is he usually out for?"

"He's normally back by four. Why do you ask?"

"Oh, I was going to give him an introduction to the pop charts."

"Really?" she says, raising an eyebrow. "I hope you're not going to pollute his mind with that dreadful rapping music."

"Definitely not," I chuckle. "But I do feel a bit sorry for the lad. His upbringing seems to have been a bit ... what's the word?"

"Puritanical."

"Yes, that."

"I've never met his parents, but I did speak to his father on the telephone at some length. I'm all in favour of order, but he laid out a raft of rules he expected young Jeremy to adhere to."

"Good grief. He's twenty-two, not twelve."

"Quite, which is why I told Mr Baker I would not act as his son's keeper. I don't think he appreciated my candour, but he relented in the end; probably after he investigated other boarding establishments in the town."

"Rest assured, Sylvia, I'm only trying to help the lad. I sense he's a bit lonely."

"He's a loner, certainly. I try to chat with him, but I'm an old woman. We don't have a lot in common."

"I don't think I do either, but he deserves a chance to be young."

"Very well. Be gentle with him, though."

"I will. Scout's honour."

Sylvia disappears into the garden, and I make a beeline for

the kitchen. It would be impossible not to spot the microwave as it's the size of a small brown caravan. I set the timer to four minutes.

I then lay a place at the dining table and return to the kitchen just as my late lunch pings.

A side-effect of so much walking is a ravenous appetite, and Sylvia's roast puts most carveries to shame. I clear my plate and, like the good tenant I am, wash it up and put it away. I only hope it passes my landlady's stringent standards.

With a full belly, I plod out to the garden to compliment Sylvia on her culinary skills and ask if I can borrow her radio. I find her digging weeds from a border. Permission is granted on condition I re-tune it to Radio Four once we've finished listening to the charts.

Her radio turns out to be a set from the dark ages. It's slightly better than the one I owned as a teenager in that it's mains powered, but we'll be listening in glorious mono as it only has the one speaker. I unplug it and take it up to my room.

I've been in Comaland for two days now and understandably, a lack of access to music hasn't featured highly on my list of concerns. That doesn't mean I haven't missed it. I plug the radio in and place it carefully on the bedside table. The beauty of technology this old is you don't need a degree in computer sciences to operate it, unlike the wireless headphones I bought myself for Christmas.

I turn one of the knobs on top, and after a satisfying click, a cut-glass voice emanates from the speaker: a Radio Four play in mid-scene. There are no buttons to choose a pre-set station, not that Sylvia would have saved Radio One, so I make a note of where the dial is set and turn the second knob in search of the correct frequency.

After some trial and error, I finally catch the end of a Radio One jingle.

I lie back on the bed and listen to a highlights show called More Time, hosted by Mark Goodier. Although I listened to the chart show religiously in my teens, I never tuned in till late afternoon. Therefore, how do I know this show even existed, let alone who presented it? How can I remember something I never knew before? Is this just my brain filling a hole in my memories with a creation of its own making?

I turn those questions over and over until I sense a headache brewing.

At three-thirty, More Time ends, and Backchat begins; the radio version of a gossip column, presented by Liz Kershaw and Ro Newton. I've heard of the former but not the latter. I close my eyes. Ms Kershaw and Mr Newton's inane chat isn't interesting enough to prevent the sands of sleep drifting back.

The voices fade, and I nod off.

At some point, a knock on the bedroom door wakes me up. Groggy, I sit up and wait for the inevitable realisation to dawn — courtesy of my own mind, I'm currently in a rented room in 1988.

"One sec."

The radio still playing, I turn the volume down a notch and stumble over to the door.

"Oh, hi, Jeremy."

He checks his watch.

"Sorry. Am I too early?"

I check my watch. Ten minutes until the chart show is due to start.

"No, it's fine. Come in."

I invite him to take a seat on the bed. I notice he's brought a pocket-sized notepad and pen with him.

"I just need to grab a glass of water. Do you want one?"

He declines the offer. I scoot down to the kitchen and locate a glass at the third attempt. One pint of water and a bathroom break later, I return to my room.

"All set?"

He nods.

With nowhere else to sit, I perch next to him on the bed; a

comfortable distance apart.

"I hope you don't mind me asking, Jeremy, but how did you make it all the way through university without being exposed to pop music?"

"I studied at the University of Kent and lived at home. If I wasn't in a lecture or the library, I was there."

"You never went to parties or pubs?"

He shakes his head.

"My parents frowned upon unnecessary distractions, and I was forbidden from drinking alcohol."

Perhaps his parents were literally Puritans. I don't ask.

"They wanted the best for me," he adds, unconvincingly.

"I'm sure they did," I reply, just as unconvincingly. "So, are you completely oblivious to every chart act?"

"Occasionally, I'd overhear conversations about music in the corridors, so there are a few names I've heard of."

"That's a good start. Can you remember any?"

"Um, Madonna, Boy George, Wet Wet Wet Wet ..."

"It's just the three wets."

"Oh, right."

"Any others?"

"Michael Jackson, Rick something-or-other ... and yes, T'Pau. I distinctly remember T'Pau because it's also the name of a Vulcan diplomat in Star Trek."

"You had a television at home?"

"No, but I've read all the Star Trek books."

"Star Trek and Asimov? You a big fan of sci-fi?"

"Yes."

"I thought you science-types were only interested in scientific facts."

"A popular misconception. We like to occasionally suspend belief and fantasise about the infinite possibilities of the unknown."

"Like aliens and time-travel?"

"The Drake Equation calculates the chances of us being the

only advanced life force in the entire Universe as remote. It's likely we've not yet found proof because of the vast distances involved."

"Right, and time-travel?"

"Piffle, I'm afraid."

"Yep, that's what I thought."

The voice of Bruno Brookes leaks from the radio.

"Sounds like we're about to tee-off."

The notepad is readied.

"Are you taking notes?" I ask.

"I thought it would be prudent. I can make a note of any particular songs I find appealing."

I detect a teeny hint of enthusiasm in his voice.

"That's a good idea."

The first song starts. Down twenty places to forty, James Brown with *The Payback Mix*. I'd all but forgotten the mash-up of the soul legend's hits, sampled, and set to a dance track. An abomination and Jeremy agrees.

"It's rather noisy," he remarks.

The next half-dozen songs are also poorly received. I can't remember half of them; probably because we're listening to the top-40 equivalent of the bargain bin in Our Price. It also strikes me we're two grown men, perched on the edge of a single bed listening to the radio, and one of us needs to somehow convince the other to meet a random young woman for drinks tomorrow night.

Salvation finally comes in the form of Fleetwood Mac's *Everywhere* — down a criminal twenty-one places to thirty-two.

"I do like this," Jeremy comments, as Christine McVie's note-perfect vocals fill the room.

"You've got good taste."

The next set of songs are a mixed bag, and Jeremy only makes a handful of notes. It's a strange situation. I'm listening to tracks I've heard a thousand times, yet Jeremy is hearing them for the first time.

Back when I thought I might one day be a father, I often daydreamed about introducing my son or daughter to the music of my youth. They'd have hated most of it, I'm sure, but I reckon they'd have begrudgingly admitted a liking for a few of my favourites. I'll never know for sure, and this is as close to that experience as I'm ever likely to get.

We enter the top-30, and Patrick Swayze's *She's Like The Wind* is up next. Jeremy isn't keen. In fairness, neither am I. It's as good a time as any to broach the subject of tomorrow evening.

"Tell me to mind my own business, Jeremy, but do you get out much?"

"Out?"

"You know, socially."

"Not really."

"Not really, or not at all?"

"Not at all," he murmurs sheepishly.

"Because you've no one to go out with?"

He nods.

"I was thinking; I know this girl about your age, and she knows all the places you youngsters hang out. We're meeting for a quick drink tomorrow if you fancied coming along? She's a lovely girl, and I'm sure she'd give you a few pointers."

"But tomorrow is Monday."

"Yes."

"I have work on Tuesday."

"We'll be back by ten at the latest."

He stares down at the notepad, mute.

"Jeremy?"

"Can I think about it?"

I've got all evening to convince him it's a good idea. There's no sense in pressuring the lad just yet.

"Sure."

The next ninety minutes fly by and, admittedly, it's an enjoyable stroll down memory lane. As Bruno wraps up, Jeremy shows me a list of the songs which piqued his musical interest.

Alongside *Everywhere*, he's put a tick against *Heart* by Pet Shop Boys, *Circle in The Sand* by Belinda Carlisle, *Oh Patti* by Scritti Politti, *Somewhere in my Heart* by Aztec Camera, and New Order's *Blue Monday '88*.

"These were my favourites," he says.

"That's a good selection."

"You think?"

"That's the thing about music, Jeremy — it doesn't matter what anyone else thinks. For the life of me, I can't understand why some folk like Shakin' Stevens, but many do. You'll find there's plenty more music you'll like and just as much you hate. Discovery is all part of the adventure."

"I understand. Thank you for taking the time to do this."

"This is just the start, lad. Do you fancy going into town on Saturday and picking up a few albums?"

"Um, I'd like that, but I don't own a record player."

"Cassette player?"

"I've got an old one I used for my computer."

"That'll do for starters. We can buy cassettes and maybe you can upgrade to a half-decent hi-fi once you've built-up your collection."

"Yes, I like that idea. Thank you."

His nervous smile appears genuine, but his fidgeting suggests Jeremy isn't used to expressing emotion. Maybe now is the time to remind him of my offer.

"And what about tomorrow evening? Any further thoughts?"

"I, err … it's not that I don't want to."

"What is it then?"

"I'm not good with people, especially new people."

"Says who?"

"Mother. She says I'm an awkward bumbler."

"In her opinion," I reply dismissively. "But I happen to disagree. I wouldn't try to help if I thought you were a lost cause."

His eyes drop to the notepad again.

"I'm particularly bad with girls," he confesses.

"And you always will be until you make an effort. Jackie is a lovely lass, and I think you and her could be good friends. And to be honest, she could do with a friend at the moment."

He finally looks up from the notepad. I make one final plea.

"It's just a few drinks. If you don't feel comfortable, make an excuse and leave. You've got nothing to lose but everything to gain."

I'm left hanging for several seconds before he responds.

"Okay, I'd like to come."

"Good lad," I beam, patting him on the shoulder. "I'm sure you won't regret it."

I, however, might.

21.

Monday mornings are grim whatever the decade.

This Monday morning is particularly grim, and I don't want to get out of bed. It's just gone eight o'clock, and I've been lying awake for twenty minutes, listening to the comings and goings beyond my bedroom door.

I suffered another restless night's sleep although it might have been self-inflicted: heartburn.

After we finished listening to the chart show yesterday evening, Sylvia laid on ham sandwiches and homemade fruitcake. We were allowed to eat in the lounge while watching television, but our landlady chose the channel. Not my ideal Sunday evening's viewing as we caught the end of Praise Be! with Thora Hird, and then had to sit through a truly awful quiz show with Ken Dodd and Larry Grayson.

Having been denied access to a television most of his life, Jeremy enjoyed both shows.

At some point Sylvia commented on my empty plate, saying Paul Daniels couldn't have made the fruit cake disappear any quicker. I was allowed a second slice to test her theory and that too disappeared sharpish.

No one wants to start the day with Paul Daniels floating around their head, but that's where mine begins.

The diminutive magician was a permanent fixture on our screens throughout the seventies and eighties. I must have been in my early teens when I first watched one of his shows on television. At that age, you know you're not watching actual magic because there's no such thing. Yet, I couldn't explain how Daniels performed his illusions.

In many respects, it's the same as Comaland.

I'm living the ultimate illusion, but I can't explain how it works, any more than I could explain how Paul Daniels cut Debbie McGee in half, or why she married him. It simply defies all logic.

And yet, here I am, lying in a strange bed listening to a pension-age woman hoovering the stairs … in 1988.

I get up.

Not wanting to terrify Sylvia, I get dressed before heading to the bathroom. I have a pee, brush my teeth, and take a quick shower; a series of mundane tasks conducted in the most extraordinary of circumstances.

With the hoover still whining somewhere downstairs, I retreat to my bedroom. The first thought that comes to mind as I sit on the bed relates to Jackie. A week today she's set to end her life.

While I'm determined to do whatever I can to stop that happening, once again I'm forced to consider the futility. When this is over, I'll likely wake up, and nothing will have changed. Jackie will still have committed suicide decades ago, no matter what events unfold over the next seven days. This is merely a deception of my own making.

Then, for the first time since I woke up in the nook, I ask the question: is it really a deception?

I brush my hand across the duvet cover and feel every fibre. I sniff the air and determine there's a faint whiff of mothballs and furniture polish. I smack my lips and taste traces of peppermint toothpaste. Then, I get up and step over to the window. I place my hand on the pane; cold to the touch. I blow a warm breath against my hand and a mist forms on the glass. When I remove my hand, a perfect impression remains.

From Harry Houdini to Derren Brown to Dynamo, no magician has ever performed such a perfect illusion. Not even close.

The words of another illustrious performer spring to mind.

In the opening lines of *Bohemian Rhapsody*, Freddie Mercury questions if life is real or just fantasy. He goes on to state there is no escape from reality.

Is this now my reality?

Overlooking the impossible elephant in the impossible room,

it is no different from the reality I left behind. I see, I hear, I feel, I taste, I smell. The characters I've encountered are authentic human beings — no different from those I've met throughout my life — the interactions typically ordinary.

Miracle or madness?

There's a knock at the bedroom door.

"Sean?"

"Yes, Sylvia?"

"What time are you due at work?"

Bugger. I hadn't even considered a fake reason why I'm not at my fake desk.

"Err, I'm working from home this week."

"I beg your pardon."

Idiot. Who works from home in 1988?

"Um, one moment."

I use that moment to prepare another lie and open the door.

"I mean, I have to complete an induction course over the next two weeks. It's just reading manuals and familiarising myself with the technical aspects of my role. All rather dull."

"Oh, I see."

"Is there anything you wanted me to do while I'm around?"

"No, but help yourself to tea, and there's a sliced loaf in the bread bin if you want toast."

"Thanks."

"And if you don't mind me asking, what do you have planned for Jeremy this evening?"

"He told you?"

"Yes."

"It's no big deal. Just a few drinks in the King's Head with a friend."

"He's not a drinker, you know?"

"He can have pop if he wants. I'm just trying to help the lad forge a social life."

"That is admirable, but please don't force him to do anything he's uncomfortable with."

"You have my word."

"Thank you. I'd better get on with the housework."

I close the door and flop back down on the bed. I stare at the ceiling for another five minutes and then trot down to the kitchen for a cup of tea and toast. Breakfast complete, I return to my room and stare at the ceiling again.

It's only just gone nine. If I'm not already insane, I sure as hell will be if I don't find something constructive to do.

I ponder the options, and my thoughts lead me back to my earlier deliberations. Just how real is this fantasy? There is one true test.

Grabbing my shoes, I thump down the stairs and shout up the hallway to Sylvia in the kitchen.

"I'm just heading out for a while."

"Do you have your key?"

"Yes … Sylvia."

I leave the house, knowing I came within a whisker of saying Mum rather than my landlady's name. It's no coincidence. Eighty miles away in Bournemouth, my parents should be alive and well.

My thoughts are so scattered I'm already halfway to the train station before common sense prevails. As I left Cline Road, I had every intention of getting on a train and heading straight down to Bournemouth. The intervening ten minutes have given rise to several issues regarding such a trip.

In 1988, both my parents still worked full-time, so neither will be home. Even if they were, their apartment is on the fifth floor, so it's not as though I'm likely to see them. If by some miracle I happened to spot them on the street, what would I do? In this reality, I'm older than they are, and a stranger. Even if I caught a glimpse of them leaving their apartment block, what good would that do? It would be the cruellest of tortures seeing them and not being able to interact in any way.

Why in God's name would I put myself through that?

No one ever truly conquers grief, but you learn how to live

with it. If I saw my parents, even for a few seconds, it'd be like going back to the first day of grief school, and I'd have to relive months of anguish.

Is it worth it?

It's not, I conclude, but there is another way to ascertain if my parents are still alive.

I change direction.

Fifteen minutes later, I pass through the gates of Stoke New Cemetery. On my last visit, I couldn't have walked any slower, with any greater reluctance. This time I dash along the path towards the far side of the cemetery. I stop ten yards short of the boundary hedge and stare open-mouthed at a patch of bare ground currently shaded by a tall conifer.

No headstone.

Never in my life has the sight of nothing summoned such mixed emotions. On the one hand, I know for sure my parents are not dead. On the other, I must accept they are not my parents — they are the parents of a young man currently living in Exeter. He loves them, and they love him. I am a nobody, but I do know that in a little under five years from now, Ian and Ruth Hardy's names will be etched on a headstone, erected in this exact spot.

Without consciously deciding on any course of action, I begin constructing the opening lines of a letter in my head: *Dear Ian and Ruth. On 17th February 1993, you will board a ferry in Haiti. It will capsize, and you will both die.*

If I received such a letter, I'd instantly dismiss it as ridiculous. However, if I then found myself in Haiti on that exact date, without question, I'd take that letter seriously. Who wouldn't?

As crazy as it is, maybe I can save my parents as well as Jackie. But what if I do wake up and discover I've been living in my own head? How heart-breaking it would be to think I'd saved three people I loved, only then to learn it was all just a figment of my imagination.

When everything around you is unbelievable, the word itself loses credibility. Sending a warning letter to my parents is no more insane than having a drink with my dead ex-girlfriend or browsing albums in a record store which hasn't existed in years.

What's there to lose?

I kick a divot from the soft soil; an act of defiance if nothing else.

"You won't see me for a long, long time," I mumble. "At least I bloody hope not."

My plan is simple. I'll walk into town and buy a notepad and an envelope. I'll pen more or less the lines I had in my head and then send the letter to my parents, recorded delivery.

As I sacrifice more shoe leather, I consider whether I could or should send a second letter — to my younger self. In principle, it seems a good idea, but then I think about the consequences. The jury is still out on whether there will be consequences of anything I do, but to completely dismiss them would be foolish.

I've made it to this point in my life relatively unscathed. I've not broken any bones, suffered any severe illness and, apart from losing my parents and finding my wife in bed with her best friend, I've not endured any significant trauma. With the first letter addressing the issue of my parents, I suppose I could tell the younger me not to waste his life with Carol. Would he take heed? Probably not.

What else could I tell him? Invest in Google or Apple shares? Bet on specific sporting events? Play certain numbers on the Lottery?

I know plenty of people I'd describe as wealthy but they aren't necessarily happy — the divorce statistics bear that out. Superficially, Carol and I enjoyed a comfortable lifestyle, but where did that get me? What good is a big old house in the country if you're sharing it with someone who doesn't truly love you? The same could be said of all the exotic holidays we took together. They were enjoyable at the time, but now I can't look back on them with any great fondness because the memories are tainted.

Giving my younger self the key to unlimited riches won't make him happy, I know that.

I conclude it would not be sensible to mess with my younger self's life. There's too much risk and so many ways it could backfire, conceptually or otherwise.

Back on the High Street, I return to WHSmith.

Before I browse the stationery, I grab a can of Top Deck shandy and a packet of Golden Wonder cheese and onion crisps. I pay and return both items to their respective shelves — an act of reverse shoplifting. Conscience clear, I go in search of the materials needed to pen a letter.

All the years of corporate frugality have left their mark, and I can't bring myself to buy a pad of writing paper and a whole pack of envelopes for just one short letter. I settle on a blank greetings card and the cheapest biro on the shelf.

A short walk later, I perch on a wall near the Post Office and transfer the sentences from my head to the card, altering my handwriting just in case my parents recognise it and assume my younger self is playing a warped prank. I then swap the card for a recorded delivery receipt. The small slip of paper is significant in two ways. The card it relates to could be the difference between life or death for my parents, but it has a greater significance in the here and now. It is tangible evidence I have bought into my illusion. I turn the receipt over, just in case the words 'sent by a certified nutter' are printed on the back. They're not.

I snort a self-satisfied chuckle.

I've officially lost the plot.

22.

Carol and I once enjoyed a three-week luxury cruise around The Caribbean. A week before we set sail, the cruise company sent us final confirmation of our itinerary, outlining the various ports of call and timings. Next to each of the port names, it said: a day at leisure. It meant we were free to come and go as we pleased and do whatever we wanted.

I've just spent a day at leisure, or an afternoon at least, as a tourist in 1988.

Embracing the madness, I toured the sights of my youth: our former family home, my old school, the outdoor swimming baths, and the shop where I used to buy games for my Atari console. Sadly, it wasn't how I remembered it. There were still plenty of games to browse, but they were nearly all for home computers. I had a brief chat with the bloke behind the counter, and he told me consoles like the Atari were old hat. I resisted the temptation to say Sega, Nintendo, and Sony would soon prove him wrong.

The highlight of my sight-seeing proved to be a little cafe by the station; the one Jackie and I used to frequent on rainy days. The lunchtime rush had passed by the time I got there, so I almost had the place to myself. I chose a table by the window and ordered what we always ordered: a milkshake and a plate of chips, although I had no one to share them with. I then spent an hour playing the fruit machine and burned through a tenner trying to win the five quid jackpot. I could have spent a hundred quid, and it would have still been worth it for the memories.

Now it's nearly seven o'clock, and I'm lying on my bed having just feasted on bacon roly-poly, mashed potato, and spring greens. Sylvia deserves a Michelin star or two.

There's a knock at my door.

I roll off the bed like a walrus and open it.

"I'm ready," Jeremy says nervously.

I look him up and down. The lad has no concept of casual.

"You might want to undo your top button," I suggest.

"Oh, okay."

The loosening of his collar helps, but there's not much I can do about his patterned V-neck sweater or brown Harrington jacket. He looks more sixty-two than twenty-two.

"Shall we make a move then?"

Jeremy nods. His eyes disagree.

We say goodbye to Sylvia, and she shoots me a look just as we're about to depart, enforcing her earlier point about taking care of Jeremy.

Ahead of schedule, we stroll along Cline Road with Jeremy remaining typically silent.

"You okay, lad?"

"A bit nervous."

"You'll be fine. We're just having a few drinks and a chat."

"But what if I don't know what to say, or I say something stupid?"

"No one is going to judge you, Jeremy."

"People do judge, though, don't they? I had it all the way through college and university."

"Did any of those people know you?"

"Not really."

"Then, who are they to judge you?"

He doesn't answer.

"Listen, I don't want to sound like your Dad …"

"Thank heavens," he snorts, a slight edge to his tone. "You're nothing like him."

"Should I take that as a compliment?"

"Most definitely, yes."

"You don't have the best relationship with your dad?"

"We have no relationship. Same applies to my mother."

It's the first time Jeremy has displayed any strong emotion, albeit negative.

"Do you want to talk about it?" I ask.

"I'm not much of a talker."

"Because no one usually listens?"

"Why do you say that?"

"Just a hunch. Am I right?"

We cover fifty yards of pavement in silence, and I've all but given up on the conversation when Jeremy finally addresses my question.

"I had a particularly sheltered upbringing," he says. "My parents are devout Christians, and they worried about external influences."

Not quite Puritan but not far off Sylvia's assumption. Knowing how sensitive some folk can be about religion, it's best I don't offer an opinion.

"Oh, I see."

"They never wanted me to attend university at all, but we agreed on a compromise, which is why I ended up at the University of Kent. Even so, I had to adhere to their rules."

"Had to? At eighteen, you're an adult."

"You've never met my parents. They expect me to lead a lifestyle which fits their world view."

"How come you managed to escape to Guildford?"

"There aren't many opportunities in the biochemistry industry, particularly around Maidstone, so I had to look further afield. My parents were not happy about it."

"Are they ever happy about anything?"

"Not that I can ever remember."

"That's bloody sad," I blurt.

"Swearing is on my father's list of rules. It's forbidden."

"Right. Sorry."

"Please don't be. I'm the one expected to follow those rules."

"And are you?"

I'm sure his shoulders rise an inch as he turns to me.

"Not this evening."

"Good lad. What's the point of rules if you can't break a few?"

"That may be true, but it doesn't help with my ... my lack of self-confidence."

"It'll come with time. Trust me."

As we walk, Jeremy tells me a little more about his strict upbringing. Not being a parent I don't want to judge his, but they sound like right tyrants. It's one thing being principled, but Jeremy cites several examples of his parents' behaviour I consider downright cruel.

By the time we turn in to King's Road, my sympathy for Jeremy has ratcheted up a notch or two.

We enter the pub fifteen minutes before Jackie is due. In all the concern for Jeremy, I'd put the reason we're here to the back of my mind. Now it's front and centre.

"What can I get you to drink?"

"Can I have an orange juice, please?"

Should I encourage him to try a beer? With Sylvia's warning still fresh, I decide against it.

Drinks acquired, we find a table.

"What's she like, your friend?" Jeremy asks.

I'm about to tell him what an amazing girl Jackie is, or was, but I stop myself just in time. I barely know her in Comaland. If I say too much, and Jeremy repeats it to her, I'll have a heck of a lot of explaining to do.

"I don't know her that well, but she seems a lovely girl."

"How do you know her?"

"I met her in Our Price, and she agreed to …"

I freeze.

"Um, I'm just nipping to the loo."

I dash off.

The problem with lies is they have a nasty habit of biting you on the arse. Jackie thinks I'm a music journalist, but I told Sylvia I work for a hotel chain. Did she mention that to Jeremy? If so, and my career comes up in conversation, it'll be clear I've lied to someone.

I need a cover story and quick.

Checking my watch, I dart back to the table.

"Sorry about that."

Jeremy nods.

"Um, did Sylvia happen to mention what I do for a living?"

"No, she didn't."

His disclosure makes my life a bit easier. I still need to concoct a reason why I lied to our landlady, but that can wait until the journey home.

"Okay, no problem. I'm a music journalist, just for the record."

"That explains how you knew so many of the songs on the radio yesterday."

"Err, yes. That's exactly why."

He doesn't ask any further questions. I'd wager his nerves are of more immediate concern. I need to offer him a few conversational pointers.

"What's your favourite meal, Jeremy?"

He stops fidgeting and considers my question for a moment.

"Sylvia's full-English, I think. Then again, I do love her cottage pie. Why do you ask?"

"Wrong question. You're supposed to ask what my favourite meal is."

"Right. Um, what's your favourite meal?"

"I can tell you what it's not — cheese and onion crisps."

"I have to disagree with you. They're my favourite flavour."

"Better than sausage and tomato?"

"Hmm … you make a valid point."

"Actually, my point has nothing to do with crisps. See how easy it is to spark a conversation just by asking a simple question, and then following it up with more questions? Before you know it, you're holding a conversation."

He looks at me like a child seeing snow for the first time.

"Just ask questions," he repeats, as if he's just discovered the missing element in a formula. "It's so ridiculously obvious."

"It's just a pointer."

The door swings open and a blonde-haired young woman

breezes in.

"Jackie is here," I declare, getting up. "Back in a moment."

Before I make the introductions, I need to check the right Jackie has just walked in. I step over to the door as she scans the room.

"Hi, Jackie."

"Alright."

"Shall we get you a drink and then I'll introduce you to Jeremy?"

"Sure."

I usher her through to the bar area. I notice she's dressed-down for the occasion: baggy jeans, trainers, leather jacket, and minimal makeup. It's the complete opposite of how she looked on our first date, asserting her previous statement that this definitely isn't a date.

"Thanks for doing this, Jackie."

"Don't thank me yet. I haven't met the guy."

"True, which is why I wanted to have a quick word with you, alone."

I relay the basics of my earlier conversation with Jeremy about his strict upbringing and controlling parents.

"It's a shame we can't choose our parents," she remarks. "His sound horrible."

"They do, and it's such a shame as he's a genuinely decent lad who just needs a few friends."

"As long as he knows friendship is all I'm offering. I'm done with men."

"Yes, you said."

Even if we were here alone, I don't think I'd be inclined to enquire why she's so resentful. Hearing about my shoddy behaviour in the third-person holds little appeal.

"As long as he knows."

"He does, but please be gentle with him. He's as nervous as a kitten but just as harmless."

"That's okay then," she replies with a grin. "Who doesn't

like kittens?"

The barman asks what we'd like.

"Half a sweet cider," Jackie replies.

I request the same again. Our drinks are duly served, and we head back to the table where a young man in age-inappropriate attire is nervously waiting.

"Jeremy, this is Jackie."

He immediately stands up and offers his hand. Outside of a work environment, no one under the age of thirty introduces themselves with a handshake. Thankfully, Jackie plays along and takes his hand.

We sit.

Jeremy looks everywhere but at our guest, like he's back in school and waiting outside the headmaster's office for a ticking off. This is a critical moment. If there's anything left of the Jackie I knew, she'll chatter away, and any awkwardness will quickly fade. I cross my fingers beneath the table.

She takes a long sip of cider and glances over the rim of her glass towards Jeremy. I'm about to fill the silence with a few inane words when Jackie poses a question.

"Where do you buy your clothes, Jeremy?" she asks in a flat tone.

His eyes widen and then flick in my direction as if begging for help. I expected Jackie to lead with a few banal questions, rather than jump straight into a critique.

"I, err … I'm hopeless when it comes to fashion."

"You're not kidding," she scoffs. "You dress like my granddad."

All ten of my toes curl up while Jeremy visibly shrinks in his seat. 'Bad Jackie' is at the table, 'good Jackie' absent.

"Saying that," she adds. "My granddad is the loveliest man you could meet. Well, he was before he got ill and lost his marbles. Now he thinks he's the Archbishop of Canterbury."

There's a slight pause while Jeremy assesses if it's appropriate to chuckle at Jackie's remark. She leads the way, and the tension eases a little. Slightly late, but I think 'good Jackie' has just arrived.

Half my toes uncurl, but I don't share in the chuckling. I knew Jackie's granddad well, and her casual quip about the poor bloke suffering dementia is like a punch to the stomach. He was such a funny, carefree bloke, and I really liked him.

"So, are you going to tell me then?" Jackie pushes. "Where do you buy your clothes?"

"C&A."

"That explains it. First things first, we need to do something about your dress sense. Give you a fresher look."

"Um, why?"

"Because if you want to meet other young people, you need to dress like they do. I know it sounds a bit superficial, but what we wear sets a first impression."

"I understand."

"You might be the life and soul of the party type, Jeremy, but if you dress like Jimmy Tarbuck, you'll never get an invite to the party."

Jackie turns to me.

"Isn't that right, Sean?"

"You're asking a man in his fifties to comment on fashion?"

"Good point," she sniggers, turning back to Jeremy.

"Confidence breeds confidence. Look the part, and you'll feel the part."

If Jeremy had a notepad, I'm confident he'd be jotting down her advice.

"Now, tell me a bit about yourself. What kind of things are you in to?"

"Science fiction books."

"Cool. What else?"

Despite his intelligence, he struggles for an answer like a class dunce. I mouth one word.

"Yes, music. I like music. We listened to the charts yesterday."

"Who are you in to? If you say Sinitta, I'm leaving."

Oblivious to Jackie's Sinitta reference, Jeremy reels off the list of artists we discussed yesterday.

"Do you ever get to see live music?"

"Unfortunately not, but I do play the piano."

Jackie and I both simultaneously respond with the same measure of surprise.

"Really?"

"Yes, to grade eight standard."

"Bloody hell, Jeremy," I bluster. "Grade eight is as good as it gets. You kept that quiet."

"It's what happens when you don't have a television or radio in the house growing up. I had no way of listening to music unless I played it myself."

"That's amazing," Jackie coos. "I used to play the electric keyboard but … I kinda lost interest in it."

"That's a shame. Why?"

"Because I was hopeless. My first boyfriend played the guitar, and we used to make up silly songs in my bedroom. We were awful."

Up until now, Jackie hasn't made any reference to my younger self. Arriving like a jolt of electricity, her recollection casts me back in time to a suburban bedroom in the early eighties. Musically, we were woeful, but the lyrics of the love songs we wrote for one another were sincere.

"If you'd like lessons, I'd be more than willing," Jeremy says.

"I'd like that. I think the keyboard is up in the loft somewhere."

"I'm free most evenings and most weekends. Actually, I'm always free because I have no social life."

There's the slightest undercurrent of self-deprecation in Jeremy's words. His subtle humour strikes a chord with Jackie, and she laughs just the way she used to laugh. It's heart-warming and heart-breaking in equal measure, but it appears to help with Jeremy's confidence.

Remarkably, the conversation continues to flow, and I become a bystander. I don't mind. Slowly but surely, Jeremy creeps further out of his shell as does the Jackie I once knew. Watching her effervesce about a Terence Trent D'Arby gig she attended in Hammersmith last year, no one would guess they're looking at a girl on the brink of suicide. Equally, no one would guess Jeremy is a lonely soul with no friends and no self-confidence.

"I'm just nipping to the loo," I say.

They're so deep in conversation; my announcement only receives a nod of acknowledgement. I don't know how it happened, but I now feel like a third wheel. They're getting on though, and it appears to be doing them both a world of good.

I make my way to the toilets and take a leisurely pee. With no hand drier, I'm forced to use paper towels with the absorbency of rubber and texture of sackcloth. Tossing a third useless towel into the bin, I notice a dispensing machine on the wall. For one pound, I can buy a tiny sample of cologne should I have left home unscented. I had a thing for aftershaves in my youth, and some of the names are like old friends: Jazz, Kouros, Cacharel, Aramis, and my personal favourite of the period, Paco Rabanne. My parents thought I was odd when I put a bottle on my sixteenth birthday wish list.

I'm tempted to buy a Paco Rabanne sample and dab a little on for old time's sake, but I don't think Jackie would appreciate me returning from the toilet smelling like the boy who messed up her life.

I make my way back to the table.

"Oh, there you are," Jackie says before emptying her glass. "We're off."

"Sorry?"

"We're going to The Britannia as they've got a jukebox and a pool table. I'm going to teach Jeremy how to play."

"Oh, right. Let me just finish my pint."

She glances at Jeremy, who in turn looks sheepishly towards the floor.

"Actually, Sean," Jackie says. "We were going on our own. No offence, but it's not really a pub for older guys."

"I'm just going to the toilet," Jeremy squeaks.

He hurries off, leaving me alone with Jackie.

"I'm not sure this is a good idea."

"Why not? You said he wanted to make friends and have a social life."

"Yes, but …"

"He's not a kid, Sean. Don't treat him like one."

I realise I have no defence. I'd be no better than Jeremy's parents if I protest too much. What Jackie doesn't realise is that I want to hang around for her sake, not Jeremy's. I still haven't had an opportunity to talk about her mental health, let alone work out how to stop her suicide.

"Fair enough," I concede. "But can I ask you a favour?"

"You can ask."

"Is there any chance we could meet in the next day or two, for a coffee?"

"What for?"

"Nothing sinister, I swear. I … um … you mentioned Terence Trent D'Arby, and I'd like to pick your brains. I'm supposed to be doing a piece on him next month, but I've never seen him play live."

"Yeah, okay. I'm off on Wednesday."

It's cutting it short but better than her flatly refusing.

Jeremy returns.

"All set?" Jackie asks.

"Ready when you are."

She then turns to me.

"Twelve o'clock at the Wimpy Bar?"

"On Wednesday," I confirm with a smile. "Thank you."

To my surprise, Jackie stands on her tip-toes and plants a kiss on my cheek in the same cursory manner you'd usually reserve for elderly maiden aunts. No more than a faint trace, I catch the scent of her perfume. The sweet floral notes trigger a montage of memories and, as they float through my mind, a ravenous yearning to be a young man follows. I would give literally anything to be here now, with Jackie Benton, and to be Jeremy.

Unaware of the emotional turmoil she's just unleashed, Jackie picks up her bag.

"See you then, Sean."

With that, she takes Jeremy by the arm and leads him towards the door. He just has time to mouth an apology at me.

I'm not sure Sylvia will be so accepting of my apologies when I return to Cline Road without her prodigal tenant.

23.

I am a coward.

Rather than return to Cline Road on my own and face Sylvia's inquisition, I sunk a few more pints in the King's Head. On reflection, the alcohol only stoked my wistful malaise.

First love, I concluded, is like a dream holiday: idyllic, and untainted by the boring practicalities of everyday life. You don't think back and remember the queues at the airport, the daily battle for a sun lounger, or heat stroke. You only remember the picture-postcard moments, and they stay with you forever.

Eventually, I left the King's Head and wandered back to Cline Road. Under dark skies, I continued reminiscing about the five wonderful years Jackie and I shared together. Stretching my own analogy, it was akin to enjoying the holiday of a lifetime and the plane crashing on the way home.

I waited outside the house until Sylvia's bedroom light went out. Then, I quietly unlocked the front door and crept up to my room. I waited again for Jeremy to return.

The last time I remember checking my watch, it had just gone eleven o'clock. I must have fallen asleep soon after as I don't recall hearing the front door opening or Jeremy's footsteps on the stairs.

There were two reasons I wanted to wake up early. I needed to tell my housemate why I lied to Sylvia about my profession, and ask him to keep my white lie to himself. More importantly, I wanted to ask how he got on with Jackie.

I woke up at eight-thirty; the house silent.

Having showered and dressed, I need caffeine.

I plod down to the kitchen and put the kettle on. Just as I open the bread bin, I hear the front door latch click.

"Sean?" Sylvia calls out.

"In here."

She bustles in with a carrier bag in hand. I suspect I'm about to receive a lecture about abandoning Jeremy, so I attempt to defuse the situation.

"Would you like a cuppa? I've just put the kettle on."

"Yes, please."

She puts the bag on the side and begins decanting the contents.

"Did you have a pleasant evening?" she asks.

"Jeremy didn't tell you?"

"No, he was in a bit of a rush this morning."

Result. One less challenge to overcome.

"It was … good. I think he enjoyed himself."

"I'm glad he had a nice time. I went to bed at ten with a migraine."

"Are you feeling okay now?

"Much better. Thank you for asking."

Shopping unpacked, she then plucks a receipt from the bottom of the carrier bag and examines it.

"Prices these days," she tuts. "Fifty pence for butter. Outrageous."

"Is that expensive?" I mindlessly reply.

"Very, but I suppose we should be grateful. At least I can now buy more than two ounces a week."

I don't remember, but maybe dairy cows went on strike at some point in the previous decade. Everyone seemed to be on strike in the seventies, from what I understand.

"Was there a butter shortage?"

"I'm talking about wartime rationing, Sean," she replies curtly. "Or have you forgotten?"

I do the maths. I'm fifty-four today, which means I would have been five years old when World War II began and eleven when it ended. Bloody hell — Sylvia thinks I lived through it.

"Oh, of course. My memory isn't what it used to be."

"Surely you must remember the end of sweet rationing? I don't think I've ever met anyone your age who doesn't remember that day."

"Yes, amazing," I blurt, turning my attention to the boiling kettle.

There's a moment of silence. If I'm to avoid more unanswerable questions about a period I wasn't even alive, I need to get a question in myself.

"What did you do during the war, Sylvia?"

Having met very few people who lived through the war as an adult, my question isn't just an avoidance tactic. I am genuinely interested in her answer.

"I was in QAIMNS."

"Err, you might have to remind me."

"Queen Alexandra's Imperial Military Nursing Service. I served in Africa and Burma."

"Gosh, you must have seen … actually, I dread to think what you've seen."

"More horror than any woman should have to witness. I spent most of the war on the front line."

"All six years?"

"Not quite. I caught the unpleasant end of a grenade blast in January 1944. That was the end of my war; almost the end of my life, too."

"Jesus Christ, that's …"

"No blaspheming, Sean. Not in this house."

"Sorry."

"And, before you rephrase your response, it's not a period of my life I wish to dwell on."

"Understood."

I pass her a cup of tea. As she takes it by the saucer, a slight tremble in her hand, my eyes linger on her wedding band and engagement ring. I've already established Sylvia is a keenly observant woman, and accordingly, she asks me a question.

"You're wondering where Mr Butterworth is?"

"It might have crossed my mind."

"He passed three years ago. Three years, five months, and seventeen days to be precise."

"I'm so sorry to hear that."

"Don't be. We had forty-six wonderful years together. My only regret is that Royston went first."

"It must be hard being alone after so long."

Very different circumstances, but I can certainly relate.

"One mustn't grumble, but yes, I can't deny the months after he passed weren't challenging. Still, my generation is adept at getting on with it, and there's no sense moping around feeling sorry for one's self."

"Which is why I'm now standing here in your kitchen?"

Her eyebrows arch.

"There are no flies on you, are there?" she says with a thin but knowing smile. "It's the little things you miss the most, like having someone to cook for, to look after. Having a few select guests in the house makes me feel useful."

"For what it's worth, it's also nice being cooked for and feeling looked after."

"I hope so."

There's another moment of silence as Sylvia sips from her teacup. Reflective rather than uncomfortable.

"Did you and Royston have children?"

"Sadly, I lost more than a few pints of blood in that grenade blast. My lower torso bore the brunt and … let's just say God decided I should follow a different path."

I'm about to apologise, but I sense it would be wasted on Sylvia. As she implied herself, folk of her generation don't appreciate platitudes and self-pity.

"Do you have children?" she asks.

I shake my head.

"You never said if you were married."

"Divorced."

"Oh dear," she says with a heavy sigh. "That is a shame."

"For the record, I wasn't to blame. My wife had an affair."

"That must have been difficult."

"Not compared to being blown up, or losing a partner after forty-odd years together."

"I suppose not, but I'm sure it must have hurt."

"It did, but I'm okay now."

"Glad to hear it. It pays to retain one's faith, Sean, even when you feel like the world is conspiring against you."

Sage advice, particularly in this world.

"Duly noted."

Another sip of tea and Sylvia snaps back to her usual self.

"I've got a long list of chores to complete, and I'm sure you have studies to be getting on with."

"Sadly, yes."

No longer in the mood for toast, I take my cup and saucer up to my room.

Tea drinking fills eight minutes of my day. Now I just need to fill another eight hours before Jeremy arrives home, which could be problematic as I've nowhere to go, no one to see, and nothing to do.

As the bedroom walls begin to close in, I decide a walk in to town is as good a way to waste time as any. I might even build up an appetite and treat myself to a cooked breakfast in the little cafe by the station.

My plans decided I tell Sylvia I need to visit the library and I might be out for a while.

The walk in to town and breakfast kills an hour. I then wander up to the library and spend a few hours reading an Isaac Asimov novel. It's not my bag, but it'll give me something to chat about with Jeremy. It's hard going, and I'm only a fifth the way through it when lunchtime arrives. Needing a break, I wander aimlessly around town until I pass a newsagent. I'm not particularly hungry, but a can of pop and a bag of crisps will keep me going until dinner.

I grab a can of Coke and peruse the selection of crisps on offer, questioning what became of Golden Wonder? Oddly, they were the most popular brand of crisps throughout my youth and yet, all of a sudden, they were replaced on every shelf in every shop by Walkers and their confusing packet colours.

Not to be foxed again, I choose a packet of ready salted in a dark blue bag.

At the counter, there's a wide selection of confectionery on display. I don't want to spoil my dinner, but a few forgotten products prove intriguing enough so I stop and browse.

Despite the change of name, I doubt a Marathon tastes any different from a Snickers, and I know for sure Opal Fruits taste the same as Starburst. Most of everything else was available when I entered a newsagent last week although the packaging has changed a bit. However, one or two chocolate bars do tempt me. It's been many decades since I last chomped on a Banjo — a twin bar like a Twix but with peanuts — or a coconut and cherry Cabana Bar.

I reach a compromise when I spot another blast from my past and snatch a packet of Pacers from the display. Being chewy rectangular mints, they're not as filling as a chocolate bar. There's also a degree of sentimentality behind my choice as I used to chew on a Pacer every time I met up with Jackie, just in case my breath wasn't at peak freshness.

I pay and leave the newsagents, loitering outside to eat my crisps and drink the Coke. It turns out ready salted crisps are ready salted crisps and Coke is Coke, whatever the decade. The first spearmint Pacer, however, summons many happy memories, and a few not-so-happy memories of the dentist's chair and lost fillings.

I stroll back to the library and stay there until four o'clock, having endured quite enough Isaac Asimov for one day.

After a slow walk back to Cline Road, I return to my room and doze.

It's almost half-five when the front door opens and closes. Jeremy is back from work. I sit up and listen to the low murmur of voices from the kitchen. The conversation is brief, and barely a minute later, I hear footsteps on the stairs.

Dashing to my door, I open it just as Jeremy reaches the landing.

"Evening, Jeremy. Good day at work?"

"Productive, thank you."

"Have you got a minute for a chat? I just wanted to hear how last night went."

"Yes, of course."

I follow him into his room.

"I'm sorry we left you," he says, hanging up his jacket. "I hope you weren't offended."

"I spoke to Jackie while you were in the loo and she explained the reasons. It's fine."

"I felt bad about it all evening."

"Not all evening, I hope. The whole point was for you to get out and enjoy yourself."

"And I did," he replies, beaming. "I had a great time."

"You got on okay with Jackie?"

He sits down on the edge of the bed.

"She's amazing. So kind, considerate, and funny."

His tone is too close to dreamy.

"But she did make it clear ..."

"Yes, yes, I know," he interrupts. "Jackie explained her situation vis-à-vis boyfriends at some length, and why she doesn't want to get romantically involved with anyone at the moment."

"She did?"

"Her first boyfriend treated her badly."

"Oh."

"He cheated on her with a girl at university."

"What an arsehole."

"That's more or less what she said. It happened some time ago, but I think it permanently damaged her trust in men."

"She said that?"

"Not in so many words, but I could hear the resentment in her voice whenever she talked about him."

"Did she mention his name."

"Come to think of it, no. I think she's tried hard to erase the inconsiderate fool from her memories."

"Understandable."

I don't think I want to hear any more about Jackie's first relationship, or my inconsiderate foolishness.

"Apart from her relationship woes did she seem happy enough?"

"She did. Why do you ask?"

"Just curious."

"I don't know her well enough to judge, but she seemed perfectly happy. We talked for a while and then spent a good half-hour browsing music on the jukebox. After that, we played pool until closing time."

"Did you win?"

"Just the final frame," he chuckles. "But only because Jackie's injury flared up."

"Her injury?"

"Yes, to her arm. I noticed the bruise when she removed her jacket."

My mind flashes back to Saturday evening in The Britannia when Gary grabbed her by the arm.

"How did she injure herself?"

"At work, apparently. She tripped and fell against the counter."

She might be telling the truth, but isn't it common for those in a toxic relationship to blame their injuries on a trip or a fall? If Gary walked into the room this moment, I'd make damn sure he left with a few bruises of his own; the piece of shit.

I try not to let the anger reach my face.

"But, apart from Jackie's injury and your dreadful pool skills, you both had a good evening and got on okay?"

"Well enough she asked me to drop by her house on Thursday evening. She wants to learn how to play her keyboard properly."

"Oh, right. That's good."

It is good because people on the brink of suicide don't

usually take up long-term hobbies. Maybe, just maybe, meeting Jeremy has helped rekindle Jackie's positivity. I can only speculate, but the signs are promising.

Sylvia calls up the stairs to say dinner will be ready in ten minutes.

"There's just one other trifling matter I needed to discuss with you, Jeremy."

"Of course."

"I might have told Sylvia a small white lie about my profession. I told her I worked for a hotel chain."

"Can I ask why?"

"People who work in the music industry are often seen as a bit flaky, unreliable. Knowing Sylvia, I don't think she'd have let me move in if I told her the truth."

"You're probably right," he says with a smile. "And I won't say anything."

"Thank you."

He clears his throat and glances down at the carpet.

"Really, it should be me thanking you," he says in a low voice. "I've always found it difficult expressing my emotions but I … I do want you to know how grateful I am, for your help and for introducing me to Jackie."

"You're more than welcome, but you might not be so grateful once you've heard her hammering the life out of that keyboard."

"You've heard her play?"

"Um, no. I've got a good imagination."

With the strikingly accurate aroma of steak and kidney pie wafting up from the kitchen, I must possess an incredible imagination.

24.

Day six of this madness. How easy it is to slip into a routine.

Last night, after dinner, we watched television until nine-thirty when Sylvia went to bed. I had a chat with Jeremy for half-an-hour before he retired. I managed another hour of television, but with only four channels to choose from, there wasn't a great deal on to pique my interest. At eleven o'clock, I plodded up to bed.

This morning I got up at the usual time, conducted my ablutions, and had a breakfast of tea and toast. God knows why she does it every day, but Sylvia was too engrossed in her cleaning regime to chat, so I went back to my room and did nothing for an hour. Thankfully, I've got one appointment in my diary today, with Jackie. I don't know if I'm looking forward to it or not, but there is one minor issue on my mind — of all the gigs she's ever attended, why did she have to single-out Terence Trent D'Arby?

I leave the house at half-ten.

I'm due to meet Jackie in ninety minutes, and I only know two facts about the supposed subject of our conversation. He had a number one with *Wishing Well,* plus a handful of less successful singles, and he wore ridiculously tight trousers if my memory of Top of The Pops is reliable.

Seeing as I'm supposedly writing an article about the man, I need more. For that reason, I'm on my way to a record shop that isn't Our Price.

I don't recall fact-finding missions being such a chore in the eighties, but maybe they weren't. Perhaps, like investigative journalists, we savoured the satisfaction of proper boots-on-the-ground research you just don't get from a five-second search on Google. Or, more likely, we just didn't give a shit. Are our lives any better for knowing every sodding detail about every sodding facet of human existence?

Still, I wouldn't mind a quick peek at Wikipedia about now.

I arrive at the record store and search the racks for D'Arby's one and only album to date — well, this date — rather pompously titled, *Introducing the Hardline According to Terence Trent D'Arby*. After memorising the track list, I read the sleeve notes and jot down a few snippets of info on a notepad I purchased from WHSmith, where I also picked up a copy of this week's NME. After a quick shuffle through the pages, I didn't find anything relating to D'Arby. Perhaps he's not as big a star as he thinks he is. He certainly won't be beyond this decade.

I'm early, but with nothing else to fill the time I traipse up the High Street to the Wimpy Bar. It's busy but not overly so. The waitress offers me a choice of two booths, both of which Jackie and I have frequented at one point or another in the past. Not ideal but I choose one with a view of the High Street.

At five-past-twelve, Jackie arrives looking beautiful but flustered.

"So sorry," she pants. "I missed the bus."

She slides across the vinyl bench opposite and dumps a canvas tote bag down next to her.

"You're doing me a favour. No apology required."

The waitress is on us in a heartbeat. I order two large Cokes.

"And what would you like to eat?" she asks.

Being I'm in a booth with my former girlfriend, separated by many decades and any rational explanation, I'm not hungry.

"Do you fancy anything, Jackie?"

"Why do you think I suggested we meet at twelve?" she grins.

"Order whatever you like. It's on me."

She orders a cheeseburger and fries. The waitress frowns when I say I'm not eating so I relent and order a plate of fries. She hurries away.

Although I'm a long way from comfortable, the atmosphere at the table is markedly lighter than it was that first night at The Britannia, mainly because Jackie appears less angsty. However, the hair twiddling suggests she's not entirely relaxed in my company. For that reason, I start the conversational ball rolling.

"Shall we talk about your gig experience first, and then maybe you can tell me about your evening with Jeremy?"

"If you like."

"Great. So, you said you saw Terence Trent D'Arby last year, right?"

"Yeah, at the Hammersmith Apollo."

"What was it like?"

Such a basic question but it's like lighting a firework. Jackie explodes with enthusiasm as she recounts every minute from the journey on the Tube to D'Arby's encore. I'm sure a proper music journalist would have brought a tape recorder with them, but as I'm not a music journalist, I scribble lines in a notepad while Jackie gabbles away. She only draws breath when the waitress arrives with our Cokes.

"I'm hoping to see him again next year," she then declares. "And I've got a long list of other artists I want to see live, too."

"Next year?" I reply, somewhat taken aback.

"Definitely."

Not only is Jackie about to begin keyboard lessons, but she's also making tentative plans for next year. This doesn't compute. I need to swing the conversation around, and an album I spotted in the record store has given me an idea how.

"Do you want to know the best gig I ever attended?"

"Go on."

"Joy Division, in '79," I lie.

"*Love Will Tear Us Apart*, right?"

"That was their only commercial hit, but they'd have been massive if tragedy hadn't struck."

"What tragedy?" she asks, poking the ice cubes in her glass with a straw.

"You don't know about Ian Curtis, the lead singer?"

"Oh, wait. He's the guy who topped himself, isn't he?"

"He's the guy who fought a long battle with depression and lost, yes."

"That's sad."

"Yep, such a loss. I can't imagine how he must have felt in those days before taking his own life, can you?"

"No idea," she says, matter-of-factly. "But topping yourself is a bit selfish if you ask me."

"Do you really think that?"

"Yeah. He must have known how much it would hurt his family, yet he still did it. That's selfish in my book."

"Unless you've suffered depression, Jackie, I don't think you can say how anyone feels, and you certainly shouldn't judge."

"I'm not judging him. I'm just saying I could never do that to my mum."

"That's the thing about depression: everyone thinks they're immune from it, until one day they're standing on top of a multi-storey car park trying to find just one reason not to jump."

"That's a grim thought."

"Grim, but it's the truth. And, if people only talked more and shared their fears, there would be many fewer suicides."

She looks up from the table and fixes me with a hard stare.

"You're not thinking of killing yourself, are you?"

I almost choke on my Coke.

"God, no. I'm just talking generally."

"Can we talk about something less depressing?"

Her casual attitude towards depression and suicide has thrown me. Is she in denial, and that's why she wants to change the subject?

Our lunch arrives, allowing for a break in the conversation and a chance to regroup my thoughts. Those thoughts then veer off in an unexpected direction as I surreptitiously watch her eat. I observe the peculiar way she holds her fork, like a pen, and the way she stirs her drink with the straw before every slurp. I observe the way she closes her eyes every now and then, savouring the taste of her food, and the way she dips each end of every fry into a pool of tomato ketchup.

These are the little quirks I've long forgotten, yet they all contribute to Jackie being the girl she is — the girl I fell in love with.

The cheeseburger no more, I try re-engaging the conversation.

"Did someone skip breakfast?"

"How'd you guess?"

"Sixth sense," I chuckle.

"I do love a Wimpy cheeseburger. A rare treat."

"Obviously."

Silence returns as the last few fries are polished off. I can't stomach any more and nudge my plate to the side. As Jackie does the same, the waitress returns.

"Are you all done?" she asks.

"Yes, thanks."

"Would you like any desserts?"

I catch Jackie's eye. I probably shouldn't, but it would be worth it to see her face light up.

"You ever tried a Brown Derby?" I ask her.

"Are you kidding me!" she replies excitedly. "It's my all-time favourite dessert."

I turn to the waitress.

"One Brown Derby and two more Cokes, please."

I turn back to Jackie, and she appears genuinely excited at the prospect of an ice-cream topped doughnut.

"You realise you've made my day," she coos.

Thinking back to all the high-class, ludicrously expensive restaurants I've dined in, I don't recall Carol ever being as pleased or grateful as the young woman opposite.

"Just repaying the favour."

Without the distraction of food, I move the conversation along.

"You had an enjoyable evening with Jeremy, I hear."

"Yeah, it was good. He's a nice guy."

"He is."

"Terrible at pool, though."

"So I heard. In fairness, I don't think he's ever played before."

"There's a lot of things Jeremy has never done before."

"Such as?"

"Do I need to spell it out, Sean? Kinda sad, really, at his age."

"Ohh, right. You got on to that subject?"

"In a roundabout sort of way. We were talking about cheating, and he admitted he's never had a girlfriend, but if he did, he'd never cheat on her."

Feeling slightly warm all of a sudden, I gulp a mouthful of Coke.

"And you should have warned me," Jackie continues. "I didn't mean to let it slip, but I thought he knew."

"Err, knew what?"

"About your wife."

"Christ. You told him *that*?"

"You never said it was a secret, and I thought you and Jeremy were friends."

I should be annoyed, but what does it matter? Five days from now, none of this will matter.

"Forget it. As humiliating as it was, it's ancient history now."

"Never goes away, though, does it?" she says quietly. "That feeling you weren't good enough."

"I felt like that for months, but I've come to realise it was never about being good enough. We just weren't right for one another."

"How long were you married for?"

"Twenty-five years."

"She took a long time to decide you weren't right."

"People change."

"They do," she sighs. "More's the pity."

Any other person in my seat would ask the obvious follow-up question. I let Jackie's sigh hang in the air. A mistake, as it turns out.

"My first boyfriend met someone else," she says. "He was at university in Exeter, and the bastard just called out of the blue one day and told me."

"I'm sorry to hear that."

"So was I. It's not as bad as what happened to you but … even if I had caught him and that bitch in the act, I couldn't imagine feeling any worse."

"I'm sure he never meant to hurt you."

"Yeah, right," she huffs. "To this day, I don't think he's ever given me a second thought, or the pain he caused. The shit didn't even say sorry — he just hung up on me."

"We all make mistakes."

"Shagging someone else isn't a mistake, it's the cruellest thing anyone can do in a relationship — you should know that."

No part of me wants to pursue this subject — no part except my conscience.

"The thing about mistakes, Jackie, is it's sometimes hard to accept you've made one."

"In what way?"

"I don't want to sound like a condescending old git, but when you're young, you have no concept of how little you really know about life. You might have a degree, a responsible job, maybe even your own home, and because society says you're an adult, you think you've learnt all there is to learn. At your age, I thought I knew what I wanted from life."

"And now?"

"Now I've lived that life, I realise I made mistakes. Some because I was naive, some because I lacked judgement, and one or two because I was a bloody idiot."

"Being an idiot is what men do best."

There's a smile on her face, but it lacks conviction.

"My point is: because I was young and pig-headed, I couldn't even admit to myself I'd made mistakes. It was easier to live in denial. Perhaps that guy who broke your heart realised soon after he'd made a mistake … he just didn't possess the emotional maturity to accept it."

"Maybe you're right but, as you put it, it's ancient history."

"You're over him?"

"He was the first guy I ever loved, and in a way, I don't think I'll ever stop loving him, but I hope one day I'll meet someone else and love them even more."

"That's the right attitude."

"And maybe you might love someone more than you loved your wife."

Probably best not to tell Jackie I already have met someone I loved more than my now ex-wife, or that she is that someone.

We swap smiles.

"His name was Sean," she then says.

"Who? Your first boyfriend?"

"Yep."

"It's a common name."

"It's weird because you kinda remind me of him a bit. You've got the same eyes and the way you say certain words is, I dunno … familiar."

"Sadly, I'm not twenty-two."

She suddenly shifts in her seat as a line creases her forehead.

"How do you know he's twenty-two?"

"Err, I don't. Aren't you about that age?"

"Twenty-one."

"Right, well, I guess I just said the first age that popped into my head."

She fixes me with a stare; the kind of stare I'd imagine a dog owner might deploy when asking their pet if it pissed on the carpet.

"One Brown Derby," the waitress announces. "And two Cokes."

I've never been so glad to see a waitress. Jackie's attention swiftly shifts to her dessert.

"That looks so nice," I remark. "I wish I'd ordered one now."

"Why don't you?" Jackie replies, already digging into the

doughnut.

"I'm trying to watch my weight."

She spoons the first mouthful home and closes her eyes.

"Oh, my God," she purrs. "It's so good."

"Are you taunting me?"

"Maybe a bit."

For the next five minutes, Jackie commentates on her dessert, telling me in detail how delicious each and every morsel is.

"What a shame you couldn't have one," she says, laying her spoon to rest. "That was lovely."

"Glad you enjoyed it."

"I'm just nipping to the loo. One too many Cokes."

She gets up and then hesitates.

"Oh, I almost forgot."

After rummaging around in her tote bag, she pulls out a printed envelope and hands it to me.

"I took some photos of the gig. Have a browse; they might give you a better idea of what it was like."

"That's really useful. Thanks."

She hurries off to the loo.

I don't have much interest in the photos, but I flick through them anyway. Some are out of focus, some oversaturated, and all of them poorly framed. Unfortunately for Jackie, she's some twenty-odd years away from the dawn of smartphone cameras, and all the filtering and editing tools, not to mention the ability to take the shot repeatedly if you're not happy with it.

I return the photos to the envelope and lean across the table. As I drop the envelope back into Jackie's bag, I catch sight of a small, leather-bound book with two words embossed in silver letters on the front: 1988 DIARY. My eyes instinctively flick towards the toilet door across the room, and then back to the diary.

Should I? Could I?

Whatever is going on in Jackie's head, surely the truth lies within the pages of her diary. If I could just scan the last dozen entries, there might be clues to why the happy-go-lucky young woman I've just had lunch with is about to descend into a suicidal state.

I glance towards the toilet door again.

I've likely got no more than seconds before Jackie returns — nowhere near long enough to read what I need to read. I could take the diary and peruse it at my leisure, but what if she notices it missing, and where would I hide it? It's too big to fit in the pocket of my trousers, and if I stuff it up my jumper, it'll stick out like a sore thumb.

Other options spin around my head, but they're even less practical. Then, one possibility dawns. I could hide it under the seat, wait until Jackie leaves, and then return for it.

With no time to think any further, I reach into the bag and grab the diary. In my haste, I pull it out of the bag too quickly. It catches the table edge. I watch in slow motion as the diary slips from my fingers and drops to the floor.

"Bugger!" I hiss.

Just as I'm about to duck below the table, I glance towards the toilets again — Jackie is closing the door behind her. I've got five seconds.

Four, three, two, one.

I emerge just as Jackie approaches.

"Sorry," I say, holding up the diary. "I put the photos back in your bag, and this fell out."

She stares at the diary, and then at me.

"I hope you didn't read it," she snaps, snatching it from my hand.

"No, of course not."

She returns the diary to her bag.

"I just noticed the time," she then says flatly. "I need to get going."

"Right, okay."

My reward for buying lunch is the curtest goodbye imaginable.

"Seeya."

She glances at her watch again and hurries away.

I sit back down and puff a resigned sigh, unsure what to make of the last hour or Jackie's sudden departure.

On the one hand, I'm even less convinced she's suffering from depression, but I'm also struggling to read this version. One minute I'm with the girl I used to know and the next, a barely recognisable version returns from the toilet. I wonder if there's another mental health issue at play; one I'm in no position to recognise. All I know is in five days, she'll jump in front of a train. Logically, something must happen between then and now to trigger that desperate act.

Despite the last few minutes and her chippy attitude, I'm also disappointed she's gone.

I could have easily spent the entire afternoon with Jackie, although she obviously didn't feel the same. I also doubt it would have been good for my stress levels. I almost blew my cover with the remark about her first boyfriend's age, and then she came close to catching me red-handed borrowing her diary. Two close shaves are enough.

I summon the waitress and pay the bill. Overall, I'm not sure it was money well spent. Then again, I'm no longer sure of anything.

25.

I can feel the clouds of a bad mood gathering.

It's ten o'clock in the morning, and I'm in my room; the house empty.

I don't want to be here.

The last six days have undermined my sanity to such a degree I've simply had enough. Last night, I had to listen to Jeremy wittering on about keyboard lessons, and Sylvia complaining about the price of groceries. This morning, I had to suffer the postman's tuneless whistling and birds chirping relentlessly in the garden.

They can all fuck off, but not before I've told them in no uncertain terms; I'm sick of this madness.

I want it to end. So does Jackie Benton, apparently.

Why?

Tired of staring at the ceiling, I get up from the bed and wander over to the window. The scene outside is as dismal as my thoughts, and it's not helping. I can't even go for a walk unless I fancy a soaking.

I feel like a prisoner; not trapped in the physical sense, but mentally.

Is that how Jackie feels?

I've replayed our conversation in the Wimpy Bar many times, and all I can conclude is the last few minutes were bizarre. Why the snarky comment about reading her diary, and what provoked the sudden mood swing after I denied it?

I don't think I'll ever understand women.

Watching droplets of rain race down the window pane, my thoughts turn to the letter I delivered to Anna. I couldn't have made my concerns clearer, but there's no obvious sign she's heeded the warning. If I received a letter stating someone I loved was on the brink of suicide, I wouldn't let them out of my sight. I certainly wouldn't let them meet up with random strangers. Anna doesn't know Jeremy and I are harmless.

Did Anna simply dismiss the letter? Perhaps she did discuss it with her daughter, and Jackie just scoffed at the notion she'd take her own life, much like she did when I broached the subject.

Too many questions.

I continue to stare out of the window in the hope my ever-reliable problem-solving process delivers inspiration. Long minutes pass, but nothing comes; a lack of data no doubt. I can't fix a problem if I don't know the cause.

The front door slams shut. Sylvia has returned.

It's highly unlikely my landlady can help solve a psychotic time-travel puzzle, but she might be able to lend me an umbrella. Being holed up in my room isn't improving my mood.

I grab my shoes and head downstairs to the kitchen.

"Morning, Sylvia."

"Oh, good morning."

"Rotten day, eh?"

"If you're referring to the weather, it is."

She plucks the kettle from the side and fills it at the sink.

"I was wondering if you had an umbrella I could borrow?"

"You're off out, are you?"

"Just for a walk. I need to clear my head."

"Royston's old umbrella is still in the stand. You're welcome to borrow it."

"Thank you."

"Cup of tea before you go?"

"What I really need is a triple shot of espresso."

"I have no idea what that is."

"Doesn't matter. Tea would be great, thanks."

I'm not in the right frame of mind for tea and small talk, but I'm mindful of Sylvia's admission about needing company. Besides, a ten-minute delay is unlikely to change my situation.

As she prepares the cups, Sylvia asks me a question over her shoulder.

"You don't seem yourself this morning, Sean. Is everything okay?"

"I'm fine."

She turns around.

"Is that so? You have the face of a man who's lost a shilling and found a penny."

"It's nothing. Work stuff."

"Having problems?"

"In a manner of speaking, yes."

"Discuss with or deal with," she replies crisply. "That was Royston's philosophy when it came to problems."

"You might need to expand on that."

"It's simple enough. If you have a problem there are only two ways to address it: you either discuss it or you deal with it. Dwelling or dithering does not help."

"I see."

"So, can you deal with your problem?"

"Um, I'm struggling."

"In which case, you only have one other option — discuss it."

If only it were that simple.

"Thing is, Sylvia, it's a complicated situation."

"Ahh, and I'm just a feeble-minded woman; too preoccupied with cake recipes and household chores to be of any help?"

"Not at all," I protest. "That's not what I meant."

"Then don't presume your problems are so unique I might not be able to offer a few words of advice."

"I don't. It's just … if Albert Einstein popped in for a cup of tea, I don't think even he would be able to help."

"If Mr Einstein were to grace us with his presence, I'd be mightily impressed seeing as he died thirty-odd years ago."

"Granted, but my point remains valid. My problem is ridiculously complex."

"Then make it less complex. That would be a good place to start."

The kettle boils, and Sylvia returns to her tea preparation duties. A fresh perspective wouldn't do any harm but simplifying my problem is a problem in itself. I focus my attention on it.

By the time Sylvia hands me a cup and saucer, I think I've got a vaguely coherent way of explaining my predicament.

"Thoughts?" she asks.

"Are you sure you want to hear them?"

"It would be preferable to your glum face."

"Okay, you believe in God, right?"

"I do."

"Imagine you had a premonition about Jeremy. In that premonition you witnessed something awful happen to him at work tomorrow. In your heart of hearts, you are one hundred per cent certain this awful event will happen, but there's no way to prove it. What would you do?"

"Why wouldn't I just tell him?"

"You could try, but would he believe you?"

"I don't know. How do you convince someone of an impending fate without categoric proof?"

"Exactly. That's the crux of my problem."

"I see."

She takes a sip from her cup.

"This event," she continues. "It happens at his workplace, correct?"

"Yes."

"And in this premonition, I'd be absolutely certain of that?"

"Right again."

"Then, the solution is simple."

"Is it?"

"Of course. No one can be in two places at once, Sean. I'd find a way to stop Jeremy going to work tomorrow."

"And how would you do that?"

"I'm sure there are plenty of ways. I could feign illness and ask him to stay home to keep an eye on me."

"Doesn't lying go against your religious principles?"

"I said I *could* feign illness, but it wouldn't be my preferred option."

"What would?"

"For someone to be in a place other than they're supposed to be, you have to give them a strong enough incentive. If, for example, Jeremy's favourite author happened to be signing books down in Southampton tomorrow, perhaps that might convince him to take the day off work."

I let Sylvia's advice sink in while tallying it with Jackie's situation. I've seen her death certificate, so I know for sure she'll die on Monday, in Guildford. But what if she's in Peterborough, or Cardiff, or Hereford, or anywhere that isn't a train track in Guildford?

So simple. So obvious.

"Sylvia, you're a genius!"

"You have a solution?"

"It needs some fine-tuning, but I think so."

Out of politeness, I stand and finish my tea, but the minute Sylvia puts her cup down, I dart back up to my room and grab the notepad.

Perched on the edge of my bed, the silence is now a welcome aid to concentration. Thanks to my landlady's fresh eyes, I can now see how simple my problem is: how do I ensure Jackie isn't in Guildford on Monday?

Another problem comes to mind; one Sylvia wouldn't have identified from my analogy.

"Shit."

I know Jackie commits suicide on Monday, in Guildford. If I prevent that happening, what's to stop her trying on Tuesday, or next week, or next month? Am I set to spend the rest of eternity guarding my former girlfriend in this illusionary nightmare?

Then again, what did Jackie say at the Wimpy Bar yesterday? She couldn't understand why anyone would take their own life. Maybe, Monday is the one and only time in her life she'll think differently; a never-to-be-repeated trip to rock bottom.

Who knows? Not me.

As real as it feels, I remind myself this cannot be anything other than a self-produced illusion. This is Comaland, and I have one task to complete if I'm to escape — prevent Jackie from committing suicide on Monday. I do that, and absolution from the guilt will surely follow. There's no telling what will happen to Jackie in the long run, but it's beyond my control and therefore beyond my conscience.

Breathing a little easier, I return my attention to the notepad.

The first word I jot down is kidnap. A ridiculous notion but if Jackie is locked up all day, she sure as hell won't be anywhere near a railway bridge. If I were to apply a grading system to my ideas, it would only merit one out of a possible five. There are so many complications, so many ways it could go wrong, but I'm not about to dismiss it. I might need more than one back-up plan.

Next idea.

As I chew my pen, Sylvia's suggestion about Jeremy's favourite author and a book signing lingers at the back of my mind. If kidnapping is the bluntest of sticks, what would be the juiciest carrot I could dangle in front of Jackie? I need one so tempting she'd find it impossible to resist.

I invest an hour jotting down ideas and eventually settle on the most practical contender. Mulling it over, the carrot is good enough, but there are several practicalities I need to address. The first will require the use of a telephone.

I hurry back downstairs. Sylvia is in the lounge, ironing.

"I'm not interrupting, am I?"

"Not at all."

"I've got a possible solution to my problem, but I need to make a few phone calls. If I give you some money, can I use the phone?"

"Help yourself. You know where it is."

"Thanks."

"They are local calls?"

"Yes."

"Keep it brief, please."

"Will do. Oh, and do you have a Yellow Pages?"

"It's next to the phone."

Returning to the hallway, I brace myself for an experience I haven't endured since I left the family home many decades ago. I sit down on the telephone seat and open a weighty volume of the Yellow Pages. After a quick thumb through, I find what I'm looking for and dial the first company.

"Hi, I'm looking to hire a car on Monday."

"For how long?"

"Twenty-four hours."

"And what kind of car do you need?"

"Something like a Ford Focus would do."

"A what?"

"A Ford ... a Ford Escort."

"No problem. We have one available on Monday."

"Can I book that, please?"

"Of course. I'll just need a credit card number, and we'll need to see your driving licence when you arrive to collect the car."

Bugger.

"Um, can I get back to you?"

I make three more calls, and speak with three more hire companies who all require a credit card and a driving licence. My credit card won't be valid for many years, and my driving licence is the plastic card type rather than the paper version used in 1988. Besides, my date of birth will raise unanswerable questions. I don't think I'll pass for twenty-two.

Without a car, the rest of my plan falls apart.

I get up and return to the lounge.

"That was quick," Sylvia comments.

"Yes, and unsuccessful."

I delve into my pocket and hand over three pound coins.

"I wasn't eavesdropping, but I heard you enquiring about a hire car."

"Yes, but I have an issue with my driving licence in that I don't have one. No licence, no car."

"You can't drive?"

"I've been driving for years. I just don't have a paper licence."

"Why not?"

"I … err, I sent it off for a change of address."

"I see. Can you not borrow a car, or take the train?"

"No, the train is impractical, and I don't know anyone in Guildford to borrow a car from."

Her attention turns back to a stubborn crease in a blouse.

"I have a car," she then says casually.

"You do?"

"Well, it's not my car as such. It belonged to Royston."

"And you've kept it?"

"I know it's silly, but we had so many lovely days out in that car, so many memories, I couldn't bring myself to sell it. And, I promised myself I'd learn to drive one day."

"It's never too late."

"I'm not so sure, but that's beside the point."

Whatever the point is, the blouse takes priority.

"If you give me your word you'll look after it, you can borrow the car. It probably needs a good run out."

"Really? That's incredibly kind of you, Sylvia."

"Give me ten minutes to finish this, and I'll introduce you to Austin."

"Austin?"

"The car."

"Ah, right."

"Ten minutes is sufficient time to make a cup of tea, wouldn't you say?"

Taking the less-than-subtle hint, I scuttle through to the kitchen. My plan is back on.

The kettle takes five minutes to boil, and I'm about to pour when Sylvia enters the kitchen.

"Come on then. We'll have tea afterwards."

"Righto."

She grabs a bunch of keys from a hook, and I follow her out the back door to the rear of the garage.

"The main door is a bit stiff," she remarks, sliding the key into the lock. "You might need to oil the hinges."

The garage itself is larger than a standard single, and the rear section contains a workbench which I suspect hasn't seen any work since Royston passed away. In front of the bench, there's a car-shaped object covered with a tarpaulin.

"Can you do the honours?" Sylvia asks.

"Sure."

Like an unveiling ceremony, I grab the tarp with both hands and give it a firm yank. The car beneath momentarily steals my breath.

"Isn't he a beauty?"

"Oh, that's Austin?"

"Yes, indeed," she replies proudly.

I am grateful, but as I stare at the sage-green Austin Allegro, that gratitude doesn't reach my face.

"Great."

26.

I've been to a few classic car shows over the years. I can admire a perfectly restored Triumph Stag or a Jensen-Healey as much as the next man, but an Austin Allegro? Notwithstanding its notoriously poor reputation for reliability, I can only assume the designer took inspiration from a bowl of dumplings.

I feigned delight as Sylvia handed me the keys. She then informed me Austin hadn't left the garage in almost six months and I might want to give him a once over before Monday.

With nothing else better to do, I said she'd better leave me to it.

Unsurprisingly, Austin wouldn't start; the battery as dead as Royston. I returned to the kitchen and informed Sylvia I needed a jump start. We then traipsed to a neighbour's house where my landlady conscripted a portly retiree called Donald to help. As luck would have it, Donald used to serve in the Royal Engineers and knew a thing or two about the oily parts of a car.

After a lot of tinkering, a few litres of fresh petrol, and much resistance, the sad old Allegro finally spluttered into life. Donald suggested my first journey should be to a parts shop as he had little faith the battery would hold a charge. He then gave me directions to one such business on the other side of town and waved me off.

It took less than a mile to establish why you never see an Austin Allegro at a classic car show — all the owners are probably dead, too embarrassed to be seen driving such a god-awful vehicle in public, or the car itself broke down on the way. It's not so much a car engineered, but thrown together by a handful of disinterested Brummies one Friday afternoon after a lengthy lunchtime session in the pub.

Still, I made it to the parts shop where a cheery bloke in brown overalls sold me a replacement battery and even helped me fit it. I then drove to a petrol station and filled the tank to the brim, paying just thirty-five pence for each litre. Rather than drive straight back to Cline Road, I pootled around for an hour to get better acquainted with Austin and his myriad quirks.

Having spent a chunk of the day doing something constructive, and my plan for Monday looking good, I returned to my room in better spirits than when I left it. There I spent the remainder of the afternoon working on a deployment strategy.

At half-five, a vital component of that strategy arrives home from work.

A creature of habit, I hear Jeremy saying hello to Sylvia and then his footsteps on the stairs. I've got half-an-hour before dinner to set the wheels of my plan in motion.

I wait five minutes before knocking on Jeremy's door. He invites me in.

"Good day at the lab?" I ask casually.

"Yes, thank you."

"Good, good. You're off to Jackie's house later for her first keyboard lesson, aren't you?"

"I'm due there at seven-thirty, yes."

"Can you do me a favour?"

"Sure."

"Tell her those concert tickets will be with me by Friday of next week, and I'll post them on as soon as they arrive."

"Concert tickets?"

"Gary Numan is performing a show at the Civic Hall in September, and I said I'd get Jackie a couple of tickets through a contact."

"Oh, yes. Jackie did mention something about a concert, but I couldn't share in her enthusiasm for Gary Numan on account I'd never heard of him."

"She's quite the fan."

"Yes, I gathered."

I pause for effect.

"Jeremy, how do you fancy making Jackie's day?"

"Um, how?"

"By pure chance, I'm heading up to Manchester on Monday

to interview Gary Numan's tour manager. There is a chance the man himself might be there so if Jackie has a question she'd like me to ask him, just tell her to jot it down."

"You're meeting with this Gary Numan chap?"

"Possibly. It's not a formal interview as such and nowhere near as glamorous as it sounds. I'll be spending most of the day on the road, for just an hour of interview time."

"Gosh, Jackie will be jealous."

"If only she were a music journalist's assistant, eh?" I reply with a chuckle. "Anyway, it might be a chance to ask a question, so just mention it to her."

"Will do."

"Right, I'll see you at dinner."

The first seed sown, I return to my room.

On Saturday, I'm planning to visit Our Price, and while I'm browsing the racks, I might accidentally bump into Jackie. If she's anything like the girl I once knew, she won't be able to resist asking about the interview. That same girl also once told me she'd willingly crawl naked through a field of stinging nettles for a chance to meet her idol.

I plan to tempt her with that chance.

The Jackie I knew also possessed a trait vital to my plan: innocence verging on naivety. I've no bloody idea where Gary Numan will be on Monday, but it won't cross Jackie's mind to question my claim. Even if she did, there's no way for her to check. Besides, she'll be far too excited when I casually suggest she might like to accompany me to Manchester.

I'm as sure as sure can be she'll jump at the chance.

I intend to pick her up at the crack of dawn, and then we'll embark on a tortuously slow drive to Manchester. By my reckoning, it'll take the best part of five hours to get there. I'll then park up near the city centre and ask her to wait in the car while I check if it's okay for her to join me in the interview. I'll then disappear for an hour or two and return with the news Gary Numan couldn't make it. By way of amends, I'll take her into the city and let her shop for a few hours, at my expense. Then, we'll have a long three-course dinner before setting off for home. On that journey, we'll stop at the services, and I'll have problems starting the car, delaying us by another hour.

If my calculations are correct, Monday will be over by the time we return home. Jackie Benton will not throw herself in front of a train in Guildford because she won't be anywhere near that bridge. It'll be impossible.

My only concern is what happens on Tuesday; not to Jackie, but me. Will I wake up in a house on Cline Road, or a hospital bed, or the nook? Will I wake up at all? Having faith in a plan is one thing, but having faith in the unknown consequences of that plan is quite another. All I can do is trust my own judgement because I cannot see any other way out of Comaland.

Sylvia calls up the stairs to say dinner is ready. I climb off the bed and draw a deep breath. I've done all I can do now, apart from wait and hope events unfold in the way I've planned. For now, I have a belly to fill.

We enjoy another home-cooked meal with a smattering of small talk. Despite being three very different people who barely know one another, we rub along surprisingly well. I think I might miss our shared evening meals. I'll definitely miss Sylvia's cooking. And, illusionary figure or not, I'm also a tad curious what will become of Jeremy. In just a few days he seems to have woken up to the possibility there is a life beyond his room. I doubt he'll ever come close to being a party animal but little by little, he's gaining confidence.

Once dinner is over and the table cleared, Jeremy tells Sylvia he's off out for the evening, explaining where he's going and why. Just as he's leaving, I remind him about the concert tickets and my possible meeting with Jackie's hero. He assures me he won't forget.

Having made significant progress today, and not wanting to spend another evening in front of the television, I decide a couple of pints might be in order. Out of politeness, I ask Sylvia if she'd like to join me but she declines my invitation. As much as I'm warming to my landlady, I can't say I'm disappointed. As I bid her goodbye, she changes the television channel to BBC One. Her eyes roll as we catch the tail end of Top of The Pops with Gary Davies and Simon Bates. I don't think Sylvia is a fan.

I set off for the nearest pub, which is only a few streets away. In 1988, every town in the country had roughly a thousand pubs, so you're never far from one.

Minutes later, I enter my temporary local. As is customary for any backstreet pub of this era, the air is thick with cigarette smoke and the stench of stale beer. I can almost guarantee the landlord's name is either Dave, or Mick, or Steve, and he'll have heavily tattooed forearms.

"Yes, mate. What can I get you?"

I scan the limited selection of pumps.

"Pint of London Pride, please."

"Not seen you in here before?" he says, tugging the pump with a heavily tattooed arm.

"No, I've just moved back to Guildford."

"From where?"

"Devon."

"Thought I could detect an accent. I'm surprised you didn't order a pint of scrumpy."

"Maybe later. I need to check if you've got any Wurzels on the jukebox first."

"Doubt it," he shrugs, oblivious to my sarcasm. "That'll be ninety-five pence, mate."

I place a pound coin on the bar.

"Keep the change … sorry, I didn't catch your name."

"I'm the landlord. Kev."

That would have been my fourth choice.

"Of course. Nice to meet you, Kev."

I decide not to ask if my combine harvester will be okay in the car park and find a quiet table.

Settled, my thoughts turn to what is currently occurring on

the opposite side of town, in the bedroom of a council house on Fir Tree Road. I can still picture it: the diagonally striped wallpaper and the dark-red carpet, the self-assembly wardrobe, and the dressing table with a mirror. Jackie never was one for clutter so, unlike my bedroom at the time, there were no posters on the walls or clothes on the floor, no dirty plates or cups. I'm curious how much it has changed; no longer a teenager's bedroom but that of a young woman. It's highly unlikely I'll ever know unless I quiz Jeremy.

I finish my drink and order another one. Kev asks if I want a ticket for tomorrow's meat raffle. I decline.

Having a swift pint on your own is perfectly acceptable but sitting alone and supping a second infers you're a sad loner. I could stay at the bar, but I don't think Kev is big on conversation. On the far side of the room, a quiz machine blinks at me. I amble over.

Over the next hour, I realise just how little of the eighties I remember. I'm okay with questions on science and nature, geography and history, but sport, entertainment, and current affairs thwart my progress towards the ten-pound jackpot. I'd forgotten Everton won the old First Division title in 1987. I'd forgotten Dudley Sutton played Tinker in the television drama, Lovejoy. And, I didn't even know British Caledonian merged with British Airways.

After the fourteenth failed attempt, I call it a night. As I'm about to leave, Kev says he'll see me again. For many reasons, I hope not.

Under dark skies, I lumber back to Cline Road and arrive just after nine-thirty. There's light leaking between the lounge curtains, so I assume Sylvia is still watching television. If his last evening with Jackie is anything to go by, I doubt Jeremy is home yet.

I unlock the front door and kick my shoes off. My priority is a visit to the bathroom, but it would be rude not to inform Sylvia I'm back. I open the lounge door and poke my head in.

The scene isn't what I expected to find. Sylvia is seated next to Jeremy on the sofa; her arm on his shoulder as if consoling the young man. His head remains bowed like he can't bear to look at me.

"There you are," Sylvia says in a scornful tone.

"What's going on?"

"It's that young woman you introduced to Jeremy. I had a feeling she'd be trouble."

"Why? What's happened?"

Jeremy slowly lifts his head; his cheeks pink and eyes puffy.

"I'll tell you what happened, Sean," Sylvia continues. "Her father assaulted poor Jeremy."

"Bloody hell. Are you okay, lad?"

He slowly nods.

"I don't understand. Why would he have any cause to assault you?"

"No idea," Jeremy croaks. "He just stormed into Jackie's room and hauled me off her bed."

I perch on the arm of the sofa.

"For no reason?" I ask, my intonation clear.

"People like that don't need a reason," Sylvia interjects. "If Jeremy had told me where he was going, I'd have warned him against it. Thugs, the lot of them."

"You mean people who live on a council estate?"

"Yes, exactly."

As distasteful as I find her bigotry, now is not the time to confront it.

"Jeremy, can you tell me exactly what happened?"

He begins to speak, but the words catch in his throat and come out as a cough.

"Would you like some warm milk?" Sylvia asks.

He nods.

Our landlady departs for the kitchen, fixing me with a disapproving glare on the way out.

Jeremy rubs his neck.

"Nothing happened," he says. "We were just listening to music and chatting. I was on the edge of Jackie's bed, and she was on a chair across the room."

"And Derek just barged in?"

"Derek?"

"Her dad. She, um, she must have mentioned his name to me."

"Yes, he just barged in and grabbed me by the throat. The next thing I know, I'm pinned up against the wall, and he's yelling in my face."

"Yelling what?"

"I can't remember exactly. He was so angry and I … I was terrified."

"What was the general gist?"

"He'd had enough of … he'd had enough of wankers like me messing with his daughter."

I think back to Derek's rage in the kitchen as he presented me with the page from Jackie's diary. I only encountered a bitter pensioner that day, but in Comaland, Derek is a comparatively fit, forty-something man. Clearly, he's an overly protective forty-something man with a foul temper, but even so, I don't understand why he flew off the handle at Jeremy.

"Can you start at the beginning? What did you do while you were in Jackie's bedroom?"

"We set up her keyboard and spent probably an hour covering the basics. At that point, I mentioned the tickets and your trip on Monday, and she quickly lost interest in the lesson."

"What happened next?"

"Jackie put on a cassette, and we listened to the first side of a Gary Numan album while discussing questions she'd love to ask him. There were dozens, and she couldn't pin it down to just one. She then got up to turn the cassette over, and that's when her dad stormed in."

"And he just went straight for you?"

"Yes, and then Jackie started screaming. He then dragged me

down the stairs and shoved me out of the front door, yelling he'd kill me if I go near his daughter again."

"Where was Jackie's mum while all this was kicking off?"

"At work."

"And you came straight home afterwards?"

"Not quite. I stood outside for a minute or so, trying to get my breath back. I could hear Jackie and her father arguing inside the house. I say arguing, but Jackie was screaming and her father yelling. I didn't want to hang around in case he tried throttling me again, so I just staggered off."

"They sound dysfunctional," Sylvia spits, returning from the kitchen. "You must report that animal to the police, Jeremy."

"I don't want to," he replies, taking the cup of warm milk. "It'll only make matters worse for Jackie. She's done nothing wrong."

"You don't know that. Sounds to me like she's rather too keen on inviting young men into her bedroom."

"We're just friends. Or at least, we were."

Sylvia then turns her glare on me.

"You shouldn't let this go, Sean. If my Royston were alive, he'd head over there and have a stern word with that man. He can't go around attacking innocent young men for no good reason, and I'd keep well clear of that daughter of his if I were you. She's trouble, or troubled. Either way, Jeremy won't be going back there if I've any say in the matter."

I don't immediately answer because my mind is racing ahead; chasing answers to questions I'm only just formulating. There's clearly a lot of hostility in the Benton household, but I must take some responsibility for what happened this evening. It wouldn't have happened at all if I hadn't introduced Jackie to Jeremy.

"I might have messed up," I mumble. "I'm sorry."

"You should be."

I'm not apologising for my part in Derek's attack on Jeremy. I'm sorry because my actions — well-intentioned as they were

— might have accelerated proceedings. I've set up a chain of events in the hope of preventing Jackie's suicide on Monday, but what if tonight proves to be the final straw; one argument too many?

I might have just altered the date on Jackie's death certificate, but not in the way I intended.

27.

The conversation in the lounge petered out once Sylvia said her final piece, and we all retired to our bedrooms at half-ten.

I knew it would be impossible to sleep, and so it proved.

Twice I climbed out of bed, intending to head over to Fir Tree Road and check on Jackie. Both times, I talked myself around. I'd likely do more harm than good turning up at the Benton house in the early hours of the morning.

I must have dozed off at some point, but I woke up again at six o'clock and got up. After a quick shower, I left the house with Sylvia and Jeremy both still asleep.

Stoked with anxiety and adrenalin, I'm now marching towards the town centre. I had considered going straight to Fir Tree Road but, knowing I might have already fractured destiny, I can't risk a doorstep confrontation with Derek, or Anna or Jackie for that matter. The best I can do is wait until Our Price opens and hope Jackie arrives at work. That's assuming my worst fears haven't already been realised.

With that thought circling overhead like a vulture, I make a slight detour towards the railway station. If, God forbid, anything untoward did take place last night, there will be evidence: police cars, the local press, and cordons.

I cross the road and head towards the Farnham Road bridge, the place I suspect Jackie ended — or intends to end — her life.

With anxiety turning to nausea, I round a slight bend in the road, and the full span of the bridge comes into view.

All there is to see is traffic trundling back and forth in both lanes. The bridge hasn't been closed, and that must be a positive sign.

I approach the metal guard barrier and peer towards the station a hundred yards away. At first glance, it looks like just an ordinary morning at a suburban railway station with commuters lined up along the platforms and three stationary trains waiting to depart. A shrill whistle sounds and one of the trains slowly pulls away. In the distance, another approaches.

I cross the road and check the view in the opposite direction. I've never been so relieved to see such an uninteresting vista. All evidence suggests Jackie is probably at home, in bed, and not lying dead on a railway track.

Nausea dissipates. I turn around and make my way to the little cafe. Our Price won't be open for two hours so I've time to kill.

I spend an hour in the cafe, and then potter around the town centre, window shopping like Jackie and I used to do. The windows aren't so different from those I browsed in Exeter not too long ago, although some of the goods on display will soon fade into obscurity. Folk no longer pop in to town to buy a gold-plated cigarette lighter or a carpet sweeper.

It's a similar story for the electronic goods in Currys' window. One day, mobile phones will replace the calculators and the camcorders, the personal stereos and the digital organisers. Progress, I suppose, but I wonder if any teenager has ever unwrapped a mobile phone on Christmas day and felt the same joy I did when my parents gifted me a Sony Walkman. Unlikely.

I check my watch — only ten minutes until Our Price is due to open. With a final wistful gaze in Currys' window, I set off for The Friary Shopping Centre.

When I arrive, the floppy-haired sales assistant is just opening the shutter.

"Morning. Is Jackie in yet?"

"Yeah. She's sorting out a display over there."

He turns and nods vaguely in the direction of the counter.

I nod back and cross the shop. Jackie is fixing a poster to the wall, promoting A-ha's latest album, *Stay on These Roads*.

"Jackie."

There's a slight pause before she turns around. I'm not expecting the warmest of receptions considering how she left the Wimpy Bar.

"Hi," she says in a subdued tone.

"Sorry to drop by unannounced but I was wondering if we could have a quick chat?"

"Can it wait till my break?"

"What time?"

"Half-ten."

I don't want to loiter around for ninety minutes, but it's better than being told to piss off. I'll take it.

"Sure. I'll come back then."

She replies with a nod which isn't quite a nod, and a smile which isn't quite a smile. Judging by her body language and panda eyes, I'm not the only one suffering after a poor night's sleep.

I leave her to finish the display.

With no appetite or energy for more window shopping, I go in search of strong coffee. That search leads me to a cafe just off the High Street where I sit with a second-hand newspaper, a cup of lukewarm coffee-flavoured water, and a flurry of emotions to process. The first of those emotions is relief because Jackie is in work. As solemn-faced as she looked, her ordeal with Derek and Jeremy yesterday evening could have tipped her over the edge. Somehow, she's still clinging on.

I need to ensure Jackie keeps clinging on until Monday morning. Once she's in Austin's passenger seat, her destiny will be in my hands.

As awful as the coffee is, I endure two more cups and read the newspaper back to front. I leave the cafe with a better grasp of current affairs — useful, should I ever play that damn quiz machine again. Then again, the only reason I'd venture back to that pub would be because I'm stuck in Comaland.

That gut-churning thought follows me all the way back to the Friary.

I enter Our Price a minute before half-ten. Jackie is at the counter and spots my approach. She says something to an older guy messing with the adjacent till and then beckons me to follow her through a door marked Staff Only.

"Where are we going?" I ask.

"Staffroom. I've only got ten minutes."

We pass through a short corridor and Jackie pushes open a door on the left. The windowless room has a kitchenette area to one side and a cheap-looking table and chairs on the other. Frankly, I'd be depressed if I had to spend every lunch break in such a cheerless space.

"Tea, coffee?" Jackie asks.

"I'm good, thanks."

"Take a seat."

I grab the chair nearest the door, and Jackie flops down opposite. With no time for small talk, she gets straight to a question.

"Is Jeremy okay?"

"A bit shaken up and confused, but he'll live."

"Can you do me a favour?"

"Sure."

"If I give you my phone number, will you pass it on to him? Even if he never wants to see me again, I'd like to apologise."

"I can do that."

Jackie then leans over and grabs a handbag hanging from the back of a chair; significantly smaller than the tote bag she had in the Wimpy Bar. She then extracts a scrap of paper and a pen. I watch her scrawl down the ten digits I used so frequently, they remain permanently etched in my mind.

"Here."

I glance at the slip of paper and tuck it into my pocket, wishing I could remember names, faces, and events as well as I remember numbers.

"You know what might help calm the waters before you call Jeremy?"

"I'm guessing an explanation about what happened?"

I don't know or care if Jeremy wants to see her again, but I do need to judge Jackie's current state of mind. Knowing what happened last night might help.

"Yep."

"My step-dad. He's overly protective."

"That much I gathered, and to a degree, I can understand, but Jeremy? You only have to look at the lad to see he's harmless."

"I know, and … it's my fault. My step-dad works shifts, and I didn't think he'd be home for hours. I got it wrong."

"It's not your fault he assaulted Jeremy. There's no excuse for his behaviour."

"I know."

"It's not my place to say, but you should suggest he attends an anger management course."

"I'm not making excuses. It's just … it's complicated."

"Our landlady was all for calling the police."

Jackie swallows hard.

"She's not going to, is she?"

"No, and you've Jeremy to thank."

"And I will if he's still speaking to me."

"I'm sure he'll accept your apology, but I don't think he'll be popping around your house again."

"No, probably not. Maybe that's for the best."

"Has your step-dad acted like this before, with other male friends?"

Her gaze falls to the floor as if she's looking for something under the table.

"Jackie?"

"I'd rather not talk about him if it's all the same."

"Fair enough, but if you do ever want someone to talk to — someone a bit older and a bit wiser — I'm only a phone call away."

"Right, thanks," she replies, half-heartedly.

"I mean it, Jackie. As I said, I've got a daughter myself, and I'd hate to think of her bottling up problems. It's not healthy."

There's the slightest nod of acknowledgement before her demeanour completely changes.

"Is it true, what Jeremy said?"

"About?"

"You, interviewing Gary Numan on Monday."

"That's not quite what I said. I have an interview booked with his tour manager on Monday. There's a chance the man himself might be there, which is why I asked Jeremy to check if you had a question you'd like me to ask."

"I've got about fifty questions."

"Sadly, I can only ask one."

"Oh, God," she whines. "I don't know which one to choose. Let me think for a sec."

As Jackie mentally whittles down her options, an opportunity presents itself; to ask the questions I planned to ask her tomorrow.

"What are you doing on Monday?"

"Working."

"Could you get the day off?"

"Maybe. Why?"

"Ah, forget it," I say, dismissively. "It was just a throwaway thought."

The Jackie of old could never let such a statement rest. She'd pester and beg until I gave in.

"Don't do that, Sean. Please, what was it?"

"Honestly, Jackie. It was a silly idea."

"Tell me," she pleads, her hands clenched together.

"Alright," I sigh. "I was going to suggest you might like to come up to Manchester with me. I can't make any promises, but if Numan does show his face, I might be able to arrange for you to say hello."

"What? I'd get to meet him?"

"Yes, for a few minutes, but bear in mind it'll be an early start and a long …"

"I want to come!" she blurts. "I'd happily quit my job for good if that's what it takes."

"Well, if you're sure," I reply nonchalantly. "But I'm leaving at six in the morning. If you're not ready, I'm leaving without you."

I struggle to recall the last time I saw Jackie quite so excited; a remarkable contrast to the sad figure putting up a poster ninety minutes ago. So much so, it's as if the first part of our conversation never took place.

She gets up from her chair and throws her arms around me. It's only the briefest of hugs and lacks any real affection, but it still summons a warm glow.

"You might have just reinstated my faith in men," she says with a smile.

"Good to know. So, I take it you're definitely up for it?"

"A million per cent, yes."

"Right, in that case, I'll see you Monday at six sharp. Make sure you're ready."

"I doubt I'll sleep so I'll be ready, and I'll supply the barley sugars."

"Barley sugars?"

"You know, sweets, for the journey."

"Ah, right. Great."

She checks her watch.

"I'd better get back to the shop floor."

I get to my feet.

"And you will speak to Jeremy for me?" she adds. "I am sorry. Really sorry."

"It's your step-dad who should be apologising."

"Fat chance of that," she scoffs. "Derek does whatever Derek wants, and sod anyone else."

The opportunity to press her on that statement vanishes as Jackie ushers me out of the staff room.

Back on the shop floor, she thanks me again before a customer approaches with a question. I leave her to it and make my way towards the exit, passing the floppy-haired kid as he restocks the racks. I throw a smile his way and stride on out to the concourse.

I've covered barely twenty yards when a voice calls out.

"Hey, mister."

I carry on walking but instinctively glance in the direction of the voice. The floppy-haired kid is jogging towards me.

"Have you got a sec?" he asks, as we both slow to a standstill.

The badge on his lapel confirms his name as Russell.

"I've got all the time in the world, lad."

"Right, um, you're Jackie's uncle, aren't you?"

Did I say that? I must have.

"Not in the biological sense. More a close family friend."

"Oh, so you're friends with her dad?"

I can't quite decipher the intonation in his voice, but it sounds almost accusatory.

"I don't think I'd call Derek Benton a friend. Why do you ask?"

"It's ... I don't know if I should say anything."

"About?"

"I'm worried about Jackie."

"Why?"

He glances back towards the store and then draws a long breath.

"If I tell you something, will you promise not to tell anyone it came from me?"

"Who is *anyone*?"

"Anyone, especially not Jackie or her dad."

"He's not her real dad, you know. He's her step-dad."

My correction seems to add weight to his conviction.

"That explains it."

"Explains what, Russell?"

"You swear on your life you'll keep my name out of it?"

"You have my unconditional word. If Jackie is in any kind of trouble, I need to know."

"If you do, I'll just deny it."

"Jesus, lad. You're worrying me now. What the hell is it?"

He takes another furtive glance back towards the store.

"So, on Tuesday evening we all had to stay late for stocktaking. It took a couple of hours and then our boss said he'd buy us a beer. They lock the centre doors after seven o'clock so we had to leave through the rear door of the shop."

"Okay."

"We opened the door, and this bloke is waiting in the service yard. It turns out it was Jackie's dad … step-dad, but she didn't look pleased to see him. Anyway, we thought she'd forgotten he was picking her up, and that's why she was pissed off; she couldn't join us in the pub."

"She didn't go with you?"

"No, they wandered off to the far side of the service yard and … hard to tell but I think they were having a barney. We waited for a minute or so and then shouted across to Jackie we were off."

"And you left?"

"Yeah. They were still talking."

I wait for Russell to continue.

"We got halfway to the pub when I realised I'd left my wallet in the staff room. My boss gave me the shop keys so I could go back and fetch it. That's when I saw … I can't even think about it."

"Think about what? What did you see?"

"There's a ramp which leads up to the service yard, but they turn the lights off after six as there are no more deliveries. It was getting dark, which is why they didn't see me."

"Who?"

"Jackie and her step-dad."

"They were still there?"

"Yeah, and things were getting a bit heated. Jackie was trying to push him away, but he grabbed hold of her and …"

Russell's lips purse, as if sucking on a rancid lemon.

"And?"

"He was trying to kiss her."

"What, like on the cheek?"

"No, like a bloke would kiss a bird ... while grabbing a handful of her arse."

28.

I can scarcely find the words. I do, however, find the right facial expression: disgust.

"Is this some kind of twisted joke?"

Russell holds his hands up, palms out.

"Don't shoot the messenger, mate. I'm only telling you what I saw."

"You said it was dark. It could have been anyone trying it on with Jackie."

"Yeah, but there were a few lights at the back of the shops, and the bloke's jacket was a giveaway."

"His jacket?"

"He wore one of those luminous orange jackets, same as the blokes who work on the motorway. Bit of a coincidence Jackie's step-dad was wearing one when we found him waiting at the back door of the shop."

I'm not sure Russell is the sharpest pencil in the case, but he's young, and therefore his eyesight is probably close to perfect. Even so, his claim is ridiculous. Ridiculous and sick.

"I'm not doubting your word, lad, but you must have got the wrong end of the stick … he's as good as her dad for crying out loud."

"I know what I saw."

He points over my shoulder.

"See that woman there, with the pushchair?"

I turn around and, maybe twenty yards away, there's a youngish mother dressed head-to-toe in stonewashed denim, leaning up against a shop window.

"What about her?"

"That's how far away they were from the top of the ramp. You telling me I didn't see his hands grabbing hold of her arse or his face as he tried to kiss her?"

I can't deny it. Russell's demonstration is convincing.

"Have you spoken to Jackie about this?"

"Have I hell!" he scoffs. "She's only been working with us for a month so I don't know her that well. And even if I did, how do you ask about something like that?"

"Probably best you don't say anything."

"Fine by me, but I had to tell someone."

"Did you? Why?"

"I don't want to get in to the details, but a few years back we found out my uncle had been touching up my kid sister; the filthy fucking nonce. I don't know what's going on with Jackie and her old man but what I saw ain't right, is it?"

"No, it isn't."

"Are you gonna talk to her?"

An obvious question. The answer is anything but obvious.

"I don't know."

"Someone needs to say something. The bloke is a sicko."

"Perhaps, but there's no evidence he's done anything. And, if you want to stay out of it, there isn't even a witness."

"Yeah, but you'll help her, right?"

There's enough sincerity in Russell's eyes to suggest he cares. Whether those same eyes witnessed what he thinks he witnessed remains debatable.

"Yes, I'll help her."

Absolved of responsibility, he seeks one final assurance I won't mention his name, and then he hurries back to the store.

I haven't the faintest idea what to do next so I make for the nearest bench to think. It happens to be the same bench I waited for Jackie on Saturday — a dozen yards from where I spotted Derek entering Our Price. I remember thinking he seemed agitated but put it down to a missed lunch meeting with his step-daughter. Then, when I dropped by the Benton house with Anna's letter, Derek was in the midst of an argument with Jackie, and she stormed out. What did he say as he stood on the front path and yelled after her? I can't remember.

Then, there's last night's incident and the assault on Jeremy. Including the alleged incident Russell witnessed, that's four times in the last week Derek's behaviour has veered from agitated to aggressive to potentially deplorable.

What the bloody hell is going on?

I think back to when Jackie and I were dating. Derek wasn't exactly friendly towards me, but he never pinned me up against a wall, and I did a lot more with Jackie than show her how to play the keyboard. And, although he'd occasionally snap at Anna or swear at the television, I never witnessed any physical aggression.

What's changed?

Two people would know the answer to that question. One of them is only a stone's throw away but confronting Jackie with Russell's allegation could badly backfire. If Russell has grasped the wrong end of the stick, she'll likely be offended by such an accusation, and I can't even tell her who told me. If there's any truth in it, why on earth would she discuss such a deeply uncomfortable topic with a man she barely knows? In her shoes, I'd either deny it, clam up, or go on the defensive. In each case, it would destroy my plan for keeping Jackie out of harm's way on Monday.

There is only one person I can talk to: Anna.

I get up and stride briskly towards the exit. It's a good twenty-minute walk to Fir Tree Road; twenty minutes to plan a deeply unsavoury conversation with Jackie's mum.

Halfway there, doubts begin to creep in. Assuming Anna even invites me in, how do I broach a subject no mother would ever want to hear, or possibly believe: her husband is acting inappropriately towards his step-daughter? The only advantage I have is the letter and my warning about Jackie's mental health. If Russell's allegation is true, it would certainly explain why Jackie is so vulnerable and why suicide looms on her horizon.

I turn into Fir Tree Road and, a few minutes later, the Benton residence comes into view. There's no Morris Marina parked outside. Derek isn't home.

I cross the street and make my way up the front path

knowing the next few minutes could literally spell life or death for Jackie if I can't convince Anna her husband is a threat to her daughter.

I rap on the glass and wait.

The knot in my stomach tightens as the seconds pass. I count to ten and rap on the glass again with slightly more force. The door remains unanswered. I try a third knock and count to ten again. Still, the house remains silent.

Maybe Anna is in the back garden putting the washing out.

I pass the lounge window and turn in to the narrow passageway between the right flank of the house and the brick boundary wall; the same place I hid on my last visit. This time I continue to the end and the small rear garden. There's no washing on the line and no sign of Anna.

"Bugger."

As disheartening as the scene is, it also prompts a few happy memories of the times Jackie and I spent sunbathing in her garden. Being here now, I can almost smell the coconut-scented lotion I used to rub on her back, and envision the tiny bikini she wore.

I shake off the memories. Now I'm back in Jackie's life as a flabby, middle-aged man, such thoughts are highly inappropriate. Unlike Derek, I have boundaries.

Deflated, I plod back down the passageway, passing the side door Jackie used whenever she forgot her front door key.

I come to an abrupt halt.

"No key," I blurt.

Squatting down, I reach for a half-brick; seemingly dumped next to the edge of a drain a few feet from the door. I lift it to reveal the single brass key left here for the next time one of the Benton family forgets their front door key.

Earlier, I thought only two people might know why Derek is acting the way he is. That much remains true. I can't speak to either woman, but I know only too well one of them documented her daily thoughts in a diary. If so, is that diary inside the house?

The handbag she plucked from the staffroom chair didn't appear large enough to contain a diary so maybe it is. Then again, it never ceases to amaze me how much a woman can fit in a handbag.

It's the longest of long shots. In all likelihood, Jackie's diary is currently in her handbag, back in the Our Price staffroom. But, maybe it's not.

I pick up the key.

I'm about to slide it into the lock when I stop to consider what I'm doing. Beyond the ethics of reading Jackie's diary, I'm about to enter someone's home without their permission. What if a neighbour notices and calls the police? What if Anna or Derek return home while I'm upstairs?

I remind myself this is Comaland. Why should I be worried about the law or ethics? I have one job here: to prevent Jackie's suicide.

Whether I'm on the moral high ground or not, my heart still thumps hard in my chest as I turn the key and step into the kitchen.

Closing the door, I stand for a few moments and listen, just to be sure no one is home. Besides the thumping of my own heart, it's as good as silent.

Not knowing how much time I've got, I don't hang around in the kitchen to reminisce about all the times Jackie and I prepared our tea in here. Now is not the time to think fondly of Pot Noodles or boil-in-the-bag curry.

Creeping slowly, I climb the stairs to the landing. There's no reason to creep as no one is home, but it feels appropriate; a measure of my inexperience when it comes to illegally entering a property.

Unlike most burglars, I know the layout of this home better than I know my own — five doors: three bedrooms, a bathroom, and an airing cupboard. The door to my right is the bathroom, but the door directly ahead leads to Jackie's bedroom.

Steeling myself, I open it and step inside.

On the scale of remarkable steps, mine are no less significant than Neil Armstrong's. He might have been the first human to set foot on a celestial body but how many people have stepped into a room decades in the past? As I drink in the scene, I get a sense of how Armstrong must have felt; the same awe and astonishment. I'm standing in Jackie Benton's bedroom, and it's exactly how I remember it.

I'd love nothing more than to sit on the edge of her bed and let the memories wash over me: every kiss, every cuddle, every laugh, every song we listened to on Jackie's stereo. Then, there were those occasions when we had the house to ourselves. Both Derek and Anna worked shifts, and occasionally, those shifts would coincide. We'd spend long, lazy afternoons in bed, doing what young people do but always alert, listening for the sound of a key in the door.

Here I am again, still alert, still listening for the same sound. The stakes are much higher now.

I start with an obvious location for a diary and make straight for the bedside table and its three drawers. The top one is full of general odds and ends, the second toiletries, and the third stuffed with magazines. The next best bet is the chest of drawers by the window. Five drawers to check but they're all full of clothes apart from the top one which houses Jackie's collection of cassettes. No diary.

I check the wardrobe next.

There's a row of shoes and trainers at the bottom and, tucked away in the corner, a canvas tote bag. I grab it with my right hand while crossing the fingers of my left.

Besides the usual odds and ends you'd expect to find in a handbag, there's nothing useful to aid my investigation, let alone a diary.

This is either a good omen or a bad one, being it's the same bag Jackie kept her diary in when we had lunch. Did she transfer it to the handbag back at Our Price, or is the diary somewhere in this room?

I place the bag back in the corner of the wardrobe and continue the search.

The shelf above the hanging rail contains a couple of other bags for different purposes. They're all empty.

Closing the wardrobe door, I slowly scan the room for the less obvious places the diary might be hiding. Rather than frantically search, I stand and think. Where would Jackie hide something she doesn't want anyone to find?

The answer comes when I think back to those lazy afternoons when we had the house to ourselves.

I step over to the single divan bed and kneel at the side. There are two drawers in the base which, if memory serves, contain spare bed linen and clothes Jackie hoped might come back in to fashion one day. I pull open the left-hand drawer as far as it will go and then jiggle it left and right until it slips off the runners. Putting the drawer to one side, I can now gain access to the void between the two drawers — the same void we used to hide packets of condoms.

Laying on my stomach I squint into the dark space. There are no packets of Durex, but there are five leather-bound books stacked on top of one another.

"Gotcha!"

I reach in and grab all five. My joy is short-lived when I realise the five diaries cover the last five years, but not this year.

I place them on the bed and continue the search. I check every square inch of the room but to no avail. As I suspected, Jackie's current diary is elsewhere.

It was worth a punt, but I won't find answers in this bedroom.

As I gather up the five old diaries from the bed, I notice the top one is from last year. I pause and wrestle with a moral dilemma. There's no reason for me to nose through it, except one — morbid curiosity.

I'm here because of what I did to Jackie, but I escaped the aftermath. I listened to Anna's second-hand account, but will I ever get a better chance to understand Jackie's perspective? Do I want to? Am I supposed to? There has to be a reason I'm now looking at a diary from 1987.

I agree with myself — it's wrong to read someone's diary, but as I'm trying to save that someone's life, the means justify the end. Besides, the diary might contain the first clues to Jackie's deteriorating mental health.

My investigation switches from Derek to Jackie's life last year.

I get up and move over to the window so I can keep an eye on the street while scanning the diary pages. Standing just to the side, out of direct view, I open Jackie's 1987 diary. I've already read one page after Derek shoved it in my face and I can't say I relish reading the rest, but I do feel a sense of moral obligation. I broke Jackie, and I deserve to know how badly.

I begin in January and the days before I returned to uni after the Christmas break. The first dozen pages contain a smattering of random thoughts and an overview of the day's events — all fairly benign.

Next, I read about the day I left for Exeter. Jackie describes how she felt walking away from the platform after waving me off. I'd rather not know, and I'm about to skip to the next entry when a word leaps off the page: propose.

Jackie thought I might propose to her before heading back to uni.

"Bloody hell," I murmur.

Like kids do, we'd discussed marriage but never seriously. At the time, I couldn't imagine marrying anyone other than Jackie, but I wanted to complete my degree and forge a decent career first. Ever the pragmatist, I wanted to do it the right way at the right time.

It seems my girlfriend had other ideas, and she committed her disappointment to this page.

The weight of guilt returns. I flip forward.

Over the next fortnight of entries, her emotions ebb away,

and the content returns to the mundane. This continues throughout February and in to March when she first mentions my return for the Easter holidays. As the pages move towards the end of the month, her excitement builds.

April is the last month we will spend as boyfriend and girlfriend. Most of her entries recount what we did together, and although Jackie's words prompt some fond memories, she also mentions the times I appeared distracted or distant. She put it down to the stresses of my coursework.

I turn the page to May, and another tearful goodbye as I return to uni on the fourth day. Jackie wouldn't have known it at the time, but it would be the last time we'd kiss, the last time we'd hold one another. We were parting for the final time.

Over the next six days, her emotions peak and fade. Then, there's the one entry in Jackie Benton's diary I've already read.

Perhaps even more than the first time, her entry on this particular day stokes a plethora of emotions: regret, shame, sadness, but above all, guilt. Reading it the first time in the Benton's kitchen, long after Jackie took her own life, those emotions were laced with shock. Now, being this side of her suicide, the shock is replaced by resolve — I just cannot let fate play out the same way.

I draw a deep breath and continue turning the pages.

I've read some incredibly emotive novels in my time; works from history's most talented authors. For all the critical acclaim and awards and commercial success, not one of those novels moved me in quite the same way as Jackie's diary pages. I recognise her pain as she journeys through the rest of May and in to June. It's a similar journey to the one I endured post-Carol. I suffered without my wife; Jackie suffered without the boyfriend she expected to marry. Her raw, harrowing emotions mirror those I experienced so closely I could have penned her words myself.

I put the diary down for a moment.

There's a pressing need to get on with the next instalment of

Jackie's life but not before I wipe my eyes and swallow back the lump in my throat.

I continue.

July begins in a similar vein to June; Jackie's mood dark and dejected. As the month progresses, her language becomes angrier as the self-pity fades to resentment and bitterness. There's no hiding from the fact Jackie despised me, and by early August almost every page is littered with offensive remarks and callous statements. I can tell what she's doing — the best way not to love someone is to convince yourself you hate them.

Then, I turn over to a page which is blank bar five words: *The end, finished, no more!*

Reading between the lines, I'd guess this is the day Jackie decided to move on with her life — to stop wasting it on me and what might have been.

From that page onwards, each day describes a positive change in her life: meeting new people, going to new places, new experiences. There's talk of nightclubs and bars, warehouse parties and raves, the various new drinks she sampled and, to my bewilderment, drugs.

Without reading another word, I know this is the period in Jackie's life Anna referenced — her daughter going off the rails.

I guess it's common for folk to over-compensate when they suffer the breakup of a long-term relationship. They want to prove to the world, and maybe to themselves, how amazing their new single life is. I've seen it before with middle-aged friends who go on a crash diet, buy a wardrobe of new clothes, and start partying like they're a carefree teenager.

In Jackie's case, her diary confirms she partied with wanton abandonment.

There's almost a weekly reference to drink and weed and coke, and graphic descriptions of sexual encounters with random lads. For months, Jackie enjoyed a truly hedonistic lifestyle. Reading about it, I feel physically sick.

Her wayward behaviour continues well in to the autumn until

she loses her job with the local newspaper due to a poor attendance record and lacklustre work ethic. Her party lifestyle catching up with her, Jackie becomes one of the three million unemployed and is forced to sign-on.

At the end of October, she secures a temporary job at the Debenhams department store for the run-up to Christmas.

As November begins, most of the entries relate to her new job and how she can't wait for her first pay packet at the end of the month. In the final week of November, Jackie mentions a new drug a friend has promised to source for a party they're planning to attend at the weekend. That drug is acid. I skim through the weekday pages only to find the next five, including the weekend, are all blank.

The next entry is on Thursday 3rd December, and the entire page is written with tightly spaced lines of text from top to bottom. Whatever happened in the previous five days, it appears condensed down to one entry.

It begins with her hazy memories of the party. It's hard to accurately tell what occurred as Jackie herself seems unable to clearly recall the facts after she swallowed a single tab of acid earlier in the evening. She mentions being dropped off at home sometime after midnight; so out of it, she couldn't open the front door. The next recollection is in her bedroom, and someone helping her get undressed. She then recounts one memory so aberrant it broke through her drug-induced stupor: the moment Derek began tugging at her knickers.

I move on to the next line.

"I drifted in and out of it, like I wasn't there and then I was. I couldn't believe it was real so I didn't react. I just lay there and shut my eyes as tight as I could, thinking it was a nightmare and I'd wake up any moment. But who has a nightmare where their step-dad touches them up?!?!"

29.

If I hadn't already visited the bathroom in this house hundreds of times, I wouldn't have found it in time. On my knees in front of the toilet, I dry retch until my stomach has nothing more to give. Still in a state of disbelief, I then stumble over to the sink and splash cold water on my face.

I thought I'd already felt the sharpest needles of shock that fateful day last year. By comparison, finding my wife in the throes of passion with her best friend now feels no more shocking than a three pence rise in the price of petrol.

Derek sexually assaulted his step-daughter.

Even thinking the words induces another turn of my stomach.

Sick and stunned as I am, I'm still where I shouldn't be, and I need more information. The assault took place six months ago, so why does Jackie take her life next week?

I dry my face on a hand towel and return to Jackie's bedroom.

Gulping back the last remnants of bile, I pick up the diary and continue where I left off. I'm torn between not wanting to read another word and needing to know the full facts. I skim the pages, in the same way I might read an online news article; picking out the salient points and brushing over the insignificant details.

In the days following the assault, her diary implies Jackie survived by adopting a state of denial and by hiding herself away in her bedroom. Then, when Anna had to do a double-shift at work, Derek and Jackie were left alone in the house. That evening, Jackie had no choice but to confront what happened after Derek barged into her room.

Her writing becomes harder to decipher as she relays what took place. As best I can tell, Derek insisted they had done nothing wrong, and Jackie enjoyed the attention, as he put it.

Then came the most deluded of suggestions — if they were

careful, they could pick up where they left off, and Anna would be none the wiser. Appalled and disgusted, Jackie screamed at her step-father to get out of her bedroom, making it clear she would tell her mum what happened if he so much as looked at her again. True to form, Derek responded with a threat of his own. If Jackie said a word to her mother, he would claim it was all of her doing. He would say Jackie led him on by walking around the house in her underwear and showering with the bathroom door ajar. He would remind Anna of Jackie's recent promiscuity, and how she'd dress provocatively and come home so drunk, she didn't know what she was doing. He would then tell Anna he couldn't stand living in the same house as her lying slut of a daughter, and he would leave.

Four words are written in capital letters: WHO WOULD MUM BELIEVE?

With an impasse reached, the next two-dozen entries are dedicated to Jackie's loathing of Derek and how uncomfortable she feels even being in the same house. There's no mention of any further incidents as her focus turns back to partying with drink and drugs playing a significant role — perhaps her way of blotting out what happened.

On Christmas Eve Derek's name crops up again, but the context changes. Just as Jackie is getting ready to go out for the evening, her step-father enters her bedroom with a confession. The last paragraph describes Derek on the edge of Jackie's bed, admitting he's fallen in love with her and how he's saved enough money for them to run away together. At that point, Jackie leaves.

Still struggling, still sick to the pit of my stomach, I'm about to turn the page when I catch movement in the corner of my eye. I look up and, outside on the street, a mustard-yellow Morris Marina has just pulled up outside the house.

"Fuck!"

Every part of me wants to confront Derek Benton here and now. I'd love nothing more than to meet him at the front door and pummel the deviant fucker until my knuckles bleed. That would be a mistake. I need to think, to consider what I do with this information, so it doesn't negatively affect Jackie in any way.

The car door opens.

Snapping out of my pummelling fantasy, I fall to the floor by Jackie's bed and stash the diaries back in the void. With my hands shaking, I try to line up both the small wheels with the respective runners. On the fourth attempt, both wheels line up and the drawer slides into place.

I get back up and risk another glance out of the window. Derek is standing on the pavement, trying to light a cigarette. I have maybe five or six seconds to make my escape.

Closing Jackie's bedroom door behind me, I barrel down the stairs, along the hallway to the side door in the kitchen. As I reach for the handle, a cough breaks the silence. The cough sounded close enough Derek must be about to put his key in a lock. I open the side door and slip out, closing it silently behind me and placing the emergency key back beneath the half-brick. Knowing Derek must be inside the house, I keep low and scamper back along the passageway.

I've only one last hurdle to conquer before my escape is complete. I race across the lawn, and glance back towards the house as I hop over the fence. Fortunately, there's no twitch of the net curtains or banging on the glass. I stride away as fast as I can without breaking into a jog and don't stop until the estate is behind me.

When I do eventually stop, my breathing remains laboured. It's not because of the physical exertion but the frothing rage in my chest. I'm so angered, I can't even pin down which sick part of Derek Benton's behaviour carries the greatest responsibility. To abuse your step-daughter is incomprehensibly evil, but then to pin the blame on her, and then use it as a blackmail tool to take further advantage is staggering.

Then, there's Jackie's suicide.

All these years he's pinned her death on me, and no doubt convinced Anna I as good as pushed Jackie in front of that train. No remorse, no contrition, no conscience. Christ, he even had the temerity to wave that diary page in …

My mind clamps down on the word diary just as my arteries flush with ice.

At some point in the future, Derek will get his hands on the diary I just read. Maybe in the weeks after Jackie's suicide, he'll take it upon himself to clear out her bedroom and, after emptying the drawers, he'll lift the bed and the stack of diaries will tumble to the floor.

I can imagine him with the diary in his hands, staring open-mouthed as he recounts Jackie's version of events from 1987. He'll thank his lucky stars he found it rather than Anna. The shame would crush most people, but I know Derek will react differently. It hadn't crossed my mind until now, but it's obvious why only one page of the diary survived. He couldn't show the entire diary to Anna as it detailed his heinous behaviour, but one page happened to mention Jackie wanted to die — the one page he could use to lay the blame at my door — the page outlining Jackie's thoughts the day we broke up.

Did Jackie kill herself because she felt ashamed? Did she feel responsible for Derek's advances? Maybe guilt played a part? I don't know if I'm only seeing what I want to see, but it's no less plausible than the situation I find myself in. Wracked with guilt and shame, and with no one to turn to and no obvious way out, Jackie Benton takes her own life.

I think back to how the pension-age version of Derek acted when I called round to offer my much-belated condolences. He couldn't have made it any clearer he held me responsible for Jackie's suicide, while Anna remained quiet. Why would Jackie's step-dad carry so much anger after so many years? The answer is now obvious — it detracted from his accountability.

I now know who drove Jackie Benton to take her own life, and it wasn't me. If only that were the end of it.

A barrage of thoughts collide as I try to make sense of it all. I wish Jackie had kept her current diary with the others as I might now have some idea how events have evolved since the turn of the year. I can only make assumptions, based upon what I've learnt over the last week.

Maybe Jackie decided to implement a few New Year's resolutions. It isn't beyond the realms of possibility she took to heart some of Derek's vile threats about what he might say to Anna if the truth came out. As twisted as those threats were, maybe Jackie realised all the partying and the drugs and the promiscuity were fuel for those threats. Perhaps she turned over a new leaf to undermine Derek's counter-allegations, should their impasse ever come to a head. However, if the scene Russell witnessed in the service yard outside Our Price is anything to go by, it seems Derek hasn't given up and is still a wholly despicable pest.

It means I still have a problem.

As long as Derek is in the picture, I can't control what happens between now and Monday. What if he tries it on again and it proves to be the final straw for Jackie? I know my presence in Comaland has altered events but thinking back, there is one alteration I made which lit an unforeseen touchpaper — introducing Jackie to Jeremy. Knowing what I now know, it's obvious why Derek reacted the way he did when he found Jeremy in Jackie's bedroom. He wasn't acting like an over-protective father, more a jealous boyfriend. That change makes the next two days unpredictable, and I need to mitigate my interference.

I conclude there's only one guaranteed way to ensure Derek doesn't bring forward the date on Jackie's death certificate, and that's to deal with him directly. It just so happens I might know someone who can help with that.

For the hundredth time, I reach into my pocket so I can check a map on my phone. For the hundredth time, I'll need an alternative solution. Scanning the street, I spot a petrol station. A minute later I have the required directions, and I move at pace towards the town centre.

I know Jackie is currently at work, but in five hours she'll be heading home, potentially to a situation which might push her over the edge. My steps quickening, I try not to dwell on how such a situation might come about. I try not to think of Anna on a double shift, or Derek being drunk, or Jackie being at a vulnerable ebb. I try not to think about Derek forcing himself on his step-daughter, or the aftermath where a young woman is so distraught, she flees the house and makes her way to a railway bridge. I try not to think of how utterly violated and hopeless she might feel. I try not to think about the final seconds of Jackie Benton's life.

Every hour now counts.

I jog the last hundred yards and arrive at my destination breathless. A few seconds to gasp in enough air, I push open one of the glass doors and bound up to an enquiry desk. The desk sergeant asks the nature of my visit.

"I need to speak to one of your colleagues, urgently."

"Which colleague?"

"Leonard Crosby."

The officer scans a list taped to the counter.

"I'll see if Detective Sergeant Crosby is free. Your name, Sir?"

"Sean Brown."

"Take a seat, Mr Brown."

I sit down while the officer makes a five-second phone call. I've no reason to feel nervous as I've done nothing wrong, but I am concerned I might have misjudged the man I'm about to meet. The last time I saw him, we enjoyed a boozy afternoon together in the King's Head as near-strangers. Back then, Leonard Crosby was a widower, well into his twilight years. Here, he's in his mid-forties with a wife and teenage kids at home.

A door swings open, and a middle-aged bloke in a pale blue

shirt and tie wanders up to the enquiry desk. The officer nods in my direction, and the man in the shirt and tie steps over.

"Afternoon, Mr Brown."

I stand up, and without doubt, I know who I'm about to address. He might be three decades younger, but his voice has the same calm authority as the one I listened to that afternoon.

"Detective Sergeant Crosby," he states, offering a handshake. "You asked to see me?"

30.

I've only met Leonard Crosby once and under very different circumstances. It takes a moment to recalibrate as I remind myself what's at stake.

"Is there somewhere we can talk?" I ask. "In private."

"There is, but can you tell me what it is you'd like to discuss?"

"It's about a young woman I'm trying to protect."

"In what way?"

"Please, can we sit down and talk about this?"

His initial reaction is to look me up and down. If I were to guess, I'd say Detective Sergeant Crosby is weighing up whether I'm a likely waste of his valuable time, or not.

"Have we met before?" he asks.

"No."

"Why ask for me then, and how did you get my name?"

"A friend of a friend said you're a decent, honest bloke … someone who can be trusted."

"Did they now?"

Not a question as such, so I nod just the once.

He takes an exaggerated glance at his watch.

"I'll give you five minutes. Come this way."

In my head, I assumed we'd talk in an interview room like those I've seen in police dramas. As I follow Leonard up a flight of stairs and through a door to an open-plan office, my assumption is proven incorrect.

"The gaffer is out all day," he says over his shoulder. "We'll use his office."

His gaffer's office is merely a corner of the main office, partitioned off with glass and plasterboard walls. I'm invited in first and instructed to sit. Leonard closes the door and lowers himself down in the chair opposite. He cuts straight to the chase.

"Let's hear it then, and keep it brief."

"Um, okay. Can I start with a question?"

"Go ahead."

"Is it illegal for a step-parent to have sexual contact with one of their step-children?"

"You said this was about a young woman, not child abuse."

"It's the same person. This young woman I know; her step-father sexually assaulted her."

"How old is she?"

"Twenty-one."

"And how long has this man been married to the young woman's mother?"

"Ten or eleven years, I think."

"In which case, he'd be looking at charges of sexual assault and incest."

"Okay, so how do I officially report it? Do you need to fill in a form or something?"

"Hold your horses. It's not that simple."

"Isn't it?"

"Why is the young woman herself not here?"

"Um, because … she's too ashamed."

"That's as maybe, but if there's no complaint lodged by the victim, there's no crime."

"What? I've just told you what happened."

"No, you've told me what you heard. Were you there when this alleged offence took place?"

"Well, no."

"There you have it," he puffs, reclining in his chair. "We can't go around arresting people on a say so. We need witnesses and evidence and most importantly, a complainant."

"Even if the complainant is too scared to come forward?"

"My hands are tied. All I can suggest is you try and change her mind, or you have a word with this fella yourself and warn him off."

"Are you kidding? You want me to do your job?"

"You're a big bloke. I'm sure he'll respond to a friendly chat if you use the right language."

Incensed, I'm about to demand he summons his superior officer when reality bites. He's already told me his superior officer isn't in, and even if he was, this is 1988. This police force is decades away from adopting a sensitive, victim-first approach to sexual crimes involving women. To officers like Leonard, all crimes are equal, and no one victim deserves special treatment. He won't be donning any kid gloves no matter how dire Jackie's plight unless I change the narrative.

"Listen, I have a plan to get this girl away, but I can't do it until Monday morning. I just need to protect her until then."

"I am listening, Mr Brown, but you're not. Unless the alleged victim comes forward and reports the incident, there's not a lot I can do."

"You think it's that easy? Don't you think most abuse victims suffer in silence because they're either too ashamed or too scared to come forward? We're talking about a vulnerable young woman here. What if she were your daughter?"

Knowing his daughter is only a few years younger than Jackie, my question catches the right nerve as his brow furrows.

I try again.

"Surely you can bring him in for questioning, and hold him until Monday?"

"You've been watching too much TV, my friend. This isn't the seventies — we can't just lock people up for no good reason."

"Would you make an exception if it were a colleague's daughter or sister? I bet you'd find a way to bend the rules then."

"I don't like what you're inferring, Mr Brown."

"I'm not inferring anything. I'm trying my best to protect a vulnerable young woman, that's all."

His expression remains unreadable.

"Come on, Leonard. Help me, please."

There's a prolonged period of silence before he responds.

"No one calls me Leonard apart from my mother and the wife. Everyone else calls me Len or Lennie."

"Oh, sorry."

"Don't be. I prefer Leonard, although it's strange hearing you say it?"

"Why?"

"You're from Devon, aren't you?"

"Yes, Exeter."

"My missus is from Torquay. Hearing you say my name is like listening to the wife."

Déjà vu strikes.

"If your wife is from Torquay, you'll know most Devonians are kind-hearted folk."

"Most, but not all."

"I'm sure your wife is, and I'm trying to do the right thing here. Give me a break, eh?"

If Leonard plays poker, he's probably bloody good at it. I've no idea what's going on behind his pale-grey eyes.

After drumming his fingers on the arm of the chair for far too long, he suddenly gets to his feet. I fear I'm about to be shown the door.

"What's this fella's name?" he then asks.

"Derek Benton."

"Where does he live?"

"Fir Tree Road, in Guildford."

"You don't happen to know his date of birth?"

"Afraid not, but he's roughly your age."

"Alright. Wait here."

With no explanation where he's going, he disappears out the door.

I check my watch three times and nine minutes pass before he returns, a buff-coloured folder in his hand.

He places the folder on the desk and retakes his seat.

"You want this Derek Benton fella locked up for the weekend, correct?"

"Yes."

"And you're sure that's all it'll take to keep the girl safe?"

"One hundred per cent."

"What about her mother?"

"What about her?"

"Does she know what kind of man she married?"

"Um, you're asking me if she knows her husband sexually assaulted her daughter?"

"No, I'm asking you if she knows what kind of man she married."

"Sorry, you've lost me."

He slides the folder to the edge of the desk and then gets to his feet again.

"Is it warm in here?" he asks.

"Err, not especially."

"I'm warm. Think I might grab a glass of water from the canteen."

"Okay."

He takes a step away from the chair.

"I'll be away for at least three minutes and under no circumstances should you open that folder," he says, his eyes dropping towards the desk. "It contains details of Mr Benton's criminal convictions."

"Right. I won't."

"And definitely don't read it, okay?"

"Understood."

"Good man," he says with the subtlest of winks. "I'll see you in three minutes."

He departs.

This isn't the kind of help I hoped to receive, but I'm not about to pass up the opportunity to read Derek's file. I snatch it from the desk.

Within seconds of scanning the top page — a summary of Derek Benton's criminal convictions — I see why Leonard felt it important I read it. The list starts in 1964 with a conviction for assault. Derek was only eighteen at the time. There's a gap of almost two years before his next date with a judge and a charge of actual bodily harm. For that offence, he received community service and a fine. I could argue Derek was just a young man with unresolved anger issues if it weren't for the next two convictions.

"Bloody hell," I gasp.

In 1969, Derek was convicted of sexual assault. There are no specific details of his crime, but he received a twelve-week prison sentence so it must have been serious. However, it wasn't as serious as the crime he committed four years later. In 1973, he was found guilty of attempted rape and received a two-year sentence. He would have been released in 1975 and, only two or three years later, he married Anna.

Now Leonard's remark makes sense. Unless Derek told her, which is unlikely, there's no way Anna would have known about his convictions. Completely oblivious, Anna invited a convicted sexual predator into her home and, as it transpires, into her daughter's bed.

There's one further conviction on Derek's record, from June last year. A month after Jackie and I broke up, he received a fine and a two-year suspended sentence for affray. 1987 was not a good year in the Benton household, for many, many reasons. And, unless I can ensure Jackie's safety until Monday, 1988 is set to be much worse.

I close the folder and place it back on the desk exactly where Leonard left it.

Barely seconds later, he returns with a glass of water.

"Sorry about that," he says, retaking his seat. "Where were we?"

"Um, I was asking you if there's any way of ensuring Derek Benton is kept away from his step-daughter until Monday."

"Can't help you with that," he shrugs.

"Oh."

"But I could paint a hypothetical picture for you."

"Right."

"What day is it today?"

"Friday."

"Correct. Now, you might be interested to know that if we were to arrest someone on a Friday evening and that individual had a suspended sentence hanging over them, we can lawfully detain them until the courts reopen on Monday."

"I see."

"But only if we're able to charge them with a crime."

"What kind of crime?"

"Anything. Say, for example, they were involved in an altercation in which they landed a single punch, that would still constitute assault."

Leonard looks across the desk with a knowing smile.

"Just to be clear," I respond. "If someone with a suspended sentence is charged with assault, they'll be held until a court appearance can be arranged?"

"That is correct, providing there are witnesses to the assault. And, if that individual has a history of violent conduct, the police have all the more reason not to grant bail."

In other words, Derek Benton is just one punch away from a spell in prison.

"Oh, and while we're talking hypothetically," Leonard continues. "I wish the law could be changed. Women have the right to know what kind of man they're getting involved with, especially if that man has prior convictions for violent or sexual crimes."

Now is not the time to tell Leonard his wish will come true twenty-odd years from now, in the form of Clare's Law. I only became aware of it when one of Carol's old school friends, Stella, exercised her right to information about her fiancé. Two months before she was due to be married, Stella discovered he'd spent six years in prison for manslaughter. Unsurprisingly, the wedding never went ahead, and Carol complained incessantly about the cost of the dress she purchased especially for the day.

"That's good advice. Thank you, Leonard."

"You're welcome."

He stands up and offers me his hand.

"Just for the record," he says in a serious tone. "Reading confidential police documents is a crime. If someone were to share information from such a file, they'd have to disclose how they obtained it, and that would put them in serious hot water. Do you understand?"

"I understand completely."

"On the other hand, a smart man might use that information to his advantage without anyone ever knowing how he obtained it."

I reply with a nod and a smile.

"The thing about us folk from Devon, Leonard, is we're not just kind-hearted — we're smart too."

"Oh, I know that," he chuckles. "My wife tells me every day."

Conversation over, Leonard escorts me back to the main entrance and says goodbye.

In need of caffeine and time to think, I find the nearest cafe.

In many respects, it feels like I've been given a gun without bullets — the information gleaned from Derek's file is only useful as a threat. I could disclose what I know to Anna, but it's unlikely she'd believe a stranger, let alone act on his accusations without proof. Even if she did believe me, would it have any bearing on Jackie's fate? Would Anna try and kick her husband out? Possibly, but Derek isn't the type to go quietly, and the situation could get very messy very quickly.

It's too risky.

That only leaves me with Derek's suspended sentence to work with, but I don't fancy taking a punch because I doubt he'd stop at one punch, knowing his criminal past. A bloodied nose or a fat lip is one thing, but actual bodily harm could see me spend the next week in hospital; ironic, seeing as I'm probably in a hospital somewhere outside of Comaland.

Again, it's too risky.

That leaves me with just threat, but there's plenty to threaten him with. I know he hasn't told Anna about his criminal past and I'd bet he hasn't told his employer either. It's a good starting point. If he doesn't buckle, I'll move on to Jackie and reveal I know what he did to her. I can threaten to tell Anna and the police. He won't know I've already tried the latter, but with two sexual convictions on his file, he'll know a third would likely result in a lengthy stretch in prison.

Confident I have sufficient leverage, where can I apply it, and what do I want from it?

The first part of my challenge is determining where I confront Derek. The family home isn't an option as I don't want Anna or Jackie walking in when I'm mid-threat.

I rest my elbows on the table and switch into problem-solving mode.

Derek is a creature of limited habit, and from what I remember, he spent most of his time either at work, in the pub, or on his arse in front of the television. Having already ruled out his home, I've got an issue as I don't know where he drinks or where he works. The obvious solution is to ask Jackie, but I cannot think of a plausible explanation for wanting to know. That leaves only one other person I can ask, but I need a cover story.

Half-an-hour and two coffees later, I give in. The best idea I've come up with is full of holes, but it'll have to do.

I leave the cafe in search of a phone box. Fortunately, I don't have to walk far to find one.

Of all the aspects of modern life, being able to communicate with anyone, anywhere, at any time is probably the one we most take for granted. I'm minded of that as I tug the telephone box door open and a waft of pissy air hits me square in the face.

I retrieve a ten-pence piece from my pocket and place it in the slot. Then, I dial the number I've rung so many times but so many years ago.

It rings six times before the beeps indicate I have to push the ten-pence into the slot.

"Hello," a female voice answers.

Thank God, Anna is home. Now, I need God to do me one more favour.

"Hello. Is Derek there?"

"Sorry, he went back to work an hour ago."

It dawns on me my earlier visit to Fir Tree Road might have coincided with Derek's lunch break. In hindsight, I should have waited.

"Ah, okay. You must be his wife, Anna?"

"That's right."

Trust established. Time to start shovelling bullshit.

"I drink in Derek's local and he lent me twenty quid last week. I was hoping I could drop it off to him."

"Why don't you give it to him in the pub later? It's Friday, and he always goes to the pub straight after work."

"What time does he finish?"

"Six."

"Right, and does it take him long to get from his place of work to the pub? I've got to be somewhere at half-six, you see."

"His depot is on Station View, so it's only a couple of minutes away."

"Great, and it's not likely he'll nip into a different pub?"

"No, he always drinks in The Drummond Arms."

"Great. Thanks Anna."

With much relief, I hang up and escape the claustrophobic latrine.

I've got a few hours to kill, but I have what I need. The walk back to Cline Road will give me time to fine-tune what I'm going to say to Derek in The Drummond Arms later. I could establish where he works and confront him on the way out, being there can't be many depots on Station View, but a pub is the better option as it'll have a ready supply of Dutch courage.

I suspect I'll need it.

31.

"It won't be as nice microwaved," Sylvia protests.

"I know, but it can't be helped."

I've just explained I need to be somewhere else at dinner time. My landlady does not like her routine disrupted or the lingering odour of haddock in the kitchen, apparently.

"Very well," she huffs.

"Do you mind if I watch television for an hour?"

"Have you completed your coursework for the day?"

"Yes, Miss."

"It was a question, Sean, not an accusation. Pardon me for showing an interest."

"Sorry, Sylvia. I'm under a lot of work-related stress at the moment. I didn't mean to sound sarky."

"As long as that's all it is. We've had more than enough drama this week."

"Yes, I know."

"Very well, and don't forget your rent is due tomorrow."

"I can give it to you now if you like?"

"Tomorrow is fine."

She returns to her dinner preparations. I wander through to the lounge.

Knowing I won't be able to think of anything other than my impending meeting with Derek, I switch the television on more in hope than expectation. I should have realised at this time of the afternoon, two of the channels dedicate their airtime to kid's programmes.

I sit through a mind-numbing nature show called Caterpillar Trail, and then a full episode of Wacky Races. Personally, I preferred Dastardly and Muttley in Stop That Pigeon, but it's nice to see Penelope Pitstop again.

Crushes on cartoon characters aside, I can't ignore the growing anxiety. On one level, I wish I'd never seen Derek's file because it only highlights the kind of man I'm due to confront.

As worrying as that prospect might be, I need to ignore it and remember he's not just a thug, but the kind of sick bastard who molests his own step-daughter. I need to harness that same anger I felt while reading Jackie's diary.

Unable to stomach any more kids' television, I retire to my room and lie on the bed for forty minutes. At twenty past five, I check the address of The Drummond Arms in the Yellow Pages and inform Sylvia I'm leaving.

I make it as far as the front gate.

"Are you off out?" Jeremy asks.

"For an intelligent lad, you do ask some silly questions."

"Sorry."

"I'm only messing with you. Yes, I'm off out for an hour or two."

My plans confirmed, he loiters in my path.

"Something on your mind, Jeremy?"

"I don't suppose, um … have you spoken to Jackie today?"

I dig a hand into my pocket and hand him a slip of paper.

"What's this?"

"Jackie's phone number. I spoke to her this morning, and she's truly sorry about what happened but would prefer to tell you herself."

"Oh, okay."

"If you are going to call her, can I suggest you do it in the next few hours. Her arsehole of a step-father won't be home for a while."

"Right, thanks."

"For what it's worth, lad, that girl really does need a friend right now."

"I know."

"And don't be worrying about Derek. A little bird tells me he's about to get his comeuppance."

"Is he? How?"

"I'll fill you in another time. I need to get going."

I leave Jeremy staring at the slip of paper like it's a lost

Shakespeare sonnet.

The walk passes by in a flash as I'm so focused on what I need to do when I arrive at The Drummond Arms. I play out multiple scenarios and all the ways my plan might backfire and what I can do to keep Derek cornered. The fact I'll be confronting him in a public space is to my advantage. He'll know there will be witnesses if he does decide to get a little punchy so I'm hoping it'll be deterrent enough.

My confidence takes a knock as I lay eyes on my destination for the first time. From the outside, it appears a shithole; the kind of pub where angry men in vests spend all day drinking — and sharing less-than-savoury political views.

I push open the door.

As I suspected, the inside is as dilapidated as the outside, as is the clientele. No one pays me any attention as I sidle up to the bar and order a pint. The barman barely mumbles a word to me; my accent marking me as an outsider in a pub where outsiders of all kinds probably aren't welcome.

In my head, I'd planned to loiter at the bar and wait for Derek to arrive, but I sense inadvertent eye contact with any of the regulars could spark trouble. Instead, I sit at a table as far away from the bar as possible. I can just about see the main door.

Six o'clock rolls around, and I dare to order another pint, knowing my foe could arrive any minute. I return to the table and regret not having a newspaper or some other method of distraction — the ale not strong enough to quell my nerves.

The door opens, and two blokes in orange, Hi Vis jackets enter. They make straight for the bar and position themselves maybe fifteen feet from my table. The first is stocky and ruddy-faced, the second a few inches taller and wiry — the low-life excuse of a man I'm here to confront.

Just when I thought I couldn't detest Derek Benton one iota more, he orders two pints of Fosters and a packet of cheese and onion crisps.

I stare at the floor while taking the occasional gulp of ale. Voices whisper in my head: one telling me I should abort, the other stoking my anger. A third voice joins the fray, reminding me this is Comaland and I have a task to complete if I'm to escape.

I'm now at the stage of my plan where there is no plan, other than to wait. I want witnesses present when I approach Derek, but I don't want those witnesses to be within general earshot. I need to pick the perfect moment. That isn't while he's at the bar chatting to his workmate.

In an effort to appear inconspicuous, I glance at my watch every five minutes as if I'm waiting for someone. Occasionally, I look up and catch one of the locals staring in my direction, but I quickly look away.

Time passes and the voice telling me to abort becomes louder as my glass nears empty. Drinking more than two pints on an empty stomach wouldn't be wise as I need to keep my faculties sharp. Conversely, I can't sit here with an empty glass.

I'm still wrestling with that problem when Derek steps away from the bar. My guess is he's heading to the toilets which are through an open archway to my left. I've already decided a confrontation in the toilets is less than ideal.

He moves across my line of sight, striding purposefully towards the archway. As I suspected he turns right; a sign on the wall indicating the direction of the toilets. Then he stops, turns to face the wall, and digs a hand into his pocket.

I can't see it from my position, but I'd bet he's standing in front of either a jukebox or a cigarette vending machine. My guess is correct. He plucks a coin from his palm and raises his right hand towards the wall.

It's unlikely I'll get a better opportunity.

I stand up and empty my glass while picturing the scene in Jackie's bedroom that night. It turns my stomach but ignites my rage.

If I pause to consider what I'm about to do, I know I'll stay where I am. This is no time for self-doubt.

Ten strides and I stop just inside the archway; a no-mans-land between the corridor and the bar area.

Derek's eyes flick from the machine to me and then back again.

Despite every nerve in my body twitching, I must appear confident and in control if this is to work. I also need to suppress my West Country accent — it's impossible to imply menace with the voice of a Dartmoor dairy farmer.

"I need a word, Derek."

He barely looks away from the cigarette machine.

"And who might you be?" he mumbles.

"It doesn't matter who I am, but you need to listen very carefully to what I'm about to say."

I pause for a second.

"I know all about your criminal past. Your dirty secrets."

He thumps a button on the machine.

"Dunno what you're talking about."

"I think you do. Remember the sexual assault and the attempted rape?"

Retrieving his cigarettes, he finally turns to face me.

"You've got the wrong bloke, and I suggest you get the fuck out my way."

"We both know I haven't, and unless you want me to tell everyone in here what you've done, you will listen to me."

"Are you deaf, or just stupid?" he spits. "I said you've got the wrong bloke."

"In which case, it won't matter if I call your boss first thing on Monday morning and tell him. You can explain how you don't really have a long criminal record, and you're not really a sexual deviant."

"Do what you like," he shrugs. "They don't give a shit as long as we turn up and do as we're told."

Bugger.

"And what about Anna? Does she know?"

Instantly, his demeanour changes. Scowling like a bulldog, he steps right up to me and wags a finger in my face.

"You go spreading that crap near my wife, and I'll fucking kill you. Clear?"

"It's not crap, though, is it? You can threaten me all you like but your wife has a right to know what kind of man she married."

"I won't warn you again."

"I'm not scared of you, Derek. You've only got one way out of this, and that's to go home, pack a bag, and get in that crappy Morris Marina of yours. Then, drive as far away as it'll take you, and stay there for the rest of your miserable life. If you're not gone by nine o'clock tonight, I'll tell Anna."

"Are you fucking threatening me?"

"Yes," I reply flatly.

He edges back a few steps and scowls silently at me. I'm guessing he's conducting a risk assessment; deciding if I pose a real threat and how he might counter it.

"Tell her," he then snorts. "She won't believe you."

"Do you want to take that risk?"

"It ain't a risk. That woman loves me, needs me, so she ain't gonna listen to the likes of you."

My bluff called, I've no choice but to deploy my nuclear revelation.

"She will if I tell her what else you've been up to."

"I ain't listening to no more of your bullshit."

He takes a step to the right to walk past me.

"How would Anna feel if she knew what you did to Jackie?"

He freezes.

"What did you say?"

"I know what you did, you sick bastard. What kind of a man …"

With Derek being so close, the punch to my kidneys lacks potency. However, it catches me off guard, and I stumble a few steps back towards the bar area. It gives me a second to regroup and instigate the contingency plan I feared I might need.

"What's the matter, Derek?" I yell. "Don't you want folk knowing you're a nonce?"

I'm betting there's a long list of people the patrons of this pub detest, with nonces at the top. It is, therefore, no surprise when the majority turn their attention to our spat.

"Come on," I taunt. "Tell everyone what you've been up to, you sick bastard."

My taunting has the opposite effect of what I hoped it would achieve. Rather than retreat, Derek leaps towards me; his face twisted, fists flying.

He catches me on the jaw and the blow judders through my skull. It's swiftly followed up with another punch to the kidneys, but my layers of flab absorb the worst of the impact. Dazed, I try to move in and grab him in a bear hug. I might not be the most agile of men but, if I can grapple Derek to the floor and use my weight, I might even up the fight.

I'm within inches of grabbing on to him when he suddenly swings his right arm in a backward arc. For a fleeting moment, I'm confused where he intends to land the punch … until it lands.

"Aghhhh!"

It's the lowest of low blows, but there is no quicker way to fell an opponent than a punch to the bollocks. I collapse to the floor.

The pain does not end there.

Unable to get up, all I can do is curl in to a foetal position and cover my head as Derek lays the boot in. I give up counting after the fifth kick because I'm struggling to draw a breath and deliberating if I'd be better off unconscious or not.

Then, suddenly, the kicking stops.

I dare to look up and catch sight of a man in an orange jacket, presumably Derek, hurrying away. I watch him all the way; long, slow, pain-filled seconds until he disappears out the door. Another man, the barman I think, then squats down next to me.

"You alright, mate?"

"No," I rasp. "Call the police."

"Won't do you much good now."

"Just call them."

The barman nods to a colleague and then helps me to sit up. A glass of brandy is thrust in my hand.

"Drink that. It'll help with the shock."

The shock isn't my primary concern.

I sip at the brandy and adjust my position to ascertain how much damage I've suffered. I don't think there's anything broken, but my torso is likely patterned with some ugly bruises. Christ knows where my testicles are.

I ask the barman to help me up.

There's a lot of wincing and hissing, but eventually, I manage to stand unaided.

"What was all that about?" the barman asks.

"A difference of opinion."

"Why did you call Derek a nonce?"

"That's between him and me. Where did he go?"

"No idea but probably to another boozer. He's usually out for a session on a Friday."

I don't care where he's gone as long as he hasn't gone home to confront Jackie.

The door opens, and two policemen enter. Every head looks away as the barman waves them over.

"We've had reports of an assault," the older of the two says.

"Yes," I gasp. "I'm the victim."

The older policeman instructs me to take a seat, and then he asks a series of questions. I notice the bar emptying while the officer's backs are turned. By the time I'm asked if I know the assailant's name, the room is near deserted.

"You say this Derek Benton is likely at another pub?"

"That's what the barman reckons."

"Can you give me a description?"

I do as I'm asked. The younger officer then steps away and mumbles into his radio.

"You should go to A&E, Sir."

"I'm okay."

"You might have internal injuries. We'll run you up there."

"Honestly, I'm fine, or I will be once I know you've arrested that animal."

"It's in hand, and I'm afraid I can't take no for an answer. It won't take long for a once-over."

Reluctantly, I concede it might be sensible.

"Good man. We'll get you looked at, and then I'll take a full statement."

"What about Benton?"

"If he's in any of the pubs in town, we'll find him."

"Can you send someone to his address? I'm worried he might assault his wife or step-daughter."

"What makes you think he'll do that?"

"Please, just send a car. I'll explain on the way to A&E."

"I'll see if there's a free unit who can take a drive past, but I can't make any promises it'll be straight away."

It'll have to do. The policeman then leads me to his car.

After an uncomfortable journey through the streets of Guildford, the officers escort me to the front of the A&E queue and share my story with a nurse. I'm then prodded, poked, questioned, and x-rayed before I'm given pain-killers and warned not to do anything too strenuous for a week. The nurse then scoots off to find the policemen, leaving me on a bed behind a curtain.

Ten minutes pass, then fifteen, and twenty. Just as I think they've forgotten about me, the older policeman pokes his head around the curtain.

"Nothing broken then?" he quips.

"Only the prospect of parenthood."

"The nurse tells me you're ready to give a statement."

"I am."

He sits down beside the bed and whips out a notepad.

"Oh, we found your alleged assailant," he remarks casually. "Although he wasn't in the mood to come quietly."

I breathe a sigh of relief.

"That bloke has issues. Serious issues."

"He's cooling off in a cell at the moment."

"Good, and I want him to stay there."

"I presume you'd like to press charges?"

"Too bloody right."

"You'd better tell me what happened then."

I don't say it, but I'm hoping what just happened is I've saved a young woman's life.

32.

Back when I was gainfully employed, one of my colleagues would regularly send emails containing inspirational quotes; a banal statement set over a photo of a sunset or mountain range. I'd usually delete those emails, unread, but as I sit here on the edge of a hospital bed, one of those quotes comes to mind: sometimes even the wrong train takes us in the right direction.

I certainly ended up on the wrong train as this isn't how I envisaged my meeting with Derek would turn out. I knew there was a chance he'd resort to violence, but I thought he'd see sense, knowing his deviant behaviour had finally caught up with him. I also figured I had nothing to lose.

What I didn't figure on was the pain.

Like everything else here in Comaland, pain is acutely real. Still, Derek is now locked up, and he won't be getting out before Monday, if at all. I'll take that as a victory.

I relay most of what happened to the officer, excluding the part where I provoked Derek. He might be a disgusting human being, but I doubt he's stupid enough to tell the police what triggered our row. To them, it'll appear an unprovoked attack; an open and shut case.

Statement delivered, the policeman asks if I want a lift home. I decline the offer as I don't think Sylvia will be too impressed if I turn up at her door in a police car, not after what happened last night with Jeremy. I'll also have to come up with an excuse why I'm hobbling around the house like I've soiled my pants.

The painkillers playing their part, I stagger down to the main reception and use a payphone to call a cab.

It's almost nine o'clock by the time I clamber out of the cab in Cline Road. I pay the driver and go over my cover story one final time.

The hallway is in darkness. I kick my shoes off, hoping Sylvia is already in bed. That hope is dashed when the lounge door opens.

"Not quite an hour or two," she says, tapping her watch.

"I had an accident. I've been to the hospital."

Her agitated frown instantly dissolves.

"Oh, dear me. What happened? Are you okay?"

"I slipped on a step and tumbled to the bottom of the stairs."

"And the hospital sent you home?"

"Yes, I've just got a few bruises."

"That might be so, but they should have kept you in for observation."

With limited time to concoct a story, I might have forgotten Sylvia used to be a nurse.

"Honestly, I'm okay. They gave me some painkillers."

"Would you like me to take a look at your injuries?"

"That's kind of you, but it's nothing a decent meal and a long soak in the bath won't fix."

I should have guessed: once a nurse, always a nurse. My landlady guides me through to the dining room and waits on me hand and foot. The moment I finish the last mouthful of haddock, Sylvia bustles upstairs to run a bath.

The fussing doesn't end at the bathroom door.

"Do you need a hand getting undressed?"

"Err, I'm good, thank you."

"Are you sure? It's nothing I haven't seen a thousand times before."

"I know, and I'm sure my injuries are nothing compared to what you've seen, but …"

"I'm not talking about injuries, Sean. I'm talking about bottoms and todgers."

"Oh."

"Well? Do you need a hand?"

"I'll call down if I have any difficulty."

"Very well. I've left a towel by the side of the bath, and I added some salts to help with the bruising."

"Thank you."

She nods and trots back down the stairs.

I'm about to close the door and begin the painful but private process of getting undressed when I realise I don't have any clean clothes to put on post-bath. I cross the landing to my room and grab a pair of jeans and a sweater. On my way back to the bathroom, Jeremy opens his bedroom door.

"I thought I heard your voice," he says. "That was a long hour or two."

"Don't you start," I groan.

"Did you have a good evening?"

"Eventful."

"Me too," he replies enthusiastically. "Eventful, but positive."

"Why? What have you been up to?"

He beckons me into his room. I just want to get into the bath, but his nervous excitement wins the argument.

"I'd rather Sylvia doesn't overhear," he says by way of explanation as he closes the door.

"Hears what?"

"Well, after dinner, I went for a walk, or that's what I told Sylvia. I actually went out to find a phone box.

"Judging by your grin, I'm guessing you called Jackie, and the conversation went well?"

"It did. She invited me to a gig on Sunday evening."

"That's great. Who are you going to see?"

"Some local band I've never heard of. Mind you; I haven't heard of many bands, local or otherwise."

"I'm sure you'll have a great time."

There's a moment of silence, and I get the impression Jeremy is expecting a question. I don't ask it because I think I know what it might relate to.

"That's not the only news," he continues.

"No?"

"While we were on the phone, someone knocked on the front door and Jackie could hear some kind of tizz in the hallway. She apologised and said she'd have to call me back. Anyway, I gave her the phone box number and hung around for nearly forty minutes."

"Okay."

"Just as I was about to give up, she called back."

"My bath is getting cold. Spit it out, lad."

"Sorry. The police arrested her step-father for assault. According to Jackie, he's already under a suspended sentence so it looks like he'll be heading to prison."

"And how did Jackie react?"

"With a great deal of delight. I don't think they have the best of relationships and after he assaulted me last night, she said it was no less than he deserves."

"So, your keyboard lessons can resume?"

"Indeed, they can."

"I'm pleased for you. And now I'm going for a soak."

"Yes, of course. I thought you'd like to know."

I pat him on the shoulder, and we share a smile.

"It is good news."

Just as I reach for the door handle, Jeremy poses another question.

"Are we still going into town tomorrow? Remember, you said you'd help me select a few albums."

I'd clean forgotten about my promise of a trip to a record store.

"It doesn't matter," he then says, misinterpreting my pained expression.

"No, no. We'll go."

"Are you sure?"

"I've nothing else in my diary and to be honest, I could do with a dose of normality."

"Can I ask one other favour?"

"Shoot."

"I'd like to buy some new clothes to wear on Sunday. If we could pop into a few shops, I'd appreciate your advice on what to buy."

"Seriously? You'd like my fashion advice?"

"If you don't mind. I would ask Jackie, but she's at work."

We both know I'm the last person who should be offering fashion advice, but I don't think that matters — he just wants a bit of moral support from a friend.

"I don't mind at all."

I say goodnight and pad back to the bathroom.

Slowly, gingerly, I undress, and ease myself into the tub; letting the warm water absorb all my aches, pains, and the stress of the last week.

And, what a bloody week.

There are still scores of questions to be answered, but I think I'm close to completing my quest. Jackie is clearly in a positive frame of mind, and with Derek locked up for the foreseeable, I cannot see any reason she'd experience suicidal thoughts, let alone act upon them. In fact, inviting Jeremy out on Sunday evening implies such thoughts couldn't be further from Jackie's mind.

With that, I do wonder if I should bother dragging her up to Manchester on Monday. It's highly likely Derek will spend his day being transferred from the police station to the court and then on to prison, so it'll be impossible for him to get near her. However, Monday should be, God willing, my final day in Comaland. For purely selfish reasons, I can't think of a nicer way to spend it than with Jackie, and it's better to be safe than sorry, I guess.

My mind turns to how that day might end.

Will there be a Cinderella moment around midnight? Will the fantasy simply evaporate like a pumpkin coach and magical ball gown? Will I go to bed on Monday night and wake up back in reality on Tuesday, exonerated?

I guess I'll find out in roughly seventy-four hours. I've done all I can, changed what needed to be changed, and gone way, way beyond the call of duty to protect the girl I once loved. There is nothing more I can do.

Comforted, I close my eyes and drift away.

33.

My first interaction of the day involves the handing over of five ten-pound notes.

"How are you feeling today?" Sylvia asks, tucking the notes into her handbag.

"Stiff, and a bit sore."

"Take two of these," she orders, passing me a blister pack of paracetamol.

"Thank you."

"Go and sit down in the dining room, and I'll bring you through a nice cup of tea."

"That's very kind of you, Sylvia, but please don't feel …"

"Tut, tut," she interrupts. "Do as you're told. It's for your own good."

I comply, and the promised tea is duly delivered.

"I'll make a start on breakfast once Jeremy has finished in the bathroom."

"Great."

"Full-English?"

"Yes, please."

"If you need anything else, just holler. I'll be in the kitchen."

In her usual punctilious manner, she checks my tea is to the required standard and hurries off.

I can say with absolute certainty I've never met anyone quite like Sylvia Butterworth. That conclusion raises a question: if Comaland is a figment of my imagination, how did I conjure up such a uniquely complex character?

Despite her occasional bouts of bigotry, Sylvia possesses several traits I quite admire. Some of those traits, I suspect, are age-related. I wouldn't dare ask her age, but she's certainly old enough not to care about what people think. I guess after a lifetime of lip-biting and polite tact, there comes a point where you just say whatever you genuinely believe and to hell with the consequences. We spend a lifetime trying to please everyone from our partners to our colleagues to our family, so it must be liberating to do whatever you feel and say whatever you like.

Perhaps if I'd adopted such a philosophy in my younger days, I wouldn't be here now; wherever here and now is. The trouble is, we all get swept along by life's tides, and in most cases, we just follow the current rather than kick against it — I certainly did.

From the day I first met Carol, I lost control. I let her dictate the direction of our relationship from where we would live to how we would live, who we'd accept as friends and where we'd holiday. My biggest regret, however, is letting her dictate our parental status.

There's no way Sylvia would have rolled over the way I did and yet, despite her forceful nature, she remained happily married for forty-six years. I'd love to have met Royston; the man who tamed my austere landlady. I'd bet they had more than a few disagreements over the years, but they clearly had the one thing every marriage needs to survive, no matter which way the tide drifts: mutual respect.

I'm sure Carol loved me, once, but I don't think she ever respected me.

"Morning, Sean."

"Morning."

Jeremy begins laying out the cutlery.

"What time do you want to head in to town?" I ask.

"I really don't mind."

"We'll go after breakfast, before the shops get too busy, eh?"

"Perfect."

I then explain the walk might be a slow one because of my injuries. I decide not to tell him the truth about how I sustained them.

"Are you sure you're up to it?"

"I've taken painkillers. I'll be fine."

Jeremy doesn't push the issue, presumably in case I change my mind.

An hour later, both fed and watered, we leave the house and plod slowly towards town. It's during our walk we discuss another item on Jeremy's shopping list.

"Tell me to mind my own business, but can you afford a half-decent hi-fi? That little cassette player of yours isn't ideal for listening to music."

"The benefit of having no social life is I don't spend much. I've plenty in my savings account."

"Good lad. It's wise to put a few quid away for a rainy day."

"And I'm hoping to buy a flat at some point. I'm quite content living with Sylvia but … well, I'd like my own space."

"I know what you mean. When are you hoping to buy?"

"Perhaps next year."

"Don't buy a place next year."

"Why not?"

Carol and I couldn't afford to buy our own home in 1989, but a year later we had our pick of properties after the market crashed.

"A friend of mine is a property analyst, and he's certain prices are set to peak within the next eighteen months before they tumble. The money you'll spend on a one-bedroom flat next year will buy you a semi-detached house the following year."

"Oh my. Do you think his forecast is accurate?"

"Take it from me, Jeremy, he has an uncanny knack of predicting the future. If you want to move out next year, rent somewhere. Do not buy."

"Thank you. I appreciate the advice."

"You're welcome. So, after we've been to the record store and sorted out your wardrobe, shall we pop into Currys and see if they've got a half-decent hi-fi you can afford?"

"I'd like that, if it's not too much trouble."

Despite my various aches and a tenuous grip on reality, I conclude it's no trouble. If anything, I like the idea of shopping with Jeremy — Carol had no great interest in music or hi-fis, or my advice on anything.

Having decided not to bother Jackie at work, we arrive at an independent record store, and the ever-organised Jeremy consults the list he compiled as we listened to the charts.

"Should I buy albums by all these artists?" he asks, showing me the list.

"Before you get on to which albums, you need to decide on the format."

"Format?"

"Yes. If you intend to listen on that cassette player of yours, there's no choice to make. However, if you are going to buy a hi-fi, that opens your options to vinyl, compact disc, or cassette."

"Which would you recommend?"

"Vinyl has a richer sound if you're prepared to pay for top-end audio equipment, but it's a pain having to turn the disc continually and they're a bugger to keep in tip-top condition. Cassettes are convenient, but you'll need to keep a pencil handy at all times."

"Um, why?"

"The tape has a habit of spooling from the cassette. A pencil is just the right shape to turn the reel and wind it back in."

"I see."

"And the third option, which I'd recommend, is compact disc. You might have to pay a bit more for a hi-fi, but CDs last forever and the sound quality is decent. Oh, and you don't have to turn a CD over. Trust me, that's a revelation if you've only ever listened to vinyl or cassettes."

"Compact discs it is then."

"Good choice. Now, let me see that list."

He hands it over.

"There's three I would definitely buy."

We scour the racks and grab *Actually* by Pet Shop Boys, *Tango in The Night* by Fleetwood Mac, and the New Order album, *Brotherhood*. We then stumble upon a rack which is of great interest to me.

"What are compilation albums?" Jeremy asks.

"Have you ever had a 10p mix-up?"

"A what?"

"You know, a little paper bag of random sweets from the newsagents. Cola bottles, Blackjacks, Fruit Salads, and the like?"

"No, never."

"Christ, that's tragic. Anyway, a compilation album is like a 10p mix-up. Each album has a selection of tracks by different artists. They're a great way to discover new artists, new genres."

I turn my attention back to the rack which contains every *Now* album released to date, all shiny and new. I grab a copy of *Now 11* on CD and hand it to Jeremy.

"I collect these. I've got all … all eleven of them."

"Should I buy them all?"

"Maybe just get the latest two. You can always come back and buy the rest another time, and start your own collection. Maybe one day it might be worth a few quid."

We take the five albums to the counter and pay. I leave the record store with a chuffed young man at my side.

"Right, next stop a clothes store."

"Where would you suggest?"

"Not Marks & Spencer, unless you want to dress like me."

"What's wrong with the way you dress?"

"Nothing, but you're twenty-two. I'm not. Let's try Top Man or Fosters."

We pass a branch of Fosters Menswear first and wander in. Two young sales assistants are chatting at the counter, and I suggest it might be worth seeking their advice as they'll have a better idea of what's in fashion. With slight reluctance, Jeremy agrees, and we approach the counter.

"Morning," I chirp. "My young friend here requires a wardrobe update, and I was hoping you might be able to help him choose a few suitable outfits."

One of the young women — Cindy, according to her badge — responds positively to my challenge. Before he can argue, she whisks Jeremy away with a promise he's in good hands. I retire to a chair in the footwear section and wait.

Over the next hour, my housemate is dragged before me numerous times so Cindy can gauge my opinion on each ensemble. I have little to contribute other than a few positive words.

When Jeremy's ordeal is finally over, I join him at the counter where his bank account takes another significant hit. As we're about to leave, Cindy offers a final recommendation.

"While you're in town, you should get yourself some hair gel."

"Err, okay," Jeremy replies, unsure why.

"You've got great hair, but it just needs proper styling. If you speak to Mandy in Superdrug, she'll give you some advice — she's a mate of mine, and worked in a hair salon for a while."

Another purchase to add to our list, we leave; Jeremy weighed down with carrier bags but still smiling.

We head to Superdrug next and locate Mandy. She shares her friend's enthusiasm and, after selecting a suitable hair gel and styling brush, she explains how Jeremy can swap his Young Conservative hairstyle for a contemporary look.

It's almost lunchtime by the time we visit our last port of call.

Eight days ago, I stepped through the door of Currys, believing it to be a retro homage to a company anniversary. Today, I know it's not. That's not to say I'm any the wiser what's going on but, like the break-up of a relationship, you've no choice but to embrace acceptance at some point. Today, I'm going to help a shy young man purchase a hi-fi; the like I haven't seen on a store shelf in thirty-odd years.

Just a typical day in Comaland.

I lead Jeremy over to the hi-fi section and ask how much he wants to spend.

"I've no idea."

Together, we stand back from the display and scan the price

tickets. They start at less than a hundred and go all the way up to five hundred.

"How are you, Sir?" a sales assistant asks, stepping up beside me.

I turn to a familiar face.

"Err, hello again, Dean."

"Did you find it?"

"Find what?"

"That coffee shop, Starbucks."

From the corner of my eye, I catch Jeremy's puzzled expression.

"I confused Guildford with another town. My mistake."

"Right."

"Moving swiftly on, my friend is in the market for a hi-fi."

"Genuinely?"

"Genuinely."

We begin a thirty minutes three-way conversation as Dean picks out the hi-fis which, I suspect, offer the best commission levels. I then bat away his attempts to foist an Amstrad monstrosity on Jeremy, and we eventually settle on a compact Aiwa system.

After another trip to another till, I confirm our shopping expedition is over.

"I think so," Jeremy replies.

"If we didn't have this great hulking box to carry, I'd suggest we grab a pint, but I think a cab home might be a sensible move."

I ask Dean to order us a cab and a minute later, one pulls up outside the door.

We return to an empty house. Sylvia mentioned helping at the church jumble sale so we probably won't see her until later in the afternoon. Our landlady's absence offers us the opportunity to set-up and test the hi-fi. We drag everything up to Jeremy's room and, while he unpacks the bags, I make a start on the unboxing.

Despite the age of the system, I still get that buzz of unpacking a new piece of tech. Jeremy appears equally excited as I ask him to choose which album he'd like to christen his new hi-fi with. He settles on *Now 10*.

"I'll let you do the honours," I say, handing him the CD.

Sitting on the edge of the bed, I watch on as Jeremy diligently follows the instructions in the user manual. I could tell him how simple it is, but that would rob him of the experience. Playing your first album on your own hi-fi isn't a million miles away from losing your virginity; a moment to savour, to treasure, although no one wants to pop their cherry with a fat middle-aged bloke in the room.

Jeremy carefully places the CD in the tray and presses a button. The drawer slides shut.

He turns to me, as if seeking permission, and smiles.

"Let's hear it then, lad."

He obliges.

If there is any track which sums up how wonderfully eclectic the early *Now* albums are, it's the first track on *Now 10*. Jeremy's face lights up as chimes peel from the speakers, followed by the dramatic orchestral opening to *Barcelona*. Of course, Freddie Mercury & Montserrat Caballé should take credit for the young man's wonderment; I'm just happy to have played a tiny part in it.

As we listen to the next half-dozen tracks, my mind floats away and lands at a conclusion. A few weeks back, if anyone had suggested I'd soon be spending a Saturday morning shopping with a young lad and an afternoon listening to music in his bedroom, I'd have labelled them crazy.

I'm now the crazy one.

Maybe.

Possibly.

34.

I wake up with mixed feelings. On one level, I'm hoping today will be a day of lasts because tomorrow, I'll be out of the house long before Jeremy and Sylvia are awake, and I won't be back in Guildford until the date on Jackie's death certificate has elapsed. That achieved, surely I'll be freed from Comaland. No more homemade meals, no more chats with Jeremy, no more awful television, no more 1988, period.

I get up and set about my ablutions, in readiness for my last breakfast in an unassuming house in Cline Road.

Sylvia and Jeremy are already up, and well in to their routine: Jeremy setting the table, and Sylvia busy at the hob.

"How are you feeling today?" she calls out, as I pop my head around the kitchen door.

Before I showered, I tried to inspect the results of Derek's handiwork in the bathroom mirror. Not easy when the worst of the bruising is across my shoulders and upper back.

"The pain is easing, but my back looks like the sky during a thunderstorm."

"Bruises fade within a week or two. Just be grateful you didn't suffer any broken bones."

"Trust me, Sylvia. I'm more than grateful."

"Good, now go and sit yourself down. I'm nearly ready to serve."

Over breakfast, I learn I'll have the house to myself this morning. Sylvia is off to church and Jeremy is heading to an address across town. Browsing the classified ads in the local newspaper yesterday evening, he spotted a pair of headphones for sale. With Sylvia not keen on his choice of music, or the volume he prefers to play it, they both agreed a pair of second-hand headphones would be a wise investment.

Once we've eaten, I offer to wash up. As usual, Sylvia declines the offer, but I dig my heels in.

"You deserve a day of rest."

"Nonsense."

"I insist."

"I don't care. This is my home, and I'll decide who does the washing up."

"That's not strictly true, is it, Sylvia?"

"Pardon?"

"Since the day I first arrived here, you've made me feel at home. So, seeing as this is *our* home, I should get a say in who does the washing up, don't you think?"

Her defiance melts away and, almost symbolically, she passes me the bottle of Fairy Liquid.

"I could do with getting to church a little earlier, I suppose."

"I'll do a good job. Promise."

"You'd better."

Despite her best efforts not to let it show, I catch the hint of a smile as she walks away.

By the time I've washed up, dried up, and put everything away, Jeremy and Sylvia are ready to leave. The church is on the way to Jeremy's destination, so they depart together, leaving me alone with my own thoughts and little to do. I don't have anything planned for the day, besides taking Austin out for a spin this afternoon to ensure he's in peak condition for tomorrow, and I feel at a bit of a loss.

I decide a phone call might be in order. I revisit the telephone seat in the hall and dial Jackie's phone number. Praying Anna doesn't answer, I wait patiently for someone to pick up. On the eighth ring, a female voice answers.

"Jackie?"

"Uh, hello?"

"It's Sean."

"Oh, right. Hi."

"Did I wake you?"

"Kind of, but I should have been up an hour ago, so it's all good. What's up?"

"I was just calling to make sure you're still up for

309

tomorrow?"

"Thank God for that," she puffs. "I thought you were ringing to cancel."

"No, not at all. We're still on then?"

"Absolutely. I'm so looking forward to it."

Despite having only just woken up, there's palpable excitement in her voice.

"Okay, just checking. I'll see you at six o'clock in the morning, then."

"I'll be ready and waiting."

I should say goodbye, but I want to be certain she's in a positive frame of mind.

"Please don't be angry with him, but Jeremy told me what happened with your step-dad."

"That bastard is already the talk of the estate, so it's no great secret."

"Are you okay?"

"Did Jeremy tell you he'll likely be sent to prison?"

"He did."

"When that happens, I'll throw a massive party. For now, I'm just happy he's not here."

"Have the police told your mum what happened?"

"Kind of. He assaulted some guy in the pub."

"Did they mention who he assaulted?"

"I think she asked, but they're not allowed to disclose the victim's name, apparently."

"Good to know."

"Is it. Why?"

"Um, I mean, it's good for the poor bloke he beat up. I'm sure he wouldn't want any reprisals."

"Well, whoever he is, I hope he's okay. Fingers crossed, they'll lock Derek up for a long time."

"Having had a taste of your step-father's temper, I think Jeremy would agree."

"Did he mention we're off out tonight?"

"He did, and he's very excited."

"Yeah, me too. It'll be a good night."

She sounds entirely sincere.

"Don't you stay out too late, eh. I don't want to be waiting outside your house because you've overslept."

"I'll be in bed by eleven, I promise, and I'm not drinking."

"I trust you. Anyway, I'll let you get on. See you bright and early tomorrow, right?"

"Yep, you will."

I put the phone down, convinced Jackie is as far from feeling suicidal as it's possible to be.

All being well, she'll wake up on Tuesday morning and continue her life, oblivious to what should have been. Maybe one day she'll get married, have kids, and live out her days happy and contented. Then again, perhaps this will all turn out to be utterly meaningless, and I'll return to a reality where Jackie Benton jumped in front of a train one Monday in May 1988. Who knows?

All I know is that if I think too deeply about the future, I'll end up with a ton of unanswerable questions and a migraine.

I get up from the telephone seat and wander into the lounge.

It's rare I ever get a day to do absolutely nothing and being I have absolutely nothing to do, I might as well take advantage. I make a cup of tea and slump down in front of the television. The pickings are slim: Open University or religious programmes. I switch it off.

Sylvia's radio provides a better source of entertainment. I sit in the kitchen listening to Dave Lee Travis until my landlady returns from church.

"Good service?" I ask, as she removes her coat.

"Same as every Sunday."

"Okay."

There the conversation ends.

"Can I help prepare lunch?"

"It's all in hand."

"I'm sure it is, but I'm bored witless."

She puts me on potato peeling duties. It doesn't help the boredom, and neither does changing the bed linen; the second task I'm asked to perform.

Jeremy eventually returns, carrying a box under his arm. He proudly places it on the dining room table.

"You bought them then?"

"I did. What do you think?"

I open the battered box and withdraw a pair of clunky Pioneer headphones, complete with coiled lead.

"They're sturdy. I'll give you that."

"I know they're a bit on the large side, but I didn't want to wait until next weekend. They'll do for now."

"If only shops were open on Sundays, eh."

"That'll never happen," Sylvia interjects, placing a jug of water on the table. "It's a day of rest, and always will be."

I don't dare correct her.

We enjoy another of Sylvia's spectacular roast dinners, followed by apple crumble and custard. There's no resistance when I offer to help with the washing up.

"Is it okay to take Austin out for a quick spin this afternoon?" I ask. "I want to make sure he's running well, for tomorrow."

"I don't see why not. Where are you going?"

"I've nowhere in mind."

"Can I come with you?"

I can hardly say no, so I don't.

An hour later, I'm driving along Cline Road with Sylvia by my side, acting as navigator.

With a blue sky above us and near-empty roads, I receive directions towards the country lanes which wind through the Surrey Hills. Austin isn't the quietest of cars so there's a distinct lack of conversation. It doesn't seem to spoil Sylvia's enjoyment of the ride, judging by her quiet smile. We pootle around for over an hour until my navigator suggests we head home.

As I pull onto the driveway, I wait for Sylvia to get out before returning Austin to the garage. Rather than reach for the door handle, she places her right hand on my forearm. Thrown by her uncharacteristic tactility, I look across. There's still a smile on her face, but her eyes are now glistening, almost tearful.

"Thank you for that, Sean."

"Err, thank you for what?"

"For helping me relive some happy memories."

Unsure what memories, I reply with a look of puzzlement.

"That route we took," Sylvia adds. "It's the same route Royston and I used to take every Sunday after lunch."

She squeezes my arm and gets out of the car without another word.

The rest of the afternoon passes by in a contented haze. After testing out his new headphones, Jeremy joins us in the lounge. Together, the three of us watch a black and white movie, Hobson's Choice, starring John Mills. We then enjoy a few rounds of cheese and chutney sandwiches, followed by homemade rock cakes.

After tea, Jeremy dashes upstairs to get ready for his first-ever gig, and Sylvia settles down to watch Praise Be! on BBC One. I read the paper for twenty minutes and decide my aching muscles could do with another soak in the tub.

I reach the top of the stairs just as Jeremy is exiting his bedroom, having undergone a Clark Kent style transformation.

He pauses outside the door as if waiting for my reaction.

"That's better, lad. You look your age."

And he does.

I know he's been practising with the hair gel as he visited the bathroom four times yesterday evening. Either he had a bad case of the shits, or he was washing the gel out after another aborted styling attempt. His practice has paid off.

"I look okay?" he asks, self-consciously.

His new clothes are not so dissimilar from those I wore back in the day: a chevron-patterned sweatshirt, stonewashed jeans, and a faux-leather jacket.

"Spot on. You'll be fighting the girls off."

His cheeks flush pink, and he looks down at his new trainers.

"What time are you meeting Jackie?"

"About forty minutes from now. I'm running ahead of schedule."

"No harm in being keen. This is your first gig, isn't it?"

"It is."

"No one ever forgets their first gig so make the most of every minute. Even if you hate the band, you'll always look back and remember tonight, so try to enjoy it."

"I will."

"Oh, and can I ask a favour?"

"Of course."

"Do you mind if I give your headphones a try after I've had a bath? There's nothing on television tonight."

"You don't have to ask. Listen any time you like."

"Thank you."

He glances at his watch.

"Go on," I chuckle. "Get going."

I pat him on the back as he makes for the stairs. Then, he pauses at the top step and looks back at me. I can tell he wants to say something but can't find the right words. I put him out of his misery with a knowing smile. The smile he sends back says everything, and he scampers down the stairs.

I'll never know what it feels like to wave off a son on prom night. I'll never share the buzz of excitement as he celebrates a milestone in his young life. This is as close as I'll ever get and while I accept I've had just a fleeting influence on Jeremy's life, I'd like to think it's been a positive influence. In an ironic twist, I might have woken up in 1988 convinced I had to help one youngster but the rules, if there are any, never said I couldn't help two.

Although I'll disappear from Jeremy's life tomorrow, God-

314

willing, perhaps it would be fitting to one day finish that Isaac Asimov novel I picked up in the library. We'll see.

I run a bath and lie in it until the water becomes unbearably tepid. After I've dried and dressed, I take advantage of Jeremy's offer and saunter through to his bedroom. The layout has changed slightly since yesterday. The armchair has been moved from the corner of the room and now sits to the side of the hi-fi, presumably because the headphone lead isn't long enough to reach the chair.

My attention then switches to another feature of Jeremy's bedroom. It ties in with the feeling I had this morning and the knowledge I might not be able to say a proper goodbye to my young housemate, or indeed my landlady.

I switch on the computer and after a few minutes of frustrated clicking, open the word processing program. It takes over an hour to write just four paragraphs, but I'm happy with it. It's heartfelt but apologetic. If I never get to see Jeremy or Sylvia again, they'll be left knowing how much they both impacted my brief stay in Comaland.

After saving the file with a suitable filename Jeremy can't fail to spot, I shut the computer down and switch the hi-fi on.

Rather than play albums I've already heard countless times, I don the cumbersome headphones and use the digital tuner to locate Radio One. Relaxing in the armchair, I listen to an hour of Andy Peebles, Soul Train, and then, bored of listening to the same genre of music, switch to Radio Two. Songs From The Shows has just started, and although I'm rather partial to the odd show tune, my eyelids grow heavier with every passing track.

At some point during *Don't Cry For Me Argentina*, I fall fast asleep.

35.

On every occasion I've woken up in Comaland, it's taken a few moments for the reality to sink in. In those precious moments, I'm at home in my new apartment, in my own bed. My stomach then sinks when I realise I'm not.

On this occasion, reality literally shakes me by the shoulder.

"Sean. Sean."

I open my eyes and Jeremy is leaning over me, the headphones in his left hand.

"Bloody hell," I wince, adjusting my position. "My back is killing me. What time is it?"

"Just gone eleven."

"Sorry, I'll shift my arse so you can get to bed."

"Um, I need to talk to you."

I look up and focus on his face. It's not the face of a young man who's just enjoyed a fun-filled night out.

"What's the matter?"

"I don't know. It's probably nothing."

"Jeremy?"

"It's Jackie."

I sit bolt upright.

"What about her?"

"I think she's ..."

"What? What is it?"

"I think she's angry with me."

The tension subsides, and I relax back into the armchair.

"Jesus, lad. Don't do that," I huff. "I thought something terrible had happened."

"Sorry."

He looks so dejected; I won't get back to sleep knowing he's feeling guilty for some ridiculous reason.

"Come on, what makes you think she's angry with you?"

"I don't really know. We had a great evening, and when the band finished, Jackie said we should go to another gig next weekend. We then called a cab and waited outside. They said it could be up to a fifteen-minute wait, but Jackie didn't seem to mind."

"Go on."

"Ten minutes passed, and I desperately needed the loo so I told her I'd only be a moment and rushed to the toilets. When I got back outside, she'd gone."

"Gone? Gone where?"

"That's the thing; I don't know. I must have said something to annoy her, which is why she didn't wait."

"Could she have got in the cab and left before you returned."

"The doorman said he saw a blonde girl in the passenger seat of a car, but he only got a fleeting look."

"Is that why you think she's angry? She hopped in the cab without you?"

"No, because two minutes later the cab I ordered turned up."

"Wait … whose car did Jackie leave in then?"

"It must have been her mother."

"What makes you think that?"

"The doorman said the car was either a light green or yellow Morris Marina. I'm sure that's the same car I saw parked outside Jackie's house the night her step-dad threw me out."

"Jeremy," I gulp. "Jackie's mother can't drive."

Our eyes lock as we simultaneously draw the same conclusion. Only one person could have been driving that car — Derek Benton.

"But … but I thought her step-dad was locked up?"

"So did I."

I scramble out of the armchair.

"Where are you going?"

"To use the phone."

Moving quickly and quietly, I dash down the stairs and dial Jackie's number. Jeremy follows. He doesn't quite share my levels of concern because he doesn't know I accused Derek of abusing his step-daughter on Friday evening. If the police have released Derek, he'll want to know why she shared that information with a stranger.

"What time did Jackie leave the pub?" I hiss at Jeremy.

"Half-hour ago. Maybe longer."

Finally, Anna answers.

"Can I speak to Derek?"

"What? No, he's not here," she replies wearily. "Do you know what time it is?"

"Is Jackie there?"

"I don't know. Who is this?"

"I need to know if Jackie is there."

"Call back tomorrow. It's late."

The line goes dead. I ring the number again.

"Shit!"

"What's the matter?"

"It's engaged. Anna has taken the phone off the hook."

"What's going on, Sean?"

I don't have time to explain.

"I'm just going to check Jackie got home okay. I'll be twenty minutes."

"It takes that long to walk there."

"I'm not walking."

I slip my shoes on and retrieve a bunch of keys from the kitchen.

"Can I come with you?" Jeremy asks.

"I don't think that's a good idea unless you fancy another run-in with Jackie's dad."

"Err, I'll wait up until you get back."

I'm already at the front door and flash a nod.

Praying Austin behaves himself, I tug the garage door open and fumble with the key to unlock the driver's door. I finally fall into the seat.

"Please start," I pray, jabbing the key into the ignition barrel.

One turn and Austin coughs into life. I mouth a thank you and slam the gearstick into first.

Until now, I've had no reason to test the old Allegro's performance. That's about to change.

I pull out of the driveway and press hard on the accelerator pedal. The change in engine note is discernible — the change in speed is not. The only way I can coax any urgency into the old motor is by revving his guts out while keeping one eye on the temperature gauge. Fortunately, the roads are near-deserted. At speed, Austin handles like a one-ton blancmange and I veer across the white lines several times.

Five minutes after leaving Cline Road, I screech to a halt outside a house in Fir Tree Road. There are no lights on, and there's no sign of a mustard-yellow Morris Marina anywhere on the street.

I race up to the front door and bang the glass repeatedly. Somewhere across the street, a dog barks, but there's no sign of life inside the house. I bang again, harder.

Suddenly, a muted light fills the darkness beyond the glass. Someone has just switched the landing light on. I can just make out the heavy, aggressive thumping of footsteps on the stairs. The front door swings open and Anna Benton stands before me in a dressing gown.

"What the hell are you playing at?" she barks. "Piss off, whoever you are."

"Anna, I need to know if Jackie is home."

"How do you know my name?"

"It doesn't matter. Please, just tell me if Jackie is home."

"Bugger off you dirty old man, before I call the police."

I should have perhaps thought about the optics of my visit. If I were Anna, I wouldn't take too kindly to a middle-aged man banging on my door late at night, asking after my young daughter.

"Anna, please. Is Jackie home?"

She tries slamming the door shut but I just about manage to wedge my foot in the way before it reaches the latch.

"I think she's in serious trouble," I add. "You need to open the door and listen to what I've got to say."

"What do you mean, trouble?"

"It's Derek. You don't know him like you think you do."

"What's that supposed to mean?"

"Did you know he's been in prison?"

I'm still talking to a near-closed door as Anna has her full body weight against it.

"Please," I plead. "If you don't talk to me, the consequences could be dire for Jackie."

The pressure suddenly eases on my foot, and the door opens.

"Who are you?" she snaps.

"For the second time, it doesn't matter who I am. All you need to know is I'm gravely concerned for your daughter."

"Why should I believe you?"

"I wrote you a letter a week ago; a warning about Jackie's mental health."

"I never got no letter."

"What? I delivered it by hand."

"I didn't get no letter," she repeats.

Someone must have picked it up from the doormat, and it doesn't require much imagination to work out who — bloody Derek.

"I ... Jesus Christ, just go and check if Jackie is home. If she is, I'll walk away, and you'll never see me again."

The weight of her dilemma seems to shrink Anna's frame by several inches.

"She's not home," she eventually mumbles. "I glanced in her bedroom on my way to answer the door."

"And you don't know where Derek is?"

"He came home earlier, changed, and said he had to go in to work."

"Why did the police release him?"

"How do you know about that?"

"Because I was the bloke he assaulted. Why did they let him go?"

"Some of Derek's mates from the pub came forward as witnesses and said you threw the first punch. The police dropped the charges and let him out a few hours ago."

"Where does he work?"

"British Rail Engineering on Station View. Derek is on the track maintenance crew."

Her revelation does nothing to quell my concerns.

"Did he ask after Jackie?"

"Only in passing. He wanted to know where she was."

"And you told him?"

"Why wouldn't I?"

My patience snaps.

"Because, Anna," I growl. "Your husband sexually assaulted your daughter before Christmas and he's been harassing her ever since. I swear, if we don't find her, she might do something stupid. That girl's head is a mess because of what Derek did to her."

Despite the amber glow of the streetlights, Anna's face loses all colour.

"Let me in, and I'll show you proof. I swear to God, you need to see it."

She steps aside.

"Come with me," I order before bounding up the stairs.

Now panicked, it doesn't even cross Anna's mind to ask how I know which bedroom is her daughter's. I switch the light on and fall to my knees beside the bed.

"What are you doing?"

"Just wait a sec."

I tug the drawer out and once again offer a silent prayer. The diary is where I left it. I snatch it up and hand it to Anna.

"Read from November onwards."

She takes the diary and flicks through the pages to find the November entries. I watch on silently as her eyes dart left and right; each page turned more frantically than the last.

Anna then stops turning and gasps, clamping a hand over her

mouth.

"Anna, you need to call the police and tell them Jackie is missing."

If Anna heard my question, there's no visible sign as she continues to flick through the pages.

"Anna. The police."

The diary slips from her hand to the floor, and she stands inert, staring into space.

"For fucks sake. Call the police."

"I ... um," she murmurs. "It can't ... it can't be true."

"Anna?"

No response.

"Anna!"

She continues to stare vacantly into space; her reaction has all the hallmarks of shock, possibly denial. Should I call the police myself? What would I say? Jackie is twenty-one, an adult, and I've no proof Derek abducted her apart from Jeremy's second-hand testimony. If I tell them about the diary, they might send a car, but the blue lights won't be flashing. All I have is the benefit of knowing what will be, what is unprovable — Jackie Benton will commit suicide tomorrow.

Tomorrow. Tomorrow. Tomorrow.

The word repeats in my head like an echo. To my right, red digits glow from the digital alarm clock next to Jackie's bed: 11:39 pm. When the realisation arrives, it hits me harder than any of Derek's blows — tomorrow begins in twenty-one minutes.

The image of Jackie's death certificate suddenly zooms into focus, temporarily trapping me in the gravity of Anna's paralysis. That certificate specified a date but not a time. The trains will still be running after midnight, which means ...

"Oh, no!"

There are two options open to me: I call the police and spend twenty minutes trying to explain what's about to happen and how I know it's about to happen, or I jump in the car and try to prevent it myself. I need to cover both bases and grab Anna by the shoulders.

"Anna, listen to me," I yell, my face filling her vision. "Call the police and tell them Jackie's life is in danger. Tell them she's about to commit suicide somewhere near the train station."

Her eyes remain glassy, but she responds with a slow nod.

"I'm going there now. Call the police, Anna."

With every second now precious, I don't wait for further acknowledgement.

Within thirty of those precious seconds, I'm already a hundred yards away from the Benton residence. Engine screaming, my hands tightly gripping the steering wheel, I urge the little Allegro to give me everything he's got. In return, I do all I can. I slap the gearstick, stamp the pedals, and try to remain on the thin line between peak urgency and recklessness.

I want to check the time, but I daren't move my eyes from the road, not even for a split second. If I crash, there's no guarantee anyone else will be there in time to rescue Jackie. Such is my focus, I can barely spare the mental resources to consider exactly where I'm heading and what I'll do when I get there. And, there are so few facts at my disposal.

There is, however, one undeniable fact — when I spoke to Jackie earlier, she sounded nothing like a young woman on the brink of suicide. When she went out with Jeremy, he said they had a great time and discussed going out again next weekend. Again, not someone on the brink of suicide. Tomorrow, she thinks we're going to Manchester to meet her hero.

I think back over my time in Comaland, and every interaction with Jackie. At times she's been angsty and rude and sometimes unpredictable. I put her mood swings down to her worsening mental health, presuming she'd already begun a steady decline towards oblivion. Now, knowing what she's been through with Derek, I can see her behaviour in a different light. She's not suicidal — she's angry, resentful, disgusted, and perhaps ashamed. Above all, she's trying her best to protect her mother from the truth and not let her bastard step-father win.

As the assumptions dry up, a question soon follows: the date on Jackie's death certificate might be accurate, but what if the cause of death isn't?

If someone leaps in front of a train in the early hours of the morning when there are no witnesses, who would know if it was intentional? What if they were pushed, or worse, thrown?

What if Derek Benton was involved?

My mouth bobs open as I cast my mind back to the scene in the Benton's kitchen. I thought Derek kept that diary page just to lay blame on me but what if I'm wrong? What if he kept it as evidence? At some point, there must have been an enquiry in to Jackie's death, and what better way to prove she was suicidal than her own confession? Jackie said she wanted to die.

I can only think of one reason why Derek would want the world to believe his step-daughter committed suicide.

"Shit!"

I drop a gear and press the accelerator flat to the floor.

36.

I throw the Allegro in to a bend and almost over-correct the steering as it wobbles out the other side.

The Farnham Road bridge is deserted; no traffic, no pedestrians and of most significance, no Jackie. I cross the bridge and stop at a roundabout. There's no activity on the street ahead, leading away from the town. I turn right and cruise slowly along the road. Nearly every house is in darkness and the pavements empty. There's no sign of a yellow Morris Marina either.

"Where the hell are you?"

With nothing more than a hunch to go on, I turn around and cross back over the Farnham Road bridge.

Station View is a long, narrow stretch of tarmac road which runs parallel to the railway tracks. To my right, there's a vast deserted car park which will quickly fill to capacity when the Monday morning commute begins in six hours. I slow down a fraction as the scene changes to a row of stern Victorian buildings. Grimy and weather-beaten, they appear industrial, but there's no sign any of them belong to British Rail Engineering.

I pass an area of waste ground and more Victorian buildings, but no depot.

Reaching the end of Station View, there's nothing but a set of nondescript steel gates ahead of me. Did I miss the depot? I begin a three-point turn, and as the Allegro's feeble headlights sweep past the gates, a flash of reflective material shines back. I edge the car forward a few feet, and the same reflective material lights up again. Almost completely covered in weeds, a sign confirms I'm in front of the British Rail Engineering Depot.

I get out of the car and dash up to the gates, expecting them to be securely locked. There's a chain wrapped around the midsection where the two gates meet, but there's no padlock.

I should be relieved my hunch proved correct, but I'm not. It means my worst fears are a step closer to being realised — this is where Derek Benton works, and there is a chance the gates are unlocked because he's on the other side.

After unwinding the chain, I push open the right-hand gate and squeeze past.

The view beyond does not fill me with hope because I can only make out faint outlines in the darkness. I pause to let my eyes adjust to the gloom.

Slowly, I move forward, and some of the dark shapes take on definition. There's a portacabin on the right, and closer to my left, the silhouette of wire fencing between the depot boundary and the railway lines.

I count my steps as I move closer to God knows what.

Ten, twenty, thirty.

To the left of the portacabin, there's another set of gates. I can just about make out machinery stored inside a compound; presumably for repairs and trackside maintenance. In the dark, the jagged angles and strange protrusions exude menace, like medieval instruments of torture.

Ahead, the roofline of a single-storey building cuts across the sky like a band of black paint on an inky-blue canvas. I can hear the slow clack of wheels on tracks in the distance and the wind swirling past my ears, but it's otherwise silent. Maybe I got it wrong. Perhaps someone just forgot to lock the gates.

With my low-light vision now as good as it's likely to be, I'm able to get a better fix on my surroundings. I slowly turn around in a full circle, searching for any clue to Derek's whereabouts. It's a view of buildings and equipment and fences, mounds of hardcore and stacks of wooden sleepers, twenty high and ten across. All I see is what I'd expect to see in a railway maintenance depot.

Light suddenly flickers in the corner of my eye. It's followed by the screech of metal on metal as an inbound train rumbles into sight fifty yards beyond the fence on my left. Slowing down on its approach to the station, the long line of carriages temporarily cast a few extra lumens of light on my surroundings.

Only then do I see what I previously couldn't — the rear quarter panel of a yellowish car poking beyond the side of the single-storey building.

Moving as stealthily as anyone my size can, I hustle towards the corner of the building where I can remain hidden and check the car is the one I'm looking for. Squatting down, I poke my head around the corner. The badge on the boot and the mustard-yellow paintwork confirm it is almost certainly Derek's Morris Marina. The question is: where is he, and where is Jackie?

The last carriage rolls past, taking its precious light with it.

I stand up straight and squint while my eyes adjust to the darkness again. The Marina is parked on an access road between the side of the building and the perimeter fence. Beyond the car there's not a great deal to see, apart from a steel five-bar gate with a large sign attached to it, warning of live rails beyond. The gate itself is innocuous — the fact it is wide open, less so.

Sticking close to the side of the building, I creep the short distance to the gate. As I draw level with it, I can clearly see the half-dozen lines of track serving Guildford station. Now, there's no choice but to answer a question I'd rather not: why is the gate open at this time of night when the depot is closed?

I hold my wrist up to check the time: ten past midnight. It's now Monday. Suicide day.

There's no time to worry about live rails, no time to plan or plot, no opportunity to consider how Derek might be culpable for Jackie's death. All I know is I must find them.

I step beyond the gate.

With the nearest rail only six feet away, I look up and down the tracks. To my left, some four hundred yards away lies the station and there's just enough ambient light to view the adjacent tracks, sidings, and embankments. There's no sign of life.

The view to my right is less encouraging.

As the light fades away, I can see maybe one hundred yards, but beyond that, it's just a series of shadowy shapes and the occasional glow of a trackside warning light. As little as I want to, I've no choice but to walk alongside the track, into the darkness.

Sticking as close to the fence as I can, I edge my way along a rough path littered with loose stones from the track beds. I know I'm trespassing, but right now, I'd gladly welcome the sight of a police car.

I pass a series of bulky metal boxes, buzzing with electricity, and yellow signs printed with black letters and symbols; all meaningless. Looking straight ahead, one of the shapes comes in to view: a footbridge. The entire span appears deserted. I get within fifty yards of the bridge and decide I won't go any further once I reach it because there's too little light.

I press on, and another shape emerges from the darkness, just short of the footbridge. I can just make out a squat, brick-built structure the size of a small garden shed, positioned on a patch of weed-ridden ground between two tracks.

As I get closer, I notice a sack of something dumped against the side of the structure. After another dozen steps, I have a better view.

"Oh, my Christ!"

It's not a sack but a someone; slumped up against the brickwork, motionless.

The only way I can determine who they are is to cross the tracks. I don't have the first clue which rails are coursing with electricity, so I take no chances and hop over each one like a show pony. I reach the island and dare to look up again.

The first detail to leap out of the darkness is the mane of blonde hair. My pulse reaching aerobic levels, I scramble across the final fifteen feet of waste ground and kneel down.

Jackie is unconscious, but I've found her.

I put my hand on her neck and feel for a pulse. It's faint, but it's there. I then cup her head in my hands.

"Jackie! Jackie!"

No response.

"Can you hear me, Jackie?"

Still nothing.

I look up, hoping beyond hope I might spot someone wandering across the footbridge, and I can attract their attention. At that exact moment, a significant piece of the Jackie Benton puzzle slides into place.

Anna said Jackie jumped from a bridge, and I assumed she meant the Farnham Road bridge. Could it be she jumped from the narrow footbridge I'm looking at? In her current state, Jackie wouldn't be capable of jumping off a kerb, so how did she get from here to the bridge? Why is she even here, and how did she end up unconscious?

I don't need Leonard Crosby's detection skills to work it out — Derek put her here, but why?

There are no obvious answers, but I can certainly draw some obvious conclusions. I don't think Jackie jumped off the bridge at all, but an enquiry into her apparent suicide would assume she did. How else would she have ended up on this particular stretch of track, where the public have no access?

That's one question I can answer because I've just walked here from the engineering depot. One man had easy access to this stretch of track and that same man had the most to gain from Jackie's suicide.

Bile catches at the back of my throat as the known facts drag me towards a possible truth.

Behind me, a train horn blares somewhere close to the station. The only reason I know why a driver might sound their horn near a station is to warn they're passing through at speed. The fast train from London to Portsmouth is approaching.

In the cab of that train, a driver is nearing the end of his shift. A long day, he's probably tired, and it's dark. Would he stand up at an enquiry and swear he didn't see a young woman jump off a bridge? Travelling at speed, would he notice the slightest smudge of movement in the corner of his windscreen?

My theories are irrelevant because the known facts tell a different story; one I know for sure an enquiry will accept.

A bridge. A young woman who confessed in a diary she wanted to die. A fast train on a dark track.

They will never consider that on the night of Jackie's apparent suicide, Derek Benton might have waited behind this structure. When the time was just right, he might have hurled his unconscious step-daughter under the wheels of an oncoming train; a train carrying the right amount of speed to mangle a body and destroy evidence.

However, Derek didn't factor my appearance in his plan.

I make another attempt to wake Jackie. She's still unresponsive. Indecision reigns as I consider my next move. Should I pick her up and carry her back across the tracks, or wait until a train approaches and try to attract the driver's attention?

I'm still weighing up the options when a shadow suddenly shifts across the ground to my right. Just as I turn my head, pain erupts across the back of my neck. The impact is seismic, reverberating down my spine and up to the base of my skull. I find myself floundering on the ground, trying to shake off the shock and protect myself from another blow.

It doesn't go well.

My motor skills are so scrambled, all I can do is roll to the side just as a thick lump of wood smashes into the ground I just vacated. The new position leaves me vulnerable to another blow, but it does allow me to look up in to the eyes of my attacker.

The final question: where is Derek? I have an answer.

"Stop!"

With the lump of wood raised above his head, he glares down at me with pure unadulterated hatred. Maybe I've undermined his perfect plan, or perhaps I'm just a nuisance, a delay to that plan, or another problem to solve. I don't know, but whatever Derek Benton is thinking, it seems smashing my head in is a priority.

He brings the lump of wood down again, and for a second time, I'm able to roll away just in the nick of time. Only inches from my head, the wood cracks against the edge of a concrete slab and splinters into pieces. Derek is left with a useless stub in his hands. Now my adversary is weaponless I have a chance to get up.

I manage to get part the way up when a boot lands in my ribcage. The pain is obscene, but the panic and adrenalin fuel my efforts and I manage to remain upright and stumble towards the opposite side of the brick structure. Derek is on me in a heartbeat, raining down blows like a madman. He's so out of control, there's no coordination to his attack, and most of the punches miss the target. I know he's bound to land a lucky blow before long if I don't do something.

Fortunately, Derek is a smoker and not in his prime. Panting hard, he pauses for a second to catch his breath. I use the opportunity to take four steps back and prepare a different strategy; attack, rather than defence. If I match him punch for punch, there's a fifty-fifty chance I'll land a decisive blow before he does. I ball my fists and wait.

What I hadn't figured into my plan was the approaching train. It's at least two hundred yards away, but a slight curve in the track changes the angle of the headlights. Suddenly, they're shining directly in my face, close enough and bright enough to blind. I glance away at the exact same moment Derek resumes his attack. This time, however, there is no flurry of wild punches.

He steams towards me with his head down and, right at the last second, he raises his hands but not in a pugilistic manner. Too late, I realise why he's switched tactics. His palms strike my chest in an almighty shove. The train headlights disappear behind the brick structure as I stumble a step backwards. I know it won't be the last backward step I take because I can feel gravity tugging at my shoulders. I've got one chance, a split second to grab an anchor.

My left arm already flailing, I reach out with my right arm and snatch; hoping to grab anything that isn't empty air. By pure luck, I lock on to Derek's arm, but an eighteen stone load requires more than twelve stones to anchor it. I continue my backward journey with Derek Benton for company.

I manage to stay upright for three more steps until my right heel hits a hard, unforgiving object. At that moment, I know gravity has won, and all I can do is brace for impact.

The pain of landing on the jagged stones of the track bed is bad enough, but an errant elbow lands square in the centre of my stomach as Derek falls on top of me. Our faces only inches apart, I gasp for air. He opens his mouth to shout something but it's drowned out by the sound of a train horn. We both turn our heads to the right, in the direction of the horn.

The train is no more than forty yards away, bearing down on us like a monstrous mechanical Giganotosaurus.

Humans are hard-wired to survive no matter what the circumstance. When faced with our own demise, we'll go to unimaginable lengths to avoid the cold hand of Death. Some people have turned to cannibalism rather than starve. Some have self-amputated limbs to prevent death by gangrene. Some, trapped in a burning building, have leapt from windows hundreds of feet above the ground.

Derek Benton's survival instincts kick in, and he tries to wrestle his arm from my grip. I know there's no way I'll get up in time. My fate is sealed. It would be the right thing to do, to let Derek escape.

I wrap my left arm tightly around his neck.

As much as I want to tell Derek it's over and he'll never harm my Jackie again, I can already hear the gates of hell screeching open.

My brain's final ever function is a thought: Jackie Benton won't die today. What a pity I will.

37.

Constant, rhythmic, like the ticking of a clock.

Unlike a clock, the intermittent sounds are not mechanical. Not a pendulum or the turn of tiny cogs, but … I don't know.

They drift away, and I follow.

Time passes. Minutes, hours, possibly days. I've no way of measuring.

I know I exist, but my grip on existence is fragile; my thoughts just murmurs, my body inert.

In the swirl of indistinguishable sounds, I thought I heard voices. I couldn't say who they belonged to, their age or gender. They came, and then they went.

There are periods I feel nothing, hear nothing. Those periods are interspersed with flashes of light and wispy clouds of colour. Nothing has form, no distinguishable shapes.

Again, the flashes of light fade and the clouds of colour disperse. Still, there is nothing.

I return once more, and the rhythmic sound is different: faster, like the electronic beat of a tune.

Tune?

My mind latches on to the word. Tune … I remember music, and if I remember music, it means I'm capable of remembering.

The electronic beats settle down to the familiar rhythm, but there is a change, a thread to cling to. I try to remember the words of a song, any song, but the world descends into the abstract and too soon, nothingness.

And then everything happens.

It begins with a single sound: a door closing. The electronic beats respond at tempo, and the voices return. This time they are distinct, but I pay them little attention as the first signs of physical sensation arrive: pressure around my mouth, a dull pain in my arm, a severe itch near my inner thigh. I want to open my eyes but daren't; the risk of sensory overload too much. My nostrils fill with an odour like sour milk and the pain I felt in my arm has moved … moved everywhere.

"Sean? Can you hear me?"

The voice is female, soft.

I dare to move, a test. Nothing too much; just a slight turn of the head in the direction of the voice.

"Try not to move."

I want to ask why, but I'm now sure the pressure across my mouth is a mask. Why is it there? Why does it feel like I've been trampled by a herd of cows, and where the fuck am I?

"Can you open your eyes?"

Yes, no … probably.

I let my eyelids flicker open and quickly shut them again. Too bright.

"Take your time."

Millimetre by tortuous millimetre I open my eyes, and an oval face comes in to focus. The woman, whoever she is, smiles. I then feel a hand curl around mine.

"Don't try to talk, but I'm going to ask you a few simple questions. Squeeze my hand if you understand, okay?"

I tense the muscles in my right hand. To my relief, it responds.

"My name is Emily, and I'm an intensive care nurse. You're in hospital. Do you understand?"

In some way, Emily's revelation is a relief. It's not that I want to be in hospital, but it's better than being trapped in my own head.

"Do you remember how you got here? Squeeze once for yes and twice for no."

I squeeze her hand twice.

"Are you suffering any significant pain anywhere? Once for yes and twice for no."

I don't know what she means by significant. I hurt all over, but it's at a bad hangover level, and not so intense I can't bear it.

Two squeezes.

"That's great. Now, I'm just going to fetch the doctor so he can take a proper look at you, and make sure everything is working as it should. Okay?"

I squeeze her hand once before it gently slides from mine.

Emily departs, and I survey my surroundings. There's hardly anything to see but beige walls and fluorescent lights. With nothing to look at, my mind returns to an assessment of my condition.

I can breathe. I can see, I can feel, I can smell, and I can hear. This is all good. A relief.

Most of my core functions enabled, I return to Emily's statement. Why am I in hospital?

Panicked, I try moving each of my limbs. My legs are leaden, but I can turn my feet and wiggle my toes. My left arm responds as efficiently as my right, but the movement is hampered by a transparent tube, embedded in my skin just above the wrist.

Legs work, arms work, senses are functioning. I relax a fraction.

Now I'm awake, the mask covering my mouth is proving uncomfortable to the point of painful. Tentatively, I raise my hand to the mask and tug it. Either I have no strength, or it's glued to my face as it doesn't want to move. I try again, but rather than tug it, I pull it down towards my chest and gasp — the sudden intake of air results in a coughing fit. There's so little lubrication in my mouth and throat, it's like choking on a mouthful of sun-scorched sand.

A nurse who isn't Emily rushes in and shakes her head when she notices the displaced mask.

"You've only been awake five minutes, and you're already causing mischief," she chuckles. "Let me get you some water."

She holds a plastic cup to my lips. I lift my hand to take over, being I'm not an infant.

"No, no," the nurse chides. "Just take tiny sips, okay."

The water tastes of metal, and it's a few degrees above room temperature. It still rates as one of the sweetest liquids to ever pass my lips. I'm allowed half a cup.

"Can I trust you alone until the doctor gets here?" the nurse asks with a wry smile. "I don't want him to find you breakdancing on the floor."

"I'll behave."

"Good. He might be a while so you should get some rest."

Rest is the last thing I want. I want to know how I got here and when I can leave. The nurse hurries away before I can ask.

Whether I want it or not, the quiet stillness in the room lures me back towards the nothingness. I fight it all the way, but I'm more tired than I can ever remember feeling. I'm about to give in when the door opens, and a grey-haired guy in a white coat enters.

"Good Afternoon, Mr Hardy," he says crisply. "Glad to see you back in the land of the living."

He snatches a clipboard from the wall and approaches the side of my bed.

"I'm Doctor Munroe. How are you feeling?"

"I've felt better, but I'm okay."

My mouth is still so dry the words come out in gravelly rasps.

"Good, good."

He examines the clipboard.

"I'm just going to conduct a few tests. Nothing too taxing, okay?"

"Sure."

He gets on with the first of those tests and shines a miniature torch in both eyes. I'm then prodded, poked, and manhandled until the doctor seems satisfied.

"You appear to be in fully functioning order, Mr Hardy."

"That's a relief. When can I go home?"

"One step at a time. I need to ask you a few basic questions to test your mental faculties."

"Right."

He consults the clipboard again.

"What's your full name?"

"Sean Ian Hardy."

"Good start," he replies, flicking his pen on the page. "And, your date of birth?"

"9th March 1966."

Another tick.

"Where were you born?"

"You mean the name of the hospital?"

"No, just the town or city."

"Guildford."

"Excellent, and can you recall which county Guildford is in?"

"Surrey."

"What is seven plus five?"

"Twelve."

"The capital of France?"

"Paris," I sigh.

"I know these questions seem ridiculous, but we need to ascertain your brain is firing on all cylinders."

"Sorry. Go on."

"Who is the current Prime Minister?"

"Margaret Thatcher."

"Best we don't dwell on that one," he snorts. "And finally, what year is it?"

"1988."

The doctor then scribbles a lengthy note.

"Well, how did I do? Is my brain okay?"

He continues writing for a few seconds longer and then taps the pen nib on the page three times.

"Eight questions, eight right answers."

"That's good, yeah?"

"It is, young man. We'll move you to a general ward soon and see how you get on over the next forty-eight hours."

"Forty-eight hours," I groan.

The doctor frowns.

"Mr Hardy, might I suggest you count your blessings? There

are many patients in this hospital who'll be with us for weeks, and some who might not return home at all."

My cheeks warm, I mumble an apology.

"Besides, we want to ensure you don't experience another seizure."

"Seizure?"

"You don't remember what happened to you? How you got here?"

"No."

"You were admitted in the early hours of the morning after suffering a seizure."

I have zero recollection of the said event.

"But … I'm okay now, aren't I?"

"Remarkably, yes. There were no abnormalities identified during your brain scan, and we've ruled out epilepsy, but the reason we need to keep you under observation is … well, frankly, it's because we have no idea what caused the seizure."

38.

As much as I didn't want to be in intensive care, I'm only an hour into my stay on the general ward, and I already hate it. I'm surrounded by five men who cough, fart, splutter, and puke every five minutes, and the place stinks of piss and cabbage.

A nurse darts past.

"Excuse me, nurse."

"Yes?"

"Is it possible to make a phone call?"

"It's on the blink at the moment," she replies, her accent Irish. "Someone is coming out to look at it later."

"Terrific."

"Look on the bright side. It's visiting time soon."

An old bloke in the bed opposite summons the nurse away. With nothing else better to do, I attempt to piece together the events which put me here.

Dr Munroe said I arrived in the early hours of the morning. Did I do anything different last night that might have triggered a seizure?

Closing my eyes, I try to blot out the noise and commotion around me, and concentrate.

I remember watching television, and Carol went to bed at about ten. The programme finished, and I decided to call it a night. I went to the bathroom, brushed my teeth, and got undressed. Carol was already asleep when I climbed into bed. I checked the alarm clock and closed my eyes — nothing out of the ordinary, just an uneventful Sunday evening.

Why then does it feel like there's something else hiding away in the dark recesses of my mind?

I can't put my finger on it, and I'm not even sure it's a memory; more an uneasy sense of detachment, like the times I've woken up after a vivid dream. Maybe it's the medication or some temporary side-effect of the seizure itself. Either way, it's disconcerting.

Visiting time arrives, and the ward fills with more old people. Most are smiling; some are not. I keep looking towards the corridor like a dog waiting for its master to arrive home from work. My parents finally breeze in.

They appear happy, or relieved, or both.

Mum skips the last eight feet and then has to adjust her final approach once she realises the impracticalities of hugging someone lying flat in bed. In the end, she kind of partly lies on top of me.

"How are you feeling, sweetheart?"

"I'm good, but you're kinda squashing me."

My mother retreats and grabs my hand. She's already close to tears and unable to find any words.

"God, you had us worried," Dad booms. "We drove up the moment we heard."

He places his hand on my shoulder. He's a stoic type, so it's quite the show of emotion by his standards.

"Who told you I'd been admitted?"

"Carol called us at lunchtime."

"Lunchtime, as in five hours ago? I've been here since the early hours of the morning."

"She had an important meeting at work," Mum says, by way of an explanation.

Dad grabs two plastic chairs and drags them over to my bedside. Mum sits nearest and retakes my hand.

"Have you eaten yet?" she asks.

"I've got that delight to come. I think they serve cabbage with every meal."

"I'm sure they don't, and hopefully it won't be for long. Would you like me to bring anything in for you?"

"I don't know why but I'm craving apple crumble. If you could sneak one in, that'd be great."

"I'll see what I can do," she chuckles.

"Have they said how long they're keeping you in for?" Dad asks.

"I'm likely to be here for a few days which is crap because I need to get back to work."

"You shouldn't be worrying about work. Just focus on getting better."

"I am, but … it took me months to get that job, and I don't want to lose it."

"I'm sure they'll understand."

I glance over my mother's shoulder towards the corridor. Ever perceptive, Mum reads my mind.

"Carol will be here soon."

I happen to catch the look in my Dad's eye. He has a way of saying so much without actually saying anything.

"What's the matter, Dad?"

"Nothing."

"She's been flat out at work," Mum adds. "But that doesn't mean she hasn't been worried sick about you."

Dad looks at his shoes; a sure sign he doesn't agree but would rather avoid a scene.

Mum moves the conversation on.

"Do you remember anything about last night?"

"To a point. I went to bed and the next thing I know, I'm in hospital."

"Do they know what caused it, the seizure?"

"No, but I've had tests, and they couldn't find anything wrong with me, so don't be worrying, okay?"

"It's a mother's job to worry," she replies, squeezing my hand. "Do you feel okay now?"

"Physically, I'm fine. It's just … it's hard to describe. I feel odd, a bit out of sorts."

"Discombobulated," Dad suggests.

"Is that even a real word?"

"It means confused and disconcerted."

"Sounds about right."

"It's to be expected," Mum interjects. "After what you've been through."

"Yeah, you're right. I'll be fine once I'm out of here."

The clack of heeled shoes echoes from the corridor. I glance over Mum's shoulder again just as Carol appears, dressed in a navy-blue suit. She stops, scans the six beds, and strides over. My parents both get to their feet. Hugs are administered.

"We'll go grab a cup of tea," Mum says. "Give you two some time alone."

They trot away. Carol leans over and kisses me on the forehead.

"What's the prognosis?" she asks. "Are you alright?"

"I've had tests, and they couldn't find anything wrong with me."

She then sits down in the chair nearest the bed.

"That's a relief. You scared the shit out of me."

"I'm sorry. If it's any consolation, you've got the bed to yourself for a few nights so I won't be waking you up."

"Just as well. I'm knackered."

"I'm guessing you didn't get much sleep?"

"Not a lot as I was here until two in the morning. They said you were unresponsive and I couldn't see you."

"They said that?"

"More or less, so I didn't see much point in hanging around."

"It might have been nice if you had. I'd have preferred to see a friendly face when I woke up."

"The nurse said she'd call the moment there was any change in your condition, and I called your parents as soon as I had a chance."

"Yeah, okay," I sigh. "It doesn't matter now."

"Do you remember what happened?"

"I don't remember a thing."

"Nothing?"

"Nope."

"Honestly, Sean, it was awful. You were shaking so badly you woke me up. At first, I thought you were messing around. I remember checking the time and being bloody annoyed with you

342

— it was twenty-past midnight. So, I yelled at you to stop being a childish dick."

"You'd make a terrible nurse," I snigger. "I don't think shouting at patients works."

"It's not funny. I thought you were having a stroke."

"Sorry."

"Your eyes were wide open, staring up at the ceiling, and you were shaking so violently."

"Jesus."

"Anyway, I jumped up and called an ambulance. By the time I got back to the bedroom, the shaking had stopped, and you were just lying there. I thought you were dead."

Perhaps I underestimated how traumatic my episode must have been for Carol. I take her hand.

"Thank you for looking out for me. If you hadn't been there, God knows what might have happened."

"You'd probably still be in bed, lying there like a cabbage."

"Grim."

"Isn't it just. Talking of grim, have you called your boss?"

"Err, no. I thought you might have called him."

"I've barely had a chance to take a pee today. I told you last night I had a frantic day ahead of me."

"It's alright. I'll call him first thing in the morning. I'm sure he'll be understanding about it."

"I hope so, Sean. We can't afford for you to lose your job, not now."

"It's just a job," I shrug. "I can get another one."

"And what about our plans?" she asks, her voice a decibel or two louder. "Do you want to live in a crummy rented flat for the next five years?"

"Come off it. It's not that bad."

"You've changed your tune. Last night you said you couldn't wait to move out."

"Did I?"

"We were looking at the brochure for that new development

down by the harbour. Don't you remember?"

"Not really."

"Anyway, we've still got a way to go before we can buy a place of our own which is why you need to call your boss and apologise."

"Apologise for having a seizure?"

"Don't be flippant. You know what I mean."

"Yes, I will."

Argument won, Carol looks around the ward.

"It's horrible in here," she whispers. "We need to get private medical cover."

"Seriously? Do you have any idea how much it costs?"

"Doesn't your company offer private medical cover?"

"I've no idea."

"Can you ask your boss when you call tomorrow?"

"It's not really a key issue at the moment. Besides, they've looked after me pretty well in here."

"Yes, but it's so grotty."

"A bit," I chuckle. "But you get used to the smell of cabbage."

"It's no laughing matter, Sean. I'd rather die than spend an hour in here, so ask your boss, please."

"Whatever," I sigh.

"Whatever? What's that supposed to mean?"

"I don't know."

She rolls her eyes.

"I hope you're not going to be one of those people."

"What people?"

"Those who have a near-death experience and then go all soft, like nothing matters in life as long as you've got a roof over your head and two square meals a day."

"It's not the worst attitude to have, is it?"

"If you want any kind of future with me, it is."

I smile back at my girlfriend. I'm sure I do want us to share a future. At least, I'm sure I did.

FOUR WEEKS LATER...

39.

I wake up with a start, my skin clammy. I've no idea what time it is, but daylight is already flooding through the thin lounge curtains. Being June, it could be any time after five in the morning.

I sit up and rearrange the cushions on the sofa. It's not in the least bit comfortable but, for the time being, it's my weekday bed.

A few days after leaving hospital, Carol said she'd had enough of being woken up by my tossing, turning, and sleep talking. She said I could either go to the doctors and ask for sleeping pills or bed down on the sofa from Sunday night through to Thursday. I've had enough of doctors and medication, so I chose the sofa.

If the nightmares continue much longer, I might have to relent. I'm permanently tired and, being honest with myself, permanently pissed off.

The sense of discombobulation Dad identified has not gone away. If anything, it's contributing to my poor sleep quality. Every time I put my head down, no matter how tired I feel, my mind won't rest. There's this constant sense of unease, and I don't know why. I tried explaining it to Carol. The best example I could come up with was to say it's like when you're on the way home from work and suddenly panic you've forgotten to do something important. No matter how hard you try to remember what it is, and no matter how much you tell yourself you haven't forgotten anything, the feeling won't go away.

When I do eventually fall asleep, it only gets worse — that's when the nightmares begin. As soon as I drift off, I'm haunted by these sketchy figures and garbled conversation. It kinda reminds me of trying to watch my old portable television when I couldn't get a decent signal. I knew there were people on the screen, and I knew they were talking, but I had no idea who they were or what they were saying.

There is, however, one person I do recognise from my nightmares — the girl I've spent a year trying to forget. I thought I'd succeeded, but Jackie Benton has gatecrashed my thoughts with alarming regularity of late, and I think I know why.

That first night in hospital, Mum and Dad left an hour before the end of visiting time so they could find a hotel. They insisted on staying in Exeter for a few days until the doctor discharged me. Fifteen minutes after my parents departed, so did Carol, citing tiredness and a need to prep for another important meeting the following day. Left on my own, I scanned the other beds. Of the six blokes in my ward, I was the only one without a wife or partner at their side.

At that moment, my mind drifted back to a prior stay in hospital. It was only a brief stay to have my tonsils removed, and I happened to be dating Jackie at the time. That girl spent every minute of every permitted visit at my bed.

"Oh, you're awake."

Carol saunters in with a mug of coffee in hand.

"Yep. Couldn't sleep."

"This is getting beyond a joke now, Sean. Go to the bloody doctors."

"The last thing I need is pills. I've got to … I need to get my head straight, that's all."

"And how much longer is that going to take?"

"I don't know."

"In the meantime, we're all expected to put up with your cranky behaviour, are we?"

It's a fair question.

On Friday, my boss called me into his office and suggested I take a week off to sort my head out. I don't blame him. I know I've not been myself, and I'm fast becoming a liability at work. Nothing makes sense to me; not since the seizure.

"Maybe a few nights in a decent bed will help," Carol suggests. "You'll have it all to yourself tonight and tomorrow."

"Possibly."

My girlfriend is off to Birmingham for three days on a management training course. Neither of us has said it, but we both know we need a break from one another. At first, I put it down to the tiredness, but there's been a noticeable shift in our relationship over recent weeks. The traits I once found desirable, attractive, are now grating. I suspect Carol feels the same way.

I haven't admitted it, but there might be some truth in her quip at the hospital. I do feel different, and I can't muster a single toss about what we both used to care about so passionately: our careers, the kind of home we wanted to buy, how much we needed for holidays, and the type of luxury car we'd love to drive. I don't even know if I wanted any of it in the first place.

"I'm going for a shower," she says. "Open a window. It stinks in here."

She's not wrong, but it's more than just the odour of dry sweat that stinks.

An hour later, we say goodbye with a half-hearted kiss at the door. I don't know about Carol, but there's a sense of relief on my part. We need a break from the sniping and the arguments. She is right about one thing, though. I do need to get my head together because I can't live like this. What I do about it is another matter, but there's one person I can trust to give me some frank, unadulterated advice.

I call my Dad's work number.

"Ian Hardy," he answers on the third ring.

"Hi, Dad. It's me."

"First thing on a Monday morning? Something up?"

"Not really but … do you fancy meeting for lunch today?"

"It's a bloody long way to drive for lunch."

"I'm off work this week and I … I need to talk to someone who isn't Carol."

"Understood. One o'clock okay?"

"Perfect."

"Do you remember that pub we went to last time you came over?"

"The Jolly Sailor?"

"That's the one. Shall we meet there?"

"Fine by me. I'll see you later."

I put the phone down and slump back on the sofa.

It's a two-hour drive from Exeter to Bournemouth, but as it's not even nine yet, I've time to kill. I'm in no mood for watching TV, so I just sit and stare into space. The space in question is the lounge of a flat Carol doesn't much like. Granted, the rooms are small and the decor shabby, but it's not that bad. It isn't a home, though.

Part of my recent malaise, I think, is that I've become acutely aware I no longer have a home in the real sense of the word. Our family home in Guildford is now occupied by a different family, and my parent's swanky apartment has never been my home. And because Carol is so obsessed with planning our next move, and the next three moves after that, we'll be living a transient existence until we finally move into a place she deems perfect.

I don't like it.

Ever since I left hospital, I've grown increasingly … I don't know how to describe it … broody? It's not that I'm desperate to be a parent — not for a good few years, anyway — but I'd imagine it's a similar feeling; a deep-rooted sense of emptiness, of longing, like there's a hole in my heart. I just want to belong somewhere, but I don't know where, or why these feelings have suddenly surfaced.

Wherever that somewhere is, I don't think it's here.

By half-ten I'm close to climbing the walls and leave earlier than I need to. For some reason, I feel like taking my time and enjoying the scenery, rather than attacking the long, winding road to Bournemouth in my usual aggressive driving style.

I open the door to my Vauxhall Nova — my first and only car to date — and slide a cassette into the stereo: *Now 11*. Tape one, side one.

With Exeter in the rear-view mirror, my mood begins to lift. It could be the music or the freedom of the open road but twenty miles into the journey, it does feel like I've left a fair amount of emotional baggage behind. I stop half-way to grab a drink and use the loo, and arrive at The Jolly Sailor five minutes ahead of schedule. Dad is already waiting at the bar.

He's not a huggy type and greets me with a firm hand on the shoulder.

"Good journey?" he asks.

"Yeah, it was. It helped clear my mind a bit."

"Did it need clearing?"

"That's kinda why I wanted to see you."

"Sounds serious," he chuckles. "Pint?"

"One won't hurt."

"What are you having?"

I scan the pumps.

"London Pride, please."

"Sorry? Since when did you start drinking ale?"

"Um, since today. I don't fancy lager."

He turns to the barman and orders two pints of London Pride.

Once our drinks are served, Dad requests a couple of menus, and we move to a table.

"So, how's life in Exeter treating you?" he asks. "Everything okay on the health front?"

"Yep, touch wood," I reply, rapping my knuckles on the table. "I had a check-up last week, and they've given me a clean bill of health."

"That's good news. Your mother will be relieved."

There's a temporary silence as we both sup at our pints.

"And, how are things at home?"

His question is asked with the slightest raise of an eyebrow as if he's already identified the reason we're here. With my head all over the place, I need Dad's advice rather than Mum's because it's usually from the head rather than the heart.

"They're not great," I reply. "They haven't been great since the seizure."

"In what way?"

"That's the problem," I sigh. "I can't pin it down."

"Okay, let's start with the symptoms and see if we can work out the cause from there."

"Well, firstly, Carol and I aren't getting on. We just seem to rub each other up the wrong way all the time."

"That happens in every relationship from time to time, Son."

"I'm sure it does, but it's like a switch has been flipped and everything I loved about Carol — her drive, her ambition — now seems so superficial. I can almost see our future mapped out and I don't know if it's the future I want."

"So, she hasn't changed — you have?"

"I think so."

"Since the seizure?"

"Yep."

"An event like that is bound to change your perspective on life. A mate of mine had a heart scare, and a month later, he quit his job and left his wife. He's now planning a move to The Shetland Isles."

"A bit extreme."

"Maybe, but he obviously wasn't happy with the life he had, and the heart scare made him realise he couldn't afford to waste another day living it."

"Are you saying that's what's happened to me?"

"I honestly don't know. My mate is in his early fifties, so he's got a lot less road ahead of him than you. At your age, you're still finding yourself, understanding who you are and where you want to be."

"And how do I work out where I want to be?"

"Process of elimination, Son." he replies with a knowing smile. "Start by working out where you *don't* want to be."

I smile back.

"You know, don't you?"

"I know Carol is a nice enough girl at heart, but I've never

351

been convinced you were right for one another. You're like your mum: you don't much like conflict. It's easier to smile and keep the peace than push back."

"Is that such a bad thing? Aren't relationships based on compromise?"

"Of course, but it has to work both ways. Carol strikes me as the kind of girl used to getting her own way. In ten, twenty years from now, I reckon you'll be living her idea of a good life, but not necessarily yours."

"Oh, for a crystal ball, eh?"

"I don't think you need a crystal ball when you've got an old fart like me to talk to. There aren't many benefits to getting old, but one of them is experience. Christ, when I was a lad, I wish I knew a fraction of what I know now."

"Would you change anything?"

"Plenty, but what you'll find, Son, is the life you end up with usually boils down to just one or two decisions you make when you're young. Plan all you like but choose the wrong career or marry the wrong person, and the consequences can ripple through your entire life, especially if you're too stubborn or too naive to admit you've screwed up. Look at my mate — he spent thirty-odd years married to the wrong woman, doing a job he never much cared for. It took a bloody heart attack for him to realise."

Deliberate or otherwise, the comparison to my situation is obvious. Like Dad's mate, I woke up in a hospital bed after a significant health scare. Unlike Dad's mate, it feels like I've been gifted a unique opportunity to appraise my life while I'm still young enough to truly change it. On one level, maybe that's why my mind has been so scrambled of late — I don't know what changes I'm supposed to make.

Or do I?

I ask Dad another question.

"You said there's plenty you'd change, given the chance. Would you still have married Mum?"

"If I lived my life a hundred times over, I'd marry her every single time."

"There's never been a time you wondered if you'd made the right choice?"

"Like you, you mean?"

Yet again, my dad is one step ahead.

"Yeah," I snigger. "Like me."

"No, I've never doubted it. Yes, we've had our problems, same as any couple, but we've always worked through them, together."

"But you've never had to choose between Mum and another woman?"

"I was young once, you know. This will probably come as a shock, but I had my fair share of admirers back in the day. And, yes, one or two might have turned my head briefly, but I stood to lose a heck of a lot more than I could ever gain. Not everyone finds love, Son, not proper love, and it rarely comes around more than once in a lifetime. Why risk losing it?"

It's a bloody good question. I had proper love, and I took a punt on a promise of something better. Why is it I'm now questioning if that punt was worthwhile? Before the seizure, I knew exactly what I wanted. What's changed?

"Anyway, shall we order some grub?" Dad asks. "Some of us do have work this afternoon."

"Sure."

We both peruse a menu. Dad takes precisely ten seconds to decide.

"Steak and kidney pie for me."

"I'll have the same."

"Eh? You don't like steak and kidney pie."

"Yes, I do."

"You sure as hell didn't as a kid."

"Oh, maybe my taste buds have matured."

He disappears to the bar to order lunch while I reflect on our conversation. When I set off from Exeter, it felt like answers were a long way away. Some of those answers still are, but I've found one or two while chatting with Dad.

"It'll be fifteen minutes," he declares, retaking his seat.

"That's enough time for you to tell me I've made the right decision."

"About what?

"I'm going to end it with Carol."

"I see."

"Well?"

"I can't tell you if it's the right decision. Only you know that, Son."

Forced to reflect, a little voice in the back of my head offers reassurance.

"It's the right decision, Dad. Don't ask me how I know — I just know."

"Now you've made it, do you feel a bit better?"

"I think I do."

"Good to hear. Anything else troubling you?"

"Yeah, but nothing I can't work through. I just needed someone to point me in the right direction."

"Glad to be of service."

We swap small talk until lunch arrives and, shortly after we've eaten, Dad has to get back to work. We say goodbye in the car park.

"You know we've got a spare bedroom, Son, and it's yours should you need it."

"Thanks, and I might take you up on that offer."

"I'm sure your mum would love to have you under our roof again. She misses having someone to fuss over."

"Apart from you."

"I'm low maintenance. I don't leave my dirty underwear on the bathroom floor or washing up in the sink."

"I'm fully house-trained now, I'll have you know."

"About bloody time."

I receive my customary pat on the shoulder, and Dad turns to leave.

"Oh, one thing I forgot to ask," he says, turning back around. "Would you happen to know anything about a card?"

"What card?"

"We received a card in the post last month, recorded delivery. All it said is if we ever found ourselves in Haiti on some specific date, we should avoid getting on a ferry."

"That's a bit random."

"Isn't it just, but it flustered your mother a bit."

"Why?"

"You know we've talked about travelling when we retire? Well, one of the places she's always fancied visiting is Haiti."

"Oh."

"It's been crossed off the visit list as your mother is the deeply superstitious type."

"That's a bit extreme, considering it's probably just some weirdo's idea of a prank."

"Exactly my view although I must admit, I thought you sent it."

"Why would you think that?"

"The handwriting looked a little bit like yours, but then I noticed the postmark. It was sent from Guildford of all places."

"There you are then. I haven't been anywhere near Guildford since Easter last year."

"Are you sure?"

"Positive."

"I believe you," he says with a wink. "Thousands wouldn't."

"Honestly, I haven't, and I didn't send any card."

"Don't fret, Son. I never wanted to visit Haiti, anyway, so whoever sent it did me a favour."

I shake my head.

"I won't tell Mum that."

"Please don't. Look after yourself and good luck with Carol. I hope she doesn't cut anything off when you tell her."

"You and me both," I chuckle.

We return to our respective cars. I sit in mine and watch Dad drive off.

With another two-hour drive ahead of me, I rummage around in the glove box for a different cassette. Right at the back, I find one I haven't listened to in over a year — partly because I'd forgotten where I'd put it but mainly because I couldn't bear the memories it summoned. As much as I love all the *Now* albums, this cassette holds a special place in my heart. It was compiled on a stereo belonging to someone I loved deeply at the time. It's the same someone I still love deeply today, although acceptance has been a long time coming.

I slide the homemade compilation tape into the slot and press play.

There are six tracks on side-A, and I sit and listen to all of them before starting the car. I then flip the cassette over and pull out of the parking bay.

When I reach the junction at the main road, I can turn left or right. A left turn will take me back to Exeter, and a right will take me towards the motorway which winds all the way through Hampshire to Surrey.

The first track begins: Dollar's *Give Me Back My Heart*.

It's the song Jackie and I danced to at a youth disco many years ago. The same song which set me on a path I should have stuck to.

I don't know if it's the right path this time, but that little voice in my head decides to intervene again.

I flick the indicator stalk upward before either of us changes our mind.

40.

I'm not a great believer in fate, which is just as well. If I did, I might have thought the various delays in my journey were a sign. An accident on the A31 meant a diversion, delaying me by at least an hour, and then I hit major roadworks on the M27 motorway.

Ten miles into my stint on the M3, the traffic came to a standstill. I switched from listening to Jackie's tape to the radio, and a far-too-happy local radio presenter confirmed an articulated lorry had broken down, about five miles up the motorway from my stationary position.

A consequence of the delays is that it's now almost five o'clock and I'm still driving. I also have to contend with Guildford's rush hour traffic as I fight my way towards the Bellfields Estate.

I reach Fir Tree Road at quarter past and for the first time on this journey, slow down of my own choice.

The extra time has allowed me to consider what I might say to Jackie … what I need to say. What it hasn't given me is the courage to say it, or work out how I might cope with the likely rejection. A year is a long time, and there's every chance Jackie no longer cares about what I've got to say. The way I ended our relationship is unlikely to have left her with much in the way of goodwill, either.

I pull up outside Jackie's house and switch the engine off. In the quiet, I reiterate to myself the main reason I'm here — to say sorry.

As I lock the car door, my stomach gurgles in the same nervous way it did when opening the envelope for my exam results. I make my way up the front path and rap on the glass. While I wait, I turn and scan the street for signs of Derek's old Marina. He was never my biggest fan and I'd rather avoid a possible confrontation. Thankfully, there's no sign of it.

The door opens.

I turn around, and for a second, I'm rendered speechless.

"Um, hi, Mrs Benton."

It's only been a year or so since I last saw Jackie's mum, but in that time she's aged a decade. Her once bright blue eyes are dull and ringed with dark circles. Where she had curves, she now has straight lines; the loss of weight dramatic.

"What are you doing here?" she asks.

"I was hoping to see Jackie."

"Why?"

"I need to talk to her."

"You should have just called … like last time."

A stinging blow from such a slight woman.

"I guess I deserved that."

"And a whole lot more."

"I know, I know. I'm a shit, a bastard. An inconsiderate, selfish, stupid moron. But, before you slam the door in my face, please let me explain why I'm here."

Anna folds her arms.

"Go on."

"What I did was unforgivable, but I'm not here looking for forgiveness. I just want to say one word to Jackie, and then I'll never darken your door again."

"What word?"

"Sorry."

Not a flicker.

"Listen, I know how badly I hurt Jackie, but …"

"Do you?" she barks. "That girl has been through hell over the last year while you've been living it up in sunny Devon with some tart. What is it she had, that my Jackie didn't? Huh?"

With Anna now riled, I suspect the conversation is about to come to an abrupt end.

"I made a mistake. A stupid, stupid mistake."

"Oh, a mistake. Is that what it was?"

"Yes, one I'll likely regret for the rest of my life, but I can't turn back time and change it, can I? I swear, if I could, I would."

"But you can't."

"No, and I have to live with that. I made a judgement, and I got it wrong — badly wrong — because I couldn't see what was so glaringly obvious. Jackie was, and always will be the love of my life."

There's nothing else I can say, so I don't. Anna, her arms still folded, glares back with such intensity it's as if she can see right through me.

She then sighs and rolls her eyes.

"You're a fucking idiot, Sean Hardy. A twenty-four-carat idiot."

"I agree, but I'm a fucking idiot who knows he did wrong. I just want to say sorry, and whether that's today or tomorrow, next week or next month, I won't give up trying. Please, Mrs Benton."

The glare eases to a hard stare.

"She's not in."

"Oh, right."

"But before you go rushing off to find her, we need to talk."

"We do?"

"You need to understand exactly what she's been through over the last year before you go wading in with your apologies."

"I think I've got a vague idea."

"Trust me; you don't."

I take the slightest tilt of her head as an invitation to step into the hallway. Anna shuffles into the lounge. I close the door and follow her into a room which hasn't changed, unlike the woman who orders me to sit.

Having made it this far, I attempt to soften Anna's mood with a smattering of small talk.

"I never asked. How are you doing?"

"I've been better."

She sits down in an armchair opposite and lights a cigarette. I don't remember her ever smoking before.

"And how's Mr Benton?"

"Dead."

"Oh … I … my God. Shit. I'm so sorry."

"You won't be when I tell you why."

Still rocked by the brutally cold manner in which Anna revealed her husband is dead, I can't find a suitable response.

"I'm only telling you this so Jackie doesn't have to. Understood?"

"Understood."

She looks up at the ceiling and mumbles a few words I don't catch.

"Derek died just over four weeks ago. The police think it was probably suicide."

"He killed himself?"

"If he hadn't killed himself, I would have killed the sick bastard."

"Why? What did he do?"

"He … Jackie came home from a party before Christmas. I was at work, and because she was so wasted, Derek had to help her to bed."

I don't share my thoughts with Anna, but the Jackie I knew has never been more than a bit tipsy.

"That's when it happened."

"What happened?"

She takes a long draw on the cigarette.

"Derek touched her up."

Her sentence makes no sense.

"What do you mean, touched her up?"

"What do you think I mean?" she snaps. "That dirty bastard sexually assaulted his step-daughter."

The walls suddenly close in as Anna's words echo in my head.

"Oh, God," I gasp. "No … not Jackie."

"That wasn't the worst of it," she continues. "For months afterwards, he kept pestering her. He got it into his head she wanted him as much he wanted her. The deluded fool thought

360

they could have a relationship."

"That's sick. Did Jackie tell you?"

"No, because Derek threatened her. Jackie hasn't been herself over the last year; she's been drinking, taking drugs, and staying out all hours, and he said I'd believe him over her if it ever came out."

"She's been taking drugs?"

Anna nods, and it's now clear why I received such a frosty reception. The shoddy way I ended our relationship was bad enough, but my actions probably contributed to Jackie's reckless and radical change in behaviour. There's no way on earth the girl I knew would touch drugs.

"You broke her heart," Anna says. "And she did what she had to do to blot out the pain."

"I'm so sorry."

"Yes, you said."

Another draw on the cigarette.

"She sorted herself out, though. Got herself a job in Our Price and stopped going out so much. Then, everything just blew up one weekend."

"How so?"

"I got a call from the Old Bill one Friday evening to say Derek was being held in custody for the weekend as he assaulted some bloke in the pub. Then, on the Sunday, Jackie went out on a date with some lad."

If Anna had rammed her fist down my throat and crushed my heart in her bare hand, I don't think it would hurt as badly as hearing about Jackie's date.

"Derek then turns up a few hours later, saying the police dropped the charges. He asks where Jackie is and then says he has to go in to work. I didn't think anything of it."

"Okay."

"At the end of the evening, Jackie was waiting for a taxi and Derek pulls up outside the pub. He tells Jackie I've been involved in an accident and I'm in hospital. She jumps in his car, thinking he'll take her there. I wasn't in no accident, though."

"Why did he want her in the car then?"

"He drove down to the road near his work depot and loses his shit."

"Why?"

"Jackie swears blind she never told a soul about what Derek did to her, but some bloke in the pub somehow knew — the bloke he beat up."

"She definitely didn't tell anyone?"

"No, and I believe my daughter. She was sick with shame so there's no way she'd have told anyone. I wouldn't have found out myself if I hadn't read her diary that night."

"And what happened in the car?"

"They had a blazing row, and Jackie gets out when she realised he lied about me being in hospital. All she remembers is trying to run away and Derek grabbing hold of her jacket. Then, the wanker whacked her around the head with a spanner."

"Shit."

"Next thing she remembers, she's sat at the edge of a railway line near Yorkie's Bridge, and blue lights are flashing everywhere. Derek carried her up there for some reason and … it makes me sick to the bottom of my stomach, thinking what might have happened."

"But what did happen, to Derek?"

"Either he tripped and fell under a train, or the guilt got the better of him, and he topped himself. The train driver said he saw someone lying on the track but it was too late to stop. Anyway, makes no odds to me, I'm just glad he's dead. He won't be harming my girl again, that's for sure."

Stunned into silence, I sit back in the armchair. When Anna said Jackie had been through hell over the last year, she wasn't exaggerating.

"Lost for words?"

"I'm still trying to take it all in," I reply.

"Don't bother. It's been a month and I ain't anywhere close

to getting my head around it all."

"And Jackie. Is she doing okay?"

"She's a survivor, that girl, and don't ask me how but she's getting on with her life. Two days after it happened, she went back to work."

"Is that where she is now, at work?"

"Nah, she finished at half-five. She was meeting a lad straight from work for a bite to eat and then going to a quiz night."

"I didn't know she was into quizzes."

"She's not really. The lad she's seeing is a bit of a brainbox, and they take turns deciding how to spend the evening. It was his turn to decide tonight."

"Have they … have they been dating long?"

"Few weeks. It's early days."

"Have you met him?"

"A couple of times. He's a shy kid, but Jackie seems to like him."

Anna leans forward and stubs out the cigarette.

"If I tell you where they are, I want your word on something."

"Okay, you've got it."

"You go in, say sorry, and leave. I don't want you messing with her head just as she's getting her life back together. You hear me?"

"Loud and clear."

"I mean it, Sean. I've let that girl down badly, but I won't make the same mistake again. You so much as make her frown and you'll be carrying your bollocks around in your pocket for the rest of your days."

"I get it, and now you've explained what she's been through, I wouldn't wish to cause Jackie another second of suffering, I swear."

"On your life?"

"You've no reason to believe me, but I would give up my life to protect Jackie. I swear to God."

She gets to her feet, but her eyes don't shift from mine. I don't know if she believes me or not, but I genuinely meant what I said.

"They're in The King's Head," she then mutters. "Close the door on your way out."

41.

I pull in to a car park with no recollection of the journey here. From the moment I left Anna, my mind has remained in a dizzying state of turmoil after our brief but devastating conversation. Even if I were to continue on and cover the hundred and fifty miles to Exeter, my mind would still be a mess on arrival.

Locking the driver's door, I pause.

Should I be doing this?

What right do I have, turning up unannounced when Jackie and her boyfriend are enjoying a quiet night out?

I work through a mental checklist, and there are plenty of good reasons to get back in the car and drive away. There's only one reason not to, and it's one I don't even understand. I know it isn't based on any logic, but I can't ignore it. I don't even know how to describe it. An urge? A compulsion? A feeling that I absolutely must see Jackie, even if it's just for a fleeting moment.

Trance like, I put one foot in front of the other and walk.

It's just gone six when I step through the door of The King's Head. It's not a pub I know well.

I scan the room, but there's just a handful of people in office attire and none under thirty. Anna said Jackie was going for a bite to eat straight from work so I could be in for a wait. I order a pint and find a table with a clear view of the door; not so close Jackie will see me the second she steps through it. Knowing she'll be with her boyfriend, I want to choose my moment.

The wait is excruciating.

Every time the door swings open my heart skips a beat, and my hopes soar. Those hopes are crushed every time as another middle-aged punter wanders in.

As the bar becomes busier, it's harder to get a clear view of the door. It's not my idea of a fun night out but quiz nights are obviously popular. What isn't so obvious is why Jackie's new boyfriend would drag her along to such a square event. I haven't even met the guy, but I don't think I like him.

My glass is nearly empty, but the minute I get up, someone will nick my prime vantage point. There's already a huddle of old farts across the way who keep looking over and shaking their heads. I smile back, but my resistance is futile as I'm busting for a piss, my shredded nerves not helping.

I relent, and I've barely covered six feet of carpet when they claim the table. Tossers.

Standing at the urinal, I recheck my watch. I've been here over an hour, and the quiz is set to start in twenty minutes. What if Jackie has talked her boyfriend in to a more exciting night out? I don't know precisely how many pubs there are in Guildford, but I don't fancy spending the entire evening checking them all. And, at some point, I need to think about that long bloody journey back to Exeter. As it is, I won't make it home much before midnight.

I decide to wait until the quiz starts and if they haven't shown up by then, I'll have to admit defeat. Either that or I find a cheap hotel and keep looking.

I wash my hands and push open the toilet door. The bar area is rammed, and I have to force my way through the crowd. Being the height I am, most people step out of my path, and I'm able to claim a spot at the bar with minimal fuss. Getting the attention of the overworked bar staff isn't so easy.

A barmaid becomes free and looks in my direction. She then steps over and asks for my order.

"I think this fella was already waiting," I reply, nodding to the guy on my right.

He turns to face me. He's roughly my age but shorter, thinner.

"Thank you."

"No worries, mate."

He orders a Coke and half a sweet cider. I glance across towards the door, but it's now impossible to see it clearly. I'll have to find a new place to lurk once I've got another drink, and I survey the room for possible options.

"There you go," the guy next to me says.

"Thank you," a female voice replies.

A bomb explodes in my chest. Just two words, but I'd recognise the voice anywhere.

Holding a breath I daren't let go, I slowly turn to my right. "Sean!"

So much for choosing my moment.

"Err, hi, Jackie."

"What the hell are you doing here?"

I've never understood what people mean by a stunned silence. Now I do. Only five feet away, Jackie is looking up at me like I'm something she's trodden in, and the guy, presumably her boyfriend, appears vaguely confused.

She looks amazing. Different, but incredible; beautiful.

"I, um … I was hoping for a quick word."

The boyfriend's expression melds from confusion to mild annoyance.

"Who are you?" he asks.

Jackie gets in first.

"Sean is an old friend from school," she replies, fixing me with a stare that implies I shouldn't contradict.

I offer the guy a handshake. He accepts it, although not with any great enthusiasm.

"Jeremy."

"Nice to meet you, Jeremy."

Jackie then turns to her boyfriend.

"Can you bear with me for a minute? I need a quick word with Sean."

Jeremy nods his agreement, and Jackie beckons me towards the other end of the bar where it's not quite so busy. She comes to a stop by a brick pillar and, like her mother earlier, folds her arms.

"You heard what I said," she says sternly. "You've got one

minute, and you don't even deserve that."

One minute. I need to make it count.

"I went to see your mum earlier. She told me what happened with Derek."

Jackie draws breath through flared nostrils and bites her bottom lip. Neither is a positive response.

"She shouldn't have done that."

"In her defence, she only told me so you didn't have to. Her exact words."

"Well, seeing as you know what I've been through, you'd better have a bloody good reason for turning up like this."

"I do."

"Spit it out then."

I reach into my jacket pocket and pull out a cassette case.

"Side two, track five," I say, handing it to Jackie. "Yazoo, *Only You.*"

Conflicted, she tries to temper the joy at seeing the cassette she compiled as a teenager with her disdain for the man who handed it to her.

"You kept it," she says flatly.

"I did, and I listened to it on the journey up here."

"You drove all the way from Exeter to give me a tape?"

"Not really. I came up from Bournemouth, and I only decided to give you the tape about an hour ago."

"Why are you here then?"

"To say sorry."

"Sorry?" she snorts. "Bit late for that, isn't it?"

"Probably, but that doesn't mean I shouldn't say it or tell you exactly what I'm sorry for."

"You're running out of time."

I clear my throat.

"Jackie Benton, I'm sorry for the abysmal way I treated you and for being a coward. I'm sorry for the pain I caused. I'm sorry for being such a fool and for throwing away the best relationship I'll ever have. I'm sorry for breaking your heart and destroying your dreams. I'm sorry it's taken me over a year to realise what a complete and utter dickhead I am. Most of all, though, I'm sorry …"

I swallow hard.

"Most of all, I'm sorry for not realising."

"Realising what?"

I nod at the cassette in her hand.

"Side two, track five, there's a line in that Yazoo song which says it all. The love you gave — it really was all I needed. I wish I'd realised that. I really do."

She doesn't say anything, doesn't even look at me. Her silence speaks volumes.

"Anyway," I mumble. "I've said it now, so I'll leave you in peace. And for what it's worth, I hope you find happiness with someone who truly deserves you."

Still mute, she tries to hand the cassette back to me.

"No, you keep it. I'd rather you remember me as the guy you made it for, rather than … well, the idiot of last year."

I take one final look at the face of my first and only true love; a face I'm unlikely to see again. Her expression is unreadable.

"Bye, Jackie."

I turn and walk slowly towards the exit. With every step, I will Jackie to say something, anything. As my hand grasps the door handle, I accept no amount of will can undo time. The damage I've done is irreparable.

On the pavement, I manage three steps before the emotions catch up with me. Many in number, they attack with a cruel and relentless ferocity. It's as if all the hurt I inflicted upon Jackie has been condensed into a toxic potion and injected directly into my heart.

It's no less than I deserve, and in some bizarre way, I welcome it. I understand the heartache, and it's preferable to the numb malaise I've suffered ever since the seizure. What isn't so welcome are the accompanying tears. I haven't cried since I was a child, but even then, I don't recall sobbing so intensely.

Long minutes pass before I'm able to get a grip.

I need a drink. God, I need a drink.

Not trusting myself to remain composed in a pub, I wander up Castle Hill in search of a corner store or off licence. I eventually find what I'm looking for, having journeyed in the same stunned stupor as my drive from Fir Tree Road. There's no way I can face the drive back to Exeter tonight, so I might as well get wasted and kip in the car. It'll likely be cold and uncomfortable, but if I drink enough, it'll blot out everything, and I need everything blotted out.

I buy eight cans of mega-strength lager; not for the taste but the anaesthetic properties.

Leaving the shop, I wander back down the hill intending to return to my car. I want to listen to music while I fade away from reality, and if I break down again, I'd rather no one was around to witness it.

Halfway there, I change my mind.

In all likelihood, this will be the last evening I spend in my old home town. There's nothing here for me now, only memories of a girl I lost. I can't think of a better way to say goodbye than in the place that girl and I enjoyed so many happy times.

I pass through the gate into the grounds of Guildford Castle and follow the path I've walked so many times before, but never alone.

When I reach my destination, the sight of it takes my breath away. The rawness of my emotions are probably at play, but on an otherwise idyllic summer evening, it's never looked so stunning, bathed in dappled sunlight.

I cross the grass and take a seat in the nook.

The first can receives short shrift. I open it up and guzzle down every drop of the syrupy lager. The taste is awful but the ensuing beer buzz welcome.

I open the second can, and it receives the same treatment as the first.

The alcohol quickly gets to work, and while it helps to numb the pain, there are side-effects. Every time I've been here, Jackie has been at my side, and there's been near-constant conversation.

Now, there's just silence, but not the kind of silence I've experienced before; like it has mass, a presence.

Jackie always used to waffle on about this place and how she could sense the energy leaking from the old stonework. She has such a fertile imagination and used to concoct little stories about the nook and the people who might have rested here over the centuries. To me, it's never been anything other than a convenient place to while away a few contented hours with my girlfriend, and indulge in the occasional amorous fumble. This evening I can almost sense what Jackie sensed.

A cold shiver runs down my spine. I shake it off and reach for another can of lager. As my hand touches the carrier bag, I catch the slightest sound of movement from the privet hedge opposite. So few people know the nook exists, I hope it's not some couple looking to do what Jackie and I used to do here.

A figure steps beyond the hedge. She stares at me, and I stare at her.

"What are you doing here?" Jackie barks.

"Reminiscing," I reply. "And saying goodbye."

She pauses for a moment and then slowly makes her way across the lawn.

"And you?" I ask.

"I needed to clear my head. Your little speech has fucked it up again."

"Sorry."

"Enough with the apologies, okay. I get it — you're sorry."

She looks at the carrier bag.

"Are you going to offer me a drink then?"

"Sure."

I pluck a can from the bag and pass it to her. She snaps the ring pull off and drops it in the bag. Anna mentioned her daughter's new-found appetite for alcohol, and I get to see it first hand as Jackie takes several long gulps.

"That's foul," she remarks, lowering the can from her lips.

"It does a job."

"And what job is that?"

"It blots out the shittiness."

"Aww, poor Sean," she says mockingly. "Were you expecting me to fall at your feet the moment I saw you? Forgive and forget, eh?"

"No."

"What were you expecting?"

"Honestly? A kick in the nuts."

She fights hard to hold back a grin.

"I don't like to disappoint. Stand up, and I'll oblige."

"Would it help?"

"Probably not, but if you'd asked me last year, I'd have jumped at the chance."

"And last year I'd have deserved it. Still do, really."

She takes a sip from the can. I prepare a question I don't want to ask, but like a kid picking at a scab, I can't help myself.

"How long have you known Jeremy?"

"Not long."

"Did he go to our school? He looks kinda familiar."

"Nope. He's from Kent."

"Well, I hope he knows how lucky he is, having you as a girlfriend."

I had intended my remark to convey sincerity, but it's met with laughter.

"I'm not his girlfriend, you idiot."

"You're not?"

"No, we're just good friends. I don't think I'm Jeremy's type."

"Why not? What guy wouldn't fancy you?"

"A gay guy, perhaps?"

"Oh. He's gay?"

"He's trying to be. His parents kicked him out when he told them, and that shattered his confidence. I'm helping him back out of the closet, so to speak."

"Right, but you're here, and he's in the pub alone."

"No, he's with Steve."

"Who's Steve?"

"A friend I met at a gig last year. He's a bit nerdy and likes a quiz, so I asked if he wanted to join our team, but really, I was doing a spot of match-making. Steve's gay too."

"That's very sweet of you."

"Yep, I can't hold down a relationship of my own, so it's the next best thing, setting others up."

"I'll keep my fingers crossed for Jeremy."

"He'll be fine. If you'd met him four or five weeks ago, you'd know how much he's changed. Poor guy was as shy as a church mouse back then."

Jackie takes another slurp of lager and then frowns down at me.

"Are you going to shift over so I can sit down or I am expected to stand here like a spare part?"

"Yeah, sorry."

Shuffling as far across the stone slab as I can, I receive another frown for another apology. Jackie sits down. Immediately, I'm cast back in time as the warmth of her body crosses the inch of space between us, and the scent of her perfume triggers so many wonderful memories. It's pleasurable but painful.

"How's Carol?" she then asks.

"Do you really want to know?"

"I wouldn't have asked if I wasn't interested."

"It's over, or at least it will be on Wednesday when she gets back from her work trip."

"Sorry to hear that."

"Yeah, right," I scoff. "I doubt you are."

"Then you don't know me as well as you think you do."

"Eh?"

"I'm not going to pretend I wasn't devastated when we broke up and for a long while I hated you with a passion. Then, I realised there's nothing to be gained from hating. In all that pain, the one thing that kept me going was knowing you were happy, and you'd met someone you wanted to spend the rest of your life with. Now, you tell me I went through all those months of agony for no reason."

"I, um … I hadn't thought of it like that."

"What happened?"

I tell her all about the seizure and the way I've been feeling ever since.

"Were you scared?" she asks. "When it happened?"

"I don't remember much about it, but I've no recollection of feeling scared. It's hard to explain, but in the days after it happened, I experienced all these weird-arse emotions … like grieving a death one minute and then celebrating a birth the next. It's taken a while, but I'm slowly getting my head together … or at least I was."

"Is the lager helping?" she sniggers.

"Probably not, but this is."

"This? You mean sitting here?"

"Sitting here with you."

Jackie doesn't respond, and I don't want to tread too heavily on delicate ground. We both sip from our cans. I change the subject.

"I'm sure you don't want to talk about it, and I'd imagine you're sick of being asked if you're okay, but …"

"I'm getting there."

"Do you remember much?"

"Like you, not a lot."

"I feel like it's partly my fault, what happened."

"How do you work that out?"

"Because if I hadn't abandoned you, that night would never have happened, would it?"

374

"Who knows, but there's only one person to blame, and he's six feet under, thank God. I certainly don't blame you."

"Thanks."

"But I do blame you for fucking up my life in other ways. I promised myself I wouldn't ask this, but why, Sean? Why did you make me feel so worthless?"

"If you'd asked me that before the seizure, I wouldn't have been able to answer it."

"And now?"

"Now, I know. I was blinded by what I thought I wanted, and I never stopped to think about what I'd lose by pursuing it. Looking back, I was like a bank robber dreaming of stealing millions, only to walk away with a tenner. All that risk for nothing."

"You obviously wanted it badly enough at the time."

"And that, Jackie, is the crux of it — I thought I knew what I wanted, but I didn't have the first fucking clue. Honestly, if I had the chance to meet that stupid, arrogant twat I was back then, I'd likely try and punch some sense into him."

"You say that like he's not you, but it was you who made that call."

"This is going to sound like absolute bollocks, but I'm convinced a different version of me made that call, and he died in an intensive care bed four weeks ago. I know because I felt the grief, but the moment I left Exeter this morning I felt ... I don't know ... reborn, I suppose."

She stares silently into space.

"Jackie?"

"At our age, we have no concept of how little we really know about life."

"Guilty as charged."

She turns to face me.

"I met this bloke last month. He told me that."

"What bloke?"

"That's a long story, but when he said it, it was with such

sincerity it kinda stuck with me."

"Clearly. Was he just a friend, or …"

"Give over," she snorts. "He was in his fifties. Nice guy but Christ, he was a weird one."

"In what way?"

"He was so smart and kind, but an absolute bullshitter with it. He said he'd take me to meet Gary Numan in Manchester and we arranged for him to pick me up one Monday morning. As it happens, it was about six hours after that shit with Derek, and I was in no fit state, but he didn't turn up, anyway."

"Why not?"

"No idea, but he said he was a journalist for the NME so I called them a few weeks back and they'd never heard of him."

"Why would he say that?"

"I never got the chance to ask. According to Jeremy, he went out to look for me the evening I ended up near the railway tracks. That was the last anyone saw of him."

"Wait … I'm lost. What's this bloke got to do with Jeremy?"

"They were staying in the same digs in Cline Road, and he took Jeremy under his wing … a bit like a father figure, I suppose. Then, he just disappeared, although he did leave a letter for Jeremy, saying he might have to leave suddenly. There was no real explanation where he was going or why; just an apology and a few words of advice."

"That's weird."

"Tell me about it. I don't know why some random stranger was so concerned about me, or Jeremy for that matter, but he introduced us when we both needed a friend, so I'm sure his heart was in the right place."

"Until he pissed off."

"Yep, but that's men for you: unpredictable, or unreliable."

The looks in Jackie's eye implies I'm probably the main culprit in her sweeping generalisation.

"Um, yeah, can't deny that," I mumble before scrabbling to move the conversation along. "Did this bloke have a name? You never said."

"His first name was Sean."

"It's a popular name."

"Yeah, he said that when I told him about you."

"You told him about me?"

"Yep, and I told him I'd always love you, even though you're a bit of a cunt."

"Bloody hell," I splutter. "I've never heard you use that word before."

"I'm not the same girl you left behind, Sean."

"No?"

"Nope," she replies, shaking her head. "But maybe one day you'll get to know the new me."

"I'm in no hurry."

Silence feels appropriate. Jackie is the first to break it.

"Oh, by the way, that Yazoo track."

"What about it?"

"I like it, a lot, but it's not my favourite of theirs."

"Okay. Which one is?"

"Remember *Nobody's Diary*?"

"I do."

"I love it because I keep a diary. Have done since the day I met you, and your name features heavily in all six volumes."

"Don't suppose you'll let me have a read?"

"I don't think so, but I might let you read one page. Actually, I might even tear it out."

"Why?"

"Because I wrote it the day you made that phone call. I never wanted it to be our ending, not really."

I pause a moment to compose the right response.

"You know, maybe it doesn't have to be."

She stares silently out across the lawn for several seconds before responding.

"We'll see."

42.

Only a fool would fail to learn from previous mistakes.

Twenty-two days ago, I ended another relationship. I did it in person rather than on the phone. During that conversation, I discovered what Carol really thought of me, and much of it wasn't pleasant. It did, however, validate my decision, and while she packed her bags, I wallowed in relief.

If it hadn't been for another conversation with a former girlfriend, I could have easily continued living in denial, maybe for years, although I'm sure my differences with Carol would have surfaced at some point down the line.

Today, having handed back the keys to our flat, I've said my final goodbye to Exeter. I'm now nearing the end of another long journey to Guildford; everything I own loaded in the back of my Nova. It's a journey I've made twice over the last twenty-two days; only possible because my employer put me on four weeks paid gardening leave after I quit.

I'm now technically homeless and jobless, but I've never been happier. Well, almost never.

The day after my chat with Jackie in the nook, we had a long conversation on the phone. I told her I would be moving back to Guildford even if she never wanted to see me again. It's my home. She agreed we could meet up as friends, and see where we went. That was all I could have asked for and more than I could have hoped for.

I pull up outside a house to the north of Guildford town centre where I'm renting a room for a month or two. As soon as I've sorted out a job, I'm hoping to rent a small flat. Jeremy did tell me there's a room going spare in the house where he lodges but his landlady sounded a bit too strict for my liking.

On my first trip back to Guildford, I met up with Jackie and Jeremy at The Britannia to watch a band. We had a great night, and despite my initial reservations, I discovered I had a lot in common with Jeremy. For starters, we both turned up wearing the same chevron-patterned pullover, which was awkward. He also collects the *Now* albums, and we spent an age talking about our favourite tracks. And, once you get beyond his shy exterior, he's a funny guy with a wicked wit. I ended the evening with two good friends — one I've known for years, the other new.

On my second visit, I met up with Jackie, and we spent an afternoon down by the river. We talked a lot, laughed a bit, and cried once or twice. Many ghosts were exorcised, and we both agreed to draw a line under the past and focus on the future. I now realise just how much I hurt Jackie, and it'll take a long time to regain her trust. I don't care if it takes weeks, months, or years. In fact, I don't care if I wake up in my fifties and I'm still waiting, as long as there's hope.

For now, I'm happy taking baby steps, as Dad wisely advised I should do.

My first of those steps takes place this afternoon. Jackie has the day off, and she's agreed to help me unpack. However, her assistance comes at a price; a meal this evening. I think I'm getting the better end of the deal as it means I have her company for the rest of the day.

There's a tap at my window. My assistant has arrived.

I open the door and risk greeting Jackie with a hug. It's warmly received.

"How was the journey?" she asks.

"Long."

"Well, you made it here in one piece. Welcome home."

Guildford is my home, but only because of one young woman who lives here. It's taken twenty-two days of soul searching to realise home isn't a physical place but a sense of belonging. Wherever Jackie is, I belong.

I open the boot, and we spend twenty minutes transferring all my worldly goods up to the second-floor room. While I begin unpacking, Jackie inspects the view from the window.

"You can see the castle from here, you know?"

I sidle up to her and check.

"Oh, yes. That's handy."

"Why is it handy?"

"Because I now realise why you always thought it so special. It's nice to know I can see it any time I fancy."

"Seriously?" she replies, her tone sceptical. "Or are you just saying that to get in my good books?"

"I mean it. When I left the pub that night, I could have wandered anywhere. I could have gone straight back to the car, or another pub to drown my sorrows, or I could have just blindly staggered around the town. Somehow, I ended up alone in the nook, and that's when I felt it."

"Felt what?"

"I couldn't tell you exactly, but think about it: I was there for no good reason, and you should have been with your friends. There has to be a reason we ended up in the nook together."

"Maybe the energy drew us back."

"I might have scoffed at that idea last year, but now …"

"Now, you think differently?"

"That's an understatement," I chuckle. "You have no idea how differently I now think."

Hesitantly, she slides her hand around my waist as we stare out across the rooftops of Guildford. I put my arm around her shoulder and pull her so tight to me; it's as if I'm terrified of ever letting Jackie slip away again.

"Then again," she continues. "Maybe we both ended up in the nook that evening because fate thought I should give you a second chance."

I look into her electric blue eyes.

"A second chance at first love? I guess that would make me the luckiest man alive."

THE END

But before you go ...

I genuinely hope you enjoyed 'A Page in Your Diary'. If you did, and have a few minutes spare, I would be eternally grateful if you could leave a (hopefully positive) review on Amazon. If you're feeling particularly generous, a mention on Facebook or a Tweet would be equally appreciated. I know it's a pain, but it's the only way us indie authors can compete with the big publishing houses.

Stay in touch ...

For more information about me and to receive updates on my new releases, please visit my website...

www.keithapearson.co.uk

If you have any questions or general feedback, you can also reach me, or follow me, on social media...

Facebook: www.facebook.com/pearson.author
Twitter: www.twitter.com/keithapearson

Acknowledgements ...

There are four people who have helped make this book possible. Firstly, Emma Silvey, who went to great lengths helping me fact-check Guildford in 1988. Secondly, two diligent beta readers who highlighted a host of issues in the draft manuscript: Phil Hodgson, and Adam Eccles. Thank you, gents.

Finally, I owe a belated thank you to my editor, Sian Phillips. I rarely add an acknowledgement to the end of my novels so this is the first opportunity I've had to sing Sian's praises. Without her help, my novels would make a lot less sense.

Printed in Great Britain
by Amazon

45578754R00219